JUDI CURTIN

FROM CLAIRE TO HERE

Tivoli
an imprint of Gill & Macmillan Ltd
Hume Avenue
Park West
Dublin 12
with associated companies throughout the world

www.gillmacmillan.ie

© Judi Curtin 2004
07171 3606 X

Print origination by
Carrigboy Typesetting Services, Co. Cork
Printed and bound by
Nørhaven Paperback A/S, Denmark

*The paper used in this book is made from wood pulp of
managed forests. For every tree felled, at least one is
planted, thereby renewing natural resources.*

A catalogue record is available for this book from the
British Library.

1 3 5 4 2

For David and Emma

SINCERE THANKS TO:

Dan;
Brian, Ellen and Annie;
Mum and Dad;
Everyone at Gill & Macmillan, and Tivoli,
for their great support and hard work;
Special thanks to my editor, Alison Walsh;
My agent, Faith O'Grady;
Caroline and Liz, for the photographs;
Kieran, for reading the manuscript and offering ideas;
Mary and Declan, for telling all their friends;
Miriam, for travelling to Greece with me
in the 1980s, when I didn't realise that I was
researching the location for this novel;
All those kind friends who stepped in and minded my
children while I was off doing exciting writer stuff;
The booksellers who promoted *Sorry, Walter*;
Special thanks to O'Mahony's of Limerick for the
launch and the window display;
Those friends, acquaintances and even strangers
who took the trouble to write and tell me
they enjoyed my writing.

ABOUT THE AUTHOR

Judi Walter comes from Cork, the setting for her
first novel, *Sorry, Walter*. She studied English and
German at UCC, before training as a primary
school teacher. She now lives in Limerick
with her husband and three children.

Prologue

Three minutes.

You get to think a lot in three minutes.

And you can dredge up a whole pile of very nasty memories as those one hundred and eighty seconds tick slowly by.

I'll set the scene.

Early morning.

A bright apple-white painted home in Douglas, nice settled suburb of Cork. A home that has a limed oak kitchen, extra plug points in every room, and a garage specially designed to be easily convertible to a play-room or extra bedroom. (Not that it will ever be done, of course.) There's a utility room, which contains a washing machine, a tumble dryer and an Everest of unironed clothing. There's an *en suite* shower room, not much bigger than your average phone box.

In this room there's a dressing-gown-clad, nervous-looking thirty-something with wild hair and badly bitten fingernails.

1

Me, of course.

I had hastily discarded the test wrappers in the not-very-clean sink, and now I stood with my back to them, and to the two tests, which lay on the windowsill next to the almost-completed crossword from last Sunday's newspaper. (What kind of a clue is 'lithe and legless'?)

Also on the windowsill lay a scrap of paper with a poem on it. Poem might be too strong a word though. 'Rush of heartfelt words,' would probably be a more accurate description. You see, as usual, when faced with a crisis, I put off the awful moment by writing a poem. This one was about the toothpaste stains on the sink.

The pregnancy test claims to be 99 per cent accurate, but, reluctant to believe the first result, I now awaited the second. Three minutes seems very long at a time like this, and all kinds of thoughts and questions ran through my mind.

Why are the lines on the test blue?

Why are the openings on the little white wand called windows? As if they were windows of opportunity.

And why is it called a wand? Is it magic?

Why is it so hard to wee on the damned thing? How many people miss it altogether and end up with two problems? They don't know if they're pregnant, and they have a big mopping-up job to do on the bathroom floor.

Do I want positive? Negative?

What will I do? Who can I tell?

Should I write another poem about the experience?

How could my eyebrows need plucking again so soon?

At the age of thirty-five, why do I still have blackheads on my chin? And why can I never stop squeezing them?

I became angry at myself then. How could I be so frivolous at a time like this?

While those three minutes dragged by, my past raced before my eyes. (I hope I never drown – I couldn't face the memories.)

As I glanced back over the years, I felt as if I were watching Gay Byrne on the *Late, Late Show*. You know the scenario – a big draw, and all the entries are gathered in a funny-shaped box. Gay smiles and makes small talk and winds the handle much in the manner of a demented organ grinder. Various brightly coloured postcards slip and slide and jostle for space. A card catches your eye for a second, only to vanish moments later to the depths of the heap, and then, out of the blue, one that was buried deep in the beginning pops up its head drawing attention to itself, shouting, 'Me, choose me', before slipping from view once more.

Unfortunately, as I sat on the closed toilet seat that morning, there was no Gay Byrne to move me on, keen to keep the show moving on schedule, careful not to miss the lucrative ad breaks, rushing to ensure that when Bono came on he'd get a respectable length of time in which to save the world and change sunglasses three times. In a studio. In October.

These memories are weighing me down. I'm weary of carrying them everywhere with me, and I want to be rid of them. They have hunched my shoulders and etched my face with premature frown lines.

Of course I thought a lot about last year. That's an important one. The psychobabble merchants would have a field day with my story of the past year. They could write papers and attend conferences titled, 'The summer Claire ran away. Thoughts and yet more thoughts.'

Then there's the story of the summer of 1986. That reared its ugly head, of course. The events of that summer seem to be inextricably linked with those of more recent times.

At last, I looked at the test again. The second window, the one that confirmed that the test was working, was definitely showing a thin, blue line. I looked at the result window with disbelief. If 99 per cent accuracy is guaranteed, what were the odds of two successive false positives? Not terribly high, I suspected.

It was beginning to look as if Lizzie's five-year reign as an only child would soon be coming to an end. Her pious repetition of 'caring is sharing' would soon have to be matched by actions.

I gathered up all of the unnecessary glossy packaging, and both tests, and the poem and the crossword, and dumped the lot in the bathroom bin. On top of the almost-completed crossword from two Sundays ago.

(Einstein couldn't get the answer to 'delirious delight', seven letters beginning with z.)

I went into the bedroom and picked up the receiver of the bedside phone. It stuck to my hand. I used the hem of my nightie to wipe the raspberry jam from my fingers. The speckled pink jam blended nicely with the cocoa stains from the night before.

My mind was trembling, but my hand was steady as I dialled the familiar number. The answering machine clicked in on the fourth ring, and my message was brief.

'Hi, it's me. Claire. I think we need to talk.'

Chapter One

All the trouble started last year.

It was April. A Wednesday morning. Just around the time of my thirty-fifth birthday – halfway to my promised three score years and ten.

The day had a nice beginning. I awoke to feel a warm body pressed tightly against mine. A leg lay languidly across my thighs. A loving hand was entwined in my long, curly hair, and short, urgent breaths fluttered against my cheek.

It was Lizzie – my precious little daughter who had perfected the useful art of slipping into a bed without waking its slumbering occupants. I peered through the golden net of Lizzie's tangled hair to look at my husband. James was as usual pushed to the furthest edge of the bed, managing to sleep while somehow clinging to his tiny allocated space. His face wore a concentrated expression, which, as I watched, changed to a half-smile. Must have been a great dream. The skin around his eyes crinkled, and his long eyelashes fluttered briefly. He was so handsome, this gentle man who shared my bed and my life and my twenty-five-year fixed-interest mortgage. I leaned over and ran a finger lightly across his cheek. His skin felt like fine-grade sandpaper. Or like one of my never-used emery boards. James opened his eyes and gave me a lascivious look, which sent a sudden pleasant shiver down my spine. I glanced at the bedside clock. It was nineteen minutes past something. I removed the sock that obscured the first glowing red digit. Seven-nineteen – plenty of time. I kissed Lizzie, and she awoke at once. She instinctively clung tighter to me, wrapping arms and legs around me like a tiny koala bear.

'How's my best girl?'

She gave the usual reply. 'Fine thanks. How's my best Mum? How's my best Dad?'

She got a few token tickles for her obedient following of our ritual. Not many though.

James's look was becoming even more intense, and there was something pressing against my left thigh that definitely wasn't Lizzie's foot. I spoke quickly.

'Lizzie, why don't you be a big girl and go down and get out the breakfast things?'

She instantly released her grip and scrambled over me to get out of the bed, kicking James in the face with her heel as she did so.

'Can I have Coco Pops?'

I smiled at her excited little voice. 'Is it Saturday?'

She shrugged her small shoulders and giggled.

James gingerly rubbed his cheek where she had kicked him, and spoke at last. His voice had an unusual husky quality. A bit like a guy in an ad for throat lozenges.

'It's Wednesday, but you can have Coco Pops if you go down straightaway. Just for a special treat. And you can put on the television if you want. Mummy and I will be down soon. We just want one more little sleep.'

Lizzie couldn't believe her luck, and she skipped happily from the room, slamming the door behind her.

James turned to me and wrapped me in a sudden, tight embrace. He spoke softly into my ear. 'And I have a special treat for you, too.'

I sighed a deep, long sigh, and prepared to be treated.

At seven forty-two James gave me a last, lingering kiss. His breath smelt faintly of garlic from the previous night's Indian takeaway. It wasn't unpleasant. He ran his hand lightly down my arm.

'Sorry, Cee. Got to go. I've a big job on today. Will I bring you up some tea and toast?'

'Mmm. Sounds lovely. But I'd better get up. Lizzie's clothes aren't sorted. For some reason, she has to wear all green today.'

'OK. I'll turn on the shower to warm up for you.'

I could hear the rush of water as he did as he promised, and then his faint humming as he went down to see just how many Coco Pops Lizzie had managed to spill onto the living-room carpet.

As I had one last luxurious stretch, I could hear the click as the toaster was pressed down, and then the buzz of the electric orange-juice squeezer. I heard James's deep voice, quickly followed by the merry peals of Lizzie's laughter.

I heaved myself out of bed, and into the bathroom. It was already full of welcoming steam. I stepped into the shower and pulled the flimsy door closed behind me. Heaven! I raised my hands towards the jets of hot water and luxuriated in how good my body felt. I closed my eyes so I wouldn't have to look at the mouldy black gunge which was sidling relentlessly along the edges of the shower. I tried not to wonder why the badly named 'shower-tidy' contained three empty shampoo bottles, four empty conditioner bottles and one small, black patent leather sandal. I lathered myself in the mint-scented shower gel James had given me for Christmas. I inhaled the cool fresh smell. I threw my head back and let the hot water run through my hair and down my back. I rubbed my arms, enjoying their slippery softness. I breathed deeply and remembered the passion of a few minutes earlier.

And I wondered why I could never be completely happy.

I stepped out of the shower and wrapped myself in a faded bath towel, then stood for a moment and watched as warm water dripped from my hair onto the cork-tiled floor. The day stretched in front of me, full of a million trivial little jobs, none of which I particularly wanted to do. Shopping, ironing, dusting – thankless, endless, repetitive jobs that I would have hated with a passion. If I wasn't too bored to feel such strong emotions.

I was bored, bored, bored.

Half an hour later, James had left for work, and I was wondering what I could put on Lizzie for her school's green day. She didn't seem to have any green clothes. I rummaged in her drawers, producing a huge pile of scarlet and orange and purple. No green though. Finally, balled up in the darkest corner of her wardrobe, I found the jumper that James's mum, Maisie, had given her for Christmas. It was a hideous hand-knitted monstrosity, all lumpy wool and intricate stitches. It was green though. Well, blue-green anyway. At least it was in the poor light of Lizzie's bedroom. I pulled it over her head and rolled the sleeves until they approximated the length they should have been. Lizzie looked like nobody's child. She looked at me doubtfully.

I smiled brightly. 'It's sweet on you, darling.'

I was only half-lying. In my eyes, she'd have been sweet dressed in dirty, torn old binbags.

'Chelsea's wearing a green dress and green tights. And Megan's dressing up as a grasshopper. And Dylan's bringing green milk for his lunch.'

My smile became less bright. I could never compete with the other mums. If I learned to stand on my head and juggle bananas, I knew they'd manage to do it blindfolded, or on the back of a speeding lorry, or while breastfeeding twins and making low-fat mayonnaise at the same time.

'Well, you'll still be the sweetest child, and we'll buy a green apple on the way to school, so you'll have a green lunch too.'

'Thanks, Mummy. Can I have a green marshmallow too?'

So easily pleased. I gave her a little hug.

'Yes, sweetheart, you can. In fact you can have two 'cause you're such a good girl.'

'Yeah.' She punched the air, and ran downstairs to get her coat.

A few minutes later we set off in the pleasant sunshine for the short walk to her playschool.

Mondays, Wednesdays and Fridays. The days Lizzie got to play with the other kids, away from the clutches of her eccentric mother.

I wheeled my bike, and Lizzie skipped along beside me. I tried to slip past the corner shop, but Lizzie was unusually determined. She had recently developed an addiction to lottery scratchcards, and took every opportunity to bully me into buying one. She loved the act of scratching, and didn't care that we never won. Sometimes it felt as if I was single-handedly financing the building of a hospital wing. Or the refurbishment of an already plush golf clubhouse in a smart Dublin suburb.

I knew that part of Lizzie's motivation was the fact that she saw her friends' mums buying the scratchcards too, and she wanted to belong.

Poor Lizzie. It must have been tough, having the oddest mummy in the neighbourhood. The one with

11

the funny notions, and the wild red hair. The one who never met the other mummies for coffee and gossip. The one who'd been wearing the same scruffy mock-suede jacket, for more than four times her daughter's lifetime. (And God knows how old it was when I bought it in a charity shop twenty years ago! For £1.50. The grandchildren of my jacket's first owner were probably going on Saga holidays already. Using their free bus passes for the trip to the airport.)

Poor Lizzie was burdened with the only mummy who didn't own a mobile phone or a people carrier or a track-suit. The only mummy who cycled around the town on a high nelly bike that had been painted pink twenty years ago, with cheap gloss paint.

The paint's all chipped now of course.

But the resulting mottled pattern is interesting. Different.

Individual.

Strange.

Just like me.

So, as a token effort at conformity, I often bought a lottery scratchcard on the way to school. We'd scratch it on the street outside the shop, and Lizzie would take the useless piece of cardboard to school. Her little trophy in the endless competition to be like everyone else.

This particular morning, we were later than usual, so when we came out of the shop with the scratchcard for Lizzie, and her green apple and the marshmallows, and the newspaper for me, Jason and his mum were already ahead of us. Lizzie shoved the scratchcard into my hessian bag, and tugged at my arm, rushing to join her latest best friend.

Jason was resplendent in a huge green papier-mâché head-dress and a long, shiny green cloak. Lizzie looked down at her jumper, which in the light of day was more blue than green. No, I lie. It was blue. Just plain blue. Lizzie looked at me with eyes too young for reproach, but which nevertheless conveyed a huge helping of bewildered disappointment.

Tactful Maureen read the situation at once. 'Lizzie, what a lovely green jumper you have on. Did your mum knit it?'

'No, my granny. The sleeves are very big.'

'No, they're just right. She's a clever granny.'

Maureen glanced at my purchases. 'And you have a lovely green lunch too. What a lucky little girl you are.'

Lizzie beamed at her.

I looked at Jason who was looking at me hopefully, waiting for me to reciprocate the compliments. I obliged. 'That's a lovely head-dress you have on.'

He carefully checked to see that it was in place.

'My dad made it. It took him three nights. And my mum made my cloak. She cut up one of her old dresses.'

Maureen shrugged in a humble I-just-ran-it-up-after-breakfast kind of way.

Lizzie grabbed Jason's arm which was clad in a real green jumper. 'Hurry up, Jason. We'll miss painting.'

Jason checked the position of his head-dress again, and rearranged it slightly. 'OK, Lizzie. Race you. Last one there's a smelly pear.'

And they set off, trotting happily ahead of us on the wide pavement.

Charming. Now I would have ten minutes in the company of Jason's mum. Ten minutes that would inevitably feel like ten lifetimes. No matter how much I snubbed her, and was smartly cutting to her, she kept bouncing back for more. This morning was no different.

She spoke with her usual earnest brightness. 'Did you see *Coronation Street* last night? It was awful sad altogether. That poor girl is pregnant again. She's only a child. And it's not her fault. Her mother's a right hussy. Two husbands and God knows how many affairs she's had.'

Maureen rambled on, as if she were talking about real people with real histories and real personalities.

'And that Jack. What he did was really out of character.'

I tried to resist the put-down – really, I did. But it sneaked out anyway. 'No, Maureen, it wasn't. He's not a person and he hasn't got a character. He's an actor and that was a plot device. A scriptwriter made him do that to move the story along.'

She gave a small shrug, as if to show that my barb hadn't hurt her. She spoke matter-of-factly. 'I know perfectly well it's not real, Claire. I just like to watch, and enjoy. It's undemanding, and it rests my brain at the end of the day. Is that so bad?'

'Yes. I'd sooner watch paint dry. I wouldn't lower myself to watch that crap.'

I could have bitten my tongue. There was no need to be so cutting. But then, there never was, was there? And yet that never stopped me. I just couldn't stop the part of me that let fly with nasty remarks. I suppose I was trying, in some pathetic way, to protect myself. But from what? Maureen was kind and gentle, and I certainly didn't need protection from her.

We'd arrived at the school, and Maureen beamed at me as if the exchange had never taken place. As if I hadn't once again breached every rule of polite discourse.

It was time for the Wednesday question. The question couldn't be asked on Mondays because on Mondays she cooked for the meals on wheels. Friday was the day she helped out at the Oxfam shop. That just left Wednesday.

'Claire, why don't you come over for a cup of coffee? The house is a tip, but sure, what harm?'

That was it. Every Wednesday. Same question. Word for word. Sometimes I wondered if she were being terribly sophisticated and clever, deliberately, self-mockingly, echoing the words week after week. Then I decided that she wasn't smart enough for that. Maureen was naive. Very kind, but very innocent. I knew she was ten times the person I was, but that only made me despise her even more.

15

And what hope did a kind, innocent person have against my smart, cold indifference?

Every Wednesday I made up some silly excuse to avoid accepting her invitation. Maybe that meant I was stupid too. I don't know. Maureen hardly needed friends. She was everybody's friend. And she certainly didn't need a friend like me.

And me? I didn't want friends. I'd deliberately cut myself off years ago. And after all that trouble I wasn't getting involved again.

'Thanks, Maureen, but no thanks. The tiler's coming, and I have to be there to let him in.'

I hoped I was right. I was fairly certain that I'd used the plumber and electrician excuses on the two previous weeks. Yes, I think it was time for the phantom tiler to visit. Mind you, if any tiler came as often as I pretended, he'd surely be tiling the garage ceiling, and the surfaces of the radiators by now. The legs of my kitchen table would be adorned with sweet little mosaic patterns, and my doors would shine in porcelain glory.

Maureen gave me a warm, genuine smile. 'Oh dear. That's such a pity. Maybe next week then.'

I smiled a small smile in return. 'Yes, Maureen. Maybe next week.'

'Bye then, Claire. I must go in and give the teacher these green buns I made for the kiddies' morning snack.'

She went into the classroom, and I stood outside for a moment. Part of me was glad to have shaken her off

16

so easily. Part of me was filled with self-hatred. Why did I have to be so mean? She was a kind, decent person. She did charity work, and baked healthy snacks for other people's children. She continued to be nice to me, no matter how mean I was to her. Every day I resolved to be more receptive to her generosity. Every day the nasty me surfaced and pushed her away once more.

And really, deep down, I wanted to go back to her house. I wanted to be fussed over, and served with coffee, and perhaps a few leftover green buns. I wanted to sit in her kitchen and look at the porridge pot in the sink, and the crumpled juice carton on the table.

I wanted to be her friend.

It was a beautiful day, so I went for a long cycle, as I often did after dropping Lizzie at school. I had no set route. No destination in mind. I just cycled until the suburbs turned to fields, enjoying the wind in my wild red hair, and the feeling that I could go wherever I wanted. The roads were mine, and the world was my oyster (as long as I was back by twelve o' clock).

I cycled fast up a particularly steep incline, deliberately tiring myself on my old-fashioned single-speed bike. I stopped at the top of the hill, and flung the long-suffering bike against a bockety wooden gate. I threw myself beside it onto a grassy bank, and tried to catch my breath. I felt free and exhilarated. At one with the beautiful world.

After a while, when my breathing had eased, and the exhilaration was edging towards boredom, and a farmer passing on a dirty red tractor was giving me strange looks, I got up, climbed once more onto my trusty bike, and went home to start the ironing.

As if I didn't feel bad enough, I had a visit from James's mum, Maisie, to look forward to that evening.

She arrived promptly at six o'clock, bringing with her a bunch of droopy celery, and a crumpled, out-of-date magazine that looked as if it might have been stolen from the hairdresser's. These she held towards me with a self-satisfied smile that would almost have been overdoing it if she were presenting me with the keys of a Ferrari and tickets for a round-the-world cruise. I kissed the lavender-scented air a few inches from her proffered cheek, and didn't even try to look grateful.

Maisie sat at the kitchen table and sniffed the air. 'Hmmm. I don't smell cooking. Don't tell me it's salad again. You know I don't like salad.'

'Sorry, Maisie. It's salad.'

I'd always loved salad, and took particular pleasure in serving it when Maisie came around. It was mean, I know, but Maisie always managed to drive me towards such pettiness.

(Our relationship wasn't really helped by the fact that years earlier, when Maisie had heard that James and I planned to marry, she had looked distinctly disappointed, and said, 'Are you sure you are suited to

18

each other?' Of course, even I knew this was mother-in-law-speak for, 'You're not good enough for my precious son,' so I immediately lapsed into a sulk which had lasted ever since.)

Maisie sniffed again. A sniff of disdain this time. 'Anyway, salad isn't enough for a working man like my James. You should make more stews. A working man needs lots of stews. Salads are only good for rabbits. And for those supermodel hussies. You be careful, Claire, or my James will fade away altogether.'

I looked across at my strong, healthy husband. He didn't look as if he'd be fading away any time soon.

James tried to smooth things. 'Salad is good for us, Mum. And anyway, Claire was probably busy today, and didn't get time to prepare anything hot.'

Maisie surveyed the untidy kitchen with narrowed eyes. 'I see you didn't get around to doing the kitchen yet.'

Ha! She should have seen it ten minutes before she arrived. Now that was a mess to be proud of.

'It's not fair on James coming home to a messy house. He never did when he lived with me,' she continued.

She took a deep breath, ready to launch into one of her tirades about her methods of housekeeping.

James dived in just in time. 'Lizzie, why don't you sing your new song for Granny? The one about the chicken?'

I handed out the plates of salad, and wondered how we'd endure Maisie's visits when Lizzie became too big to distract on demand.

Much, much later, James and I stood at the door, waving goodbye to Maisie. I was tired and tense from the effort of not saying all the things I wanted to say. (Funny how I often managed to bite back my nasty comments when Maisie was around. I suspected that I was actually a little bit afraid of her.)

As I stood leaning against the hall door, I wanted to shout out into the evening air.

'Ha! Tomorrow, James is going to work in an unironed shirt and shrunken socks with holes in them. I never make sure he wears a vest on cold mornings, and I don't care if he doesn't eat five portions of fruit and vegetables every day. And as soon as we can close this door behind you, your precious little boy and I are going in to have wild, unbridled sex. On the kitchen table. With the light on. And the curtains open. And there's nothing you can do about it.'

Of course, what I really said was a quiet, 'Goodnight, Maisie. See you next week.'

I went to close the door, but I wasn't quick enough. I still got to hear Maisie's parting words.

'And don't forget, Claire. Do a stew. You can feed your old salads to that dirty squeaky rat thing that Lizzie calls a pet.'

'Yes, Maisie,' I replied meekly, resolving to give her a bigger salad than ever the following week, with lots of greenfly for added flavour.

James sighed as he closed the door.

'Thanks for trying to be nice, Cee.'

I smiled at him and felt very small.

Chapter Two

The next day was Thursday, and Lizzie didn't have playschool. I loved those school-free days. They generally started with ambitious plans for trips to the park, or exciting, creative activities. The reality, as usual, was that we spent most of the morning thrown on a couch, reading storybooks, and drawing pictures of cows with pointy noses and stick-legs. When lunchtime came around, I half-heartedly pushed the cereal bowls into the dishwasher, and swept the toast crumbs into the corner of the kitchen, next to the fridge.

There's nothing at all wrong with being a housewife, as long as you're good at it. Trouble is, I'm completely useless. I hate cooking. I hate cleaning. Ironing drives me almost demented with its dreary repetitiveness and its endless reappearance. I never bake or knit or stencil pretty swirls of ivy onto the walls. I usually try to get by with the absolute, bare minimum of housework, while fervently wishing I were somewhere else. When faced with a completely trashed kitchen, my usual response is to sit amidst the chaos and write a poem. A romantic one, usually. About true love, and violins and bluebirds of happiness. Then I crumple the paper into a ball, fling it into a corner, where it could lie for days, or even weeks if I managed to find a far enough corner. Then I go for a cycle if I'm on my own, or draw some more cows, if Lizzie is around.

Housewife of the year I ain't.

Poor, long-suffering James would often come home from work to scenes of total chaos, as Lizzie and I romped gigglingly in the garden, or amidst the tossed clothes of her bed, or mine. And he never once complained. He'd just smile his easy, tolerant smile, and join in as Lizzie and I would scramble to restore some semblance of order to our disordered world.

That Thursday night, when Lizzie was in bed, and James had helped me to half-tidy the kitchen, we sat down to watch an old movie on the television. James put his feet up on the coffee table, and rested one arm companionably on my shoulder. He nestled into his seat and sighed.

'This is nice, Cee, isn't it?'

The film started just then, and James didn't notice that I failed to reply.

I sat on the couch, in my apple-white living-room, and wished I had a friend I could talk to. Someone with whom I could share my feelings of frustration. Someone who would understand that even though I loved my husband dearly, I couldn't find the words to share my true feelings with him. I needed someone who could help me to find a way to tell him how sad and ungrateful and lonely I felt.

The film droned on and on. I didn't even try to follow it. I half-closed my eyes, and imagined what it would be like to have a friend.

I could picture the scene. I'd feel lonely. I'd call my friend and she'd arrive at once. We'd hug – a close, sisterly hug, like in the feel-good movies. We'd both be good-looking, in an interesting, slightly weathered kind of way. We wouldn't have crow's feet, rather wren's feet, just about visible on our still glowing skin. We'd look terribly cool in our casual, but not scruffy, clothes. I'd put the Alessi kettle on, and we'd sit for hours by the comforting light of a real fire. (Smoke-free fuel of course. We'd be that type.) Miranda (or perhaps Megan) would listen to my sad tale, rubbing my velour-clad arm and handing me tissues softened with aloe vera. Her big, brown eyes would soften and glow. She'd make comforting cooing noises every now and then. She'd absently fiddle with her 'Save the Whales' badge. Then she'd offer me advice, and we'd calmly discuss what I should do. Lots of sparkling, intelligent words would pass between us. We could open a bottle of wine. A nice light Beaujolais perhaps. We'd sip it delicately from John Rocha crystal goblets, hardly smudging our pale pink lip gloss. The wine would make us mellow and wise rather than blindly, word-slurringly drunk. We'd dip crumbly breadsticks into interesting-looking concoctions made of avocado and hommmos and sundried tomatoes. We'd nibble some expensive Belgian chocolates. We'd shed some companionable tears, and then laugh a little.

I'd feel better.

Fat chance!

When had I last had a friend?

I'd scared them all away years earlier with my prickly personality, and my ever-so-clever put downs. Deep down, I craved friendship, but I had no one I could tell. No one to talk to. I had painted myself into the corner of life's living-room, and I was there alone.

The next day, Lizzie had school again. It was a beautiful day, and after I dropped her off, I climbed onto my bike and headed for the hills once more. As usual, I cycled until I was panting and breathless, then, found a convenient gate to rest my bike on, and flung myself onto the grass nearby. I reached into my ever-present shoulder bag in the vain hope of finding a bottle of water that didn't have things growing in it. As I rooted around in the hessian depths, my fingers touched the lottery ticket that Lizzie had bullied me into buying a few days earlier. For a moment I thought of saving it so Lizzie could scratch it after school. Then I decided that it was time I started to discourage this wasteful habit. I suspected that now that the hospital wing and the golf-club renovations were complete, I was now actually financing the fitting out of the presidential dog-kennels with hand-woven cashmere carpets.

I scratched the first two panels with my thumbnail. Bad luck. They both read €20,000. Now I'd never win. It was always more encouraging to get two small amounts first. Then there was some reasonable chance of a modest return on my investment. I half-heartedly scraped at the rest, uncovering various free-ticket symbols, and a few pictures of televisions and footballs. I thought of leaving the last unscratched panel for Lizzie, and then remembered my decision to wean her away from her gambling habit.

I scratched, and looked. I looked again. I turned the ticket over, and then over again. I rubbed my eyes. I read the small print. Twice. Yes, it was clear enough. Match three amounts – win that amount. I'd matched €20,000 three times, so it would appear – to any impartial, idle observer who could read – that I'd won that amount.

I gave a long whistle. (I can't actually whistle, so I suspect I produced my usual thin, wailing sound.) It didn't matter. I did it again. I leaned back on my damp, grassy throne, and looked up at the blue sky above me. I'd just won €20,000.

I closed my eyes, then opened them again. The sky was still blue. The ticket still appeared to tell me that I'd won.

I could hear the faint chugging of a tractor in a distant field. The wind rustled the leaves over my head.

An unidentified bird whistled in the hedgerow. A spider scuttled across my boot, spinning a silken thread for the long journey from my toes to the ground. My bike fell with a loud clatter, bringing two splintering wooden bars of the gate with it.

And I began to dream my crazy dream.

Chapter Three

That sunny Friday, in April of last year, I was very relieved that when I collected Lizzie from school, she'd forgotten all about the lottery ticket. Until I knew for sure what to do, I didn't want her prattling to strangers about Mummy's big lottery win. I took her home and parked her in front of the television, without even stopping to feel guilty. Then I spent the afternoon dreaming and planning. By the time James was due home, I had it all worked out.

We'd go away. The three of us. For three long, wonderful months. We could travel to Australia. The Far East. California. All the places I'd once dreamed of visiting. We'd be warm for three whole months. Three months without ironing or mopping floors. Three months without making small talk with the neighbours. We could pack three rucksacks with denim and cheesecloth and musk oil. James could grow a beard, and I could braid Lizzie's hair. I might even get my nose pierced. James could get his nipple pierced. (Well, maybe not. Not even my crazy dream was that crazy.) We could throw away our watches and our humdrum responsibilities. For three magical months, we'd be brown and happy and carefree. We could travel cheaply, and then the lottery money would last until we came back.

The timing was just perfect. James works as an electrician. He runs a small business with his partner, Liam. Liam has three strapping student sons who 'help out' every summer, driving James almost to distraction with their cool confidence, and their laid-back, arrogant, young men's ways. Liam could easily manage without James for the months of June, July and August, and James would be spared his annual penance. Lizzie was due to start school in September, so this would be our last chance to head off without worrying about her missing valuable term time.

It made perfect sense. To me at least.

As Lizzie watched her favourite *Barney* video for the third time, and I made my plans, I could hear my dear old granny's last words echoing in my head, egging me on.

I remember it so well, that icy morning in January. I was fifteen, and I had skipped school to visit my granny in hospital. She'd been there for months, slowly fading away, more from old age than anything else. I loved her dearly, but I can't pretend that was the only reason I went to visit her. There was also the small detail of a double maths class, and I had no homework done. Trigonometry. Not funny.

The nurses knew me from my previous visits. One gentle, middle-aged one rushed to meet me as I sauntered along the corridor.

'Claire. You're just in time. She's going.'

Even at fifteen I knew what she meant. I knew granny wasn't going for a walk, or for a quick macramé lesson in the occupational-therapy room. I knew she wouldn't be packing up her support stockings and her nylon nighties and her pink hot water bottle for a long weekend in Killarney.

I felt a moment of panic. I wasn't ready for this dying business. It was Wednesday though, and I knew my mum would be out shopping. Dad played golf every Wednesday, so he too was out of reach – all those years ago when Ireland was a mobile-phone-free zone.

My granny was dying and there was no one there but me.

I think my feet must have slipped into reverse, but the nurse was having none of it. She squeezed my arm gently and propelled me through the door, whispering, 'It's OK, Claire. Don't be afraid. She's still your gran. And she's not in any pain.'

Granny lay there, thin and pale. No thinner or paler than usual though, and for a brief moment, I hoped the nurse was wrong. Maybe she was over-reacting. Granny had a panicked look in her eyes though, and her shallow breathing was even more laboured than usual.

My eyes moved towards the clock over the door. Twenty-seven minutes past ten. Double maths would be over by now. At school it was break-time. I could be huddled in a corner of the classroom with my friends. We could be jostling for places to sit on the huge brown storage heaters. We could be laughing over the horoscopes in the latest *Jackie* magazine. We could be checking the 'Cathy and Clare' problem page, for nuggets of wisdom to guide us through the coming weekend. We could be sharing crisps and chocolate and pineapple chunks. And apple-flavoured drops that would blister our tongues with their sharpness.

No school for me though. I had to stay and watch my granny die.

Her eyes flickered in recognition as I approached the bed. She reached for my hand and held it – remarkably tightly, for a dying woman. Amidst lots of sighs and gasps, she uttered a stream of advice.

'Go with your instinct. Always follow your heart. If you get married, don't let yourself be fenced in. Be free and take every opportunity you get. Never be afraid to live your dreams.'

In my innocence, I thought that just because she was dying, the secrets of the universe had been revealed to her, and she was kindly sharing them with me. It was many years before I realised that I had been listening to the last drug-induced ramblings of a half-senile old lady. Unfortunately, by then I'd taken a lot of her advice to heart. I'd kind of got into the habit of living by her clichés, and it seemed hard to let go of them.

Last April, they still rattled around my brain, colouring my judgement, leading me astray.

James arrived home promptly at five, just as he always did. He put his arms around me and kissed me gently on the top of my head. He gave a little throaty laugh, and I knew he was recalling our early-morning exertions. (Our mornings were becoming quite exciting, and Lizzie was having more Coco Pops than were good for her.) I laughed too, but my mind stayed on my exciting travel plans. James gave my head another kiss, and went out into the garden.

I don't like gardening. I don't really see the point of it all – endless scrabbling around, getting hot and dirty. And what is there to show after all that? Buckets full of tomatoes, just ripe at the time they're practically giving them away in Dunne's Stores. Huge watery marrows with no taste, which James innocently expects me to transform into aromatic soups and casseroles. And runner beans. Basket after basket of runner beans. Week after week, after week. By the end of September, I am having nightmares about being choked by tough, stringy green pods.

Still, James seems to enjoy it, and I must admit that I always found it relaxing to watch him at work. That evening, I followed him into the garden. I sat on our wooden garden seat, in the still-pleasant evening sun, and looked on as he planted some onion sets. As he laboured, Lizzie sat on my knee and fiddled with my hair, winding long strands around her fingers.

James carefully raked the soil, then marked out lines with a short stick. The onion sets came in a small, brown paper bag, which James emptied onto the earth, releasing, along with the onions, a little shower of dried golden skins. Then he pushed each set gently into the soil, working steadily, stopping and straightening his back at the end of each row.

When he was finished, he came and sat with us. I ran to the kitchen to make him a cup of strong, fresh coffee. I brought him a chocolate biscuit. He should have realised then that something was afoot but – guileless man that he was – he just thanked me, and sat back to survey his work. I sat next to him, and Lizzie wriggled between us. James rubbed my knee in an absent, companionable kind of way, leaving a slight mucky stain on my jeans.

A passing helicopter crew, casually glancing downwards would have surveyed a sweet, domestic scene of gentle harmony. Of course it couldn't last.

I took a deep breath. 'Lizzie, run down to the end of the garden, hop around the apple tree twice. Pick five daisies, and sing the *Barney* song four times.'

An old trick, but it always worked. Lizzie raced off, giving me about three-and-a-half minutes to talk to James. I pulled the lottery ticket from my pocket and waved it in his face.

'Look, look. We've won twenty thousand Euro. Isn't it incredible?'

I knew James thought I was winding him up. He took the ticket from me and examined it carefully. He

32

gave a long whistle. Unlike me, he could actually whistle, so it attracted Lizzie's attention. She stopped in the middle of her hopping, and made as if to come back to us.

'No, darling. You keep hopping. Daddy and I are just having a chat.'

Lizzie obediently began to hop again, with an intense look of concentration on her small, innocent face.

James jumped up and gave me a huge hug. 'This is fantastic, Cee. Just fantastic. Think what we could do with all this money. We could convert the garage. Change the car for a newer model. We could . . .'

I should probably have realised then that things weren't going to be quite as easy as I had hoped.

I interrupted him. 'James, I've had the most fantastic idea. You're going to just love it. It's the best idea I've ever had. Let's not spend the money on the house. Let's spend it on a big trip.'

He smiled. 'Yeah, you're right. The house is fine as it is. Will we go to Lanzarote? Remember we saw it on the travel show. We could get one of the apartments with a balcony and a sea view. Now we can afford the extra. It'll be fantastic.'

I laughed. 'No, it's not that kind of holiday. It's different. Very different. This is going to be more than a holiday.'

He gave me one of his tolerant smiles. 'OK, tell me all about it.'

So I did.

I was so excited, and it seemed so right. I could see us walking barefoot on a golden beach, swinging Lizzie in the air between us. I could hear her shouts of joy. I could feel warm sand between my toes. I could smell the sea and sun oil and barbecued shrimp.

I couldn't hold back the words. They tumbled out, and, as I spoke, my plans became more and more ambitious. A year away. Maybe even more. We could rent out the house. We could go to India and work. We could trek through Peru. Live with hill tribes in Thailand. Nothing seemed impossible. We could live out all of our youthful dreams.

Finally the words ended, and James, shielding his eyes from the sun, looked quizzically at me. I could feel the first tinglings of unease.

I gave a nervous laugh. 'Well, what do you think?'

Still James didn't speak.

'Wouldn't it be great? It would be the holiday of a lifetime. Lizzie would love every moment.'

Lizzie, just back from her quest, agreed. 'Yeah, can we go on holidays? Chlöe went to Spain. Could I go on a camel? We saw camels on a video at school. They're very humpy.'

James ran his mucky hand across his brow. 'You are joking, aren't you?'

I was taken aback, and couldn't respond to his question, so he asked again. 'This isn't serious, is it Claire? You don't really think we could do this? Tell me you're just winding me up.'

I was so disappointed that I could hardly speak. I had been so sure he would share my dreams. I wanted him to join in with my enthusiasm, and to plan with me, to dream with me, but all he could see were obstacles.

'What about my work, for one thing? How could I get away?'

'That's easily sorted. Won't the three wise men be back home soon, looking to run the business until their precious college courses require their presence again in September?'

'Well, I suppose that's true. I wouldn't mind giving them a miss. But that would only cover the summer. Are you saying we could go away for a year?'

I nodded miserably. 'I'd like to, but a few months would do if that was all you could manage.'

'But what about Lizzie's hamster? Who would take care of that for months on end?'

When he asked that particular question, I knew there was something else going on. James had always hated that hamster. He'd have been quite happy for it to go and live on a nice farm in the country where it would have lots of other little hamster friends to play with. When the hamster got mentioned, I knew there had to be a reason why James was being so pathetic.

There was.

'And what about my mum? How could we leave her for all that time?'

'For God's sake, James. She's not an invalid. She's as strong as a horse. She'd be fine without us.'

'Who'd do her shopping if I wasn't there? Who'd put out her bins and cut her lawn?'

'She could do all those things herself if you weren't so available. She treats you like a baby, and yet she wants you to be the man in her life. That's not fair. And there are maintenance firms who'd be glad to tidy her garden. Hasn't she got a copy of the *Yellow Pages*? You know she'd be fine.'

He spoke appeasingly. 'But, Claire, she'd be lonely.'

'Lonely my eye. She hates me, she's impatient with Lizzie, and she spends her time giving out to you.'

'Come on, Claire. You know that's just her way. She can't help it. You know she'd miss us.'

Ha! Miss bossing us around, he meant. She'd miss having us to criticise, and put down. Clearly it was time for the Maisie argument to get one of its regular airings. The old, 'Is Maisie lonely and misunderstood, or is she a bit of a manipulator?' argument. James and I had had a hundred of these arguments in the past. We both knew the ground rules, the points past which neither of us dared to step. The arguments never went anywhere of course, and clearly this one was going to be no different. We went through the usual motions for a while, and then we wound it up.

Anyway, my heart wasn't really in it. He was right. Maisie would be lonely without us, and for all of my giving out, I knew she loved Lizzie, and I suspected that, deep down, she even felt some small, grudging affection for me. I felt uncharacteristically generous towards her.

'We could pay a maintenance firm to do her jobs for her. And we could even hire someone to come in and keep her company every now and then. We can afford it now.'

James looked doubtful. 'I don't think so. Can you imagine how Mum would feel about a hired companion?'

He was right of course. She would hate the very idea. Suddenly I had a brainwave.

'What about Bobby? Maybe he'd come home for a while.' Bobby was James's errant younger brother. His only sibling. He had cleverly flown the nest years before James found the courage to leave. He went to Australia to find himself, which was a pity as, Australia being such a vast country, he was clearly having difficulty – he'd been gone for over ten years. Even if he hadn't succeeded in finding himself, perhaps he'd make do with someone like himself, and come home and take some responsibility for his mother.

James gave a cold laugh. 'Come on, Claire. Fat chance of him showing up. If he got wind of the fact that he was needed, he'd try to find a place in the world even further away, just in case we'd track him down and drag him home.'

I smiled. Just as we always disagreed on the topic of Maisie, we were at one when it came to Bobby. He was an irresponsible charmer, and totally useless.

Then I remembered my dream, and pleaded. 'Please, James. Consider it seriously. It would be fantastic. Let's be brave. Let's live a little. I don't want to look back from old age and feel we threw away a wonderful chance. Don't let your mother spoil this for us. If she loved you, she'd wish us well.'

Looking back now, with the knowledge that always comes too late, I can see why James reacted as he did, and I can accept that perhaps I was getting a bit carried away. Perhaps I should have introduced the idea more slowly, and given him time to get used to it. Maybe my crazy enthusiasm was a little intimidating to him after a long day of laying electric cables and repairing fuse boxes. Maybe he wasn't quite ready for the mention of musk oil and the tortoise-preservation camp in the Galapagos Islands. I might even have let it slip about the nose-piercing. Probably not a good idea. Maybe I should have mentioned two weeks in Lanzarote, and progressed slowly from there.

That day, however, I was filled with a sense that we had to seize the moment, or lose the opportunity forever. Granny's words popped up: 'Never be afraid to live your dreams.'

I so desperately wanted to live that dream. I allowed my enthusiasm to inspire me, to convince me that I could do anything. Unfortunately the same enthusiasm terrified poor James. And, to be fair to him, every family needs one member with a scrap of sense. In our family, he shouldered that heavy burden.

I was very upset at his reaction, but nevertheless determined that we would make this great trip. I was determined that I wouldn't let Maisie, of all people, ruin my great plan.

Still, I think things might have turned out differently if James hadn't then said something that was quite out of character. What he said next clinched it for me in the end. I know now that he didn't mean to be dismissive, but standing there on that glorious spring day that had started out so well, he unintentionally hardened my resolve, and turned my mind to stone.

He stood up and half-turned away from me, as if the matter were concluded. He picked up his shovel and began to dig the potato plot. A few moments later, he stopped digging, rested his foot on the shovel and turned back towards me. 'It's that time of the month again, isn't it?' he said.

Sudden tears sprang from my eyes and dripped down onto my check shirt. James dropped his shovel and sat beside me again. He put his arms around me.

'Come on, Cee. You know I'm only kidding.'

I just sobbed louder in reply.

'You know I can't just up and leave. Life's not like that. Well, my life isn't anyway. We'll have a nice summer holiday. You'll see. I'll try to get three weeks off. We'll go to the travel agent's tomorrow and enquire about Lanzarote.'

I sobbed even louder. I'd never even been to Lanzarote, but all of a sudden it sounded awful. All I could picture were hordes of suburbanites like us, grimly enjoying their few weeks in the sun, dutifully attending the tour rep's meetings, drinking watered down sangria, making small talk with the roasting bodies on the neighbouring sun-loungers. I could even hear the conversations in my head.

'Oh, you're from Cork. Do you know the Roches from Douglas?'

'Are they the ones with the fish shop?'

'No, but they're their cousins. These Roches have an off-licence.'

'Oh, right. Isn't the drink here dirt cheap?'

'Yes. We bought three beers and two vodkas last night. Guess how much.'

'No idea.'

'Go on, just guess. You'll never guess right.'

'Er, seven Euro.'

This would produce a triumphant whoop. 'No. Six Euro and thirteen cent. Imagine. Guess how much that would cost in my local at home. Go on, guess.'

I ran these foolish conversations through my mind as I clung to James and sobbed ever louder. He stroked my hair and muttered soothing words.

It was too late, though. There was nothing he could do or say. I knew in my crazy, unstable kind of way that I had to do something, or that very soon I'd be no more good for Lizzie, or for James, or for myself. I had the horrible feeling that my whole world was collapsing around me, and that I had to break free or be crushed forever under huge mounds of ironing, and papier-mâché masks, and organic flapjacks and glossy brochures for package holidays aimed at the kind of person I didn't want to be.

It was as if the glue that had held me together for all those years since 1986 had suddenly begun to dissolve. I could see myself crumbling into tiny fragments that could never be reassembled. I could see my personality disintegrating and flying away on a capricious wind, like ticker tape at an American St Patrick's day parade.

I was afraid.

Chapter Four

After that, things began to move very quickly.

Well, maybe quickly isn't the word. Things just moved steadily on, like a roving glacier, grinding everything in its path, making all around it cold and harsh and chillingly inhospitable.

James apologised many times but I couldn't forgive him. It wasn't like me really. I will admit to some minor character defects, but stubbornness isn't usually one of them. For some reason though, on this occasion, I dug my heels in. I was adamant that I was going to take a trip, with or without him.

I couldn't, then or now, explain my feelings of hurt. We argued for days. We had long, emotional, tearful arguments, that left me feeling sick and tired. Sometimes, in quiet moments, I wondered if perhaps I was showing signs of some mental illness, if I might need medical help, but still, I couldn't stop. Our arguments were going nowhere. It was as if James and I were strangers from different countries, with no language in common, trying to communicate with inadequate, irrelevant phrasebooks.

In my mind, I was saying: 'Please help me, James. I'm all mixed up and upset and can't make sense of anything. I feel I have to escape or die.'

He was probably hearing: 'James, I've fulfilled all your worst fears and turned into a complete raving loony, and if you give in to this whim of mine, I'll only find even crazier ideas to push upon you.'

The words James said went like this: 'I love you but I can't go along with this eccentric notion of yours.'

What I heard though was: 'I don't love you enough, or understand you enough so I'm going to dig in my heels and veto every suggestion you make.'

Sometimes I toyed with the idea of telephoning my old travelling companion, Grace. She, of all people, should understand how I felt, and perhaps she could help me decide what to do. (The years might not have been kind to her. Her flawless looks might have faded. Her golden locks might be showing tinges of coarse grey. And that alone would have made me feel better.) But I hadn't seen or heard from her in so long, and I felt shy about contacting her now. I was so desperate that I twice took out the most recent number I had for her, but each time I put it away unused.

She'd have got a right shock if I had rung her, poor girl. Hearing my voice, after all these years, would have stunned her. Anyway, she'd probably forgotten that I ever existed. Surely she would have filed me away in her 'don't go there' file.

In the end, for all kinds of reasons, I made no contact.

Often, during that emotional time, I lay awake in the dark, listening to the suburban, night-time noises. There were regular sirens, as ambulances and squad cars raced through the empty streets. Occasionally I'd hear car doors slamming, and then whispers as my neighbours made their way home after a night out, the click-click of high heels sounding very loud on the fancy cobble-lock driveways. I'd lie there, wide awake, wondering what was happening to me. I'd stare at the ceiling, weeping many silent tears, feeling them drip down my cheek, soaking my hair and my pillowcase. (In the mornings when I idly chewed strands of my hair, they always tasted of salt.) I'd look at James sleeping peacefully beside me, and wonder why I was being so pigheaded, why I was hurting him so much when he didn't deserve any of it.

Every night I resolved that, in the morning, I would put an end to my foolishness, apologise to James, and settle back to my old, peaceful life. Every morning though, I'd awake cross and cranky, unable to step back, unable to offer any kind of compromise. Then the rows would begin again.

One Friday, about two weeks after my lottery win, I was having one of my feeble 'good mother' afternoons.

Lizzie, all wrapped up in one of James's old shirts, was standing on a chair that she'd dragged over to the kitchen counter-top. She was helping me to roll out a grey sticky mess that was supposed to be pastry. I never could make pastry anyway, so it was nice when Lizzie helped, and I could blame her for the inevitable disaster. She had gathered a large collection of plastic pastry cutters, and she painstakingly began to cut out an array of shapes. They were pressed so deeply into the work surface that I despaired of ever removing them, but it seemed a pity to interrupt her concentration by suggesting the adult notion of failure.

I heard the car pull up outside, and braced myself for yet more harsh words and arguments. James came to the back door, and made funny faces at Lizzie through the glass. She grinned briefly at him and then returned to her task. He let himself in, and I noticed that, for the first time in ages, he was whistling cheerfully. He tickled Lizzie, and then leaned across the worktop and gave me a gentle kiss. I was pleased, and then suspicious.

He pulled up a stool, and sat beside me.

'I have a marvellous idea, Cee. I don't know why we didn't think of it sooner. This way we can go away. We can follow your dream.'

I became even more suspicious. This thing between us wasn't going to be solved that easily.

I spoke cautiously. 'Well. Spit it out.'

He beamed at me. 'It's the perfect plan. Guess what I've thought of.'

I was hopeful and pessimistic at the same time, and in no mood for playing guessing games. I scraped some sticky goo from my thumb and made a small grey mountain on the worktop.

'Just tell me, James. Please.'

He beamed at me again. 'We'll bring Mum with us. Isn't that the answer to all our problems?'

At first, I thought he was joking. But sadly, no. This poor deranged man, who had seen how a day out in Crosshaven with his mother could drive me to such dreadful agitation, somehow thought that I could see my way to spending long months abroad in her company. He continued to beam at me, showing his unnaturally perfect white teeth. I didn't know whether to kiss his innocent boyish face, or to punch it hard with my pastry-encrusted knuckles. How could he get it so wrong?

'Isn't it a great idea? You know how Mum loves to travel. She's very sociable, really. She could help us with Lizzie. She could babysit, so you and I would have time together. I know she's not your favourite person, but this would be different. We'd go somewhere warm, and we'd relax. It could be the making of us.'

My perceptive little Lizzie looked up and saw my darkening face. She'd witnessed too many arguments recently. It wasn't fair.

I spoke as calmly as I could. 'Go put on your *Postman Pat* video – There's a good girl.'

She slid off her chair and padded off obediently.

James seemed to be waiting for a display of joy at his great idea. He looked as if he was holding his breath.

I spoke slowly, and quietly. 'James, I would die if I had to go on a long holiday with your mother. I'd hate every single second. It would be a long, slow torture. I would sooner stay here, locked in this kitchen for three months, having my bikini-line waxed and my teeth de-scaled, than spend a week with your horrible, small-minded, selfish, interfering mother.'

There wasn't much he could say to that, was there? He managed, 'I'm going for a shower.' And he headed upstairs.

I absently scraped the grey mess of Lizzie's creation from the grainy surface of the worktop. It seemed the pool of my tears wasn't yet exhausted. They began to drip forth again, turning the grey paste to an even slimier mess. I hoped Lizzie wouldn't want to eat it.

James came down from his shower, clean and unsmiling. We ate our dinner in silence, and part of me was glad at the break from the fighting. Next morning, though, it all began again, and we had a few days of hurt silences, intermingled with brief, vicious parries that left me feeling weak and lost. It was as if the warmth and affection that had always existed between us had vanished forever.

James cracked first. He came home from work one evening, tired and cross. He sat me down at the kitchen table, and stared into my eyes with an anger that frightened me into silence.

'OK, Claire. I give in. I cannot take any more of this. I love you more than you will ever know, but that doesn't seem to be enough. I am suffering, Lizzie is suffering, and I think you are suffering. I don't know what has caused this, and I'm not sure that I want to know. I am not taking one minute off work. I am not leaving my mother to fend for herself for months on end. I am not trekking off halfway across Europe, or the world, following some crazy dream of yours. My life is fine as it is, thanks very much. You can take Lizzie and go. Go wherever you want, and stay for weeks – months if you like. Just have Lizzie home to me, ready for school in September as we had planned.. That's all I ask of you.'

I nodded dumbly. I was drained and frightened, but still I couldn't backtrack.

It may seem strange that a seemingly happy marriage could disintegrate so fast, and I can't offer much in the way of explanation. It was a bit like an episode of *ER*. One minute, everyone is laughing and sharing holiday plans and chocolate brownies, and the next, there's total mayhem with bloodied limbs all over the shop, and screaming lunatics rampaging around the place. (And of course, being *ER*, there would be a blizzard too. It's set in Chicago, for God's sake, not Antarctica. Why is it always snowing?)

I had marooned myself on an island, depending on James and Lizzie for all of my sustenance. I was an only child, and my parents had both died shortly after Lizzie was born. My dad had a heart attack, and my mum sort of faded away six months later. I had no close friends. I had no one to tell me in a calm way to get a grip on myself. After that awful summer of 1986, I had worked hard to rid myself of close human contact. I'm ashamed to say that when James and I married, I edged his friends out of our lives. I didn't mean to do this, and I didn't realise it at the time, but I did it all right. I wormed out of invitations to parties and gatherings. I made no overtures to anyone, and when people were kind to me, as many were, I managed to scare them off with my cool exterior. The term 'Ice Maiden' was coined with me in mind. I stood with my head high, protecting my fragile ego, and soon, people stopped trying.

The sad result of my isolation and exclusion was that I had no one to listen to me except James, and when he shut me out, I felt abandoned. I was wandering blindly, not sure what to do, but afraid that if I backed down and did nothing, I would somehow get lost, adrift in a hostile world, never to be forgiven for my weakness.

I found myself making plans for a trip to Greece. This was no accident, of course. I'd been to Greece before. And you've guessed it – it was in 1986. Not exactly a successful trip, that one. Not one I'll be writing about for the 'My Best Memory' column in the *Evening Echo*. Still though, with uncharacteristic perception, I knew I had to go back.

Chapter Five

How can I begin to describe how I felt back then, in the spring of 1986?

It was near the end of my second year in college, and as my exams were due to finish early in May, I had many months of freedom stretching in front of me. I was part of a large, animated group, sitting together at a long, brown trestle table in the college restaurant, imaginatively called 'the Rest'. We sat there, nursing cold cups of tea and coffee, putting off the awful moment when we would have to return to the Aula Maxima, or the reference library, to study. The grass in the quad had just been cut for the first time that year, and this had prompted the usual panic, as college lore held that, by the first grass cut, all students should be finished their third revision. I was conscious of not losing the precious study place I'd just found that morning, with a lovely, distracting view of the comings and goings in the car park. I'd filled in a vacation slip, and wanted to get back before it expired, afraid that otherwise I'd return to find that some desperate student had unceremoniously dumped my books in the passageway. There was always a shortage of study places at college, but at least it gave us something to demonstrate about. The social highlight of the first term was always the students' union march through the Grand Parade and Patrick Street. We loved the disruption it caused, enjoying listening to disgruntled oldies griping on – 'long-haired layabouts, trying to hold us to ransom – they don't know what real work is like – things were different when I was young,' and so on. Now, though, in the last term, we fought amongst ourselves for the few available places, the marching forgotten, in our efforts to do a year's study in a few short months.

Still, we were generous to ourselves in our coffee breaks, enjoying the chat and the common yearning for the freedom of the long summer break. That particular day, everyone was discussing plans for the holidays, and most had plans of some sort – acting as camp counsellors for spoilt American children, packing gherkins in German factories, doing whatever job they would be given in a kibbutz, or waitressing in London. None of these particularly appealed to me, so when Grace leaned back in her grey plastic chair, tossed her blonde head and said, 'I'm going to Greece to lie on the beach and do as little work as possible', it seemed just like my idea of a holiday. Jessie, overhearing our conversation, also liked the sound of this, and we broke into a little subgroup to make plans.

Making those plans must have taken all of ten minutes. Plans are so easily made and broken when you're a student. I had worked part-time during the term, and had saved enough money for a return train ticket to Athens. I'd have enough then to keep me going for a few weeks, as would Grace and Jessie, and we figured we could get some kind of work to supplement this whenever times got hard.

Weeks later, we found ourselves on the ferry to France, and then a train to Athens. Grace, Jessie and I – a strange combination. Grace was tall, slim, blonde and beautiful – all the things I wanted to be. Even in our normal student attire of raggy jeans and sweat-shirts, she managed to look like a goddess. She was totally relaxed and laid-back about everything, and had a slight air of detachment, as if she didn't really belong in this ordinary, dirty world. She was just passing through, waiting until something better came along. For all this, she was good fun, and always ready for an escapade of some sort.

Jessie was a total contrast in appearance: smallish, fattish, and not particularly good-looking. Yet she too had a certain charm. She could talk to anyone on any topic, and she had the most infectious laugh I have ever heard. When she was involved in a discussion, she became so animated, it was impossible to resist her, and so whenever she had a madcap scheme, there was usually a queue of people waiting to join in with her.

And me? I fell somewhere in the middle between these two, and to be honest I was a bit in awe of them both. I was of average height, neither as slim as Grace, nor as pudgy as Jessie. My wild red curls often drew admiring glances from passing American tourists in polyester trousers, but I hated them. I'd have happily exchanged them for Jessie's sleek black curls or Grace's long mane of glistening silk. I suppose my appearance was unremarkable, in an intense, young studenty type of way, but no one ever looked at me the way they looked at Grace, and part of me was deeply envious.

We wandered down through Europe, often getting places by virtue of Jessie's eloquence, or Grace's looks, with me just tagging along behind, glad to be trailing along in the wake of two such wonderful beings. I was quiet by nature, and tended to sit back and watch the other two, happy to go along with whatever they planned.

We travelled with a great sense of wonder, and as none of the three of us had ever been abroad before, it all seemed amazingly exciting and exotic. We wandered through France, Germany, Austria and Yugoslavia. We stayed in youth hostels, lived cheaply and had a marvellous time.

In Frankfurt, we acquired some free tickets to the zoo, and we stood gazing with envy into the monkeys' cages, mouths watering at the sight of the big black buckets, piled high with fresh fruit. I thought hungrily of all the times my mother had tried in vain to make me eat more fruit, and felt I would have killed for just one slightly brown banana. Jessie made faces at the monkeys, and jumped around taunting them, in the vain hope that they might get mad and throw a few bananas or apples at us. Grace stood coolly next to the cage of one large male primate, tossing her hair and smiling. She obviously wasn't his type though, as he continued to scratch his back with a bored air.

For the next few nights, I had the same dream, always involving a big bowl of ripe bananas, just a little out of my reach.

As we travelled through Germany, we joined the dedicated Irish effort to bankrupt German Telecom. Like most other Irish students, we had brought with us a large bag of Irish five-pence coins, which worked like magic in the public payphones. As our coins were worth only about a fifth of a Deutschmark, which we were using them to replace, it made our obligatory telephone calls home a lot cheaper, and we took a certain mischievous pride in being so smart. Unfortunately, we were not sophisticated con artists. We had heard rumours that, in an effort to catch the culprits, some of the phone booths had been rigged to lock shut when an illegal coin was used. Our heads told us that this was unlikely, but we were taking no chances, so we joined the Irish army of students, distinguishable across the country by the fact that we made all of our calls with one foot wedged in the phone booth doorway, just in case.

We made only one stop in Yugoslavia, in Zagreb. We were politically naive, blissfully unaware of any tension within the country. To us, Zagreb was just a very dull city, with no tourist office (or at least none that we could find), no lively bars or restaurants, and a youth hostel which looked ready to tumble down around us. If we had looked hard enough, I'm sure we would have found lots to like about the city, but the truth was, we had no interest in history or culture – we just wanted discos, beaches and good-looking, dark-skinned men who would shower us with outrageous compliments and gentle kisses.

It was a long journey by rail from Zagreb down to Athens, and we were very badly prepared for it. We had heard that we would be able to buy food and drink on the way, and this was true, but only just about. Every time we stopped at a station, there were local people selling drinks and food on the platform. Unfortunately we had also heard about a German girl who got off the train to buy something, and was left behind when the train departed unexpectedly. The story went that, stranded without ID, she was jailed without ceremony, and remained in jail until her friends returned to rescue her some weeks later. We were real innocents abroad, easily fooled by every modern myth that came our way, and though we weren't entirely convinced, we were scared enough not to dare to leave the train. Instead we relied on the most desperate of the vendors who came to the windows holding their wares aloft, and we bought many strange things, most of which we were afraid to eat. The only drinks we managed to buy were bottles of soapy tasting, barely fizzy, warm water that never seemed to quench our thirst, and made us feel rather unwell.

On the last section of that long, hot train journey, we were joined in our compartment by a group of young Greeks. They had large flasks of fresh water, which they passed around amongst themselves, oblivious to our hot, parched stares. I came close to crying, when, feeling slightly queasy and very, very, thirsty, I had to watch one young man put his head out of the window, and pour that beautiful, precious water over it. He pulled his head in, shook it, and caught my horrified look. He was confused for a second, and then realisation dawned.

'You want?' he asked, leaning over to hand me the still half-full flask.

I nodded gratefully, and drank deeply, handing it quickly to Jessie and Grace, before he could object.

He laughed. 'You finish,' he said, and watched as I drained it.

On that single occasion, all of my friends' powers were eclipsed by my desperation, and I felt good as the train finally chugged into Athens.

We spent one unremarkable night in the city, staying in the cheapest hostel we could find. There we shared a room with two Swedish girls who had travelled the length of Europe especially to visit the Acropolis. We tried not to look bored as they gushed on about Doric columns and Pentelic marble, and temples to obscure gods and goddesses. When we got up the next morning, the Swedish girls were gone, departed early no doubt so as to see the sun rise over the Parthenon. Grace, Jessie and I lingered over our breakfast, and then decided to follow their good example and soak up some history. We followed some basic directions and found ourselves on a dusty street, straining our necks looking up towards the Acropolis. It towered over the city, beautiful and majestic. We were indeed impressed. We stood at the base of the hillside and looked up in wonder.

I sighed and rubbed my sore neck. 'They were right, those Swedish girls. It is beautiful.'

Jessie agreed. 'Yeah. Imagine how long that's been there.'

Grace shielded her eyes with her hands as she spoke. 'Years and years. It's cool all right, isn't it?'

I could feel the intense sun burning my scalp. 'I'm roasting here. Let's find the path up.'

Grace wiped one small bead of sweat from her perfect brow. 'It looks a long way up. I wonder can you get a taxi?'

Jessie shook her head violently. 'No way, Grace. We can't afford it. We spent a fortune in that pub last night. We'll have to walk.' She caught Grace's mutinous look and quickly added, 'Bet there's no taxis anyway.'

Grace was right. It did look like a very long way up. I felt tired already, just thinking about it. I didn't like to admit to being a philistine though. 'Maybe the best views are from down here.'

Grace was quick to agree. 'Yeah. Bet there's nothing up there to justify that long walk.'

Jessie wasn't too worried either. 'Anyway, it'll still be there in September when we get back here.'

'And it won't be so hot then.'

'And there won't be as many tourists.'

'So we'll be able to see more.'

'It would be a pity to go now, when we might miss something important because of the crowds.'

We all smiled, quite happy that our laziness was suitably hidden by our cleverness. Jessie put an arm around Grace and me. 'Come on, girls. We've got islands to explore.'

Grace handed her camera to a passing teenager, so he could get a picture of us with the Acropolis in the background. Just as he clicked the button, a bus trundled behind us, blocking the view. Then we turned our backs on that wonderful, historic sight, and set off to catch the boat.

We had read up about the various islands, and had trouble deciding which one to visit. It was decided for us when we were told at the harbour that the only boat leaving in the next hour was headed for Mykonos. We paid in a little office, were each handed a large, flimsy white ticket, all in Greek of course, and set off to find the boat. We got aboard, wriggled out from the dead weight of our rucksacks, sat on deck, turned our faces to the sun, and closed our eyes.

I stretched out, arranged my head on the side of my rucksack, and sighed deeply. No college. No studying. No fussy parents. No routine. No rain. No cold. I could feel contentment settling over me like a cosy old eiderdown. I thought that the dirty old ferry, with its chipped paint and greasy deck, was surely the closest to heaven that I'd ever been.

I would give a lot to be back there, then, on that boat, slowly chugging towards the islands. There's a lot I would do differently, if only I could go back.

Next time around, I'd wear sunscreen. And a sun hat.

The shoulder pads. They wouldn't make it into the replay of my life. Or the espadrilles. They didn't even look good. And they were never comfortable. The rope soles hurt my feet, and I had to shuffle along to avoid losing them. I only wore them because Grace had a pair, and they looked good on her. And that was pointless because my dad's ancient plaid slippers would have looked good on her.

And what happened later that summer. How I wish I could change all that.

But I have to face it. I can't go back and try again. I won't get the chance to be smarter this time. I won't get the chance to be cool and sophisticated and in charge. And knowing me, it probably wouldn't make any difference anyway. I'd just be getting a second chance to make a complete mess of my life. I'd probably do it even more spectacularly second time around.

In my own inimitable fashion.

That didn't stop me trying though. Last spring, as I sat with Lizzie at the kitchen table, making my plans for another trip to Greece, I had a crazy notion that I could change my awful past. Make it all right again. Make it so the bad stuff never happened.

All I wanted was another chance to be happy.

So I made my plans. I read guidebooks and studied maps and booked tickets. I continued stubbornly, trying to ignore the voice in my head that told me to stop this foolishness and to go back to my quiet suburban life.

At times, it seemed faintly ridiculous. I should have been going to the supermarket, cleaning the toilet, taking Lizzie to the park, and yet, here I was planning to leave my husband and set off on a whimsical trip to a Greek island.

James could have stopped me if he'd tried, but he didn't try. Every time I looked at him, I could see the hurt and incomprehension in his dark eyes. But he said nothing. He worked harder than ever, leaving home early, coming home late, conversing in monosyllables when silence was no longer convenient.

One evening, just after tea, I stepped out into the garden and I thought I saw James crying. He looked up and saw me and he made a big show of coughing, as if something was caught in his throat. I took a tentative step towards him, and began to speak softly.

'James, I'm so sorry. Maybe . . .' I didn't get to finish, as we were suddenly distracted by frantic wails from the kitchen, where Lizzie had just fallen off a stool. I ran in. Lizzie wasn't hurt, and she was easily calmed with a cuddle and a sweet. When I went back into the garden minutes later, James was deep in conversation with our next-door neighbour about the various ways of preventing cabbage-root fly.

I'll blame James so. That's settled.

Though it wouldn't be the truth at all.

Chapter Six

Wednesday night. Card night.

I'm not quite sure how I ended up being a permanent member of the card school. It had started innocently enough, about a year earlier. I was walking Lizzie home from the shops one afternoon, when one of my neighbours, Lily, ran out to meet me. She hadn't been living in her house for long, and I barely knew her. She made a token comment about Lizzie's red coat and then said rather abruptly.

'Can you play a hundred and ten?'

As it happened, I could. We used to play it between lectures in my first year of college.

'Mmm. A bit.'

'Great, we're short one tonight. Can you be here at eight?'

I was silent for a moment, which must have implied consent.

'Lovely. See you then. 'Bye.'

Lily skipped back up her driveway, surprisingly nimble in her high heels and flouncy skirt.

James laughed when I told him that evening. That made me feel even worse. 'Please, James. Would you go instead of me?'

He laughed again. 'No way. I can't even play a hundred and ten. Beggar my Neighbour is the most advanced game I know. And anyway, Lizzie and I fancy a quiet night in – don't we, my little sausage?'

Lizzie giggled her approval of that idea, and I reluctantly went to change into clean dungarees for my big night out.

I surprised myself by having a great time.

Lily, who looked to be about forty-five, lived a few doors from my home. She shared her house with a small, wiry-coated yappy little dog, who heralded my arrival before I got a chance to ring the doorbell. Lily showed me into her living-room, and I felt a distinct warmth towards her when I saw that the room made my kitchen seem like a haven of neatness and order. The table in the middle of the room was clear, but a heap of magazines and newspapers and junk mail on the floor nearby suggested that it had only recently been relieved of a serious mess. It looked as if she had subscribed to every alternative part work that had ever been published. *Crystal-hugging in seventy-two parts. Analyse your Dreams with Aromatherapy. Yoga for Yuppies. Feng Shui for Fanatics.*

Two of the walls were shelved, but the shelves were barely visible through the mountains of books and papers that adorned their surfaces. Tangled windchimes and dreamcatchers hung at strange angles all around the room.

At the table were seated a man and a woman. Lily introduced us without ceremony.

'This is my brother, Christy, and his wife, Helen. This is . . . I'm sorry. I don't actually know your name.'

'Claire. Pleased to meet you both.'

The couple looked sadly at me and each gave a small nod by way of greeting. I had a horrible fear that some terrible family tragedy had created the vacancy in the card school that necessitated my presence.

Lily spoke brightly. 'Thanks for coming. Eileen, who usually comes, has gone on holidays.'

So much for my theory. I was soon to discover that Christy and Helen always wore the same rather sad expressions.

And I'm not quite sure where Eileen went on her holidays, but she never returned to claim her place in the card school, and that suited me fine. I fitted in perfectly with the quiet couple and with Lily, who was also quiet, but seemed the picture of loquaciousness compared to her relatives.

So that night, a few days before I was due to leave for Greece, I sat at my usual place between Helen and Lily, picked up my cards and announced that I would be away the next week, and for the foreseeable future.

All three players dropped their cards onto the table and looked at me in alarm.

Lily spoke first. 'Claire, where are you going? We'll miss you so. What will we do?'

I was touched for a moment, until I realised that she was really concerned about the game. A hundred and ten with four players was unusual enough. With three players it was all but impossible.

Then I looked closely at Lily's face, and thought I could see traces of real concern in her eyes. I could feel my usual tears welling up. Lily touched me lightly on the arm, and when she spoke, I knew she was taking this seriously.

'Christy, Helen, why don't you go into the kitchen and put on the kettle? I think Claire and I are going to have a chat for a while.'

This was a most unusual request, as tradition dictated that we didn't get a drop of tea in Lily's house until we had completed at least one game of cards. Still, Christy and Helen, whose alarmed looks had been replaced by their customary gloom, obediently rose from the table and shuffled into the kitchen, closing the door behind them.

Lily looked at me with her clear, calm gaze. I'd spent one evening a week in her company for almost a year and yet I barely knew her. Was she happy? Lonely? Mad? I had a funny feeling that she might be gay, but somehow that never came up in conversation.

'*I'll call twenty. And by the way, Lily, are you gay*? I don't think so.

Still, something made me feel that Lily knew more about me than my clumsy way of shuffling cards, and my tendency to call a bell when the game got boring.

'Tell me, Claire. Are you going on a pleasure trip?'

I shook my head. I was almost afraid to speak for fear of unleashing the tear torrent.

'Is James going with you?'

Another shake.

'Lizzie?'

I nodded. If we continued like this, it was going to be a lengthy process.

I dug my thumbnail into my palm in an effort to stop the tears and spoke in a rush. 'You see, I won the lottery, a scratchcard, and I thought it would be a great idea to go on a fantastic trip, far away, but James didn't want to go. He wanted to go to Lanzarote and I couldn't bear that. I didn't want to be fighting with foreigners over sun loungers and spending hours discussing how much a taxi into town would cost. So I said I'd go to Greece on my own, well with Lizzie too of course, and now I've booked the tickets and it looks as if I'm going and I don't even know if I want to any more. But James doesn't care. He says I should go. Well actually, he does care. I think he's a bit afraid of me. I think he's afraid I'm going to turn into a loud, shrieking wife, and he doesn't know what to do. And in a way he's right. If I stay here, I think maybe I will turn into a loud, shrieking wife.'

I stopped for breath, and dug my nail so deep into my palm that I drew blood.

Lily spoke softly. 'Why did you want to go in the first place?'

'Because I was afraid. I'm not happy here. I love James and Lizzie but I hate my life. I always want something, but I don't know what it is. I was afraid that if I didn't do something, I'd be sucked down. You know, like into quicksand. And I'd never get out and I'd never be happy. I'm bored and I'm lonely and I don't know what to do.'

That was the first time I'd ever enunciated how I felt, and it was strangely liberating, in a snivelling, sobby kind of way.

Lily saw her opportunity. 'And why Greece especially?'

God! Now she was approaching a serious can of worms.

Because the worst thing in my life happened there. I did a terrible thing, and it's been hanging over me ever since. I went there when I was nineteen. Before I went, I was happy and free, and then I spent a few short months ruining my life forever.

I took a deep breath. I'd already said more than enough. 'I'm sorry, Lily. You're very kind, but I'm not ready to discuss that just yet. I went there once before. A long time ago. It wasn't a happy time.'

Lily nodded wisely. 'I'll take it then that you're not going back for another look at the temples?'

I tried to smile as I shook my head.

'Maybe James is right. Maybe you should go. And if you don't like it, sure can't you come straight back?'

Now that was a comforting thought. I felt better already. She stood up and gave me a pat on the shoulder. Then she rummaged in a drawer and pulled out a small, mauve, crystal-like object, which she pressed into my hand.

Oh no. Not a loony crystal. I don't believe in all that stuff. I tried to look grateful.

Lily wasn't fooled. 'I actually believe that this crystal will keep you safe. But even if you think that's only new-age nonsense, at least it will be handy for pinning the pages of your newspaper down while you're trying to read on the beach.'

She went to the kitchen door and yanked it open. Helen was just approaching it with a tray in her hands. 'No way, Helen. You haven't earned it. Put that back and we'll start. Christy's deal, wasn't it?'

The evening continued as normal, and my trip wasn't mentioned again, but when I was leaving, Lily held me in a close embrace, and whispered in my ear.

'Go to Greece. Have a great trip. There will always be a place at the card table for you. That Eileen was an awful cheat.'

Late that night, James reached for me in bed. I think it must have been a sleepy instinct. We had barely touched in weeks. I clung to him. I was glad to be close to him again – even if it was only a physical closeness. It was subtly different though. We were sort of going through the motions. It was a bit like watching the credits when a film is over. When it's over, it's over, and it's never going to be truly satisfying to drag it out until the last moments to find out who played the 'woman screaming on the corner' or who the best boy was.

When we were finished, James gave me one brief hug. He whispered in my ear, tickling me with his breath. 'Goodnight, my darling.'

I felt suddenly choked. 'Goodnight, James. I love you.'

Then we turned away from each other and slept.

Our last day at home was miserable. I took Lizzie to school as usual, trying to explain that this would be her last day, that we were going on a big trip on an aeroplane, that Daddy couldn't come, and that when we came back, she would be going to a new school, just for big girls and boys. I tried to put myself on her level, to say it in a way that she would understand, but in her little, four-year-old world, she couldn't grasp the enormity of what we were doing. She couldn't get the bigger picture, so she latched onto the details.

'Will we get lunch on the plane? Can I have pizza? Will it be a red plane like the one in my book? Can I bring my Teletubby? Can my hamster come?'

The questions flowed out fluently, and, as often happened, she didn't seem to notice that I wasn't answering; just enunciating the words was enough.

I left Lizzie at school and lingered outside for a few moments. Maureen wasn't there, and part of me was disappointed. I hadn't told her of my plans for the trip, as I assumed she wouldn't understand. Still though, I could have done with a few minutes of her chat and genuine warmth. I knew she would have been kind. I wheeled my bike home. Even the thought of a cycle in the countryside couldn't lift my spirits. It was a beautiful day, but I paid no heed to the bright flowers and the sunshine. This day seemed to hold no promise, no joy. I was filled with a sense of dread.

I went to my room to begin my packing. Everything had to fit into a backpack. (After all, how could I stage a dramatic escape from my boring suburban life if I had to do it while dragging a smart set of Samsonite matching luggage behind me? With my tickets and passport in a Louis Vuitton organiser?) So I was quite limited in what I could bring. The *Complete Works of Shakespeare* and the ironing board would have to stay behind. I packed faded summer clothes from last year. (And God knows how many years before that.) One warm jumper each. A light jacket. Suncream. Sunhats. Sunglasses. (So many sunny things, when I felt as if a dark cloud had enveloped me, folding me within its clammy blackness, never to let me go.)

When I stopped, and surveyed the clothes laid out on the bed, it suddenly struck me that I had unconsciously selected for myself the clothes that James had never liked on me – the hippy-type clothes that he always gently mocked – the loose flowery trousers, and the faded pinarette dresses. I was a bit old for that type of dress. I should have left them behind with my student days. Still though, I was kind of attached to them, and besides, I knew that Maisie hated them, and that in itself was a reason to keep on wearing them. My hippy clothes were my badge of defiance, and they were coming with me. This seemed proper anyway, as this trip, I suppose, was the ultimate in defiance.

Poor me. Other women row with their husbands and get revenge by buying up half of The East Village with their joint credit cards, before getting blind drunk on expensive champagne. I ended up packing raggy clothes into a torn blue rucksack, all the time wondering quite when I had managed to lose the plot so completely.

I wanted to bring a photograph of our erstwhile happy family, so I dragged out the big cardboard box, into which all of our photographs were thrown. Every Christmas, I resolved to sort out the photographs, and display them in albums, but Christmases came and went and it never got done. The photos were all thrown together with no labels and no order. The photo box was a scene of chaos, just like my life.

I opened a packet at random. Lizzie's eyes shone out at me. She was about twelve months old, sitting snug on her dad's lap. She was looking straight at the camera, smiling a gummy smile. James's hand rested on her still-bald head, and he was looking at her with such love that I quickly dropped that packet and opened another. Each packet I opened, though, seemed to tell a tale I didn't want to hear. Mundane scenes of family life. Holidays. Birthday parties. Christmas. James holding Lizzie as she put the angel on the top of the Christmas tree. The three of us on the beach, eating

71

ice-cream cones. James blowing out the candles on his birthday cake, watched by a bright-eyed Lizzie.

What did I expect? Families tend to reach for the camera at happy times. You don't hear cries of, 'Oh look – the hamster's died. Get the camera quick and we'll take a nice photograph.' Or, 'I'm really tired. Lizzie's been throwing up all night and the washing machine's broken. Let's take a picture so we can remember this special moment.'

When James came home much later, he found me, still sitting on the floor in the spare bedroom, adrift in a sea of glossy photographs, unable to cry any more.

'I can't do it,' I whispered. 'I can't go, I can't take Lizzie away from you, I can't leave you.'

James sat down beside me. He stroked my arm and spoke gently. 'You must go. Things may never again be right between us if you go, but they certainly won't if you stay.'

I clung to him. I wanted him to beg me to stay.

He rubbed his arm across his eyes, wiping away what might have been a tear. 'Just go. The sun and the fresh air will be good for you. You've been upset. And I don't know how to help you. We need this break, this time apart, and when you come back, then we can see what happens.'

This gentle certainty frightened me more than his anger had, and so, even though I could see my marriage crumbling behind me, like the monkey city in *The Jungle Book*, I went.

Chapter Seven

The first time I went to Greece, my mum and dad drove me to the ferry port. Mum made Dad take a picture of me in my bedroom just before we left. Dad had a funny old camera. He had to stick on a plastic flash-cube, which went all distorted after the flash, like something out of a Dali painting.

Mum didn't say anything, but I wondered if she was thinking that if I didn't come back, that would be the last photo they had of me.

In the car, Dad made endless jokes about greasy food and greasy men with greasy hair. They weren't funny, but they distracted me from Mum's barely suppressed sobs. I was impatient with her. After all, I was only going away for the summer. I'd be home in a few months and everything would be the same as before.

Or so I thought.

(Years later, when I dropped Lizzie to playschool for the first time, I felt like crying. She was going to be gone for two-and-a-quarter hours. Suddenly I knew how my mum had felt. It was too late though – she'd been dead for nearly three years by then.)

I was embarrassed walking into the terminal with my red-eyed mother and fussing father. I felt better though when I saw that Grace was similarly encumbered. (Clever Jessie had left her parents at home and got a lift with Grace.) We raced through the check-in procedures, gave our parents their final hugs, and skipped onto the boat for a celebratory drink. We each had a big black pint of Murphy's. We held them aloft.

'To freedom.'

'To holidays.'

'To doing whatever we like, whenever we like.'

Grace forced her camera into the hand of a passing barman, who grudgingly took the first of our holiday photos.

This time, Lizzie and I travelled to the airport in a taxi. James had wanted to drive us, but I refused to let him. I was afraid that I might change my mind and not leave at all. I knew that if James were there it would all end in copious, public tears.

Before he left for work that morning, James held me tight. We didn't speak. I could feel the warmth of his skin even through the brushed cotton of his work shirt. (His shirt was red check. I had one exactly like it when I was sixteen. Gallagher shirts, we called them then, after Rory. I thought it was the coolest thing I ever owned.) Lizzie came charging between us. James wriggled free and gave her the disposable camera he had hidden in the cereal cupboard the day before.

'Yeah. Thanks, Daddy.'

'You take lots of lovely photos to show me when you get home.'

'Ok. I'll take one every day. If Mummy lets me.'

Hmm. Twenty-four pictures. Would we be home again so soon?

I smiled at her. 'Of course, darling. Now give Daddy a kiss because we'll be gone when he gets home.'

He picked her up and held her tight. 'Bye, my precious. See you soon. I love you, best girl.'

'Bye, Daddy. I love you too. You're my best daddy.'

Then she ran off to put her camera into her backpack.

James was on the verge of tears. I'd stepped over the verge, and my tears were following their usual path down my cheeks. After the weeks I'd just put down, it was a wonder that my tears hadn't gouged a path down my cheeks. I could have been a diagram in a Geography book. *Crevasses: a natural feature.*

James held me again.

'Please, James. Won't you come for a week or two? You could easily get a flight. I could cancel my flight and we could travel together next week. Or the week after. I don't mind. It would . . .'

He held up his hand to stop me. 'Just go, Claire. You need this break. Go, and come back safely. I love you.'

I was sobbing uncontrollably by now. 'I love you too, James. And I'm so sorry about all of this.'

He tightened his hug, and we rocked together for a few moments. Then he let me go, and went out, closing the back door gently behind him.

The flight to Athens was uneventful. As soon as the seatbelt sign was switched off, Lizzie curled up on my lap and fell asleep. I stroked her hair, and tried to compose a poem in my head but I couldn't get past the first two lines.

Greece is a word.
Greece is a feeling.

Pathetic. Even by my low standards.

I found my mind drifting back to the day of Lizzie's birth.

She had been born by emergency Caesarean section. The doctor told me not to worry, but it was difficult not to, as I watched him pacing the floor, checking his watch, and regularly giving instructions to have the anaesthetist paged again. A pretty, fluttery young nurse with fluffy blond curls danced around in his wake, wringing her hands. I wondered if her distress was caused by worry for me, or whether she was due to get off duty soon, and was keen to go home and get on with her laundry. Maybe she wanted to check her Lotto numbers. Or maybe she and the doctor were an item and as soon as they were finished plunging their bloody, gloved hands into my abdomen, they were going to make mad, passionate love on the stripped-pine floorboards of his penthouse apartment. Then they'd sit naked on a sheepskin rug, sipping champagne and feeding each other chocolate-covered strawberries.

Finally the anaesthetist arrived and things began to move quickly.

I had made the big mistake of reading too much during my pregnancy. One of the dubious books I read implied that childbirth would be a cinch if managed properly. It was the kind of book often read by first-time mothers, stating that childbirth might involve 'some discomfort'. It said, with great authority, 'Giving birth will be a long process.' (This much was true.) 'Hospitals will often decide not to allow you to eat at this energy-sapping time, so it is important, if you must go to hospital, to have a good meal first.' The implications were clear – only total wimps who didn't deserve babies went to hospital, and hospitals deprived mothers of nourishment, not out of medical necessity, but out of some sick desire to cause pain. In my innocence and inexperience, I believed what I read, so when I felt my first labour pain early that morning, before I even woke James, I went downstairs and cooked myself a big plate of rashers, sausages, eggs and black pudding and five cherry tomatoes. I can see them now sitting on the plate in a large pool of golden fat, and I can see myself, stomach bulging, night-dress straining over my bump, standing at the kitchen counter, licking my greasy fingers, and thinking I was invincible.

The anaesthetist looked at me in disbelief when he heard what I had done. If hospitals enjoyed punishing their patients, they must really have enjoyed me. As a result of the meal, an epidural was the first option. Believe me, it is no fun being told to hunch over when the nurse who's illustrating the position has a concave abdomen. And when you try to copy her, you find that you have a bump the size of a Spacehopper in the way. And hunching over is even less pleasant when you're not even half-decent in a paper gown that ties only once at the neck, covering nothing fully except perhaps for a small part of one of your shoulders. And it's not nice when you're cold and afraid, and you foolishly glance over your shoulder to see another nurse brandishing a needle the size of the Jack Lynch tunnel. And it's disconcerting to realise that seven people in emerald-green gowns are stooped down, gazing intently at your lower back as if it's shortly going to be the scene of some major procedure. And it's hard to be terribly reassured by the doctor's blithe, 'This won't hurt . . . much.'

It is even less fun when the epidural injection doesn't work, and you need a general anaesthetic after all, although they have already told you this isn't a great idea for silly women who eat rashers, sausages, eggs and black pudding and five cherry tomatoes while in labour.

I awoke slowly, vaguely aware that someone had given birth, but not quite sure who. I felt as if I'd been run over by a fleet of double-decker buses carrying Kerry football supporters. Lying on a high-sided hospital trolley, I tried unsuccessfully to find a part of my body that didn't ache or throb. The room seemed to be very busy. People bustled by, carrying lots of dangerous-looking shiny things in kidney-shaped bowls. And I couldn't understand why everyone had masks on. Surely it wasn't Halloween. And if it was, their masks weren't very scary.

I only gradually became aware of the little swaddled bundle by my side. She slept peacefully, her face downy soft, her long, dark eyelashes curling gently. Then I slept again too.

Those early days in the hospital, I fed and cuddled her mechanically. I changed a nappy that appeared to be full of soft, black tar. I wiped sweet baby-vomit from my shoulders. I rocked her when she produced ear-splitting screams that seemed incompatible with her tiny, wriggling body. I did all I should, but out of duty, not out of love. She was like someone else's child, soon to be returned. The expected bonding did not happen, and I feared it never would. I held and cuddled her, and felt a fondness, much like I would for a helpless puppy, but nothing I had never felt before. At night, I dreamed that all the sanctimonious writers of those pregnancy books were sitting around my bed in half-lotus positions, tutting and waving cloth nappies and breast pumps, and pointing accusing fingers at me.

Then, one morning, weeks later, when Lizzie and I were at home alone, it happened. I had just lifted her out of her bath, and wrapped her in the soft white towel my mother had given me especially for Lizzie, insisting that the towels James and I used would be too harsh for her soft, sensitive skin. I was drying the little folds of skin under one of her chins when the strange, new sensation hit me. It frightened me with its intensity, and all at once I knew what the books meant. I looked at her soft, sweet face, breathed in her warm milky breath, and I knew for the first time what all the fuss was about. I had never before felt such love and devotion. This small, pink creature was the centre of my universe. Each of her little sighs the sweetest sound I had ever heard. She opened her bright eyes and looked at me as if she understood. I held her to my breast and stroked her damp downy head as she sucked. She finished feeding and nestled deeper into my arms. We played a lengthy staring game. I adored her, and she looked as if the feeling was mutual. She had no nappy on and she soaked my legs with a surprising volume of warm wee. I even loved her wee. Soon her little eyes began to waver, and then close. She slipped into a deep sleep, and I sat for much longer, wet and rather smelly, but oh so much in love.

I had planned to return to work, but this never happened. My job in the accounts section of a large department store in Patrick Street wasn't that exciting anyway, and there was a queue of girls with even more lowly jobs than mine, waiting to take my place. I took maternity leave, unpaid leave, sick leave (this was a bit dishonest), and finally I acknowledged what James had seen months earlier – I didn't want to go out to work. Minding my precious baby was work enough for me. I looked forward to each new day – bathing Lizzie, dressing her, playing with her, wheeling her on long, long walks. I enjoyed meeting little old ladies who cooed over her, telling me to enjoy her, as I would surely look back and see these as the happiest days of my life. I needed no telling, though, as I relished each moment, and savoured each of my darling's little milestones. I recorded each detail of her life in her baby book. I took countless photographs. As she outgrew her little vests and sleepsuits, I folded them in tissue paper, and stored them, I know not why, in a pink cardboard box in the highest cupboard in her bedroom.

Of course, without my salary, finances were a little more stretched at home, but we managed. Most days, I wheeled Lizzie to the shopping centre in Douglas, and I wandered around in a leisurely fashion, carefully planning which groceries to buy. I'd visit each of the two vegetable shops, carefully comparing prices for tomatoes and carrots. I was a little more careful than before in the supermarket, and in the butcher's shop, and I would head for home, pleased with my small economies. Often, however, having bought a cheap cut of meat for our dinner, and vegetables that were reduced in price because they were slightly past their best, I wandered into the baby boutique, and spent my savings on luxuries for Lizzie. James was bemused, but tolerant. 'How many pink socks does a baby need?' he would say, but he was a man of simple tastes. The slightly inferior food was fine by him, and he was glad to see me so happy.

Happy as I could be.

I sat on the plane to Athens, stroking my daughter's silken curls, barely holding back my tears.

I finished my poem:

Greece is a word.
Greece is a feeling.
A bad feeling.

Lizzie and I spent one forgettable night in a cold, functional hotel in Athens. She was quiet, wondering no doubt what had possessed her mother to bring her to such a desolate place. Her usual flood of questions was briefly stemmed. Poor child – I suppose she didn't know where to begin.

We rose early and made our way to the harbour at Piraeus. Only later did I realise that I had failed to notice the Acropolis, which would have been clearly visible had I taken the trouble to look up. The wonders of ancient architecture towered over me, but I kept my head down, lost in my own small world, pulling my small daughter along behind me.

(Of course, I'd missed the Acropolis the last time round too. But that omission was hardly the worst of my crimes that summer.)

The harbour was crowded but I had pre-booked ferry tickets, so we were quickly aboard and chugging towards the islands. Even though it was still only May, it was beautifully warm, and we sat out on deck, facing towards the open sea. Despite my gloom, Lizzie had been able to get herself into a holiday mood, and she prattled away cheerfully, managing to lift my spirits slightly. She had packed some of what she considered to be the necessities of life into a small nylon backpack, and this she repeatedly unpacked and repacked, sometimes laying the contents out neatly on the empty bench opposite us. She had picked out a photo of James in a really foolish pose, taken on her last birthday, and this she always took out first. Each time, she laid it gently down, and weighted it carefully with the crystal Lily had given me. (Lizzie had looked suitably impressed when I'd handed it to her and told her it was a magic crystal. But then, I reasoned, she was four years old, just the right age for believing in magic.) She took out the disposable camera that James had given her before we left. She had also brought a packet of colouring pencils and a pad of plain paper 'for my work'. These were joined on the bench by a collection of small *Barney* figures, a few odd wooden bricks, some toy cars, and, for some reason, a purple plastic eggcup.

Despite her vehement objections, I had covered every exposed part of her body with factor 50 sunscreen, and I had insisted that she wear a sunhat, even though it came close to blowing overboard on several occasions. Each time this happened, she laughed with glee, pleased that the wind was conspiring to thwart my ambition to protect her from the sun. Then she ran joyfully along the deck after it, tossing her curls as she ran.

I threw my head back, allowing the wind to whip my hair away from my face. I turned my face to the sun, trying to soak up its comforting warmth. I probably looked like a crazy woman but I didn't care. For a short while, I felt invincible – sure that I'd made the right decision; sure that coming to Greece was the best thing I'd ever done.

An elderly American tourist interrupted my musings, asking if she could take a picture of Lizzie. I agreed, and Lizzie obliged with a beaming smile. I'm sure the kindly old lady was rewarded with a good picture.

In a box somewhere, there's a photo of me that Grace took on the ferry to Mykonos. It was May then too. May 1986. I am standing against the white railing, small tattered rucksack on the ground next to me, containing all I had to keep me going for the next few months. I have one hand raised, holding my hair back from my eyes. My clothes are pathetic. I'm wearing very tight, very short, blue denim shorts, and my t-shirt has shoulder pads. (It was the eighties, after all). My face and skin are still pale, and I look tired, no doubt as a result of the very long drunken night we'd just had. But the most noticeable thing in the picture is my expression. Looking past the camera at I know not what, I have a look of anticipation and excitement – a look as if life were there just ready for me to grab it, with all my wildest dreams waiting for me just over the next white-tipped wave.

Lizzie's carefree antics made the journey seem short, and soon we found ourselves in the little harbour of Mykonos. There were only a few stray back-packers around as we stepped off the boat, and stood somewhat forlornly, watching the ferry prepare to leave on its journey back to Athens. My false confidence vanished quickly, and I began to feel mildly panicked. What was I doing in this strange place? I was meant to be a suburban wife and mother. Shouldn't I be at home preparing dinner? How could I have done this?

Lizzie held my hand tightly, and looked up expectantly at me, squinting in the strong sunlight, certain in her childish way that I would know what to do next. Resisting an urge to jump back aboard the ferry, I said with forced brightness, 'Come on, darling. Let's go and find a nice place to stay.'

Finding lodging didn't prove difficult, as it was so early in the season. A little old lady, whose eyes lit up when I mentioned staying a few months, led us through a maze of cobbled streets. Even with my sunglasses on, I could feel the strong glare from the whitewashed houses, and marvelled, as I am sure many had before me, at the blueness of the sky in contrast. The lady, who had looked so frail, stepped nimbly on, and soon I was breathless as I struggled to keep up. Lizzie skipped along beside me, enchanted by the quaint houses.

'Look, Mum – look at all the dolls' houses. Can we stay in one, please?'

I read somewhere that the warren of small, curving streets was designed to confuse pirates attacking the town, and I could see how effective a ploy this would have been. I found myself wondering how I would ever find my way back to the port, since the lanes all looked so alike. Then I decided that I had enough problems as it was without worrying about minor details like that.

And anyway, as far as I knew, I would be staying for quite a while. I didn't need to know where the port was.

At last, we stopped at a small iron gate, set in one of the snow-white walls. The little old lady pushed open the gate, and we stepped into a tiny sun-filled courtyard. It was paved with irregular, cracked slabs. Bright red flowers (James could have named them) tumbled from the roofs and pushed their way through every available crack. My guide led me to a freshly painted red door, unlocked it and led the way inside. We stepped into a clean, bright room. Two single beds occupied two of the corners. There were two easy chairs, and a round table with three chairs, all made of pine. There was also a tiny kitchen area, almost hidden behind the still-open door.

The old lady pushed open another door with a flourish, and said, as if this should be a great treat for us, 'Look, own toilet, own shower.'

I smiled, trying to convey a wonder, which of course I didn't feel. 'How much?' I asked.

She looked at me as if she were about to do me a great favour, and mentioned a price which was indeed quite fair. I was so relieved to have found a suitable place so quickly that I immediately paid her for two months, telling myself firmly that I would have to stay now, after such an investment. The old lady smiled a toothless smile and took my hands in hers.

'You be happy here. You and little girl.'

Her kind words brought sudden tears to my eyes. I did my best to smile. 'Yes, I'm sure we will. I'm sure we will be very happy. Thank you.'

Then she handed me the single key, patted Lizzie on the head, and left.

Lizzie pranced around the room with delight, touching everything, and opening the few cupboards and drawers. She ran to the window and looked out. 'Look', she said. 'We can see the sea.'

She was right. We were on a hill, and we could see down over the roofs of other houses, down to the harbour, and on out to the open sea. We stood together, surveying the view. She put one arm around my leg, and rested her head on my hip, as she often did.

'Do we live here now?' she asked.

Chapter Eight

The first few days in our new home passed quietly and quickly. I tried to telephone James a few times, but managed only to reach the answering machine. I had a picture in my head of him running down the hall to pick up the phone, and then stopping suddenly when the machine clicked in, allowing him to hear my voice. This hurt me deeply, but I wasn't ready to deal with it. I felt fragile, just about able to cope. Once I almost left a weepy message, but I pulled myself back just in time. Instead I left a bright, breezy message, declaring that Lizzie and I were both fine, and that I'd call again soon.

I began to wonder if perhaps I should try to buy a mobile phone, and enter the twenty-first century at last. Then I decided that having one would make life easier for James, not for me, and as I still felt betrayed by the fact that he had allowed me to leave, I decided against it.

For a while, I couldn't settle down. I wondered how soon we could pack up and return home. I knew that I should see the time as a time to meditate, a time to enjoy Lizzie, and watch her grow, but I couldn't do this. There was no sense of joy or hope in those early days. It was a time to be endured, a sentence that had to be served, my well-deserved punishment for being so selfish and irrational.

It didn't take long to arrange our few belongings in the house. We discovered a little shop at the top of our street, and that provided the essential foodstuffs for our first few days. Lizzie was fascinated by the unusual packaging, and eagerly tried any new foods that I presented her with. The shop had only one type of biscuit – small, hard and tasteless – but Lizzie in her enthusiasm for all things new, proclaimed them to be delicious.

She also delighted in using bottled water all of the time. She often reminded me (not that it was necessary): 'Don't forget, Mummy – only brush your teeth with the fridge water, or you might get very, very sick!'

Our days soon took on a simple pattern, which I found comforting after all the upheaval of the previous weeks. It was a joy not to be constantly afraid of the next argument, the next hate-filled silence. (I still had the odd argument in my head with James, of course, but that didn't matter, as in those mental spats I was always calm and clear and reasoned, and ultimately the victor.)

Mostly I didn't bother to wear my watch, so we awoke when we had slept enough. Usually it was sunny, and I just pulled back the curtains, and let the weak, early-morning sun shine in on us. Lizzie would come over to my bed and snuggle against me, wrapping both arms and legs around me. Sometimes, if it was very early, I could persuade her to sleep again. Then I'd snooze too, and awaken later to feel the clammy warmth of Lizzie's legs entangled around mine, and the gentle rush of her breath against my cheek. Often her upper lip glistened in the heat, as she twitched and sighed and dreamed her harmless dreams. When she awoke again, we would chat, and tell stories, and Lizzie would tell endless 'knock, knock' jokes, none of which made any sense at all, as she was still in the childish phase when jokes did not require a punchline to be funny. This would continue until Lizzie became hungry, and we would get up and dress at our leisure.

At home, Lizzie had perfected the art of picking my weakest moment in the supermarket, and so our kitchen cupboard was always filled with a selection of sugary cereals (hidden behind bags of porridge, as James didn't approve). These sugar-laden cereals were usually selected because of some plastic toy, wrapped in cellophane, which, despite earlier wails of 'I need it – Jason has one', managed to entertain Lizzie for about five minutes. Here, in our new simple life, these luxuries weren't available, and it seemed that Lizzie could survive without them after all.

Breakfast was always the same. We spooned natural yoghurt into our plain white bowls, and stirred in small chunks of fresh fruit. This feast was washed down with orange juice for Lizzie, and strong black coffee for me. After breakfast, I'd wash the few dishes, and Lizzie took great pleasure in drying them and replacing them on the shelf. Then, our housekeeping completed, we would pack a sandwich for lunch, and our swimming gear, and set off on long leisurely rambles.

I enjoyed getting to know my way around the narrow streets, and finding a different way home each evening. Sometimes we stayed in the town, and other days we would stroll a mile or two further, finding a different road or track each day.

Every day, Lizzie insisted on going to the nearest beach before returning home. There she would play, paddle and sometimes swim. When she swam, she always begged me to accompany her, and sometimes I did, enjoying the still-cool water. Then we would wrap ourselves in our only two towels, like mummies, and lie in the sun until we were warm again.

Later, we would wander slowly home. All the streets still looked the same to Lizzie, so when we were nearly home, I would tease her by saying, 'I think we might be lost. Run around that corner and see if there's someone to ask.' She would obediently run around and then return, shrieking, 'We're here, we're home', having recognised our little courtyard gate, the only landmark she knew. In her sweet childish way, she never tired of this game, and on the odd occasion that I forgot it, she insisted on backtracking, so we could, 'come home properly'.

For supper, we usually had fish, bought from a wizened old man who had a little stall near the harbour, and we supplemented this with fresh fruit, vegetables and salads. With my evening meal, I always had a glass of the local wine. It wasn't particularly good quality, but the sunshine, and the days of being outdoors, made everything taste better, and soon I stopped noticing its rather rough taste. After our meal, Lizzie would change for bed, and when she dozed off, I would sit in a little wicker easy chair, and read until I felt tired. Then I too would retire, and, to my surprise, I slept peacefully each night, awaking refreshed, and ready for another new day.

Every day was the same, but I didn't mind. It was easier that way. If that was my Groundhog day, I could live with it.

Sometimes, in quiet moments, I thought back to my first ever days in Mykonos, that time with Grace and Jessie.

We arrived early in May. I can still hear the scrape of the ferry against the harbour wall, and the shouts and laughs of the sailors as they threw ropes to each other, and stared at Grace's legs. I can hear Jessie's whispered, 'Wow', as she looked up a hill towards a small church, blindingly white against the deep blue sky. I can see Grace's slow smile as she adjusted the straps of her rucksack on her slender, already brown shoulders.

I blinked and sighed and looked around at the little port. It was as picturesque as it appeared in all the postcards we had seen, and I loved it at once. Even though it was so early in the season, there was a bustling air to the harbour. I caught Jessie's eye. Yes, we had done the right thing in coming to Greece.

We skipped off the ferry, full of excitement and girlish anticipation. A skinny young boy approached us at once, and offered us accommodation. We followed him a short distance from the harbour area, giggling at his serious demeanour and businesslike bargaining. We immediately accepted his offer of a small room, furnished with three beds and nothing else. Across the hall, there was a bathroom, clearly for the use of his entire family, as well as us. Grace peeped in and wrinkled her delicate nose. Jessie and I followed her eyes with ours. It was our first encounter with that most Greek of experiences – the basket on the floor for used toilet paper. We had heard that this was necessary because of the dodgy plumbing, but didn't believe it until we saw it. We were initially revolted by it, but, like everything else, we soon got used to it and, after a while, it seemed as if we would never throw paper into a toilet again.

There was a small fridge in the hallway outside our bedroom, and we soon had it filled with many bottles of water, which we decanted into a cheap, red metal flask, to sustain us on long, hot days on the beach.

That was it. We had a bed, a toilet and a fridge.

And we were happy.

Young and healthy though we were, the long train journey had tired us out, and we spent the first few days lolling on the beach, too tired to explore. We soon found a bar on the seafront where we had our first meal each day (it was usually too late to call it breakfast). Every morning, we ordered the same thing – a large omelette with cheese and tomatoes – healthy food in a vain effort to reverse the damage caused by excess alcohol on the previous night. Lunch was always a sandwich on the beach, washed down with ice-cold water from the communal flask. In the evenings, we somehow found the energy to check out the local nightlife, and we danced the night away, flinging our young bodies around in time to the beat of the music, happy in the knowledge that we could sleep the next day away to compensate.

A simple life.

Undemanding.

Innocent.

And, oh, so long ago.

Chapter Nine

The days with Lizzie passed, as they do, and then the weeks began to slip by. I began to feel less angry with James. Anger is hard to maintain at such a distance. And in such balmy weather. In my mental arguments with James, I began to give him a few of the cleverer lines, and sometimes we finished up with a small imaginary cuddle. Sometimes, especially after a few glasses of wine, I felt so well-disposed towards him that in my mental picture of him I airbrushed out the tiny scar on his left cheek. Once I even pictured him in cut-off denims and sandals, but I admit that was probably taking things a bit too far.

Still though, I didn't particularly want to speak to him in real life. The benign imaginary James was the only one I felt I could confidently cope with, even then. I telephoned every now and then, of course, but usually when I knew he would be out. I left brief messages, telling him that we were fine.

Sometimes Lizzie spoke into the telephone, her childish voice eager. 'I cut my hand. I got a new bucket and shovel. You can't get Rice Krispies here. I love you. Daddy.'

I wondered if these messages broke his heart, as I knew they would mine, but then reasoned that he knew where we were, and could easily come for a short break if he missed her that much.

If James had appeared out of the blue to sweep us both off our feet, that would have been just fine with me. No chance though. Impulsive extravagant gestures were never really his type of thing. His was always a quiet, understated kind of love. Easily overlooked.

Anyway, James had stubbornly pitched his tent in Maisie's camp, so he'd have to live with that. I bet she was savouring my absence, maximising the damage to our marriage. No doubt, she spent long evenings in my house, poking her nose under the beds looking for dust, and checking the cupboards for unhealthy food.

Occasionally, of course, I misjudged things, and James was home when I phoned. My heart always gave a strange lurch when I heard his voice, rather than my own recorded one telling me that I wasn't at home. We had cautious little conversations, about the weather, and food, and uncontroversial things like that. Sometimes he asked if I had plans to come home, but this was always in an unnaturally flippant kind of way. We both knew not to start a row on the telephone, so we were being kind to each other in our stilted exchange of words.

James always ended by saying, 'I love you, Claire.' These four words made me unaccountably sad.

My answer was always the same. 'I miss you, James.'

One evening, Lizzie and I came home from our day at the beach to find a small grey kitten curled up on our doorstep. He was dirty and thin, so we decided he was a stray, and Lizzie immediately fell in love. She fed him twice each day, and cuddled him whenever we were at home – tight possessive cuddles that must have hurt the poor skinny creature. However, Sninky, as she called him, didn't seem to mind, and ran to her whenever he saw her coming. For a while, I took to calling him Stinky Sninky, but that started to upset Lizzie, and even I didn't take pleasure in teasing a four-year-old child.

On our next trip to the shops, she acquired, by virtue of lots of smiles and gestures, a small wooden fruit box, and some straw, and made him a cosy bed. They became firm friends, and Lizzie spent long hours talking to him, and asking questions, not in the least put out by the fact that he couldn't reply. I tried hard not to think about worms and fleas and rabies, and just crossed my fingers and looked away whenever Lizzie went to kiss her little pet's fur.

As the weeks went by, the island began to get busier. Houses that had been locked and shuttered when we arrived began to open up, and the occasional backpacker began to appear down our quiet streets. Real backpackers, carefree young ones, who didn't look as ridiculous as I did in open leather sandals and long flowery dresses. Real carefree spirits who didn't have mortgages and life insurance and *en suite* bathrooms. They weren't playing at being free, like I was.

Buildings that previously had seemed to be private houses now had tables and chairs on the street outside and hand-painted restaurant signs over the door. Little shops began to appear where there had been none before. All in all, there was a feeling that the island was yawning, stretching its limbs, and awakening after a long sleep.

Lizzie was beginning to tire of our isolation. Clearly she wasn't going to grow up a social misfit like her mother. Whenever she heard voices outside our little courtyard, she would run and peep out through our gate, and wave and call. The local people began to know her, and they smiled and chatted in Greek to her, while she happily babbled back in English. She had never known either of her grandfathers, and now she adopted a local man as an honorary one. He was a tall, thin, kindly old man who always stopped to pet Sninky, and to talk to Lizzie. He passed by at about the same time each morning, and Lizzie began to anticipate his arrival, shouting, 'Grandad's coming.'

She would run down the street to meet him, catch his hand and walk with him to the next corner, which was as far as she was allowed to roam without me.

Grandad (we never knew his real name) always carried an unlikely purple shoulder bag, with 'Mykonos' printed on it in pink, and from this bag he regularly produced a little surprise for Lizzie – sometimes a piece of fruit, a sweet, or even a little bunch of wild flowers. Lizzie often had presents for him – pictures she had drawn herself, little stones she had painted, or some of the flowers from our courtyard. Once, Grandad produced a piece of brightly coloured ribbon, which Lizzie later insisted on cutting in two. Next morning, she waited proudly, with one piece tied in her hair, and the other piece around Sninky's neck.

'Look, look,' she cried, when he came. 'Twins.'

He threw his head back and laughed a deep, happy laugh. 'Twins,' he repeated, and we could hear him laughing and repeating it over and over as he went on his way. I wonder what he thought it meant.

In time, Lizzie refused to leave in the mornings until she saw her 'grandad', and her chats with him became an important part of her daily ritual.

Our daily trips to the beach became longer, as more children began to appear. In that wonderful, easy way that children have, Lizzie could communicate with them all, despite an absence of any common spoken language. They built sandcastles together, paddled, and played intricate games with feathers, shells and stones, which made no sense to me but seemed to make perfect sense to them.

The tourist population was constantly moving, so Lizzie rarely saw any child for more than a few days, and never went beyond first-name terms. This didn't bother her though. She'd say, 'D'you remember Hansi, the one with the green swimming togs? He had a cut hand.' Or, 'Andrea built a very silly sandcastle.' And even though she never saw any of these children again, their names lingered on in her conversation, long after their faces could have stayed in her memory.

Though it's a little clichéd to say it, Lizzie was a constant source of joy at this time. Our lives were so free and easy; I almost never had to reprimand her. She kept strictly to any limits I set, and never strayed. She was gentle, affectionate and great company, and she helped to give me a sense of calm and peace that no army of therapists could ever hope to match. Though I was careful to cover her with sunscreen, and she always wore a hat, she was becoming gently tanned, and beginning to look more like one of the local children. When she looked up at me and grinned from under her tattered straw hat, her brown eyes sparkling, her freckled cheeks glowing, I could have died with the love I felt for her, feeling that I was selfish to want anything in life besides this precious girl.

(How sad that in a few short years my sweet child will probably be a sulky monosyllabic teenager, and I, the mother she once worshipped, will have somehow morphed into an embarrassing encumbrance, useful only for doling out fifty-Euro notes and low-calorie dinners.)

One day, as we sat on the beach, I thought I saw Jessie. Impossible, I know, but the eyes can play foolish tricks. This woman walked by on the sand, just near to where I sat. Her figure was just like Jessie's – plumpish without edging towards fat. She had the same walk and the same toss of her head, making her dark curls shine in the sun. These dark curls, though, were touched with grey, and this woman had a toddler's hand clutched in each of hers. Jessie never got to have children or grey hairs. It's stupid I know, but I always blame myself for that.

Often, over the years, I pictured myself meeting her mother for the first time. At a wedding or a dinner party perhaps. I can hear our conversation.

'Oh, you were in UCC in the 1980s. Perhaps you knew my daughter, Jessie. Jessie Madden.'

'Yes, I knew her. Actually it was my fault that she died.'

I can imagine her shocked expression. 'Were you in India with her?'

'Well, no actually. I was in a different continent. And I hadn't seen her for years.'

I can imagine her eyes turning cold, as she wondered how to get away from this lunatic. But I wouldn't be able to let her go. I would have to explain.

'You see, she saw what a mess I made of my life, and she had to get away. She ran away to India so she wouldn't end up like me.'

In those peaceful weeks, those first weeks in Greece with Lizzie, I read like I hadn't read since leaving college. I rediscovered the joy of starting a book and reading quickly through it, with few distractions, confident of reaching the end while still remembering what happened in the beginning. I had brought only one book with me and that was quickly finished, but on one of our walks I found a treasure-trove – a small dark shop, right at the end of a dead-end lane. It was hard to see how a tourist passing through for a few days would ever find it, but obviously many did. It was a second-hand bookstore crammed with used paperbacks, many of them in English. It seemed as if a boy of about ten was running this shop, and he had a system which suited me perfectly. The price was written inside the front cover of each book, and for any book I returned, the boy solemnly returned half of the purchase price.

I visited this shop regularly, and it never ceased to amaze me what some people brought on their holidays to read. Mostly they were blockbusters and bestsellers from previous years, but mixed in amongst these was the oddest selection of books I have ever seen. There were books on bee-keeping, geology, and nutrition for cats. I think the strangest, though, must have been a 1986 copy of the Greater London bus timetable. In moments of fancy, I thought I should pay the few cent asked for this, and liberate it from the confines of this musty, dusty shop, where it was surely going to languish forever. (I could even read it. I could find out that every morning that summer, while I was busy ruining my life, a bus left Earl's Court for Marble Arch, stopping only three times on the way. Or I could discover that lost property would be kept for seven days only. And that standing upstairs was an offence punishable by a twenty-five-pound fine.)

What I did buy was the complete works of F. Scott Fitzgerald, which I read with great joy, and way more understanding than I had many years before when I had first read them. I particularly enjoyed *The Great Gatsby*, with its bittersweet tone of nostalgia and regret, and this led me back to many classic works that I had read once in youthful arrogance, quite unable to grasp many of their nuances.

The shop also had a large box of children's books, into which Lizzie dived on every visit. Once she got over her shock at the lack of film tie-ins and TV characters, she began to rummage through them with glee. She often selected books in Greek, German or languages I couldn't recognise, but as she couldn't read, this was no problem to her. It gave me the challenge of making up stories to go with the pictures, which was easy the first time round, but more difficult afterwards, as I was expected to have every detail identical on each telling.

One day, I arrived at the bookshop to be greeted with a shy smile by the young boy. He caught the sleeve of my shirt, and led me to a dark corner at the back of the shop. He rummaged in a large box and produced two ageing soft-porn magazines, with strangely coy pictures of almost naked men adorning the covers.

He smiled in a way that made him look older than his years. 'You like?'

My first instinct was to check that Lizzie was a safe distance away. I think I blushed as I answered, 'No, no. Thank you anyway.'

He looked hurt. 'You buy?'

I shook my head again. 'No, that's not really my type of thing, actually.'

I turned and saw that Lizzie was watching with interest. I said one last, firm, 'No', and hurried from the shop.

As I ran down the street, I had a sudden vision of Maisie ogling the oily beefcakes, and I found myself giggling helplessly. Lizzie ran beside me, looking at me in a bewildered fashion. Poor child. After all the scenes of sadness she'd witnessed in the previous weeks, she must have been totally flummoxed by my sudden fit of laughter. I wiped my eyes, enjoying the sensation of tears that weren't accompanied by uncontrollable sobbing and deep, black despair.

I rounded a corner and stumbled over a small, mangy-looking dog. I completely lost my balance and found myself sprawled on the cobbled lane. Lizzie knelt beside me, full of solicitous concern.

'Oh, Mummy. Are you OK? Are you leaking blood? Do you want me to kiss it better?'

I got to my feet, and dusted myself down as best I could. 'Yes, darling. I'm fine. Look – I'm not cut at all.'

'But you are. Look at your arm.'

She was right. A steady stream of blood was trickling from my elbow. I fumbled in my pockets for a tissue, but found only a clothes peg, a few coins and a dried-up marker.

A deep voice interrupted my fumblings. 'Here, use this. I promise it's clean.'

I looked up to see an outstretched arm proffering a tissue which did indeed appear to be clean. I took the tissue and dabbed at the trail of red which by now stretched from my elbow to my wrist.

Only when my dabbing was complete did I look to see who the good Samaritan was.

He was a tall, black-haired vision. Deeply tanned, with long, lean limbs, and crinkly eyes. And he was smiling at me. 'Here, take another tissue. I have plenty.'

'No, really. Thanks, but I'm fine. I think I'll just have to go home and wash this properly.'

He looked a bit doubtful. 'I live near here. You can wash at my house if you like.'

I was briefly tempted. After all, I was on holidays. And he was very handsome. In an easy non-James kind of way. But my elbow had already stopped bleeding, and Lizzie was tugging impatiently at my skirt.

'Mummy, can we go to the beach now? You promised. And that was ages ago.'

What could I say?

'Not *now*, darling. *I just want to go to this perfect stranger's house because I like his crinkly eyes, and because I need some excitement in my life. I haven't had sex for weeks and I'm mad for it.*'

Hardly.

So I did the sensible thing. I smiled and thanked the black-haired vision once more. Then I took Lizzie's hand and we set off for the beach.

And I regretted it all afternoon.

In bed that night, I composed a poem in my head. It was about a guy with hair the colour of ravens' wings.

I eased my guilt by telling myself that the poem was really about James.

Chapter Ten

Much as I enjoyed the quiet evening meals I shared with Lizzie, I should have known that the situation couldn't last forever. One evening, it became clear that I could no longer keep to the quiet routine of grilling fish for us both, and then relaxing with a glass of wine. There was nothing exciting or earth-shattering that led to this change, mind you. I wasn't discovered by a modelling agency, or struck down with cholera. I never became an unwitting pawn in a Mafia drugs scam. (Well, maybe I did, but if so, I remain unwitting.)

The change came in early June.

We'd had one of our usual, quiet days, and we'd come back home to shower and change into slightly less grubby clothes than those we'd been wearing earlier. I was exceptionally proud of the dinner that night. The fish was lovely and fresh, and hardly burnt at all, and I'd chosen a particularly wide selection of vegetables to boil.

I carried the plates to the table and busied myself opening a bottle of wine. I was surprised to notice that the usually ravenous Lizzie didn't dive straight into her food. I watched her for a few minutes but still she didn't even lift up her fork.

'What is it, love? Aren't you hungry?'

She shook her head slowly, without raising her eyes from her plate.

'Oh, dear, are you not well? Have you a pain in your tummy?'

She shook her head once more.

This was very strange. I leaned across the table and felt her forehead. It was no warmer than usual.

Then she raised her eyes and I could see that they were full of tears.

My heart nearly broke. The poor little child. I was sure it was an attack of homesickness – a sudden urge to be with the dad she loved so much. How could I be so cruel as to uproot her from everything she knew and loved? What kind of a monstrous mother was I?

I pulled her onto my knee and held her tight. Her little tears brimmed over and spilled onto her knees in a sudden shower of watery crystal.

'What is it, darling? Why are you so sad?'

She looked at me with huge, waterlogged eyes. 'I hate this dinner, Mummy. I really hate it. Why can't we have something else? Every single day we have fish and vegetables and I hate it. I hate . . .'

As she spoke, she broke into huge racking sobs. I held her tight, unsure of whether I should join in her tears, or break into hysterical laughter.

My poor little baby.

I looked over her head to the food, which was rapidly cooling in front of us. Now that I examined it more closely, it didn't look all that appealing. The fish had actually stepped far over the 'lightly chargrilled' look, and veered dangerously into the 'burnt to a frazzle' zone. I had boiled a selection of vegetables in one pot, and, on reflection, that was probably a bad idea, as they had dissolved into an ugly mush that was uncannily like the colour of *marla* after three terms in the hands of junior infants. Not pleasant. Not pleasant at all.

I spoke brightly. 'I know. Sninky looks hungry. Why don't we give him this dinner, and we'll go and eat in a restaurant?'

Lizzie's tears ceased at once and her face lit up with sudden joy. She punched the air, managing as she did so to topple the wine bottle in such a way that the contents emptied themselves all over our food. That settled it then. There was to be no going back.

I scraped the wine-sodden mush from the plates into the bin. Even Sninky shouldn't be expected to consume such awful stuff.

What a failure I was! Even though I've always loved food, my culinary skills have never been great, and in Mykonos, with no cookbooks (if people brought these to the island, they didn't sell them in the second-hand bookshop), and unfamiliar ingredients, my repertoire was very limited, to say the least. I'm not one of those natural foodie people who can rustle up a feast from a hotchpotch of exotic vegetables, experimenting with spices and herbs, and pungent things that grow in hedgerows. I never use those strange-sounding sauces you can buy only in the oriental food store, or in the market from bearded men in sandals. Some people can take unpromising ingredients, and magically transform them into aromatic delights. I am one of the select few who can take the finest ingredients and render them inedible without even trying.

I thought back to the disastrous day a few months earlier when Lizzie had caught me at a weak moment and persuaded me to make pancakes for tea. I followed all the instructions in my old school cookery book very carefully. Well, I thought I did. The book didn't mention electric mixers, but I thought I'd use mine anyway. It seemed like a good idea, and besides, I'd got it for a wedding present five years earlier and it had never been out of its box.

James was very kind about the whole affair, and he didn't even laugh once.

And he said that he was planning to repaint the kitchen that weekend anyway.

Even the ceiling.

Lucky Lizzie. If we were to avoid grilled fish and vegetables, it looked like we'd be dining out a lot.

Even though the dinner was safely in the bin, she wasn't taking any chances.

'Hurry up, Mummy. Get ready. Put on your nice clothes for going out.'

As she spoke, she was pulling the better of her two dresses from a heap of clothes that had adorned the end of her bed since we'd arrived in Greece. She pulled it on and rummaged around in her backpack of treasures for a piece of ribbon Grandad had given her. For once, she stood still while I tied it in her hair, and meekly she allowed me to wash her face.

'Now you,' she said.

Her enthusiasm was infectious, so I also selected my best dress, though when I looked closely at it, it seemed rather faded and worn. (No wonder since I'd had it for nearly ten years, and I'd bought it second-hand, but never mind. Its big claim to fame was that Rachel wore the same dress in an early episode of *Cold Feet*. Pity she was going to a seventies fancy-dress party at the time.) I rooted out a subtle-coloured lipstick – the only make-up I had with me, and borrowed one of Lizzie's ribbons to tie back my sun-bleached hair. I looked closely at myself in the mirror for the first time in ages, and was pleasantly surprised. I am a bit old to use the 'ugly duckling into swan' analogy, but I think it was true to say that I was no longer the haggard creature who had arrived in Greece just weeks earlier. The circles had vanished from under my eyes, I was lightly tanned, and I had lost weight without even trying. I smiled with pleasure, despite myself.

Lizzie ran for her disposable camera. 'Stand still, Mummy, and smile like that again.'

I laughed. 'Why are you taking my picture?'

"Cause that dress makes you so pretty. Just like a lady in a book. You'll be the nicest lady in the restaround.'

Innocent child. But if she thought that, I had no notion of disillusioning her. I smiled my best smile, and closed my eyes for the flash.

Lizzie ran to put her camera away safely, and I found myself thinking about another of the photographs that Grace took of me in 1986.

Grace never seemed to like me that much, so I don't know why she took all those pictures. And afterwards, she even got them developed, and got an extra set of copies for me. I haven't looked at them in years, but I know exactly where they are in the attic (right at the back, next to my college lecture notes), and I can remember each one clearly. Especially the one she took before I left for my big dinner date with Kevin.

The picture was taken outside the small restaurant that was my home that summer. I am leaning against a dry, stone wall. I think back and I can hear Giorgios clattering pots in the kitchen. I can hear Jessie laughing as she stands behind Grace, trying to make me laugh. I can see her frantic waving and face-pulling. I can hear Grace's impatient words.

'For God's sake, Jessie. Grow up and stop fooling around. And Claire, try to look sophisticated.'

I was trying to look sophisticated. I was trying very hard. And failing. Even then, I think I knew that.

My face is young, sweet and innocent, with a winsome, almost defiant smile. But my attire is sad. Truly sad. I looked like a little child, dressed up in her mother's clothes, none of them fitting properly, or suited to my age.

I look really pathetic.

And I remember that when Kevin arrived, Grace took one more photograph, of the two of us. I remember him putting his arm around me, and laughing at one of Jessie's stupid jokes. His arm was warm and strong. He smelt fresh and clean. He looked sophisticated and he wasn't even trying.

But when Grace gave me the bundle of photographs that cold, October day, over a year later, the one of Kevin and me wasn't there. I asked her why, and she gave one of her airy gestures and said that it hadn't come out.

Lizzie was pulling at my arm.

'Come on, Mummy, or all the restarounds will be closed.'

We set off happily, with a sense of adventure. I imagine we made a happy picture, mother and daughter hand in hand, chatting pleasantly. Lizzie wanted to stop at the first restaurant we came to, but I persuaded her to continue. I hadn't been outside our home after teatime since we had arrived on the island, and I was enjoying the novelty. It was early, so the streets weren't yet crowded, but there was a pleasant buzz in the air. I savoured the first whiffs of food, grilled as only the Greeks could do it. It was never unusually tasty, but the smell was wonderful and enticing. (Freshly brewed coffee's like that too, isn't it? Somehow it never seems to have a taste to match its delicious aroma.)

I loved the little tables set out on the streets – brightly coloured tablecloths pegged down in the light breeze. I savoured the smell of perfume and aftershave, mingled with shampoo and after-sun creams. I picked up some of the relaxed air that only holiday-makers can have – the wonderful feeling that the only item on the evening's agenda is enjoyment; the happy knowledge that tomorrow holds no drudgery, only more (a cliché, I know) sun, sea and sand.

Eventually I had to yield to Lizzie's pleas and decide on a place to eat. The restaurants were all quite alike, and there was little to choose between them. Many retained the old custom of having a small display area, just off the street, where you could see the dishes available before you committed yourself to paying for and eating them. The food looked pretty much the same in each, so I let Lizzie choose.

'This one,' she cried, pulling me a little way down the street to a small taverna. It was well located like all of those in this area, right by the sea, with tables and chairs set up all along the sea wall. After we were seated, I asked her why she had chosen this one. She gave me a disdainful look, and indicated the tablecloths.

'You know green is my best colour.'

A charming waiter brought us menus. Like all the waiters we met, he was polite and mildly flirtatious. He never once gave offence, as he smiled and bowed, and he almost made me forget that I was about twice his age. Lizzie also fell for his charm, and she quickly began to call him by his name – 'Milos, can I have some more bread, *parakalo?*' – and he would come and present whatever she wanted with a flourish and a little bow, prompting her to dissolve into giggles.

I surveyed the menu, unaccustomed to such choice. All the expected Greek dishes were there – *moussaka*, *souvlaki*, *kalamaraki*, *thalassina*. I didn't really care what I ate as long as it wasn't plain grilled fish and boiled vegetables. Lizzie didn't care what she had as long as it came with chips. In the end, I chose *moussaka*, and while it could not be described as 'haute cuisine', it was well cooked and tasty. I washed this down with a half-bottle of the local wine, then I sat back, gazed out at the sea, calm in the setting sun, and I felt I was ready, at last, to rejoin the human race.

We wandered home early, and, sleepy after the wine, I went straight to bed. Lizzie jumped in beside me and cuddled up close.

'Thanks, Mummy,' she whispered before she fell asleep.

After that, we went out more and more. After all, I had to spend all that lottery money on something. If I brought too much home, James would only want to spend it on shelves for the garage, or roof insulation, or something equally boring. Or, horror of horrors, Maisie might get her hands on it, and spend it on lavender water and Rennies and a lifetime's supply of vests for James.

We tended to visit the same few restaurants. Everyone spoke English very well, but as time went on, we learned a few simple Greek phrases, and we began to exchange polite greetings with the waiters, lording it over the passing tourists who never seemed to progress beyond 'please' and 'thank you'.

In one restaurant, which we visited often, there was a particularly friendly waiter. He was older than most (that means he was a little closer to my age), and he seemed to go a little beyond the normal level of flirtation. When the restaurant wasn't too busy, he often sat at our table while we ate, and chatted with ease. When he finally asked me to go for a drink with him, I was flattered, but I refused his offer. It was just too corny, and faintly ridiculous. Me and a Greek waiter – I don't think so, somehow. I was no Shirley Valentine – and anyway I could never manage that Scouse accent.

When I refused his invitation, he looked at me aghast, as if his life was over, and he went back towards the kitchen with slouched shoulders and his head low. I felt cruel and mean. After all, having a drink wouldn't have hurt. However, the next evening, I saw him sitting at a table with another thirty-something tourist, gazing earnestly into her eyes, and laughing at her jokes, so I felt able to relax, happy in the knowledge that I hadn't broken his heart after all.

Weeks and weeks passed by. For the first time, I felt I was on holiday, and not just trying to regroup after a time of trauma. I awoke each morning feeling refreshed and happy, and looking forward to the new day.

I painted my toenails for the first time (scarlet because, since I had left it so late, I decided I'd better do it properly). Then Lizzie insisted that I do hers also. I enjoyed these little girlie occupations with her. Now that I never had to rush anywhere, I must have been gentler, because now Lizzie loved me to comb her hair. We would sit in the courtyard, in a warm, sunny corner, and I would comb away happily, and then style her hair with ribbons and slides. This was so calming, and had a primeval feeling, as if I were a mother primate grooming her young, and picking fleas from her fur.

There was a new lightness in my step, and all of my senses seemed to come alive. I enjoyed the cocoa smell of my sunscreen, and the fragrance of fresh fruit, as if I had never smelled them before. At times I felt as if I were on a drug of some kind. Colours seemed brighter, music seemed to have an irresistible beat, and scents of all kinds evoked only happy memories. I could sit on the beach for hours, wriggling my painted toenails in the soft, warm sand, and turning my face to the healing sun. (I knew all about skin cancer, but decided to put my faith in Ambre Solaire.) I could sit and dream, and watch happy groups of people go by, and yet be quite content with Lizzie by my side. I felt like Diogenes, happy to live in a barrel, almost, even, to the envy of the great Alexander.

For a short time, it was almost as if the old Claire was back. The old carefree Claire. The Claire I used to be before my first trip to Greece. I almost felt like the Claire in the photograph that Grace had taken on the boat. Except with more wrinkles and slightly better dress sense.

Almost.

Then, one evening, Lizzie and I were in one of our usual restaurants, waiting for our meal to arrive. We were passing the time by playing 'stone, scissors, paper'. Lizzie was carefully keeping score.

'You've won five times Mummy, but I've won six times.'

'Yes, that's right. You're good at counting.'

'So I'm really winning, amn't I?'

'Yes love, you're really winning.'

I was wonderfully relaxed. I leaned back in my chair and watched a red sun slowly make its way into the calm sea. I ran my fingers through my hair, and gave a deep sigh. What a wonderful place. What a happy time.

My thoughts were interrupted by a deep, rather cultured voice.

'Are these seats free? Would you mind terribly if we joined you?'

Chapter Eleven

My hand remained in the 'scissors' position as I looked up to see who had spoken.

It was the black-haired vision who had kindly lent me the tissue the day, weeks earlier, when I'd fallen and cut my elbow. He was still black-haired. He was still very much a vision.

I became unaccountably flustered. He seemed to be waiting for a reply.

'Er, yes, I suppose so. Lizzie, move over and make some room for em . . . and . . . em . . .'

Lizzie showed more poise than her bewildered mother. (But then, that wasn't difficult. Raucous drunken teenagers vomiting in dark laneways were often more poised than I was.)

She held out her hand. 'My name is Lizzie, and my mummy's name is Claire. My daddy's name is James but he's in Cork. He's minding my hamster.'

At the last words, I could see the black-haired vision's eyebrow raise ever so slightly. He beamed at Lizzie and took her hand.

'My name is Ross, and this is my son, Alistair. My daddy's name is Andrew and he's in England. I haven't got a hamster.'

Lizzie giggled at this.

Ross busied himself with arranging chairs and place settings while I tried to recover some of my lost calm, and sneaked a closer look at my guests.

Ross really was very handsome. Now that the sun wasn't so bright, his eyes weren't so crinkly, and this allowed me to see them properly. They were the most unusual shade of pale, pale blue, almost mauve, just like the colour of the hyacinth Lizzie had brought home from playschool that spring (the one that arrived in perfect, sweet-scented health on a Tuesday and somehow managed to be completely dried-up and dead by the Thursday).

Ross's hair, by contrast, was dark – jet black. It was curly and longer than I thought was fashionable, but hey, what did I ever know about fashion? His face was deeply tanned, with little white lines around his eyes, where the sun hadn't quite reached. He looked older than me, perhaps mid-forties.

I turned to look at his son, who had happily taken my place in Lizzie's game.

'We'll start again, because Mummy was losing. I'll say one, two, three.'

He smiled and nodded his agreement.

'And you mustn't move your hand until after I say three.'

He nodded again.

'And you know scissors beats paper because it cuts it all up.'

The patient boy nodded again. He was probably wishing his dad had kept walking when he saw us. He looked to be about twelve years old, and he was almost a mirror image of his father. Same nose, same hair, same blue eyes. I looked quickly from father to son, and couldn't hide my smile.

Ross spoke. 'You didn't know cloning was available eleven years ago, did you?'

I reddened. I was embarrassed that this man could read my thoughts, even though he'd known me for only about two-and-a-half minutes.

He grinned. 'Everyone thinks the same. I guess it's strong genes or something. All the men on my side are alike. It makes the family photos very boring.'

I laughed. He had a lovely easy manner. Friendly without being pushy, with a gentleness in his speech that was strangely reassuring. And how I needed reassuring! I should be at home in Cork, sponging the worst of the day's stains out of Lizzie's tracksuit. Or scraping the morning's porridge stains from the allegedly non-stick saucepans. Or frantically spraying Mr Sheen in the air so James would think I'd been doing some housework.

How did I end up on a dusty island in the middle of the Aegean Sea having dinner with a handsome stranger about whom all I knew was that he had crinkly eyes and strong genes?

Ross spoke again. 'I really hope you don't think it rude of us joining you like this.'

I shook my head and lied. 'No, it's fine. Really.'

'It's just that Al and I get tired of each other's company. Sometimes it's nice to chat to someone who doesn't look like a different-sized version of yourself. It can get so you feel like you're talking to a mirror. And how sad is that?'

I laughed, despite myself. He seemed like a nice guy, and clearly Lizzie was already in love with his son. What harm was there in enjoying myself over an innocent meal?

Ross and Alistair ordered from the hovering waiter, and soon we were all tucking into beautiful meals that weren't grilled fish and boiled vegetables. We shared a bottle of wine like old friends, and chatted about the weather and life. I mentioned that I liked *ER*.

Ross agreed. 'Yes, it's great. But don't you think it should be turned into an audience participation show?'

'How? What do you mean?'

'You know. Wouldn't it be fun if the cameras stopped rolling in the middle of resuscitation scenes, just when Dr Kovac was raising the paddles and shouting, 'Clear'? Then you could dial a number to determine if the patient should live or die.'

I laughed. 'Ross, that is truly bizarre.'

He laughed too. 'Yes, but admit it. It would be fun, wouldn't it?'

123

'Yes, I agree, it would. But only really sad psychos would ring in, so every patient would die. Romano would have to close the ER. I'd never see Carter again.'

At this, Ross gave a sudden, huge guffaw of laughter. It's strange how you warm to someone who laughs at your witticisms.

When we were finished rewriting television shows, Ross told me that he was from the North of England. He was a graphic designer. He'd been on the island since the previous September, but Alistair had just joined him in May. He didn't mention Alistair's mother, and of course I didn't ask. After all, I was leaving lots of gaps in my own story.

All too soon, we'd had coffee and sticky dessert and after-dinner drinks of ouzo. I was having a lovely time. It was so nice to talk to an adult who wasn't a waiter or a shopkeeper or a fisherman.

Finally, when all the other tables were empty, and when the waiter was pointedly unpinning tablecloths and tidying up chairs, I reluctantly got to my feet. Ross got up too, and our tired children quickly followed suit.

I held out my hand. 'That was a really lovely evening. I enjoyed myself. Thank you.'

Ross took my offered hand. His skin was dry, but his grip was firm. 'No, thank *you*. It's been lovely chatting to you.'

A tired Lizzie leaned against my side. 'Bye, Ross. Bye, Al. Sorry that you didn't win the game.'

'That's OK, kid. You're too good for me.'

He was rewarded with a beam from Lizzie.

Then we all stood there. It was hard to know how the evening should end. A light breeze had come up, and the boats in the harbour were rocking and making gentle clinking noises. I took a few steps in the direction of home.

Ross spoke again. 'Can I see you home? Have you far to go?'

I shook my head. 'No, it's just up here. We're fine. But thanks anyway.'

We all chorused one more goodbye, and Lizzie and I set off for home.

'They're nice, Mummy. Al is very funny. He taught me a new game.'

'Yes, they were nice, weren't they?'

'Are we having dinner with them again tomorrow? Can Al come and play with Sninky?'

'I don't think so, darling. We don't really know them, do we?'

'Course we do. Al is eleven and Ross is forty-three, and Al's mum is called Harriet and she's married to a really horrid man called Darren who chews his food with his mouth open and wears a big ugly bracelet.'

I smiled. Clever girl hadn't wasted any time.

'Mummy, can men wear bracelets? I don't think they should.'

I gave her hand a little squeeze. 'No, lovey. I don't think they should either.'

'And Al's grandad lives in a huge big house. It's called a manshing or something.'

'A mansion?'

'Yes, a manshing. And one day Al's dad might go and live in the manshing but he's not sure yet.'

Hmm. Very interesting.

I shook my head to clear it of foolish thoughts. I was never going to see Ross again, so why should I care if his dad had a mansion or not?

I pulled gently at Lizzie's hand to hurry her up. 'Come on, slowcoach. It's way past your bedtime.'

'OK.'

There was a silence for about thirty seconds. A record for my loquacious daughter.

'Mummy, did you ever see a rose roys?'

'Do you mean a Rolls Royce?'

'Yeah, a rose roys.'

'Yes, sometimes you see them in London.'

'Oh.'

'Where did you hear that word?'

'Al said it. He said his grandad has five of them. And one is eighty years old. That's very old. Daddy's car is only three. I said Al's grandad should take that one to the place where they squash all the cars until they are tiny but Al only laughed.'

This was getting way out of hand. Luckily we were at our door.

'Come on quick, Lizzie. Last one in bed's a rotten egg.'

We ended the evening in a mad, giggling scramble, and I slept a deep, calm sleep until dawn.

Chapter Twelve

Next morning, I hummed as I prepared the fruit for our breakfast. I don't know why.

Lizzie joined me at the table, and half-heartedly turned her nose up at her food. She gave a sly little smile.

'I don't want this breakfast.'

'Yes you do. You love it.'

'I don't.'

She thought for a moment. 'Mum, I'm a bit fed up of fruit and yoghurt for breakfast.'

I was wise to her tricks. 'Eat it up, and no argument.'

'But . . .'

'Forget it, sunshine. You got your way about our evening meal. There's no way you're going to bully me into taking you out for breakfast too.'

She smiled, and dived into her food with gusto.

We had no agenda for the day, but that was nothing new. We pottered around the house for a while. I rinsed out a few of our dirtier clothes, and put them to dry in the courtyard. Lizzie played one of her endless 'family' games. As usual, Sninky got to be the dad.

Lizzie was the mum and also took the roles of seven very noisy children. The mum and the children shouted and fought a lot. The dad just lay in the sun and occasionally purred.

Eventually, even Lizzie tired of this game. 'Can we go to the beach, Mummy?'

'Yes, if you like.' The fifteen minutes I'd just spent on housework was more than enough for me.

'Yeah. Can Sninky come?'

'No, darling, I've told you lots of times. Sninky wouldn't like the beach. He'd be too hot.'

'He could swim to get cool, like we do.'

'I don't think so, darling. Cats don't like swimming.'

'Yes, they do. When Jason's cat had kittens, Jason's dad took them to live on a nice farm in the country where they could go swimming every day.'

Oh, dear.

'Well, they must have been special cats. Most cats don't like water, and I'm sure Sninky wouldn't.'

'OK. We have to go out for a while, Sninky. You be a good cat, and we'll play some more when I get home.'

She rushed off to get her beach stuff, and we strolled the short distance to the beach. We sat in our usual spot, quite near the water, and settled ourselves down. Lizzie immediately began to build sandcastles, and I flipped open my book. After a few pages, I realised that I had no idea what I'd just been reading. I felt unusually bored and restless. I turned onto my stomach and rolled down the top of my swimsuit to tan my back.

'Stay next to me, Lizzie, and don't go near the water.'

'OK, Mum.'

I was reassured by the scrabbling sound she made as she worked on the sand next to me. I rested my head on my arms and closed my eyes. Occasionally a light breeze cooled my skin.

A short time later, Lizzie pulled at my arm.

'Look, Mummy. Look. Al and his dad are coming.'

I raised my head slightly and looked up. Sure enough, I could see the matching dark heads advancing towards us. I grabbed my book, and pretended to be reading. After all, I knew I could rely on Lizzie to let them know that we were there. I was right. They were still a good distance away, when she let out a huge shriek.

'Al, Ross, we're over here. Come and sit on our towels.'

I couldn't pretend not to have heard that, so I looked up from my book and gave them a casual wave.

Seconds later, two shadows on the sand in front of me let me know they were close.

'Move over, Mummy. Make room.' Lizzie was using one hand to push ineffectually at my hip, while using the other hand to try to pull my towel from underneath me.

I'd have been only too happy to share my very skimpy towel with this handsome man, but I was a married woman, and I was sure that it would not have been appropriate. Especially in front of my daughter and his son.

Ross grinned. 'It's OK, thanks, Lizzie. Al and I brought our own towels.'

Alistair was already spreading his on the sand next to where Lizzie was digging, when his father spoke again.

'Slow down, son. Maybe we're intruding. Maybe we should sit somewhere else.'

Oh no! I didn't want them to leave. I sat up suddenly, forgetting that my swimsuit was rather inelegantly ruched down around my navel. Aargh! I sat on my hands trying to stop them from frantically pulling my top back up. After all, Ross had seen my breasts by then, and it was a bit too late to be prudish. And anyway, no other woman on the beach was wearing a top except for the ancient old crone who sold melons at the edge of the path. She seemed to be wearing more clothes that I did in January in Cork.

Ross squatted on the sand next to me, and held out his hand in greeting. I took it, feeling dreadfully exposed. My suit had by now slipped so low that even my shiny, pink, Caesarean scar was on display, sneaking a few inches down from my navel before disappearing behind the blue nylon folds of my swimsuit. As I used one hand to shake his, I tried to be subtle as I used the other hand to pull my swimsuit top back into place. Ross gallantly kept his gaze on my face as I struggled.

I tried not to sound flustered. 'Please, feel free to join us. We'd love company. Wouldn't we, Lizzie?'

'Yeah. Come on Al. Let's make a huge big castle.'

Al dropped to his knees in answer, and began scooping large handfuls of sand out of where Lizzie had been digging.

Ross still hesitated. 'Are you sure, Claire? Are you sure we're not intruding?'

I felt a bit happier by now. Ross had reclaimed his hand, and I had managed to pull my swimsuit top almost around my neck.

I smiled at him and spoke the truth. 'It's lovely to see you, Ross. Really.'

He matched my smile, and doubled it with a huge beam. 'OK, then. We'd love to join you.'

The morning passed very quickly. Ross made easy, undemanding conversation. Alistair was a lovely, gentle child, who showed endless patience as Lizzie bossed and cajoled and bullied him. For a while I thought that, to the people around us, we must have looked like a family on holidays, but then I realised how ridiculous that notion was. If we were a family, then surely Ross would have been reading a thriller with a shiny black cover, and I'd have been doing a crossword. If Al and Lizzie were siblings, the peace would have been shattered on a regular basis, with endearing little pleasantries:

'No, you can't have an ice cream.'

'Stop throwing sand at your sister.'

'I don't care if it's just a game – she doesn't appear to be enjoying it.'

'No ice creams. You've had enough already.'

'Stop thumping your brother.'

'I don't care if he called you bum-face. You're to stop thumping him.'

'I said, no'

And on and on and on.

As it was though, everyone was on their best behaviour, and we had a lovely time.

I had been hungry for ages, but ignoring it, when Lizzie spoke. 'Mum, I'm starving. Can we get some lunch?'

At the mention of food, Alistair popped his head up from his digging. 'Yeah, Dad, I'm famished. Can we eat, too?'

I felt suddenly bold. For me, that is.

'Why don't you both join us for some lunch? We live just near here. I have salad and fruit and cheese.'

I had a lovely bottle of white wine in the fridge too, but I didn't mention that. I didn't want Ross thinking that I was trying to get him drunk so I could seduce him.

The children looked pleadingly at Ross. I could see that he was wavering. Finally he spoke. 'I'm real sorry, guys. I have a project that just has to be e-mailed to London by six this evening. If I don't go now, I'll never get it done on time.'

There was a chorus of 'aw's from the children. I was so disappointed that I felt like joining them, but decided I'd better not.

Ross spoke again. 'How about if I cook dinner for us all tonight?'

I didn't know what to say. Ross was looking at me with an open, easy smile.

'Don't worry. It won't be anything fancy. A stir-fry maybe, or perhaps a curry. Do you like lamb?'

Huh! As if I was worried about what he planned to cook. He could have served up Pot Noodles and Angel's Delight for all I cared. The food wasn't an issue.

You see, I knew there was nothing wrong with my accepting an innocent invitation to dinner. I knew that Ross was probably just being friendly and had no sinister designs on my body. (After all, he'd already seen my scarred, rather flabby stomach. And my breasts, which had never been anything to write home about anyway, and certainly weren't improved after eleven months of breastfeeding Lizzie. That sight would surely have quenched any desire he might have had.)

The problem was, I was beginning to hope that it wasn't an innocent invitation at all. Somehow, in the intense heat of that July morning, I found myself totally and absolutely turned on by the golden-skinned vision who was sitting on the sand next to me. As he rose to pack up his belongings, I had to struggle not to stare at his broad brown chest, and the strong shoulders that were just beginning to gleam with perspiration. He stooped to pick up his towel, and a muscle on his thigh twitched in a way that shouldn't have been so fascinating to a woman who was married to someone else.

I busied myself, folding Lizzie's towel in an effort to distract myself.

It didn't work.

Ross finished packing up, and I still hadn't answered. He looked at me, and I thought I could see a rather hurt expression in his pale blue eyes.

'Will I take that as a "no" then?'

I was being foolish. What would a handsome, clever man like Ross see in someone like me? He was only being friendly. And while I fancied his body in a big way, he'd never reciprocate, so we'd both be safe. And anyway, what could ever happen with Lizzie and Alistair there?

I made a snap decision. 'Yes. I mean no, that wasn't a no. We'd love to come.'

Ross seemed very pleased. 'Great, that's great. Does seven o'clock suit?'

'Yes, that's fine. Seven is fine. Where do you live?'

Ross described where he lived, only a few minutes' walk from the beach, and then he and Al set off.

Lizzie and I had a quiet lunch on a shady patio outside a taverna, during which I wondered whether I'd just made the best, or the most stupid, decision of my life.

Chapter Thirteen

Getting ready for my hot date didn't take long. I had a quick shower, and then I just had to choose between my dirty dress, my torn one, and the one with the broken zip. I decided on the one with the broken zip, as the offending item was on the back and easily covered with a cardigan. Lizzie insisted that I paint my nails, and wear lipstick.

She failed to notice that I wasn't resisting.

As we walked through the harbour area, something made me feel I should phone James. Guilt, I suppose. As usual, he sounded happy to hear from me. We made small talk about the weather. He didn't ask when I was coming home. I didn't ask if he would come out to see us for a few weeks. We'd asked those questions so often before, without either of us getting satisfactory answers. There wasn't really much point any more. It was as if our relationship was on hold, trapped in a world of tinkly recorded music and encouraging messages. There was no real, live operator to propel us forward. There wasn't even a '*dial two for messed-up marriages*.' I handed the receiver to Lizzie, and after a brief, giggling chat she hung up.

We resumed our walk. I couldn't quite make up my mind whether the telephone conversation made me feel better or worse. Then I put it out of my mind completely, as we reached Ross's house, and rang the bell.

Ross greeted us warmly, and accepted the bottle of white wine I brought. He ushered us into a small living area, and refused my offer of help.

'No, thanks. We're fine. Al and I are quite happy in the kitchen. You just make yourselves at home while we finish up.'

We sat on a cushion-covered couch. The television in the corner was on. What a novelty – I hadn't watched TV in weeks. And, even better, *ER* was on. It was in Greek, but that hardly mattered. The characters still just saluted each other by saying 'Hey', and giving each other meaningful looks. After a while, the camera zoomed in on Carter's face, as he completed some difficult procedure. With a face like that, who needed words? Even 'Hey' wasn't necessary.

I'd be happy, any time at all, to have Carter bend over me, the way he does. I'd recline on the crispy white sheets, and look at him trustingly. His big brown eyes would narrow slightly with the effort. A lock of hair would slip over one eye. He'd hold his breath, and I'd certainly hold mine. He'd put on that concentrated look, which moments later would change into his toothy boyish smile . . .

'I'm in.'

And the screen would go all fuzzy.

Ross walked in, interrupting my fantasy. Inspiring an entirely new one. What was it about this guy? I just couldn't keep my eyes off him. Luckily, he didn't appear to notice this as he showed us onto a patio which seemed to hang out over the ocean. There was a table, and four chairs. The table was set beautifully, with a small bunch of wild flowers in the centre. The patio was bounded by a low stone wall, and along the length of this was a line of flickering nightlights in delicately painted jars. I was touched, and then realised that it probably wasn't even for my benefit. Perhaps they dined like this all the time.

Ross served the food. Lamb stir-fry with rice and salad. It was probably lovely. I have no idea, as I tasted none of it. My plate was full, and not long afterwards it was empty, so either a passing wild cat ate it, or I did. I suppose it was me. I just don't remember.

The children giggled over trivial childish stuff, and Ross made easy conversation. I sipped my wine, and basked in the warmth of his personality.

As usual, wine loosened my normally obedient tongue. 'Lizzie tells me your dad lives in a manshing.'

Ross smiled, but looked rather uncomfortable. I felt bad for being so direct.

'I'm sorry. Perhaps I shouldn't have said that.'

'No, it's OK. I suppose it's true.'

Alistair jumped up. 'I'll show you a picture of it. You won't believe it.'

Ross looked as if he was going to stop his son, and then thought better of it.

He shrugged. 'Why not? Let Claire see the awful truth.'

Alistair returned with a large framed photograph. He held it in front of us. Ross covered his eyes, as if in shame.

I looked. I took a deep breath, and then looked again.

It was like the house in *Brideshead Revisited*.

With knobs on.

And turrets.

And west wings and east wings and stables and conservatories and chapels and orangeries.

I spoke quietly. 'You were brought up here?'

Ross still looked embarrassed. 'Well, no actually. We're new money. My dad's factory made a fortune in the sixties. I was well into my teens before he bought the stately home.'

I gave a nervous laugh, and tried to lighten the suddenly tense atmosphere. 'You won't believe this, but Lizzie says your dad has five Rolls Royces.'

Ross hesitated. 'Well, that's not quite true.'

I relaxed a little, before he continued.

'Actually, he just e-mailed me this morning to tell me that he's bought two more. Now he's got seven. He's a bit of a fanatic.'

I looked behind me at the admittedly pretty, but very small cottage that appeared to be Ross's home. Something didn't seem quite right.

Ross fixed his pale blue eyes on mine. 'Would you like me to explain?'

What could I say? It really wasn't any of my business. Ross wasn't much more than an acquaintance, and didn't owe me any explanations. On the other hand, I was intrigued, to say the very least.

My silence was answer enough.

'OK. Al, why don't you take Lizzie in to watch some television?'

The children set off obediently, carrying their empty plates with them.

Ross took a deep breath, indicated the photograph, and began.

'That's Wyndham Hall. My parents live there.'

He suddenly looked very troubled. I was sorry I'd started the whole conversation.

'Please, Ross. Why don't you leave it at that? It's making you uncomfortable. I shouldn't have been so nosy. I . . .'

He raised his hand to stop me. 'Actually, I need to talk about this. If you'd listen, I'd be very grateful. I would really welcome some impartial advice.'

I shrugged. 'Happy to oblige.'

He leaned across the table, and took my hand. 'Thank you so much, Claire.'

My hand tingled at his touch. I felt a sudden urge to throw myself into his arms. Reluctantly I pulled my hand away. If I kept it in his while he was telling his tale, I couldn't concentrate for a moment – he might as well be reciting the soccer results.

He looked for a moment at the space in his hand where my hand had been, and then he continued. 'I had a lovely childhood. My dad worked hard, and my mum stayed home to take care of me – I'm their only child. Then Dad made his fortune. He set up a factory to make parts for heavy machinery. It seemed he could do no wrong. He became incredibly wealthy.'

I couldn't stop myself blurting out the rude question. 'How wealthy, exactly?'

He shrugged. 'Really, you don't want to know. Just trust me. We're not talking small change here.'

I nodded wisely, as if I understood.

'Dad's still running the factory, but he needs to retire. He's in his eighties, and his health is failing. He wants me to go home and learn the business, while he's still well enough to show me the ropes. I'm not sure I want the job though. I don't want to live in England and be a manager. I like it here.'

'Why go back, then?'

'I feel I owe it to my dad. He worked so incredibly hard to build up the business.'

I interrupted. 'Yes, but that's his dream. Not yours.'

Ross gave a half-smile. 'I know. Part of me says I should just tell him I'm not interested. But part of me remembers how he used to bring me around the factory when I was a little boy. He was so proud of me. I know he did it all for me. It would break his heart if I turned my back on his empire.'

He refilled my glass, which seemed to have emptied itself very quickly. I thought for a moment.

'What if you went back, and took over until . . .?' I wasn't sure how to finish the sentence.

Ross gave a sudden, incongruous guffaw. 'You mean go back until Dad pops his clogs, and then sell up?'

I nodded, embarrassed. It didn't sound very nice when he put it into words.

He saw my embarrassment. 'Don't worry – I've often thought about it. But then I'd just be there, putting in the time until Dad dies. Perhaps wishing for his death. That wouldn't be fair to any of us. If I go back, I have to do it whole-heartedly. I'd have to go back meaning to stay.'

I hesitated, and then spoke. 'What does Alistair's mother think?'

'Who knows? We married young. We had a lot of fun together at first. She was pretty and flighty and had expensive tastes. She wanted us to move into the west wing of the manshing. She left when she realised I wouldn't shower her with the trappings of my father's wealth. She married a man with even newer money than ours. He has a trucking company. He loves her and buys her everything he wants.'

'Ross, I'm so sorry.'

He shrugged. 'It's OK. She's not a bad person. I just shouldn't have married someone who spent so much time looking in the mirror.'

He leaned back in his chair and took a long drink of wine.

'So that's my story. What do you think? Should I do the decent thing, and go back? Or should I stay here and enjoy the simple life?'

What could I say? At home, I struggled to decide what to have for tea. Or whether to buy spearmint or freshmint toothpaste. I often came home from the video shop with nothing more than a headache because I couldn't commit ninety-seven minutes of my life to any of the films on display.

'God, Ross. I don't know. I don't even know where to begin thinking about it. I'm not very good at this kind of thing.'

'That's OK. I feel better just for talking about it. I think I know what I have to do. I think I'm going to go back. Sometimes I just like to think I have a choice.'

We sat in silence for a while. I emptied my glass again, and Ross got up to open another bottle of wine. When he returned, he sat next to me. For the first time that evening, I got to concentrate on the scenery. The sun was just setting over the sea. The air was warm and sweet-scented. I could feel the warmth from Ross's shoulder even though we weren't touching.

Alistair interrupted us, popping his head through the half-open patio door. 'I'm going to bed, Dad. Lizzie's asleep on the couch. Goodnight, Claire.'

I was impressed once again by his gentle manners.

'Goodnight, Al. And thank you for being so nice to Lizzie.'

'Oh, that's OK, Claire. She's a cool kid. I like her.'

Ross rubbed his son's shoulder affectionately. 'Goodnight, son. Sleep well. See you in the morning.'

Al left, closing the patio door behind him, and Ross and I lapsed into a comfortable silence. A motor-bike chugged past on the road outside.

Eventually Ross spoke. 'Well, Claire, I've told you all my deepest, darkest secrets. Well, my deepest ones anyway. You'd need a few more drinks before I burdened you with the darkest ones. Do you want to tell me your story?'

Oh no. Just when I thought there would be no need to talk about myself. What could I say? Scenes flashed through my mind.

James almost crying, the day I left.

Maisie's triumphant smile.

Maureen's gentle kindnesses.

My mum and dad, worn-looking and sad.

Lizzie smiling her first gummy smiles.

The recent memories floated up easily into the soft evening air. Then I got to the old stuff. The brain-sludge.

Grace tossing her blonde hair.

Jessie laughing with tears in her eyes.

Kevin, with his confident air.

Kevin laughing with his friends.

Kevin in the restaurant.

Kevin on the beach.

Then the worst day of all. The day . . .

Ross edged his chair closer to mine. He put a finger to my lips. 'Don't tell. Don't tell if it upsets you that much.'

He produced a tissue and wiped a single tear from my cheek. He stroked my head and carefully untangled the lock of my hair that had caught in the strap of his watch. A Rolex, I suddenly noticed. I was slow to pick up on that kind of thing. Bet it wasn't a fake.

I wanted to fling myself into his arms. I wanted to cling to him, and I wanted him to hold me tight. I wanted him to rock me, and stroke me, and calm me. I wanted him to rip off my clothes and make fierce, passionate love to me, in the gentle, sweet-scented air.

I stood up and said, 'I think I'd better go. It's been lovely.'

Ross stood too. He took my hands in his. He spoke in a lilting voice, gently mocking my Cork accent.

'It's been lovely. You are lovely. Please . . .'

I took my hands back and clasped them primly in front of me. Even I could see where this was leading. Where I really wanted it to lead. But I'd never been unfaithful to James before. Of course I had hurt him in all kinds of ways, but I'd never been unfaithful. I'd never even thought about being unfaithful to him (except with sultry, white-coated *ER* doctors, and surely that didn't count?)

I went through the patio doors into the living-room. The television was still on. *Star Trek* now. Lizzie was curled up on the couch, with a blanket over her. Ross followed me.

'I'll just check on Al,' he said as he opened a door, and peeped through.

He closed the door gently again. 'Fast asleep.'

He looked at Lizzie. 'Does she sleep soundly?'

I nodded. I knew he wasn't just making conversation.

He took me by the hand and led me down a small corridor. I went willingly. We were in a bedroom. He closed the door behind us. He dropped my hand and looked closely at me. I inclined my head in agreement. Suddenly anything he wanted to do was fine with me. More than fine.

He leaned past me and turned the key in the door. A definite statement of intent. Clearly he wasn't going to show me his stamp collection, or his wedding photographs.

There was a small light next to the bed. It cast a gentle orange glow. He slipped my cardigan from my shoulders and kissed my arm. I put my hands under his t-shirt. His skin was warm. I could feel wiry hair. I could feel his heart beating. I could feel his chest rising and falling with deep, heavy breaths – almost sighs.

I sat on the bed. Ross knelt in front of me. He gathered my hair in his hands, and held it back from my face. His voice was hoarse with emotion. 'You are so beautiful, Claire. So beautiful.'

I felt beautiful. I felt beautiful and brave and happy, as I broke the rest of my zip in my rush to take off my dress.

Some time later, I was almost skipping along the road from Ross's house to mine. His step was slightly heavier, as he was burdened with the not inconsiderable weight of my sleeping daughter.

I let us into my little house, and pulled back the covers of Lizzie's bed. Ross laid her gently down, and covered her. He kissed his fingers and touched her lightly on her forehead.

She stirred and spoke in a sleepy voice. 'Goodnight, Daddy.'

Ross looked genuinely frightened as he tip-toed from the room as quickly as he could.

I followed him into the courtyard.

'Don't worry. She always talks in her sleep. She won't remember anything in the morning.'

He put his arms around me. This was beginning to feel very familiar. Familiar and nice. I rested my head on his shoulder and inhaled his smell of soap and lemons and lamb stir-fry. I'd have happily stood there for the night. For days even. Or weeks. Rocking gently, with the still warm wall behind my back and Ross stroking my hair.

He spoke. 'I have to go. I can't leave Al alone too long.'

I reluctantly released my grip. 'Goodnight then, and thanks for dinner.'

'Goodnight, Claire. It's been lovely. Really lovely.'

He gave me one last gentle kiss, and left.

I stood in the courtyard for quite a while. Then I went in to bed.

That night I dreamt of Kevin. He was on an island, and I was swimming away from him. I was swimming with clean, confident strokes that I can't do in real life. He was calling me, but I wasn't paying any attention.

I was laughing.

Chapter Fourteen

I slept later than usual and awoke to find Lizzie curled around me in her usual boa-constrictor-like way.

I smiled at the memory of the previous night. Then I grimaced as Lizzie rolled over and poked her knee into my thigh. Ross had been very gentle, but I had some very strange aches and pains. Parts of me were feeling very delicate, to say the least. And some delicate parts of me were feeling particularly delicate indeed.

I lay as still as I could and relived the previous evening. I must be honest and say that in my mental video replay, the first few hours were fast-forwarded, while the last hour was watched slowly, frame by frame. I had just got to the part when Ross said I was beautiful, when I was rudely interrupted.

'Mummy, Al let me play with his Gameboy.'

'Mmmm,' I murmured, hoping she'd go back to sleep.

No chance. Lizzie had just had one of her split-second transformations from sound asleep to completely, talkatively awake. 'I was asleep in Al's house. How did I get home? Did you lift me?'

Oh dear! The first dilemma of a cheating wife and mother. I decided to tell the truth. At least the truth was easier to remember.

'No, darling. You were too heavy, so Ross carried you home. Wasn't that nice of him?'

'Yes. Is he coming to our house today?'

'I don't know, darling.'

'Can we go to the beach then? I want to dig another big hole.'

Clever girl. She wasn't going to dwell on possibilities and half-hopes. She was going to get on with her life. Pity I couldn't emulate her four-year-old's wisdom. I was already wondering how I could face Ross again. Or if I'd get the chance to face him again. I had a horrible feeling that I'd seduced him. Or maybe he was a serial seducer who was so good at it that he made the woman feel that it was all her doing.

Lizzie rolled out of my bed, and pottered around the room. I lay for a while, wondering what it would be like to wake up next to Ross.

Very nice, I imagined.

Not that I'd ever know.

I wondered how I could fix it to see him again. Should I hang around the beach, hoping he'd come for a swim? Should I lurk on the street outside his house, hoping he'd come out? Could I find the courage to knock on his door and invite him to my place for dinner? Would I ever lie on his bed again, in complete sensual abandon?

I shook myself to put such bad thoughts out of my mind. How could I do this to James? Skipping off to Greece was one thing. Cavorting in stone cottages with wealthy visions was a different thing altogether.

I jumped out of bed and busied myself with preparing breakfast. I had just finished scraping the seeds from a soft, sweet melon, when there was a knock at the door. Before I could respond, Lizzie ran over and flung it open.

It was Ross.

I became completely embarrassed and flustered. I was wearing a very short, faded old nightdress with unravelling lace at the neck, and a large coffee stain down the front. (Though why that should embarrass me, I'm not quite sure. After all, the night before, Ross had seen me wearing nothing only a very self-satisfied smile, and he didn't seem to have a problem with that.)

He stood in the doorway, looking rather bemused.

'Perhaps I should call back later.'

No way. Dirty nightie or not, I wasn't letting him escape. What if he never came back?

'No. It's fine. Come in. Sit down. Lizzie, get a plate for Ross, and give him some melon.'

As I spoke, I grabbed some clothes from my bed and ran into the bathroom, banging the door shut behind me.

Bad idea. I dropped the clothes onto the floor and surveyed them. I was faced with the choice of wearing jeans with no top, or a dress with no knickers. I settled for the dress. After all, if we got to the stage where he knew I'd no knickers on, I'm sure we'd both be past caring if I was a slut or not. I ran a comb through my hair, and returned to Ross and Lizzie.

Ross was happily ensconced in a seat by the window, eating a huge slice of melon. Lizzie was sitting opposite him, chattering happily.

I was desperate to know why he was there. Had he come to declare undying love for me? Or was he here to say that he'd made a terrible mistake, and that we should forget all about the previous night?

Suddenly a horrible thought struck me. Had he come to tell me that he'd found a broken condom under the bed?

Adult discussion was impossible with Lizzie there, so I tried not to be impatient as she very, very slowly ate her fruit. She made little patterns on her plate with orange segments and slices of apple. Each time she ate a morsel, there followed a lengthy rearrangement of the remaining pieces.

Finally I cracked. 'Lizzie, why don't you go out into the courtyard, and eat your fruit there?'

'No, Mummy. I can't. You know you said I shouldn't eat my fruit outside because there are too many flies.'

'Well, actually, it's not so warm this morning. There might not be any flies.'

151

'Yes, but Sninky might jump up and knock over my plate. You know you told me that might happen if I eat outside.'

'Well, Sninky looked tired when I saw him earlier. I don't think he'll bother you.'

'And what if a wasp came? He might go on a fruit and I might eat it and he might sting me, and my tongue would get all big and I'd choke.'

I hadn't realised that she paid so much attention to all of my dire warnings.

'Why don't you leave your fruit? I think you've had enough for now.'

'No, I've only had a little bit. And you said I have to eat five pieces every day.' As she spoke, she slid all the fruit to one side of her plate and started to make a new pattern. It looked very complicated. And very slow. Ross was sitting back in his chair, enjoying the scene.

Suddenly I couldn't take any more. I jumped up and removed her plate and put it into the fridge. Before she could protest, I rummaged in the food cupboard and produced a packet of Smarties and put them into her hand.

'Now. You can eat these outside. Flies and wasps and cats don't like Smarties, and they're lovely bright colours so they're probably full of fruit.'

Even Lizzie knew this to be untrue, but in the face of such a sudden, unexpected treat, she wasn't about to argue. She skipped off happily, and I was left with Ross.

I sat at the table where Lizzie had been. Now that we were alone, I didn't quite know what to say to him. He sat with his head resting on one hand, and we looked at each other for a few moments. I was struck yet again by the pale blue of his eyes. A bloody genetic blip, and I was completely helpless. If he'd been born with brown eyes, like most dark-haired people, I could probably have resisted. It was those impossibly blue eyes that did it for me. Without them, surely my marriage vows would be unbroken, and my conscience clear.

We sat in silence. In the brief time that I'd known Ross, we'd had lots of silences. Up to this, they'd been of the companionable kind. This was different. This was like the silence after a child has sent a football crashing through a stranger's window. Clearly there was going to be a reaction, but it was hard to predict what kind. Would it be the, 'Don't worry, it could happen to a bishop' kind? Or would it be the 'How could you possibly have done this dreadful thing?' kind?

It was easier for Ross. He was English. He was used to the stiff-upper-lip-let's-all-sit-in-dignified-silence vibe. My family were always the ones who broke a rare ten-second silence with a bright, 'Why doesn't someone say something?'

I kept to the family tradition, and blurted out the first non-contentious thing I could think of.

'That was a lovely meal last night. You're a good cook.'

'You're a good lover.'

I thought I had misheard him. 'Pardon.'

He smiled. 'I said you're a good lover. Very good actually.'

I could feel the blush spreading rapidly. I think it reached my toes. It clashed with my nail varnish.

How does a girl respond to that kind of a statement?

'Well, you know how it is, I did my best.'

'You weren't so bad yourself.'

'You should see me when I'm sober.'

'Tell all your friends, I do groups.'

Nothing I could think of sounded right. And anyway, the blush was distracting me. And I was remembering that I had no knickers on.

'Er. Thanks.'

Ross leaned over and took my hand. 'I'm sorry. That was rude of me. I shouldn't have said it. I just wanted to get it out of the way.'

I put on a pretend hurt look. 'Thanks a lot.'

Ross grimaced. 'I'm not doing this very well, am I? Forgive me. It's just that my mind is racing this morning, for all kinds of reasons. I really came to say that after I talked to you, I made up my mind about a few things. I phoned my father first thing this morning. We had a good talk. We hadn't talked properly for a long time. I've agreed to go back home for a little while. I'll stay for a few months, and come to a proper decision then. And anyway, Al has missed too much school – he needs to catch up, or we'll all be in trouble. And he hasn't seen his grandparents for quite a while. Going back will be good for all of us.'

Ross continued to speak. I was glad that he had made the beginnings of a decision, and that he seemed to be happy with it. But mostly I wanted to know when he was leaving. I'd have been very upset if he had announced that he was leaving on the next ferry. After all, I'd already done the unfaithful thing, and there was no going back. Might as well do it a few more times and get value out of the guilt I would surely feel when I got back home to reign once more in my apple-white kingdom.

Poor Ross. While he was telling me of plans that would change his life and that of his son, I was wondering if there was any hope of a quick shag.

He picked up a piece of melon and ate it. I could see his perfect, sharp teeth. I knew from personal experience just how sharp they were. I watched as he licked the juice from his fingers. I remembered exactly what he had done with those fingers the previous night.

I hoped he'd washed them.

He looked at me. I suspect that my naked desire was visible on my face. Whatever he saw, it made him stop his monologue. He leaned over and kissed me gently on the lips. I could taste the melon, and faint traces of alcohol. He held my head tightly in both of his hands, and kissed me fiercely.

Eventually, in the interests of getting oxygen into our systems, we pulled away from each other. My stomach felt very strange. Ross was breathing heavily. Heavily enough to get himself arrested if he happened to be on the phone.

'I told my father that I'd need a few weeks to pack up things here.'

I replied to this statement with a huge smile. I had a few ideas as to how I'd like to spend the next few weeks.

And none of them involved packing.

Chapter Fifteen

There followed two marvellous weeks.

Ross may indeed have done some packing but, if so, I didn't see much evidence of it. All I could see was us packing as much sex as was possible into fourteen child-encumbered days.

It was very difficult. We lay on the beach, almost naked, rubbing oil onto each other's backs while Lizzie and Alistair romped in the shallows, and made endless sandcastles. I found myself almost whimpering with desire when I felt Ross's hands on my skin. He often had a hungry look in his eyes that sent very strange sensations right through my body.

Most evenings, we ate in Ross's house, as the extra rooms there made it easier for us to indulge our illicit passions. We had to be careful that neither child would see us kissing or touching. They took our sudden friendship quite for granted, but neither Ross nor I wanted them to know just how friendly we really were. After our meal, they would watch television, and Ross and I would wait impatiently for them to fall asleep.

On more than one occasion, I thought seriously of getting a child-friendly sedative to speed up the process. It would be easy to slip something into their orange juice, and they'd drift quickly into peaceful sleep.

Then I found myself picturing tabloid headlines – 'EVIL MOTHER DRUGS CHILD FOR SEX ORGY WITH LECHEROUS TYCOON.' Tabloids were hardly likely ever to know, but even thinking about it made it seem too sleazy for words, so I abandoned my drug plans and made sure to wake Lizzie early every morning, to ensure that she'd be good and tired when night came.

Of course, Ross and I didn't have the perfect relationship. He was always kind and considerate, but it quickly became clear that his views and mine, on a huge range of subjects, were very different. He could barely hide his impatience at my total lack of interest in politics. I could hardly bear to hear him speaking about world leaders as if he knew more about their internal affairs than they did. And he was constantly playing Bruce Springsteen CDs, and singing along completely out of tune. Very loudly.

At night, when the children were safely asleep, I used to fling off my clothes in wild abandon, tossing them to every corner of the room in my hurry to be rid of them. Ross only turned his full attention to me after he had carefully folded all his clothes and placed them neatly on a chair at the end of the bed. Admittedly, once he had carefully placed his socks onto his shoes, he showed remarkable inventiveness and passion, but I could have lived without the time he spent fussing over his clothes.

But none of this mattered. This was not going to be a long-term affair. I knew that when I got to sixty, I wouldn't be watching Ross fold his underpants, or listening to him putting the world to rights. I wouldn't be enduring his hummed version of 'Hungry Heart'. He had booked his flights back to England, so I knew that, in total, this affair would last for precisely seventeen days.

And that suited me fine. Much as I craved and desired his body (and how I craved and desired his body!) I didn't want our liaison to last forever. It was as if he were a box of rich Belgian chocolates. I planned to savour every morsel to the very last. And when they were gone, I wouldn't mourn their loss.

I rang James every few days, and we had rather guarded conversations. At first, I feared that Lizzie would mention Ross, and I had a casual 'just friends' story ready, but I never needed it. She just prattled on about Sninky, and the beach, and what she had for breakfast.

Of course I felt guilty. Not all the time. But every now and then, a tidal wave of guilt would wash over me. Luckily, like all tidal waves, these passed quickly, and everything seemed clean and fresh and new when they were gone.

And anyway, an affair in Greece wasn't quite like one at home. It wasn't the same at all. And besides,

Ross was like therapy. Since I'd met him I'd become free and happy. Ross was beginning the curing process for my melancholy. And cavorting with him was much cheaper than checking into a home for the bewildered.

And, most importantly of all, being with Ross was making me strong. I almost felt ready to face my awful past. Soon, I knew, I'd be strong enough to go back to San Stefanos one last time. And the clever part of me, the part of me that read a few psychology textbooks before dropping out of college, knew that only when I had faced my past would I be ready to go home and face the future.

A few days before Ross was due to leave, Lizzie and I arrived as usual for our evening meal. Lizzie carried the salad I had made onto the patio, and stayed there chatting to Al. Ross took me by the arm and led me to the kitchen where a huge pot of something was bubbling noisily. His pale eyes were unusually bright. He spoke in an urgent whisper.

'I have a marvellous surprise. Please agree. Please just say yes.'

I laughed. 'How about if you run it by me first?'

'You know Christa, the lady who lives up the road?'

Of course I did. She was the gentle old German lady who sometimes babysat for Alistair.

'Well, she has invited Al to sleepover in her house tonight. A kind of a goodbye treat. And she says Lizzie

160

can go too. Do you think she'd go? They can stay until lunchtime tomorrow.'

All kinds of wonderful thoughts ran through my head. They all involved sex. 'Of course she'll go. She'd love to.'

Even if I had to drag her there screaming and kicking and crying blue murder, she was going. That much I knew.

In the event, Lizzie was charmed by the idea. She worshipped Alistair, and would have gone to the ends of the earth with him. Going three doors up the road for an evening of popcorn and videos, followed by a sleepover was hardly going to be a problem.

We ran back home to pack a small bag with her pyjamas, a toothbrush and a teddy. When we got back to Ross's, Lizzie flung her arms around me and hugged me tightly. One of my tidal waves of guilt was building up, getting ready to swamp me. My poor baby. I was packing her off to a stranger's house so I could indulge in a night of passion with a man I'd only just met.

Lizzie disentangled herself. 'Sorry, Mummy. No more cuddles. Al and I are going now. We can't be late because Christa has made the popcorn already. See you in the morning.'

'OK, darling. Be good. Brush your teeth and go to the toilet before you go to bed. See you tomorrow.'

She gave me one quick kiss, and skipped off with Ross and Al. I contemplated ripping off my clothes and jumping into bed, ready for Ross, when I realised that

that was stupid. After all, we had the whole night in which to make sweet music together. And what kind of a symphony would it be if the wonderful, crashing climax came just as the first notes were played?

So I busied myself setting the table. I found a huge box of night-lights, and I arranged them on every free surface of the patio. When I lit them, they even stayed alight, barely flickering in the still, evening air.

I poured myself a glass of cold white wine and sat back, enjoying the view. Ross seemed to be gone for ages. I was more excited than any child on Christmas Eve.

Finally I heard the front door open, and Ross came through to the patio, looking very pleased with himself.

'I'm so sorry, Claire. Christa asked me in, and insisted I have a glass of wine with her. I didn't like to refuse. I didn't want to look too eager to get away.'

'It's fine. We have the whole evening. Just for us.'

'Yes, you're right. Just for us.' He sat beside me, and gathered my hair back from my face. He kissed me gently on the forehead. I had to fight the urge to fling myself on him.

I spoke brightly. 'Why don't we eat?'

He looked like a little boy who'd been told to take his hand out of the cookie jar. 'Let's eat later. It'll keep.'

I smiled as sexily as I could. 'No. Please, let's eat. We have the whole night. And I want to do it out here, under the stars. Please.'

The mention of sex under the stars seemed to work. Ross got up, and returned very quickly with the food.

And so we ate. As usual when I was with Ross, I could concentrate only on him. I could tell you now the exact shade of blue of his eyes. I could pick the colour from a chart of hundreds of blues. I can picture his smile. I can see his bottom tooth on the left with the tiny chip missing. I can picture the exact way his hair curled over his ears.

But, not to save my life, could I tell you what I ate that evening. Anything I ate passed my lips without being tasted. The food wasn't a taste experience – it was just energy, fuel for the night of passion that lay ahead.

Finally, when it was almost dark, Ross got up and cleared the plates from the table. I was for the ancient Greek tradition of throwing everything into the corner of the patio, sending them crashing noisily against the stone walls. He wouldn't hear of it though. He insisted on carrying them into the kitchen, though he made the supreme sacrifice of leaving them soaking in the sink – a slovenly habit he normally would not allow.

He returned with a large puffy quilt. Having pushed the patio furniture to one side, he spread the quilt on the ground in its place. Then he took me gently by one hand and led me the few steps to the quilt. We sat together and looked out towards the sea. The moon left a delicate trail on the still water, like a pathway to heaven. There was a smell of charred food, and strong, sweet flowers. I could hear crickets and distant music.

Ross gave a deep sigh, and carefully guided me so I was lying down. He leaned over me, obscuring the moon and the stars. He unbuttoned my dress.

For one brief moment, I was reminded of Kevin. That was a clear starry night too.

Then Ross kissed me ever so gently on the lips, and all thoughts of Kevin vanished into the warm night air.

Much later (as they say in the best trashy novels), I awoke. I'm not sure how long we had lain there, but the moon had obviously tired of our high-jinks and had decamped to a different location, behind some trees. The stars still twinkled, and the sky still looked like dark grey velvet. I heard a familiar sound. Familiar but not pleasant.

How could I have lain outside with neither clothes nor mosquito repellent on? I ran inside to inspect the damage. It could have been worse. Two bites on my face, three on my right arm, two on my right foot, and five vicious ones on my left knee. (There was also one on my left breast, but I think Ross had done that.)

I rummaged in Ross's neat wardrobe and found a huge t-shirt to wear. As there was no quilt on his bed, I had an excuse to wake him. He sleepily got up, and we moved to the bedroom. We snuggled together in his bed. He wrapped his arms around me and we slept.

Next morning, I awoke to find something hard pressing against my leg. How had we managed to trail an empty wine bottle into the bed with us?

I watched Ross for a while. In sleep, even when I couldn't see his eyes, he was still beautiful. His dark lashes curled on his cheek. His longish hair was rumpled and slightly damp, like a little boy's after a bath. His skin was so perfectly clear and golden that I couldn't resist stroking it. The pale blue eyes opened, and stared at me in wonder. I stroked and sighed and smiled, just like the heroine in a made-for-TV movie.

Just like the hero in a made-for-TV movie, he quickly tired of this, and led the way as we indulged in a few pleasures that would definitely never be seen in a made-for-TV movie. Even in Sweden.

Afterwards we dozed. When I awoke again, the sun was streaming into the room and across our naked bodies. It was still pleasant, not yet hot. One of my legs dangled over the side of the bed, and the other was draped languidly across Ross's thighs. He had one arm flung behind him, and the other was around my shoulders. We must have looked like the survivors of a drunken game of Twister.

I rearranged my limbs, and snuggled more comfortably next to Ross. In his sleep, he did a similar realignment. I lay and watched his chest rising and falling easily. He had a dreamy look on his face. (Perhaps because he was dreaming?) His arms were a perfect golden colour, like pancakes made by a better cook than me.

I sighed deeply. It was perfect. Well, perfect until the sun all of a sudden became much hotter, and my mosquito bites began to itch furiously. I was terribly hungry. Then I felt a dreadful urge to go to the loo. An urge I was too lazy to give in to. Then Ross awoke. He smiled at me, snuggled closer, and began to sing in my ear. The words were definitely those of 'Born to Run'. The tune was not one that Bruce Springsteen was likely to own up to. I think it was actually 'Thunder Road' in the wrong key. I decided it was definitely time for the loo.

We had a leisurely breakfast on the patio. I often found myself smiling, thinking of the night before. After breakfast, I could see that Ross fancied another bed or patio-session, but I resisted his enticing smiles. I was a little ill at ease about Lizzie, and keen to see her again. I wasn't used to being away from her for so long.

Ross agreed to collect her from Christa's house, while I tidied up the kitchen. The dishes from the previous night were still wallowing in the greasy sink. Whatever we had eaten was brownish in colour, and it had a lot of garlic. I was just finishing up when Lizzie rushed in and launched herself at me.

'Mummy, I had a great time. We watched lots of videos, and Christa has three cats and four kittens, and I slept in a bunk bed and we had Rice Krispies and can I go there again?'

I laughed at her enthusiasm. 'We'll see darling. Now give me this morning's hugs and we'll go home.'

'OK. Bye, Al. Bye, Ross.'

Ross walked us to the gate. The next day was Lizzie's fifth birthday, and I really thought we should spend the day on our own. I didn't think it would be fair for me to spend her special day ogling Ross, and wondering when I'd get up close and personal with him again. I was just wondering how to explain this, when he spoke.

'Thanks so much for last night. It was great. The best.'

The children were engrossed in a noisy game of 'stone, scissors, paper', so I sneaked a quick kiss on his lips. 'Yeah. It was fantastic. Do you think . . .?'

He interrupted me. 'Would you mind awfully if we didn't meet tomorrow? I have to finish my packing and sort out things in the house.'

I nodded my agreement. 'That's fine. I want to spend the day with Lizzie anyway.'

'That's settled then. How about if we meet here the next evening? I'll cook us a farewell dinner. Is seven o'clock OK?'

'That sounds perfect. I'll bring a salad. See you then.'

We sneaked one more quick kiss, and Lizzie and I set off for home.

Chapter Sixteen

The next day, 8 August, Lizzie's birthday, dawned bright and sunny, just as we were used to. Lizzie woke me excitedly.

'Mummy, Mummy, wake up! It's my birthday. I'm five. Wake up!'

I grunted from under the blanket. 'Happy birthday, darling.'

'No, Mummy. Look at me. Look how big I am. I'm five.'

It was very early, but no one could resist such an onslaught. Reluctantly I shook myself free of my dreams. Pulling myself up in the bed, I gave Lizzie a birthday kiss, and a tight hug.

A few weeks earlier, I had bought her two small dolls, and some dolls' furniture. One afternoon, when she was playing in the courtyard with Al, I had made a little house out of an old cardboard box, decorated with sheets of brightly coloured wrapping paper. Now I wriggled out of Lizzie's exuberant clutches and silently pointed to them, hidden under her bed. She pounced on them with joy. She was so easily pleased (not yet of an age to appreciate only Nike trainers and Playstations), it was as if I had handed her the crown jewels on a plate. The poor child was still too young to realise that making houses was not exactly my forte, and that this was a particularly feeble effort at creativity, with a crooked roof and side walls that were distinctly warped. (When Ross first saw it, I think he thought it was a joke. He began to laugh, and only stopped when he noticed that I was looking cross and hurt. He did the thing that never worked in school either – turning a laugh into a fit of coughing.)

Lizzie immediately began to rearrange the furniture, talking to the dolls as if they were old friends. She called to me often, showing me different pieces of furniture, as if I hadn't selected, bought and paid for each piece. When I was finally able to tear her away from her toys, we had her birthday breakfast. It was yoghurt and fruit as usual, but Lizzie had little fruit jellies dotted around her plate as a treat. Also, as a special treat, Sninky was allowed inside for breakfast, and he solemnly lapped a saucer of milk as if he knew this was a special occasion.

I felt it was important for Lizzie to speak to her dad on her birthday, so I had left a message on the machine the day before, saying that we would phone early this morning. Now we hurried to the payphone, and for once I was praying silently that he would be there. I dialled, and held the receiver to Lizzie's ear. Seconds later, her expression of deep concentration changed to one of joy.

'Daddy. Daddy. I'm five. I got dolls and a house. Mummy made the house. Sninky came into the kitchen. I'm getting ice cream.' On and on she rushed, as if life were too short to say all she had to say. I'm not sure if James got to say anything. Then she handed the receiver to me.

'Daddy wants to talk to you.'

I felt even guiltier than usual. Somehow spending a whole night with Ross seemed a lot worse than anything I'd done previously.

'How are you?' I asked tentatively.

'Fine.' Noncommittal.

'Lizzie's doing great. You should see her. She's grown. She's so sweet. She's being a little angel. She can nearly swim. I can't believe she's five already. She . . .' I stopped when I realised that I was prattling on like she did.

There was a pause, and then James spoke. 'How are you?'

'Fine.' I could be noncommittal too.

'Any plans?'

'I'm feeling a lot better. I might come home soon.'

'OK. Come home when you're ready. See you then.'

'I'm missing you, James.'

Suddenly I realised that this was true. I couldn't tell if he heard my last words, as they had to compete with a series of loud beeps, and then the line went dead.

I wasn't sure how to take the conversation, if it could be called that. James didn't sound so excited at the prospect of our return, but then, maybe he didn't want to put pressure on me. And his voice had that hurt tone that bothered me so much. He didn't have much to say to Lizzie either, but maybe he didn't want to upset her when it was clear how happy she was in Greece with me. There were too many maybes, so I decided that since nothing could be settled until we got home, I should put it out of my mind until I was in a position to do something about it.

We went to the beach. Lizzie sat cross-legged on the sand in front of me and said, for about the fiftieth time that morning, as if she had to prove it to herself, 'I'm five. I'm five.'

She held her hands in front of her, and examined them closely, turning them over and back. Then she held them together, as if to measure them. She waved her right hand in the air. 'Look, Mummy. I think this one is bigger already.'

I looked at her with love, and found my thoughts drifting back, as many mothers do on their children's birthdays, to the day she was born. You know the kind of stuff. The kind of stuff that's really best forgotten. The kind of stuff you never share with the non-mothers amongst the women you know.

'This time five years ago, I was given an enema.'

'This time five years ago, the enema started to work and the only toilet was engaged.'

'This time five years ago, the epidural needle went into my back.'

'At this moment five years ago, I threw up on a student nurse's shoes.'

Just when I was reliving the delightful moment when my catheter was removed, Lizzie interrupted, pulling at my arm impatiently. 'Where are we going today?'

The answer jumped into my consciousness unexpectedly, as if it had been there all the time, hiding, lurking and waiting for the correct moment to pounce, catching me unawares. The words popped out without thought.

'Let's go to San Stefanos.'

The taxi dropped us near the beach. A lot had changed. It was still beautiful, but there were more buildings than I remembered and more activity. The taverna with no name was gone, replaced by a tasteful row of whitewashed cottages, but behind these, virtually unchanged, was the little olive grove.

Lizzie was quiet for once, as she held my hand. We walked up the rough, stony lane and climbed over the low, crumbling wall into the grove, dislodging a shower of dust and stones as we did so. Lizzie stopped to sit in a patch of dappled sunshine, where she began to play with some shiny white pebbles.

It was easy to find the spot, though I had never been in the grove before. One tree, the largest, grew a little

172

away from the others, as if it were more important than they, and they dare not come too close. It was here, under this tree, that I bent down, and felt the cool, powdery earth under my fingers.

I knelt in the shade of the tree, and my tears rolled onto the dusty soil. A line of ants ran for cover as the huge drops plopped all around them, darkening the soil in a random pattern of dark brown blobs and blotches. They must have thought it was the end of the world.

Chapter Seventeen

I suppose the tears were a dead giveaway. It looked like the time had come. I'd have to dust down those old memories and give them the decent airing they'd been waiting for, for all those years.

I had to go back to that fateful summer. The summer of 1986. The summer that started out so well, and ended so very badly. The summer whose memories never got sorted out. Those old memories had just rested at the edge of my brain like so much ugly, black sludge, totally useless, distorting everything else. It was time to dredge through that sludge to see what I came up with.

The beach. Grace, Jessie and I spent a lot of time on the beach that summer. In the early days, we went to the town beach. We knew there were many others, but it seemed like too much trouble to go and look for them, and anyway, we were simple Irish girls, easily pleased. We would lie on the beach, on the obligatory straw mats with green canvas trimming, often too tired and hungover to read. (Anyway, after a year in college, reading just seemed like too much hard work.) We had long, unhurried conversations on all kinds of topics.

Typical conversation:

'Thank God we didn't go to America. Imagine having to work.'

'Yeah. I think work would kill me.'

'Can you die of work, I wonder.'

'Dunno. I might die of thirst. Isn't it your turn to refill the flask, Jessie?'

'No way. I did it last. It's Claire's.'

'Nope. Not me. It's yours, Grace.'

'No way. Anyway, if you go to sleep, you'll forget about your thirst.'

'Do you think?'

'God, I'd love a beer. Whose turn is it to go for beer?'

'Not mine. I went yesterday.'

And so on. And on.

Lying there, we felt that we could change the world.

If only it weren't so hot.

And we weren't so lazy.

Putting on suncream was another job that took up much of our time. We had a blue cotton drawstring bag, 'the factor bag', filled with an assortment of oils and lotions. Applying these was a little like painting by numbers. Factor 8 for noses, factor 4 for arms and legs, and factor 20 for white Irish breasts, exposed to the sun for the first time ever.

Sometimes a young English woman sat on the sand near us. She had small twin girls of about two years old – Heather and Hazel. They were pretty little children, all blonde curls and dimples. The mum played untiringly with them, digging holes and making sand-castles. Then she'd lie them on a check rug, and rub their tummies, and sing them to sleep.

I used to smile secretly at the cute scene.

Grace and Jessie used to shudder ostentatiously.

'What a life! That poor woman's life is over.'

'She's given up her identity for those two ungrateful creatures.'

'What does she do for fun? Watch *Sesame Street*?'

'No.' Grace spoke with haughty disdain. 'I bet she goes to parent and toddler group.' She shuddered again at the very thought, and even I had to agree. Parent and toddler group sounded a bit grim.

Many years later, Maureen persuaded me to go to toddler group. She had caught me at a weak moment one morning, as I queued to pay for the newspaper.

'Claire. Good to see you. Jason and I are off to parent and toddler group. Why don't you and Lizzie come with us?'

I had no excuse ready. 'Em, I don't know, Maureen. We . . .'

'Come on. You'll enjoy it. We'd love you to come – wouldn't we, Jason?'

Jason nodded in happy agreement.

She was so kind, and I'd been particularly cutting to her the day before, so I couldn't bring myself to refuse. 'OK, thanks, Maureen. We'd love to come.'

It was only a short walk to the church hall, where the weekly meetings took place. Maureen led the way in, and pointed Lizzie and Jason to the play area, where they were immediately surrounded by a group of kiddies. She then led me to the table where the mothers (no dads, I'm afraid) were gathered. The kiddies were all clean, and nicely dressed in cute outfits with matching socks. The mothers, I'm sorry to say, were a different matter altogether. Most were dressed in shapeless tracksuits, with the odd pair of Lycra leggings or blue jeans thrown in for variety. Several looked as if they hadn't combed their hair in days, and one lady had a large porridge stain down her front. The only jewellery in evidence was a collection of well-worn wedding rings, adorning reddish, washing-up-damaged hands.

Maureen introduced me to everyone, and someone passed me a cup of tea and a chocolate biscuit. Conversation around the table was animated. There was a lengthy discussion on the merits of fabric conditioner. Then ten minutes were spent on the exciting topic of oven cleaners. Next we had a nice chat about constipation. One tired-looking woman with pretty eyes and greying hair set the ball rolling.

'Poor Amy. I don't know what to do with her. She's had terrible constipation. She hasn't been in two days.'

There was a chorus of sympathetic clucking from the track-suited gathering.

Grey-track-suit said, 'Have you tried apple juice?'

Pink-track-suit offered, 'Boiled water, six times a day.'

Black-and-white-track-suit joined in, 'What about . . . Chelsea, stop kicking Danny . . . sieved prunes?'

Everyone at the table had a suggestion. Pink-track-suit turned to me. 'What do you think, Claire? Have you any ideas?'

Oh, no. I felt like a bold schoolgirl who hadn't been paying attention. What could I possibly say? Had someone mentioned brown rice? I could feel my cheeks redden as I muttered, 'How about exercise? Is she getting enough exercise?'

The woman with the pretty eyes looked at Amy in her arms. The child was about six months old. The mother smiled and said gently, 'They don't get much exercise at this stage, do they?'

I blushed even more. I felt incredibly stupid. Maureen gave me a rueful grin, and the conversation meandered on through topics ranging from the mildly boring to the mind-numbingly boring. It was a cold day, but the room was lovely and warm. The children played happily, and the whole scene was cosy and welcoming. All the mothers were kind to me, making an effort to include me in their conversations. There were moments of warmth and closeness, as women with similar small everyday problems found kindred spirits and relaxed for a while away from the endless ironing and sweeping and vacuuming. The women in the room managed to look worn-down and spirited at the same time. They dealt easily and calmly with their small daily crises. They were cheerfully getting on with the lives they had chosen or slipped into accidentally.

I hated every moment. I thought I'd never get out into the cold air. The women's kindness threatened me. I feared their benign friendliness more than I feared being alone. I couldn't lighten up and join in. If I'd made an effort, I could have found a niche in that group. I'd have found some kind souls who would have befriended me, and included me in their narrow social lives. I was too afraid though. I had to bite my tongue to keep the barbs from flying forth. The cold, aloof me wanted to mock these women and everything they stood for.

The lonely me was close to tears as I left with Maureen, lying as I promised to return the following week. Vowing to avoid these decent, content women.

In my misguided way, I decided boredom was preferable.

Grace, Jessie and I were never bored as we lay on that golden beach in May of 1986.

As the evening progressed, and the sun began to lose some of its heat, we would roll up our mats, pack up our factor bag (gathering our traps, as my dad used to say), and head for home. We took turns to shower off the sand and salt, and then we would anoint our hot bodies with after-sun soothers, splash on some anti-mosquito liquid, and dress up in our finery for the night.

179

Our taste in food was unsophisticated in the extreme, and dinner most nights was pizza with chips for Jessie and me, and moussaka with chips for Grace who always had to be different. This fine food was washed down with copious amounts of the local white wine. As we sat in a lively restaurant, looking out over the ocean, this wine tasted like the most wonderful drink in creation, and, as though we were connoisseurs, we selected the same bottle each night.

Some years later, someone brought me a bottle home from their holidays, and I saved it for months, waiting for a moment special enough to justify opening it. When the time came, and I opened it with great ceremony, it was one of life's great disappointments. Without the Greek breeze blowing my hair, and the Greek waiters attending me, and Grace and Jessie giggling beside me, I experienced it as it really was – rough and fairly unpleasant, with a nasty metallic aftertaste. Back then, though, in Greece, we couldn't get enough of it, busily lowering the Greek wine lake and raising the country's mountain of empty green bottles.

Soon we had tried out each of the discos, with each of us having a favourite. This was never a cause of strife, however, as we visited at least three each night, dancing to the same tunes all night long. My favourite was called 'The Windmill'. This was reached by climbing a few whitewashed steps up from the street, and then entering directly into a huge, dark room, which seemed to shake in time with the loud beat of the music. The darkness pleased me, giving me a little more anonymity, and a little more confidence, and I would dance away quite happily until Grace or Jessie would haul me away, keen to get going to the next spot. When we had finally exhausted all of the possibilities in terms of nightlife, and when most establishments were ready to lock up for the night, we would set off for home, often a little unsteady on our feet. There we would fall into bed, sometimes fully clothed, ready to dream the sweet dreams of innocent youth, rarely disturbing each other as we stumbled in turn to the toilet, all through the long, hot nights.

These were great days to be alive, probably the best of my life, but of course I didn't appreciate it then. We didn't sit around counting our blessings, saying, 'We are so lucky: young, healthy, vibrant. We have enough to eat, more than enough to drink, and we are on holidays in one of the most beautiful places on earth.'

No, we just got on with it, and if we thought about it at all, it would have been on the premise that this was just the beginning: that there would always be days like these.

I know now that our lives were just beginning, but, in many ways, the best was already over. We just didn't know it then.

And we were so happy, that if we had known it, we wouldn't have cared anyway.

Chapter Eighteen

We lived this soft life for about two weeks, and, inevitably, our money began to run out. Clearly the impossibly cheap wine we were downing by the litre wasn't quite cheap enough. We all muttered occasionally about getting jobs, but even looking for a job seemed like too much hard work. Sometimes I thought I was born to lie forever on a Greek beach – that I had at last found my true destiny. I wondered whether, if I simply stayed there, passing kind people would give me food and the odd bottle of rough red wine to sustain me.

One day, Jessie left Grace and me on the beach, and set off up the town, mumbling something along the lines of 'I have to do everything for you.' We didn't pay her much attention, only breaking off our conversation about the merits of white chocolate over milk to ask her to bring back a fresh bottle of water. Thus we were most surprised when she marched back in triumph a short time later. She sat down, deliberately blocking the sun from our slowly cooking bodies, fully aware that this would grab our attention.

There was a cross duet of, 'Jessie, get out of our sun.'

Jessie sat still, ignoring us. 'It's all sorted,' she said with a little satisfied smirk.

Grace jumped up in horror.

'What's sorted?' she asked, looking worriedly at the smug bearer of this news.

'Our new jobs,' replied Jessie, enjoying the effect this was having on us.

'Jobs?'

Grace looked vaguely unwell, rather as if Jessie had told her that someone had emptied the dirty toilet-paper basket onto her bed.

'Yes. Jobs.'

Jessie was beginning to sound like my secondary-school headmistress with her echoing of our words.

I was a bit worried too. 'What kind of jobs, Jessie? I'm not sure that I want a job, now that you mention it. Unless you've found someone who needs volunteers to test suncream.'

Grace continued. 'Yeah. Or maybe we could get a job as wine-tasters. We'd be good at that.'

Jessie was putting on her impatient face.

'Guys, get real. We need money. Lovely though this sand is, please don't continue to bury your heads in it. We are all almost broke. If we don't work, how are we going to survive the next few months?'

Grace lazily stretched her long limbs. 'Couldn't we write home, and ask for loans? They'd never refuse us.

183

We could say we're desperate, and we could worry about repaying them when we get back.'

I agreed. 'Anyway, we are desperate, aren't we? I can only afford three more pizzas and two bottles of wine.'

Grace gave a big yawn. 'Maybe you could go on a diet and make that one pizza and four bottles of wine.'

'Mmmm. Or maybe a very strict diet. I could skip the pizza altogether and have five bottles of wine.'

Jessie sighed, and admonished us as if we were bold children. 'You are both pathetic. Wait until I tell you.'

Grace lay back on her beach mat, arranged her hair in a golden fan around her head, wiggled her dainty hips until she was comfortable, and drawled lazily. 'OK, then. We're all ears.'

'I met this Greek guy. A nice friendly fellow. He needs some help in his taverna for the summer.'

I interrupted her. 'No way, Jessie. No way. I'm not slaving in a taverna all summer. I've got a suntan that needs daily attention.'

Jessie gave me an impatient look, and I thought again of my school headmistress. She continued. 'It's only a small place. We just work for an hour in the late afternoon, helping to set up the restaurant, and then one of us stays on to serve, and the other two go out on the town and get pissed. And on Sundays, the taverna is closed, and none of has to work. It's perfect.'

Even Grace had trouble finding fault with this plan. 'What's the pay like?'

Jessie waved her hand airily. 'It's not exactly a fortune, but we get a place to stay, and all our food. He'll even give us wine to set us up for our nights out. This way we can stay here until it's time to go back to college, and we won't even have to work hard.'

I looked at Grace, and she slowly nodded her agreement. 'If we must work, I suppose that's as good as it gets. Can you find the guy and tell him we accept?'

Jessie shrugged. 'That's OK. I've already accepted for you. We start tomorrow. Now who's got the factor 4?'

Next day, we packed our belongings (this took about five minutes), and set off for San Stefanos, a small village about a mile and a half from the main town. When we arrived, we had no trouble finding our new home. It was a small building, with only a faded wooden sign, swinging on a rusty chain, to indicate that it might be a taverna. (We spent a good part of that summer there, and despite constant pointing to the sign, and wringing of hands by the owner, he never got around to painting it, and we never knew what the name of the taverna was.)

We knocked, and the owner came out to greet us. He fitted the stereotype of a chef quite well – round and jolly – and he spoke with lots of waving hands and dramatic facial expressions. Our interview consisted of a shake of the hand, and a quick 'You will work hard, no?' When we nodded, he beamed and gave us each a big hug that threatened to crush ribs, arms and assorted internal organs. Then he effortlessly slung all three of our rucksacks over his shoulder, and led the way around the side of the building, to our quarters. To us it was luxurious – a large room, with a wooden floor, a bed each, and, wonder of wonders, just off it was another small room with our own bath, shower and toilet.

The shower was in almost constant use over the next few months. In the mornings, we took turns to dive in, using the tepid water in a vain effort to shake off the fuzzy feeling which was the result of too much drinking. In the evenings, we all showered again, rinsing off the day's sand and sweat, ready for yet another night's overindulgence. The bath was used only once. I used it. Much later that summer. When everything had gone so horribly wrong.

We settled in quickly. The work was not demanding, and Georgios, the owner, was not a hard taskmaster. We started work at about five each evening. My job was making the Greek salad, which suited my level of cookery skills. I chopped up huge, juicy red tomatoes, and mixed them with cucumber and delicious crumbly Feta cheese. Georgios, doubting my ability, took over from there, adding pepper and oils until he was satisfied with the taste. Grace and Jessie also got menial peeling and chopping jobs, and then we all helped to set up the tables outside, clipping down the tablecloths, and laying out the cutlery. Whoever stayed on to serve always had an easy night, for the restaurant was small, and we were never rushed off our feet. (In fact, it was probably just as well, for the sake of our health, that each of us had one night in three without drinking and carousing until the early hours.) The fact that we couldn't speak a word of Greek was never a problem, as the dinner guests were never Greek anyway. Though Georgios had only limited English, he never had any problem making us understand him, using ever more flamboyant gestures and mimes to get his simple messages across.

As I was nineteen, and unattached, romance was always near the top of the agenda for me. I had spent the previous two years in college, always with a 'fancy' for some boy or other. These were usually boys I hardly knew – boys I bumped into at lectures or in the restaurant. My feelings were rarely reciprocated, but I was slow to accept this sad fact. I would do careful strategic planning, checking the times of the beloved's lectures so I could be 'just passing' when he came out, or casually turning up when I knew he would be at lunch. When I finally accepted that he wasn't just shy, or slow on the uptake, I would retire, hurt and sorry for myself. I would stay home for a few days, writing soppy, gushy poems to my lost love, and then I'd emerge, declaring myself free of such foolishness.

Inevitably, someone else would smile, or just be kind to me, and again I would read too much into this, and off I would go again, more precious months of my life wasted on someone who barely knew I existed. Of course, I was asked out occasionally, but never by anyone who reached the ideal of my perfect man, and, in my youthful idealism, I wasn't ready to accept anything less than perfection.

Grace and Jessie were also, for various reasons, unattached, so whichever two of us were off duty on a night were generally on the prowl, manhunting. It was the kind of place where it was easy to pick up a man. Grace practically had to beat them off, and even Jessie and I did well, especially on the nights when our beautiful friend was safe at work, serving mediocre food and wine to undiscriminating tourists.

We always went into the main town, where we spent the time drinking and dancing and giggling. Most nights, we would both have an offer of company on the way home, which we usually accepted, as it was nice to have a strong shoulder to lean on, as we trudged up the slight hill out of the town. Those were innocent days, not like now. Most men were happy to go as far as they were allowed, but they rarely took offence when we drew back.

All three of us were virgins, back in those innocent days when virginity didn't imply religious fundamentalism or complete social and emotional dysfunction. The only permitted activities were hugging and French-kissing, with occasionally a less-than-chaste grope, if we'd had enough to drink, or if the groping hand belonged to someone attractive enough.

One night, when I refused the offer of a walk home by a pompous young Greek, he looked pained. 'It's

188

OK,' he said. 'I know you Irish. You Catholic so no fucky, fucky. I understand. Is cool.'

This incident entertained us girls for weeks, as we admonished each other at the start of each evening: 'No fucky, fucky.' Then we would fall around with laughter, as if it was the first time we had ever heard it.

Innocent days indeed.

Jessie was studying English in college, and she loved to quote *Paradise Lost* to us, as we lay on the beach. One day, after a particularly long and obscure passage, Grace had had enough.

'For God's sake, Jessie! Give us a break from that Milton fella. Don't you know any poems that were written this century?'

'But Milton's great, Grace. Listen to the words. "Groves whose rich Trees wept odorous Gumms and Balme." Isn't that good?'

Grace shrugged. 'I suppose. But why always *Paradise Lost*?'

Jessie lost her lofty half-smile and looked cross. 'Because I bloody learned lines and lines and lines of it. I spent hours in the library studying it when I could have been lying in the quad, or drinking cold tea in the Kampus Kitchen.'

Grace wasn't impressed. 'So what? We all had to study, you know.'

Jessie looked even crosser. 'Yeah, but after all that, it didn't even come up in the exams. All that bloody work, and it didn't come up.'

I tried to soothe her. 'Look on the bright side, Jessie. Maybe it'll come up next year.'

She smiled. 'Yeah, maybe it will. I'd better keep on quoting it, so I won't forget. "Of Man's First Disobedience, and the Fruit . . ."'

Grace shook her head and pointedly moved her beach mat a few feet further away from our poetic friend.

Jessie must have been a diligent student because she managed long, long quotations, none of which I can remember now. What I do remember is that a lot of them were about pride and how this caused man's great downfall.

I should have listened more closely, as we lay for long, happy hours on that warm, golden sand, instead of dreaming about Greek waiters and soft music and sweet cocktails. I should have paid attention to Jessie's endless recitations of Milton's wise words, because, in the end, pride was the cause of my downfall too.

OK, so I'm getting ahead of myself. I can't compete with Milton's version of downfall. My downfall was a lot humbler. I didn't bring the entire human race crashing down with me. I went down all on my own.

And no one even noticed.

Chapter Nineteen

My Greek god came sailing in from the sea.

Well, actually he was American, and he was no god, that was for sure. But that didn't matter to me then. I just liked to romanticise.

He arrived one afternoon, not too long after our arrival in San Stefanos, as Grace, Jessie and I lay in our usual spot on the local beach. Jessie had spent the previous few evenings in the company of a hunky German, and now that he had left for the fatherland, she was missing him.

'I didn't want to spend the rest of my life with him,' she wailed. 'But another few days would have been nice. He had a sexy tongue.'

I was interested enough to look up from my book. 'Aren't all tongues sexy?'

Grace joined in. 'Yeah. What makes one tongue more sexy than another? Was his longer or wetter than usual?'

I giggled. 'Does colour matter?'

Jessie smiled a slow smile. 'No, girls. You wouldn't understand. It's more what he did with it that made the difference.'

The three of us sniggered, as we each pictured possible scenarios. Jessie declined to elaborate on this last comment, so we paid her no more attention, and we all lapsed into musing about our recent conquests. I was thinking about a nice, quiet Greek student called Dimitris, who I had met a few days before. We had met at a disco and danced together for hours. The next day, he showed up on the beach at San Stefanos, sauntering along the sand, and waving happily when he saw me. He spent the afternoon with me and the girls, lying on a brightly striped towel, and being utterly charming and chivalrous. His presence made us too embarrassed to sunbathe topless, but we all generously allowed him to rub suncream on our backs. Later, he and I swam together, and walked hand in hand along the beach. We sat down in the dappled shade of a small dead tree. I felt like a girl in a Bounty ad. Then he took my towel and gently and carefully dried my face, as I gazed in besotted wonder at his deep, almost black eyes. He slicked back his longish shiny hair and gave a slow smile.

I thought for a moment of the pasty-faced intellectual type I'd fancied in Cork before I left. The guy who looked like he hadn't seen a ray of sunshine in months. (But it was Cork, so he probably hadn't.) This guy, Damien, wore his college scarf every day, carefully winding the thick red, black and white woolly garment around his thin neck, even in May. He was once heard quoting Camus in the college bar. Damien wore his thick glasses like a badge of honour, and his favourite record was by an obscure Indian psychic, chanting to the beat of a gong. I wondered how I had lain awake every night for three weeks dreaming of being kissed by that guy.

Then Dimitris took my head in his hands and kissed me ever so gently on the lips. All thoughts of Cork and pasty-faced intellectuals slipped from my mind.

The girls and I were always a bit careful about dalliances with the locals, because we knew they wouldn't be on the next ferry off the island, and none of us wanted anything more than a brief fling, and a bit of a laugh. In Dimitris's case, however, I was prepared to make an exception to our rules. I didn't get the chance though, as despite flowery promises that he would return to the beach the next day, he never showed up. Maybe he had rules of his own, and didn't want anything to do with a girl who was likely to be around for more than a few days. I suppose even insincere Greek charmers have standards to keep.

My musing was interrupted as I gradually became aware that Jessie was sitting up, looking out to sea with a concentration unusual for those laid-back days. A very flash cruiser was pulling into the bay, and mooring just offshore. Moments later, a group of eleven Americans had disembarked, and arranged themselves decoratively on the sand not too far from us. We spent the rest of the afternoon, rather rudely, staring at them, and listening to their conversation. They were all tanned and good-looking, and everything about them seemed to scream 'Money', in a loud but ever-so-tasteful fashion. They wore well-cut, well-pressed shorts and t-shirts, and deck shoes, all of which made us feel rather scruffy in our faded cut-off jeans, skimpy t-shirts, and worn out espadrilles. While we liberated our sandwiches from their greasy paper wrappings, and drank water from our ever-present flask, the Americans assembled a barbecue, grilled some fish, and drank wine from real glasses, which they unpacked from sturdy wicker baskets.

Their conversation, though we knew the meaning of all the words, was completely foreign to us. There was talk of skiing trips, summer-houses in Martha's Vineyard, shopping excursions to Bloomingdale's and Sachs. We knew of these things only from television, from years of watching shows like *Dallas* and *Dynasty*, and here were these people talking as if the glamour and wealth these programmes portrayed were just what they expected from their lives, as their due. We looked on in awe, no less impressed than if a helicopter had just landed on the beach, delivering Bobby, Pamela, John Ross and Miss Ellie, in all their flashy glory, right at our feet.

Since we were staring and eavesdropping for so long, we quickly discovered the dynamics of the group. They were all in their mid-to-late twenties, and they seemed to be five couples, with one unattached male. Once we realised this, we all devoted most of our attention (no point in wasting it on men who already had pretty, well-dressed girlfriends with tinkly laughs), to this one – the single one, the one they called Kevin.

Like the others, he was tanned and handsome, with bleached blonde hair. He was stocky in build, but strong and athletic looking. To look at him was to see generations of good genes (carefully engineered by bossy matriarchs, no doubt), helped along by years of healthy food and active, outdoor life. His easy confidence was no doubt bolstered by long seasons of being shrieked at by leggy Lycra-clad cheerleaders. He probably had a youthful-looking, golden-haired mom who ruffled his shiny hair and said, 'I love you, honey,' every time he went out the door of their tasteful colonial-style home.

Kevin was quieter than the others, but when he spoke, they all seemed to pay attention. He sat a little away from the group, closer to us, and read most of the time, only occasionally joining in the conversation.

The girls and I were unusually quiet. We stopped talking about tongues and kisses and foreplay. (Though is it right to call it foreplay when all that follows it is a prissy, 'That's far enough – I'm a Catholic'?) We just sat there, watching, trying to keep our mouths from hanging open. Whenever it became too hot, instead of lots of splashing and screaming which were our usual antics, we demurely sauntered to the water, swam a few metres, and tried to look elegant as we returned to our places, edging our beach mats a little closer to Kevin each time.

Eventually, when it was nearly time for us to pack up and start work, the American group began to move. They were going to the main town to eat and check out the night clubs (discos to us, but night clubs to these sophisticated newcomers). They stood up, and each one managed to look neat and fresh, as if they had just changed and showered, as opposed to hot and grimy as I knew we looked. One stunningly attractive girl gingerly brushed a few grains of sand from her perfect golden arm. Another looked like a ballerina as she gracefully folded a leather-trimmed rug. I looked in dismay at my beach mat, which was fading unevenly, and ostentatiously fraying at three corners.

To our delight, Kevin decided not to go with the others.

'You all go ahead,' he called. 'I'll just chill out here and I'll catch you all later.'

The others set off, and the beach was deserted in the early-evening sun, except for Kevin, Jessie, Grace and me. Our repeated shuffling had brought it about that now only a few small feet of sand came between us. If Kevin had bothered to look, he'd have seen a wide beach-mat-shaped trail illustrating our furtive progress across the beach.

Predictably, Jessie made the first move. 'Is that book good? I was thinking of reading it when I've finished the one I'm on.'

It wasn't a very original approach, but it did fine, as an ice-breaker. Kevin looked up, as if he had just realised that we were there, though how he could have missed our naked, adoring stares was hard to imagine. He stood up, and crossed the few feet of sand that separated us.

'May I sit down?'

We all nearly killed ourselves, scuffling quietly, trying to make space for him on our beach mats, but he didn't appear to notice this as he just squatted on the sand in front of us, and beamed at the three of us. I hadn't seen such teeth since Donny Osmond hung up his microphone, and as I smiled weakly back, I mentally promised myself, yet again, that I would get my overlapping front teeth straightened as soon as I got home. Kevin seemed quite unaware of the reaction he was causing. Maybe he thought that we were slightly dim and flustered all the time. Or maybe it was just that he had this effect on everyone he met, and noticed nothing strange about us.

'I'm glad they're gone. Three weeks on that boat is beginning to seem like a very long time. I could do with some new company, some new topics of conversation.'

I thought my brain would explode with the effort to find something smart to reply to this, but the best I could manage was, 'What do you like to talk about?'

This was a bit feeble, even for me, but Kevin didn't appear to notice. He looked at me as if it was the smartest question he had ever been asked. 'Where should I start?'

I glowed inside, and, as I was prone to blushes, I suspect that my cheeks glowed also. Inside my espadrilles, my toes were probably even suffused with a nice deep shade of pink.

Our conversation juddered on, though if conversation is defined as an exchange of ideas, this didn't qualify. It was more a vicious vying, as each of us three girls tried our hardest to be the wittiest and smartest. Kevin just lapped this up, smiling benignly like an indulgent father with a group of competitive toddlers.

After a while, I was beginning to think he was a bit conceited, and not even all that good-looking, once you ignored the perfect teeth and the golden tan. I was looking forward to mocking him later, laughing with the girls over his posh accent and his exquisite fingernails.

Finally, he made a move that saved our jobs. (For, as long as he was there, none of us was going to be the first to make a move towards work.) He waited for a rare gap in our babbling and said, 'I need to meet the others, just to tell them I'm not going to join them for dinner. Then maybe you would care to join me for a drink and something to eat?'

I automatically looked towards Grace, who was looking at me in a quizzical, rather cross manner. Jessie caught my eye and shrugged. There was no mistaking it though. Kevin was looking straight at me in a way that made it clear that he didn't mean the three of us. He meant just me, on my own – me and him, together for the evening. This time I think my mouth really did hang open in surprise. It wasn't just that he was older than us, and so sophisticated and worldly wise. It wasn't just that he was handsome in a rich, privileged way that was totally new to us. It wasn't even the fact that I felt like I was talking to a film star rather than a real, human person like myself.

Of course, I only realised this later, but I now know that I fell for Kevin because, on that fateful, sunny day, he sat on a beach with the stunning Grace, with the vivacious, confident and funny Jessie, and with me, and he picked me.

I foolishly thought that he could see something special in me, something that no one else had ever been able to discern. I was proud that at last someone had made the effort to see past my quiet, shy exterior to the wonderful person my mother always told me lurked underneath.

And that, I'm afraid, is the sad and sordid truth – I fell for Kevin, and met my downfall, because he chose me above the friends I was always half in awe of.

Kevin made arrangements to come back and pick me up later, and then Grace, Jessie and I raced back to the taverna where Georgios brushed off our laughing and breathless apologies.

'You work now. Work fast,' he said, shrugging to let us know that he wasn't cross, just mystified at our strange behaviour.

Jessie and Grace were gracious in defeat. They must have been surprised that I had somehow bagged the most eligible male we had yet seen on the island, as they had never seen me as a threat, but they tried not to show it. Jessie made the ultimate sacrifice. It was my turn to work late that night, but she insisted on doing it for me.

'I don't feel like going out tonight,' was her unlikely excuse.

They raced around, doing most of my work, while I sat and watched them, wondering if I had imagined the previous few hours.

When the restaurant was ready, we retired to our room to plan my clothes for the evening. Jessie dramatically emptied the contents of our wardrobe onto her bed. It was a sorry sight – a not very large collection of faded t-shirts, jeans and shorts, and one pink dress, which belonged to Jessie, and which she had only brought to please her mother. It was agreed that in the absence of any real alternative, I should wear the dress, even though it was much too big for me. Draped over my shoulders, *à la* Grace Kelly, I should wear Grace's white lacy cardigan. They wanted me to wear Grace's best shoes – gold strappy sandals, which were totally unsuitable for a beach holiday – but they were much too small for me, and I didn't want to look like one of the ugly sisters, masquerading as Cinderella. Reluctantly they agreed that I would have to wear my only shoes – my faded blue espadrilles – even though they didn't quite fit in with the sophisticated image I was trying to project. Then Grace tied up my hair, scraping it all back from my face, and tying it with a scrap of blue velvet ribbon, the only piece we could find. We felt that I should be wearing make-up, but as none of us possessed any, this wasn't an option, so I just pinched my cheeks and bit my lip, as I had read in some trashy novel that this would give me some healthy-looking touches of colour.

The girls stood back and surveyed their handiwork. Even kind Jessie couldn't force an admiring expression onto her face.

'You look really different, Claire. Doesn't she, Grace? Isn't she completely different?'

Grace only managed, 'Yeah you look very, em . . . I'll get the camera and record this moment for posterity.'

I was ready much too early so I waited, sitting on the low whitewashed wall at the edge of the taverna, fiddling with the buttons of Grace's cardigan, half-afraid that Kevin wouldn't show up.

Also, though I didn't like to admit it to myself, I was half-hoping that he wouldn't appear. What I really wanted, deep down, was for him not to come, and for us girls to have a good laugh about it. Part of me wanted to run inside and hide in our bedroom. I wanted the girls to tell Kevin that I was violently ill, and unable to join him for dinner. But I didn't want to let the girls down, after all of their efforts to make me look well. And besides, how could I pass up on this golden opportunity – this one time when I got the guy they both wanted?

So I sat there, biting my lip and giving my cheeks an occasional pinch. Wishing I was somewhere else.

Chapter Twenty

My mum always used to say that if something seemed too good to be true, then it probably was.

Kevin arrived, as he had promised, at eight o'clock. He was wearing white trousers, with a dark polo-necked top under a white cotton cardigan, and freshly polished deck shoes. If one of my college friends had shown up on campus dressed like this, he would have been laughed out of it without ceremony, and marked forever more as a social pariah. Somehow though, on Kevin, these clothes looked right. His hair was slightly damp after being washed, and he was freshly shaven, with a barely perceptive scent of expensive after-shave. (By that, I mean he wasn't wearing either of the two I could recognise – Old Spice which my dad and all of my uncles wore, or Brut which everyone else I knew, including the girls, wore.)

'You look great,' he said as he kissed me on the cheek, and I blushed with pleasure, even though I was already feeling a bit cheap and tacky next to his easy, moneyed elegance.

I tried to be smart. 'Well, you know how it is. My Chanel suit is at the cleaners, and a cat ate my Dior dress.'

Kevin looked a bit puzzled for a moment. A deep furrow appeared on his forehead, just above his eyes. Then it dawned on him. 'You're kidding, right?'

I nodded. I was beginning to dread the evening even more.

Jessie and Grace had 'accidentally' come out just as he arrived, and they overheard this exchange. Jessie gave me a sympathetic look that made me even more worried than I had been before. Grace ran for her camera again, and took the photo of me with my debonair date, and then we set off to walk the short distance into town.

Kevin spoke first. 'I want to make it clear. This night is my treat – you will not be allowed to pay for anything.'

'No, Kevin, that's not really fair. Why don't we go Dutch?'

Kevin put on his puzzled expression again. 'Dutch?'

I began one of my small mental panics. Maybe 'going Dutch' meant something very strange to Americans. Had I just promised him a night to rival page twenty-seven of the Karma Sutra? Or had I unwittingly questioned his mother's honour?

'I mean, why don't we split the bill?'

'Oh, I get it. No, I insist. I'm paying.'

I breathed a deep sigh of relief, and didn't protest any more. Georgios hadn't got around to paying us yet, so I had very little money left. I had borrowed from both of my friends to fund this evening. If I had to pay for anything more than pizza and chips, I'd be in debt to Grace and Jessie for months.

Kevin walked a bit too quickly for me, and I almost had to run to keep up – not easy in espadrilles. After a while, I perfected a sort of running shuffle, which can't have looked terribly elegant. I was too shy to ask him to slow down, and consoled myself by thinking that at least I'd have a good appetite for the food he was going to buy me.

As we walked, Kevin did the talking, mostly about himself. He told me about his sporting activities – football, swimming and racquetball. He told me about all the trophies he had won that season. He ran me through the last twenty minutes of the last football match of the season. 'And then I picked up the ball, and everyone was cheering, and . . .'

I smiled. I knew about this stuff. My dad always watched *Match of the Day*. I could even hum the theme tune.

'That was a foul, wasn't it?'

'Excuse me?'

I repeated. 'That was a foul. Sure you can't pick up the ball.'

'Of course you can. Anyway, where was I? Oh yes, I picked up the ball, the crowd went crazy, and . . .'

'Oh, I get it now. You were the goalie.'

The puzzled expression got yet another outing. I wondered did he practise it in front of the mirror. This time the look was overlaid with a cross, impatient glance. I wasn't quite sure what I'd said wrong, but whatever it was, clearly Kevin wasn't impressed. I didn't interrupt again, and didn't listen that closely either, as I found the subject dreadfully boring. What I did glean was that Kevin had been the hero of the day, and that he was the centre of some very strange laddish rituals in the dressing-room later. He headlined the sports section of the local newspaper the following morning, but apparently there was no mention of the dressing-room escapades. Top secret, apparently. Or at least until now. Once Jessie heard, half Europe would be in the know within hours.

When Kevin had eventually exhausted his sports stories, he began to talk about his job. He had some important-sounding position that I had never heard of, in a merchant bank. He tried to explain the significance of what he did, but I was afraid to get too involved. I was afraid that he'd discover that I didn't even understand the difference between a merchant bank, and the bank on the South Mall where I lodged my student grant, so I did my best to steer the conversation away from this topic. I scrambled wildly for something that might impress him, though I was no longer quite sure why I felt the need to do so.

We quickly exhausted the topics of films (his all-time favourite was *First Blood, Part 2*), music (he liked John Cougar Mellencamp), television (he lamented the demise of *The Greatest American Hero*) and books (he thought, *Jonathan Livingston Seagull* was the 'neatest book ever'). Luckily we'd reached the town by then or we'd have been reduced to talking about the weather, which would have been very sad, since this was supposed to be such a hot date.

Kevin brought me to a restaurant I had never seen before. It was a little out of the central part of town, up a small lane lined with beautiful flowering trees and shrubs. It looked like a very fancy private house, and there was no sign or menu outside to indicate otherwise.

'My brother came here last year,' he explained. 'It's a well-kept secret. They don't want too many people coming and spoiling the exclusive atmosphere.'

I nodded agreement. 'Oh, yes. Very sensible of them.'

Oh dear. Surely my scruffy, studenty presence would spoil the exclusive atmosphere. I began to worry that a beefy bouncer would appear and refuse to admit me. I pinched my cheeks again, and tried to tidy the tendrils of hair that had escaped from the not-very-strict confines of the blue velvet ribbon.

Kevin rang a bell set into the wall. A narrow gate opened, and we were admitted. Clearly Kevin's suave appearance was enough to neutralise mine. A fawning waiter bowed as he guided us through a narrow leafy passageway. I'd never been fawned over before, and wasn't quite sure that I liked it. We were led to a small terraced area, set out with only five or six tables. Tiny white lanterns lit up the surrounding trees, and instead of the loud bazouki music I was used to, the only sound was the gentle tinkling of tiny bells, whenever the soft breeze shook the branches. The tablecloths were of crisp white linen, and the tables were beautifully set, with crystal and silver, and a small vase of flowers in the centre of each. Part of me wished I'd brought Grace's camera, so I could have some visual aids for later when I was boasting to the girls. The sensible part of me decided that the production of a camera in these surroundings would probably earn me my walking papers.

Instead of the cheerful, friendly waiters I was used to, we were served by distant formal men, wearing white shirts, starched as stiffly as the tablecloths. None of them even tried to chat me up. The menus they handed us were bound in wine-coloured leather, and I could see no prices. Neither could I see any of my favourite, familiar dishes. There was no sign of pizza, Greek salad or kebabs. I didn't know where to start, and, aware of the haughty, unfriendly waiter hovering nearby, I whispered desperately (this was the kind of place where whispering seemed essential), 'I can't decide. You choose for me.'

Kevin quickly took control, speaking with authority to the waiters. He ordered a large selection of dishes, none of which I had ever heard of before, then he closed the menus, and called the wine waiter with an authoritative click of his fingers. I thought they only did that in the movies, and was surprised when the wine waiter materialised at Kevin's elbow, like a genie summoned from a bottle. I half-expected to see a puff of smoke.

I agreed happily when Kevin suggested a cocktail before dinner, but was sorely disappointed. The cocktails I knew were large, sweet, brightly coloured, and always, but always, adorned with a paper umbrella. Usually they had a crust of sugar around the edge of the glass, making the contents seem even sweeter. The ones that were put in front of us here were of a different breed altogether. Mine was dry and bitter, with only an olive in the bottom of the glass as decoration. I drank it down speedily, despite its unpleasant taste, choking violently as the olive tipped out of the glass and down my throat. Kevin kindly beat me on the back until the olive reappeared amidst a spray of alcohol and spittle. I gave a few more coughs, and then giggled nervously. Kevin did not appear to be amused.

Whatever the vile concoction was, it was clearly high in alcohol, and within minutes I could feel it going to my head.

So there I sat – scruffy, shy, intimidated, nervous, and now well on the way to being drunk too. The writing was on the wall. It had to end in tears.

I still don't know why Kevin bothered with me. He couldn't have found it difficult to get girls to go out with him – girls who would fit in a bit better with his fancy ways. Grace, for instance. She would have sat there, saying little, looking haughty and beautiful, and she would have fitted in fine. Jessie would have confidently bluffed her way through the evening, never letting on that she was used to anything less. I couldn't carry it off though. I was so hopelessly out of place in this fancy establishment, and my feeble attempts at scintillating conversation must have been really boring to the worldly-wise Kevin. My jokes were lost on him, never producing anything except his puzzled expression. Even worse, any time I laughed at something he said, his amazed expression indicated that as far as he was concerned, what he had said wasn't meant to be funny at all.

I began to wonder if he had invited me out of boredom. Or even worse, was it just so he and his posh friends could have a laugh about the sad, silly Irish child-bumpkin who had jumped at the chance to go out with him? A few times I looked over my shoulder, half-afraid that I'd see his friends peering over a wall, tossing their sleek heads and trying not to laugh out loud at my discomfort. I began to feel sick with embarrassment and hurt pride. All I wished for was to be back with my friends, where I could be comfortable and at ease, and could stop all this foolish pretence. I wished a reverse fairy godmother would appear and magic me away from the fancy restaurant, back to the humble taverna to scoff pizza and swill back cheap red wine. This Cinderella should never have gone to the ball.

A year later, I was watching a late-night movie on television, and a similar scenario arose. Two smart, cool guys were surveying a group of girls, trying to decide which they should go for. One guy zoomed in on the prettiest girl, but the other guy whispered quietly as he smiled a sensual smile at the plainest girl in the group.

'No. No. Don't go for the pretty girl. Go for the mousy one. She'll be more grateful.' I felt like crying.

I'm sure that the meal must have been very expensive, but I didn't like it. Very little of it was familiar to me, and maybe this type of food required practice to be enjoyed. There were strong flavours, and funny fishy things I didn't recognise. Truffles appeared a few times, but I only recognised them because, at each reappearance, Kevin gushed, 'Truffles. Don't you just love truffles?' Repeatedly failing to notice my spectacular lack of enthusiasm.

I ate very little, and spent most of the time pushing the food around my plate, hoping no one would notice. At the back of my mind lurked a dreadful fear that the chef would suddenly appear, screaming and waving knives, demanding to know why I didn't like his food. Unfortunately, though the wine was also unfamiliar, I suffered no such pangs about consuming it. I suppose it was nerves, but whatever the reason, I know I drank considerable quantities of it, smiling meekly at the snooty waiter who appeared regularly to top up my glass.

After I had emptied the first few glasses, everything seemed to happen faster, as the alcohol made an

efficient buffer between me and my sense of being o
of my depth. Soon the meal was over, and I found
myself back outside in the lane, feeling queasy and
wobbly.

I looked up at the sky and gasped in wonder.

'Wow, look. Look at all those shooting stars. It's
incredible. They're all over the sky.'

Kevin looked up. 'I don't see any.'

I leaned against a convenient wall and the stars were
still again. I muttered something pathetic about optical
illusions.

'How about a night club?' asked Kevin brightly,
seemingly unaware of how tipsy I was.

'No,' I replied, shortly. 'I think I just want to
go home.'

'That's just fine by me. Home it is then.'

He gallantly put his arm around me, giving me some
welcome extra support, and we set off for the walk
home.

The walk did nothing to clear my head, though I
began to relax a little, relieved to be free from the stiff
atmosphere of the restaurant. I waffled on about
I know not what, and Kevin humoured me, answering back no matter how foolish I was being, as if he
were dealing with a prattling child. It was one of those
strange occasions, often associated with alcohol,
when a road seems to stretch out far ahead, but then,
a moment later, you find you have reached your
journey's end.

We stood together near the lane leading to the beach at San Stefanos. I was leaning on Kevin for support, and now that I didn't feel I had to pretend any more, I was reluctant to leave him. I was enjoying the warmth of his shoulder next to mine, enjoying being in Greece, enjoying the balmy evening. And a quick snog would have suited me fine. The girls and I were keeping count, and Grace was getting too far ahead. And surely a harmless fling with a good catch like Kevin would negate at least two of her greasy student conquests.

I must be honest too and admit that I was embarrassed to return to my friends too early – afraid to admit to them that I couldn't carry off the sophisticated-lady act.

That old devil called pride again. Too proud to admit that I was a failure. Too proud to go home and laugh at myself.

'Let's have a walk on the beach,' suggested Kevin.

I didn't reply, so he led me on to the sand anyway. The beach was, of course, deserted, and he led me to the farthest edge, to where there were some small, scrubby trees. He walked purposefully, and later I began to wonder if he'd planned this all along. Had he picked this spot that afternoon, while Grace, Jessie and I did our adoration act?

He sat down, and pulled me down onto the sand beside him. I lay with my head in his lap and closed my eyes. He gently untied the blue velvet ribbon, and stroked my hair. It was so peaceful there, I was full of drink, and I very quickly dozed off. When I was a teenager, I could fall into a deep sleep quickly and I was very likely well into my first dream, and snoring peacefully, when I half-awoke to realise that Kevin had undone all of the buttons on the front of my dress. I sat up, but was hit by a wave of dizziness, as the beach and the beautiful starry sky began to spin out of control.

'It's cool. It's cool,' he murmured as he eased me down onto my back again.

The drink had done a good job of masking my inhibitions, and it did feel nice lying there in his arms, so I lay back and let him caress me. My mind wandered a bit. I was worrying that if there was tar on the beach, I might stain Jessie's dress. It occurred to me that my mum had some clever way of removing tar stains from clothes. I wondered what it was. Was it something to do with petrol? Or vinegar? I thought I could see a satellite on a slow trajectory over my head. A sharp stone pressed against my left thigh. I tried to tell Kevin about the satellite, but he didn't understand. Or else he wasn't interested. His caresses became more urgent. He didn't look sophisticated any more. His eyes were half-closed, and he seemed to be clenching his teeth. I thought vaguely about telling him to stop. The edges of my mind seemed to be filled with fog as I wondered what words to use. He pulled off my shabby, grey, Dunnes Stores panties, climbed on top of me, entered me, and was finished

213

in moments. He gave a small grunt, then he rolled over and lay on his back on the sand next to me, panting.

I rearranged my clothes, but continued to lie next to him, too shocked to get up and leave. Completely sober, now that it was too late.

I wondered if Armani made knickers. If so, had the cold, elegant man who lay on the sand next to me ever touched anything less with his beautifully shaped fingers?

When I was about fifteen, a regular topic of conversation amongst my classmates was whether we would like our first lover to be tender or passionate. This was, of course, purely speculative, as we were all young and totally inexperienced, and the little knowledge we had came from romantic novels or trashy films. We spent much time discussing this, debating the relative merits of urgent, hot passion, or more gentle caresses, perhaps with soft piano music in the background. I usually went for the tender option, picturing a gentle, oh-so-considerate lover, treating me as if I were so delicate that I might crush under his weight.

Never, in my most pessimistic moments, could I have pictured what turned out to be the truth – sleepy, drunken fumblings with a selfish, uncaring stranger.

A few minutes later, as if nothing had happened, Kevin took out his cigarettes, and offered me one. I accepted even though I hadn't smoked since I'd enjoyed a few sneaky ones behind the school bicycle shed when I was fourteen. We lay side by side, smoking in silence. Kevin blew perfect smoke rings into the warm night air. I watched them drift and grow, until they disappeared from my sight. I wished that I could float upwards with them, and vanish forever into the starry blackness.

We smoked a few cigarettes each, and then Kevin walked me the short distance to my room. He patted my cheek in a rather patronising fashion as I stood at the door. His hair didn't even appear to be tossed.

'It's been great. Really great,' he said, and he flashed me one of his perfect smiles. His teeth glowed strangely in the dark. Then he sauntered off, back towards town, whistling softly as he went.

He didn't use my name. I wondered if he even remembered it.

I lingered for a while, watching until he turned the bend and disappeared from view. Then I lingered for another while, looking at the stars twinkling at me through the velvet sky. I could hear the lapping of small ripples on the wet sand. I could hear the regular grumble of Georgios's snoring, through the open window of his bedroom. I pressed my cheek against the rough wall of the house. The slight pain was almost comforting.

Mercifully, Jessie and Grace were sound asleep, and didn't stir when I entered the room. I tiptoed into our bathroom, and vomited twice, as quietly as I could. I caught sight of my greyish, frightened face as I cleaned my teeth in an effort to freshen my mouth. I threw

Jessie's dress and Grace's cardigan into the back of the wardrobe, under our empty rucksacks. Then I pulled on my nightie and went to bed.

I lay there for hours, wide-awake now, staring at the ceiling.

And try as I might, I couldn't get the sound of Kevin's insouciant whistling out of my mind. Over and over, I heard it, in an endless, joyless loop.

All through that long night, hour after hour, I heard it, rattling ceaselessly around my sick head.

And now, almost seventeen years later, I can still picture Kevin clearly. I can still see his white cotton cardigan slung casually over his shoulder. I can see his carefully groomed hair curling gently behind his ear. I can see his soft-soled shoes, which made no sound on the rough, gravelly road. I can see him striding confidently away from me, stepping lightly in time with his whistling.

Chapter Twenty-One

I awoke next morning, feeling sick and tired. I lay on my bed trying to ignore the throbbing in my head, while Grace and Jessie battered me with questions, none of which I felt like answering.

'Did you have a good time?'

'Did he have a sexy tongue?'

'Or a sexy anything else?'

I didn't answer, as the girls laughed with abandon at Grace's wit.

'Ha,' crowed Jessie. 'She's so in love, she can't talk to us. Are you leaving on the next cruiser for Barbados?'

'Have you packed your deck shoes and your wind-cheater?'

'And a little black dress for soirées?'

'And your life-jacket?'

'And your sick bag?'

At those last words, my stomach began to heave tentatively, but the girls didn't seem to notice. They were having too much fun. They didn't mean to upset me, but this was payback time. This was my punishment for grabbing the guy they considered to be the catch of the season. In different circumstances, I'd have laughed along with them.

'No,' said Grace. 'He's flying her to his country home in the Hamptons to introduce her to Mommy and Daddy.'

'Yeah, that's it. They'd like to check out her pedigree. They wouldn't want their pure blood tainted with the blood of an Irish commoner. Can she prove that she wasn't born in a bog? Has she got her papers with her? Can she trace her family back to Brian Ború?'

Grace gave a sly smile. 'Maybe not Brian Ború, but she's had very close links with Brian O'Connell from second-year law.'

How did Grace know that I'd fancied that guy for months? I thought it was a secret. I'd have protested, but didn't have the strength. Anyway Grace was more interested in the present than in the ancient history of college romances. She changed tack slightly. 'No, that's far too boring, that old "Mommy and Daddy" scenario. I bet Claire and Kevin are eloping tomorrow, to get married on an uninhabited island.'

She gave a dreamy sigh and continued. 'The simple, but deeply meaningful service will be conducted by a Greek Orthodox priest. The deliriously happy couple will stand hand in hand in a meadow, surrounded by wild flowers, and babbling brooks. There they will declare their undying love, with wild goats bleating in the background and bluebirds of happiness flitting in the warm air around them.'

'Ha, yes. Then they can roll in the flowery meadow and consummate their marriage . . . and . . . and . . .' Jessie could hardly continue for laughing. 'They'll get covered in goat-shit, and die slow painful deaths from goat-shit poisoning.' She looked as if she'd do herself an injury she was laughing so much. She hunched over, holding her stomach with one hand, and wiping tears of laughter from her eyes with the other.

Grace ignored her and gave another exaggerated, dreamy sigh. 'And they'll live happily ever after, in a little thatched cottage, with their ten perfect, blond children.'

The girls were having such fun at my expense, they didn't notice that I wasn't responding. But what could I say? How could I tell them how horrible it had been?

The arrogance of Kevin's boring, self-important conversation.

The stiff, unfriendly restaurant.

The awful food.

And then the worst part – the beach.

How could I begin to tell them about that?

I felt so humiliated, and so stupid. What could I have been thinking of, going off with a guy like Kevin? How could I have thought that he really liked me? Why did I let myself get so drunk when I was out with a virtual stranger? How could I have let him do what he did? I could have made him stop. I could have screamed. I could have run away.

And did I?

No, I just lay there like a passive fool and let him do what he wanted.

How typical of me. My first sexual experience and was it a marvellous meeting of minds and bodies? Fat chance. It was more of my usual behaviour – just go along with what someone else wanted, too pathetic to say what I felt. Too stupid to have a mind of my own.

I was filled with a nasty mixture of self-pity and self-hatred.

The girls giggled on for another while, very pleased with their comedy double act, and then Jessie finally noticed. 'What's wrong, Claire? Why aren't you telling us? What happened?'

They were my friends, and I suppose I should have told them. They could have talked to me and helped me. Perhaps if I'd talked to them then, things would have been different. But I didn't talk. I shut them out, and they stayed out.

I don't know why I felt so ashamed. It was the eighties, hardly the dark ages. A bit of uncomplicated nookie on the beach was no big deal for a lot of people, even back then. But it was for me. The whole thing had been so casual, so heartless and so cold. I felt as if I had sold myself for a fancy meal and a few drinks.

So I didn't tell them. When they questioned me again, I just told them that Kevin was terribly boring, and that I hadn't enjoyed the night. They weren't really convinced, but I stuck to my story and, in the end, they got tired of asking.

We all lay in our beds for a while longer. Grace and Jessie chatted on about other things, soothing in their banality, until I almost began to convince myself that the previous night was nothing more than a bad dream, brought on by too much alcohol.

Then I decided to get up.

If the earth didn't move for me the night before, it certainly did now. I rolled out of bed, stood up and fell down. I remained on the floor for a few moments, enjoying the coolness of the tiles against my cheek. I was no longer drunk, but I was dreadfully, over-whelmingly hungover.

A concerned Jessie leapt to my aid. She helped me to get up, and I rolled gratefully back into bed.

I lay there for another while, waiting for the weakness to pass. Smiling weakly, I tried to make little of my condition.

As soon as Grace could see that I wasn't going to keel over and die, she started to tease me again.

'Now we know why you won't tell us about last night. You can't remember. You got drunk and you can't remember.'

I wanted to scream at her. 'I was drunk but I can remember. I only wish I could forget. I just want to forget.' But of course I didn't. I just pleaded that I had a headache, and finally they let the matter lie. After a while, they got up and dressed. Jessie came to my bed and spoke softly.

'I don't suppose you fancy any breakfast?'

I shook my head weakly, and turned towards the wall. They tiptoed from the room, and left me alone. I could hear them whispering outside, but I didn't care. I lay in bed for hours longer, unable to sleep, unable to get up and face the day. The wooden shutters were closed, but a crack allowed through a narrow stream of bright sunlight, which moved slowly across the ceiling, as the morning turned to afternoon.

Much later, Jessie came to the door and whispered, 'Quick, they're leaving.'

I knew at once who she meant. Before I could answer, she grabbed my arm, and pulled me out of bed and outside and around to the front of the taverna. From there we had a good view down to the beach, where we could see Kevin and his friends getting ready to go back aboard their boat. They weren't looking in our direction, but I shrank back into the shadows to make doubly sure that I wouldn't be seen.

They were efficient in their packing, and were quickly loaded up. I could hear trills of easy laughter, and confident American voices. I couldn't make out what they were saying. As they set off, I could see Kevin on deck, leaning casually against the guard-rails. He was looking steadfastly out to sea, never once turning back towards the island, towards me.

We watched until they were out of sight, and then, because there was nothing else to do or say, we watched the empty horizon for another little while.

I never even knew his second name.

And, for all I know, Kevin wasn't his real name anyway. Perhaps it was a silly, false name, made up on a whim, to fool the sad Irish fool he met that summer in Mykonos.

Who had vanished from his mind long before he unwrapped his first caviar sandwich, or sipped his first glass of chilled champagne, as he sailed in idle pleasure through the calm, sparkling waters of the Aegean Sea.

Much later that evening, I strolled across the beach to where the scrubby trees were. There was an indentation in the sand where I had lain the night before. I could see the deep marks where the toes of Kevin's deck shoes had dug into the sand. Our discarded cigarette butts lay together.

I felt suddenly angry. I trampled the butts until they were hidden from view. Then I kicked and scuffed at the sand until there was no more trace of where we had been.

As I stepped away, something brushed against my cheek. My blue velvet ribbon hung sadly and limply from a dry twig. Just next to a faded crisp bag. They seemed to taunt me in unison.

'*Ha, thought you could forget so easily! Dream on, girl. Dream on.*'

Chapter Twenty-Two

For the next few weeks, I tried hard to put the whole episode out of my mind. Those were the happy days before anyone knew a whole lot about AIDS. Back then we thought it was a disease only gay men caught. I was neither gay, nor a man, and since Kevin fulfilled only one of those criteria (as far as I knew), I didn't feel the need to get too worked up about it.

And everyone knew that you couldn't get pregnant the first time. Well, actually, I knew for sure that last notion was a myth. Or maybe not so much an old wives' tale as a story put about by desperate young men whose desires were being thwarted by cautious young women.

So, of course, I did worry, but I tried not to.

Jessie and Grace might have known more about these things than I did, but as I still hadn't told them what had happened, I couldn't ask them. I couldn't pretend to be asking for a friend, or casually wondering, just out of idle interest. They'd know something was up, for sure. And, somehow, I felt that talking about it would only make it more real.

They continued their mocking occasionally. Their favourite, regularly repeated jibe was, when entering a disco or bar, one of them would say casually, 'No point Claire looking for a man here. Mr Perfect from Boston wasn't good enough for her.'

Then the other would peer through the door, and exclaim in mock disappointment, 'No, just ordinary mortals in here.'

'Oh, there's a likely guy. Nope just saw his feet. Made of clay like ours. Sorry.'

'No one suitable for you, Claire. Why don't you go home and read your Bloomingdale's catalogue?'

'Or weave yourself a nice wicker picnic basket?'

They weren't nasty girls, and they weren't trying to hurt me. All the teasing was meant in fun, so I tried to ignore it. Soon Jessie fell for a Scots fireman, and took over the role of chief target for mockery.

Before long, Kevin was forgotten by everyone.

Except me.

And so life in Greece rambled on. We worked (not too hard), sunbathed, drank and partied. Gorgeous Georgios shook his head sometimes when he saw us heading out yet again for a night on the town.

'You go out all nights. Why you not have rest?' he asked one evening.

Grace looked at him in horror. 'Rest?'

Georgios shrugged his large shoulders. 'You stay home and read books. Sleep.'

Jessie and I spoke together.

'Read books?'

'Sleep?'

Grace dismissed the thought with an elegant wave of her arm. 'The very idea!'

Georgios laughed, shaking his head again. He always treated us kindly, and he appeared to be fond of us, sometimes addressing us as, 'my children', but I expect he could never have stood back and watched children of his own, drinking and gallivanting each night as we did.

We knew that he had no wife or children. He lived alone, over the restaurant, but when he wasn't sleeping or working, he was rarely there. Sometimes we saw him, sitting in the shade outside a quiet taverna, playing cards with a group of old men, but otherwise, we had no idea of how he spent his time. He was very tolerant, as I have to be honest and admit that we were not great workers. We often showed up late in the afternoons, when we were meant to be getting the restaurant ready for the evening. We made silly mistakes when he gave us the simplest of jobs to do in the kitchen, and often when setting up tables, we forgot crucial items like knives or salt. However, we were always friendly to the customers, and he liked to see that, so he forgave us almost everything else – living in hope, I suppose, that soon we would have to improve.

A vain hope, as it happened.

The weeks went by, and gradually the gnawing worry at the back of my mind became more persistent. All the sun and retsina in the world couldn't stop the march of time and reality. My periods were always regular, and I knew that I was a few days late. I still tried not to worry too much, telling myself that worry had only upset my cycle. This thought kept me going for another few days, and then I began to worry again.

I tried telling myself that the change of air, and different food had finally kicked in and affected my hormones, but this excuse was too feeble even for me, and after entertaining it for another few days, I had to admit to myself the awful, unbelievable truth – I must be pregnant.

The horror of this was so great, that I couldn't think straight. How could I possibly go home and tell my family? How could I go back to college and finish my degree? How could I care for a baby when I couldn't even look after myself?

Making a mess of my own life took all my time and energy. How would I manage if I had a baby to think about too?

I sank deeper and deeper into myself, and felt only half-there whenever I went out with Jessie and Grace. Soon they could no longer ignore my strange behaviour. They had obviously discussed it between themselves, and one day they very pointedly cornered me in our room, where we had retired for a respite from the fierce heat of the afternoon sun. I was sitting on my bed, and the two girls sat on Jessie's bed, facing me. Grace looked quietly concerned, while Jessie went for the direct approach.

'OK, Claire. Spit it out.'

I shrugged, and didn't meet her eyes. 'What do you mean?'

'What's wrong with you? You're going around with a face like a wet week.'

'It's nothing. I'm just a bit tired. That's all.' The old habit of secrecy and subterfuge was hard to break.

Jessie spoke softly. 'Come on, Claire. You can tell us.'

Grace was beginning to look rather nervous. 'Maybe she doesn't want to tell us. Don't bully her.'

Jessie shot her an angry look, and came to sit beside me. She put her hand gently on my arm. 'Come on, Claire. It can't be that bad.'

She was rewarded with a sudden shower, as I began to sob uncontrollably. She rubbed my arm, and didn't speak. Finally the words came, working their way out between streams of spittle and tears.

'I'm pregnant. My period's late, and I know I'm pregnant.'

It seemed that in their whispered discussions they hadn't considered that particular scenario. There was a silence, interrupted only by my occasional sobs and hiccuppy gasps for breath.

Eventually Grace stepped into our bathroom, and returned with a toilet roll. She unwound a long stream of paper and handed it to me. 'You'll feel better if you blow your nose.'

I tried it, but it didn't help. Still, maybe it helped her. She was always very fastidious.

Soon my gasps and sobs gave way to quiet sniffs.

Grace and Jessie recovered from their shock. But then, as I said to myself in bitter moments, it wasn't their lives that had just fallen to pieces. Jessie tried to be positive, in her usual chirpy way, but that was rather difficult, under the circumstances. After all, what possible good could come from the situation? I was single. A student. Still a teenager. Pregnant by a barely-known passer-by. Not much to be positive about in that, was there?

After much discussion, and a few more showers of tears on my part, Grace spoke with authority. 'There's no point in getting too worked up until you've done a test. You'll have to do a test and then you can decide what to do.'

I nodded in agreement. I knew in my heart that there was no need for a test, but at least I would feel as if I were doing something.

Of course, I didn't know the first thing about pregnancy tests. I remembered my mum joking with a friend once about rabbits dying as a result of pregnancy testing, but surely times had moved on? Surely some intense activists would have put a stop to that kind of carry-on? Surely there would have been protest marches and 'Save-the Bunnies' badges? And cute, big-eyed bunny faces gazing sadly from the pages of left-wing newspapers?

Jessie brushed away my talk of dead bunnies. 'Don't be ridiculous, Claire. This is 1986, you know. I'm going into town. I'll find out what you have to do.'

She set off on her mission, glad, I think, to be able to help. I could hear the crunch of tyres on gravel as she manoeuvred Georgios's bike onto the road. Then all was quiet again.

I lay on my bed, tired after my emotional outburst. Grace began to potter around our room, picking up stray items of clothing, and stuffing them into the wardrobe. Then she too lay on her bed, and we dozed in the afternoon heat.

Jessie arrived back some time later. 'Do a pee first thing in the morning, give it to me, and I'll bring it to town. You'll have a result in two days.'

I was so glad that she had done the research for me that I didn't ask how or where, but just did as she said.

The next two days were very difficult, as I prayed for an undeserved miracle. I had happy visions of waking one morning to find that my period had started. I dreamed of waking up with blood on my knickers and joy in my heart.

That didn't happen though, and the afternoon of the result came.

Jessie went to collect the result, and Grace was left with the more difficult job of staying with me.

I wonder did they pull straws? Loser gets to stay with the weeping one.

Grace and I went down to the beach, as we did every afternoon, but we didn't even bother to bring the factor bag or the mats. We didn't change into our bikinis either. We just sat there, absently playing with pebbles, and drawing patterns on the sand, trying not to keep looking towards the town. Grace tried to distract me, but gave up when it became clear that she was wasting her breath. Jessie had borrowed Georgios's old bike again, and we figured that if she were only going into town, the longest she should be was one hour. I tried not to keep looking at my watch, but failed. I just kept on hoping and hoping that Jessie would come back laughing, and shouting happily. 'It was a false alarm. You're free. You're free.'

Then we could all hug, and we'd go on a big boozy session to celebrate my narrow escape.

And everything would be all right.

I made my sweatshirt into a pillow and lay back on the sand. I closed my eyes and pictured the happy, not-pregnant scenario over and over. I prayed every prayer I knew, and even recited a decade of the rosary. I promised to be good forever. I prayed as I had never prayed before, and then settled into a slow mental chant. 'Let it be negative. Please let it be negative.'

My eyes were closed when Grace tapped me on the shoulder. I jumped to my feet. Jessie leaned the bike against a wall, and walked slowly towards us. She wasn't smiling. She didn't need to say anything. Her look of genuine pity said it all. She might as well have been carrying a banner declaring: 'It's official. Claire is not only a weak idiot. She is also pregnant.'

'I'm sorry,' was all she could mutter as she came near and gave me a hug of comfort.

There could be no more hiding from the truth. I knew it and they knew it, and it wasn't going to go away. I was going to have a baby. I had been stupid and vain and this was my punishment.

I sat down on that beautiful beach and gazed out at the perfect, deep blue sea. A gentle breeze cooled my face. I let a handful of fine, warm sand slip through my fingers. I hunched over and gave in to the tears. Deep sobs shook my officially pregnant body. The girls loyally sat either side of me. Jessie leaned her head against mine, and Grace rubbed my back with her long, slim fingers.

It was no comfort at all.

Chapter Twenty-Three

I spent long hours trying to decide what to do, though that was a bit sad, as there weren't exactly hundreds of options open to me. Grace and Jessie showed endless patience as I repeated the same non-arguments over and over again. Occasionally they offered advice. Grace had no doubt in her mind.

'If it were me,' she stated in her ever-so-pragmatic way, 'I would go to Athens and get on the next plane to London and have an abortion. You don't want this baby, and it's going to ruin your life. It's not a nice thing to have to do, but the alternatives are worse. Sometimes you've got to put yourself first.'

By now, I had realised that no matter what happened, Grace always put herself first, but that observation wasn't much use to me.

For me, an abortion wasn't really an option. I would have loved a simple way out of my predicament, but an abortion didn't appear to be that simple. I have to confess that I wasn't so much concerned about taking the life of my unborn child as I was about what might happen afterwards. I was very superstitious, and the last vestiges of my vanishing religious beliefs still rattled around my brain. I felt that I would somehow be punished for such a terrible crime. I felt sure that if I did have an abortion somehow, some day, I would have to pay the price.

Having the baby and keeping it wasn't really an option for me either. I had at least one more year of college to go, and I couldn't finish that if I had the baby. If I didn't finish, my employment prospects wouldn't be great, and I did not relish the prospect of living in poverty with the unwanted child of a man I'd known for only a few hours.

Loyal Jessie sometimes took flights of fancy, saying she would track Kevin down and tell him about the baby. Then he would return to sweep me off my feet, and we would live happily ever after.

'I don't want to be swept off my feet by him,' I protested. 'He wasn't even nice. I don't even want to see him again. Ever.'

So Jessie changed tack slightly. 'That's fine then. I'll just track him down, tell him about the baby, and he can support you both. He can put you through college. It's the least he could do, considering the mess he's got you into.'

This plan had several major flaws. Firstly, I knew so little about Kevin that it was most unlikely that we could ever find him. Jessie could hardly stand in the lobby of every Bloomingdale's store shouting, 'Anyone here know a Kevin? Good bone structure and dodgy morals. Anyone know where I could find him? I just want to give him some good news.'

(Strange one that. I knew next to nothing about this man, yet I was carrying his baby. The baby could grow up to look just like Kevin, carrying his genes, and perhaps a tendency towards sinus problems, and yet I didn't even know his address.)

The other problem with Jessie's plan was that in those innocent days before widespread DNA testing, in the unlikely event of our finding Kevin, he'd hardly throw his hands up and say, ' Sure. Great. That's fine. The baby's mine. How much money do you need? Private school? College fund? Just name your figure. It's the least I can do.'

Jessie was a persistent, inventive planner, but even she had to admit reluctantly that, whatever happened, Kevin was not likely to feature in my future plans.

That left only the option of having the baby and having it adopted. Because of my circumstances, I felt no bond with my unborn child. I felt nothing for this child, except annoyance. I just didn't want to give up a year of my life for this alien, unwanted being. It was an inconvenience. It was messing up my life in a big way, and while I could not bring myself to kill it, I just wanted for it not to be there. I wasn't upset at the thought of future grief at having to give my child to strangers. I wasn't worried about the possible heartbreak of turning my back on a tiny, precious newborn. I wanted to be rid of it as soon as possible.

I know that sounds heartless, but I'm being honest. That's exactly how I felt.

The thought of going home to face my parents was daunting. I wasn't afraid of their anger; it was just that I knew that they would be so disappointed in me. I could see it already – their incomprehension, their looks of pity and regret, their feeling (echoing my own) that I had ruined my life. I knew that they would be supportive, but I also knew how it would upset them, how they would dread telling their friends. Some of their friends were of that smug sort who could manage to say, without really saying it, 'How careless. That would never happen to our daughter.'

Then their knowing looks. 'I always knew they were too soft on that Claire. She needed to be taken in hand.'

And so on and so on.

I didn't want to visit this scenario either on my parents or on myself, so I decided that I had to figure out a way to have the baby without my parents finding out. I know now that this was a crazy idea, a desperate idea, but I was desperate. My parents weren't ogres. They would be very upset if they knew I was pregnant, but I know now that they would have been more upset if they had ever discovered that I had a baby and didn't tell them. Back then, though, I fixed my mind on the idea that if I could somehow have the baby without their knowing, and give the baby away, then I would be able to pick up the pieces of my life as if nothing had happened.

And everything would be all right.

Gradually, a desperate plan began to take shape in my addled brain. I had a cousin in London who could perhaps help me. I could nip home from Greece in a few months' time, and visit my family, hiding my thickening waist with the loose sweatshirts I often wore anyway. If anyone mentioned my increased weight, I could pretend I'd just been eating too many pizzas.

I could concoct a story about a year out from college, a year for work experience. I could then head off to London, stay with my cousin until the nasty business was all over, and then go home.

Nice and neat. No mess. No one need ever know.

It was only seventeen years ago, but times have changed so much since then. Now an unplanned pregnancy would be only a small glitch – something to be built into one's life, requiring just a little re-arranging. Back then, things were different. Now, while I can vividly remember my feelings of despair – my feelings of desperation – it is hard to see right back into those times, to see why it needed to be such a big deal. It's hard now to see why it wasn't possible for me to be brave, to have the baby, and to weave the new situation into the existing threads of my life, without necessarily changing the whole pattern.

My mind was made up, though. My family would never know, and then we could all get on with the important business of living happily ever after.

I thought about leaving Greece immediately, but I decided to stay for a while. Grace put my feelings on this into words. 'If you're going to be pregnant and miserable, you may as well stay and be pregnant and miserable here, where it's sunny, and where the wine is cheap.'

So that's what I did.

I had no unpleasant symptoms of pregnancy, so I went about life pretty much as before. I worked, sunbathed, read trashy novels and ate chocolate. I still went to discos, because that's what Grace and Jessie wanted to do, and I didn't fancy staying at home on my own. I no longer looked for romance though, and I didn't bother surveying the seething crowds for possible love objects. I danced with men when they asked me, but when they held me close for slow dances, I didn't know whether I should laugh into their innocent, boyish faces, or rest my head on their warm shoulders and cry buckets of self-pitying tears.

One night, a tall, thin German pressed his body against mine and sang in my ear along with Elton John. Little did Boris know that deep inside me, where I couldn't yet feel it, some other man's baby was squirming and wriggling like a small red tadpole. Staking its claim on my insides. Binding itself to me. Becoming part of me.

The darker side of me said that I might as well have some fun and sleep around, now that I had nothing left to lose, but I had no interest, no desire.

Years later, when I was expecting Lizzie, I followed her growth with such interest. I had a book with line drawings showing the stages of the baby's development at weekly intervals. I watched each one, seeing the little limbs forming, and picturing the same happening inside me. When I got to the stage where, according to the book, the baby would be the size of my closed fist, I would lie in bed looking at my hand, and picturing the baby growing within me, picturing it with love.

And now, of course, it's happened again. There's yet another life inside me. Alien to me, and yet part of me. I hope I'll be able to love this one. The way I love Lizzie. But back then, with that poor, unwanted child, I knew nothing about its development, and wanted to know nothing. If I thought of it at all, it was just as a blight on my life. A major inconvenience. I was young and afraid. I wasn't ready to love a child because I was too close to being a child myself. I was too busy being selfish, lying on a beach, working on my tan, trying to bleach my hair with lemon juice, and trying to be normal.

When I was expecting Lizzie, not one drop of alcohol passed my lips, because I was so terrified of harming the precious creature inside me. The first one was different though. I drank as if it wasn't there. In fact, I probably drank more, just because it was there.

Every night there was beer, wine, and ouzo. The more I drank, the better I felt. Perhaps it was an unconscious effort to hurt the baby.

To damage it.

To punish it for ruining my life.

Chapter Twenty-Four

Looking back over the years, I think I did quite a good job of ignoring my unborn baby. I did my best to deny the existence of the life growing inside me. It caused torrents of crazy hormones to rampage around my bloodstream, but I pretended not to notice.

Of course that couldn't last forever. The first outward signs began to appear, and it became harder to pretend.

My breasts expanded, and for the first time ever, I actually filled the cups of my size twelve bikini top. All of a sudden, I had a better cleavage than Grace, though, in the circumstances, I didn't feel like gloating.

I found that my appetite had increased greatly, and I ate as I had never eaten before. All day long, as I sat on the beach, I gave in to overwhelming cravings for crisps and ice cream and chocolate. Every evening, I ate a Greek salad, and then a huge pizza and a large plateful of chips. Not content with that, I'd then pick at Grace and Jessie's leftovers, before finishing up with a huge, chocolaty dessert. Or three.

'Eating for two,' I'd mutter by way of explanation as I stuffed my face with food.

Two elephants by the look of it.

I had always been fairly skinny, but I couldn't remain so while eating like this. One morning, as I lay on the beach, eating a huge choc-ice, I became aware of a little bulge above my bikini bottoms, where my flat tummy used to be. My comfy, old denims, which had been like a dear friend to me for many years, betrayed me soon afterwards. For a while, I could lie on my bed, breathe in, and manage to close them, and spend the day in mild, constricted discomfort. But then one day the moment of truth arrived. Grace watched as I lay on the bed, wriggling and grunting. She raised one neatly plucked eyebrow.

'One pizza too many?'

I stopped struggling to take a deep breath, then I muttered through clenched teeth, 'No. I think they shrank when I washed them. I knew that water was too hot.'

Grace's expression showed what she thought of that little piece of self-delusion. But even I knew that the jeans hadn't shrunk.

I gave a few more token tugs at the zip, and then admitted defeat. I tried my only other pair, with similar lack of success. I grabbed the two offending pairs of jeans and threw them crossly into the turmoil of the wardrobe. Grace had finished plucking her other eyebrow, and was admiring her handiwork in a small, chipped hand-held mirror.

'Maybe Jessie would lend you a pair of hers.'

'A pair of my what?' Jessie had just wandered in from the beach. I had a funny feeling that she wouldn't be pleased at Grace's suggestion, and I shook my head at Grace in a poor effort to silence her.

Grace wasn't easily intimidated, and she spoke airily.

'I just suggested that you might lend Claire a pair of your jeans, now that hers are too small for her.'

Jessie reacted as I had expected.

'Thanks a bunch, Grace. Claire's pregnant, for God's sake. Are you saying my jeans would still fit her?'

Grace's cool gaze lingered for just a second too long on Jessie's rather pudgy frame. She chose discretion rather than truth. 'Well, maybe not. I don't know what I was thinking.'

I was quite sure that Jessie's jeans would have fitted me with room to spare, and I particularly liked her faded Levis, but I didn't want to offend her any more than necessary.

'Forget it, girls. I'm fed up of jeans anyway. I think I'll wear my new skirt.'

I rooted in the wardrobe and pulled out a long, loose skirt, with an elasticated waistband. It was made from a soft, silky fabric, patterned all over with swirls of cream, gold and brown. I had bought it a few days earlier from a French girl who was selling most of her belongings to raise the money for her train fare home. I could see that she was sad to hand it over, but she was desperate, and she was selling all of her clothes except what she was wearing. I handed over the few drachmas she asked for, and for one brief moment I felt sorry for her. Then I reasoned that perhaps it wasn't such a great tragedy. Surely handing your favourite skirt to a stranger could not be quite as traumatic as giving away a baby. Even a baby you never wanted.

This was around the beginning of September, and the season was starting to wind down. There were fewer tourists, and life on the island began to move even more slowly than before. Some days the girls and I were completely alone on our little beach.

One evening, as we chopped vegetables and made salad, Georgios pointed to the grease-spattered calendar on the kitchen wall. He rested his chubby finger on 30 September, and repeated sadly, 'I close taverna. I close taverna. Winter.'

Grace didn't care. 'That's fine. We have to get back to college then anyway.'

Jessie looked pointedly at me, and Grace corrected herself. 'Well, we all have to leave then anyway. College or not.'

I felt sadder than ever. I had always known I'd have to leave, but now there was a deadline. When the taverna closed, I would have no choice but to pack up and go home to my parents, and spend a few dreadful days pretending not to be pregnant, before setting off to London for a bleak, lonely few months.

The Greek salad must have been extra salty that night, as I cried a few furtive tears into the cucumber

I was chopping. I hope none of the taverna's diners suffered from high blood pressure.

The days passed slowly, and the nights became longer. There was a slight chill in the air one Sunday evening when we set off for our usual walk into town. Jessie shivered as she pulled the door closed behind us.

Grace laughed. 'Better get used to it, Jess. Think of the draught in the Aula Maxima.'

Jessie shivered even more. An exaggerated, theatrical shiver this time. 'Don't mention college, please, Grace.'

I smiled at her. 'Don't worry, Jessie. I don't mind. I'd love to go back, but I know I can't. You can still talk about it.'

Jessie made a wry face. 'Well, Claire, I wasn't just thinking of you. I can't bear the thought of college anyway. The summer here has been so free, so lovely. So warm. The thought of the cold just kills me. I don't know if I can face November in Cork. I'm not sure I can bear to walk down the Western Road every morning in the rain and the wind.'

Grace smiled. 'But what about the two great loves of your life? Milton and the blond med student with the blue racer?'

Jessie blushed slightly. How did Grace know these things? For someone who was apparently so self-preoccupied, she always seemed to have a fair insight into our supposedly secret love lives.

Jessie sighed deeply. 'I think that guy might be gay. In any case, he never looked crooked at me. Doesn't matter anyway. Gay or not, even he couldn't compensate for the endless drizzle, and the lectures on Anglo-Saxon runes. But still, bet I end up back there anyway. I've no other option, have I?'

She didn't sound very convinced.

Towards the middle of the month, we met a group of English students who had spent some time on a kibbutz, and Jessie began to get a strange gleam in her eye. She questioned them at length, asking them all kinds of questions that went beyond polite interest. I noticed that she became prone to untypical bouts of meditative silence.

One coolish evening as we sauntered home from the beach, our shadows long on the dusty golden sand in front of us, Jessie announced her decision. 'I'm going to Israel. I won't ever have a chance like this again. I need to travel.'

I was surprised. 'What about your degree?'

She shrugged. 'My degree can wait.'

This made me feel unaccountably sad. How I wished I were in her position. All I wanted was to go home again, back to college. To be the same girl who'd left Cork four-and-a-half months earlier. Jessie had this option and she was turning her back on it. How I envied her.

I think she saw what I was thinking. She spoke gently. 'You'll have your year out too, Claire. You'll come back next year. Things can be the same again. We can do our final year together. We'll graduate together and we'll go on to be rich, famous and happy.'

Grace smiled. 'And I'll just be one year ahead of you both. I can suss out the future, and have it ready for you when you arrive.'

Jessie spoke pensively. 'Anyway, I'll probably understand a lot more of my texts after a bit of experience of life. Sir Gawain doesn't speak to me the way he should. *Beowulf* is beyond me. And I'm too young to understand the torments of Emily Dickinson.'

Grace quoted in a forced theatrical voice. 'You don't have to be a chamber to be haunted.'

Quick as a flash, Jessie replied, 'You don't have to be a chair to be wooden.'

The three of us laughed, glad of the release.

I wasn't forgetting Jessie's plans though. I still wasn't sure that her idea was a good one.

'What about your folks? Won't they mind?'

She gave a careless shrug. 'They'll learn to live with it. I'm going to go home, explain to my family, borrow some money, and go. One year out and then I'll go back to college, a better person.'

She was far too polite to say it, but I was sure that her decision was partly because of me. She could see how trapped I felt, and she needed to get away. She needed to live, to be young.

'*Carpe diem*,' she kept saying, showing off her great learning. 'I don't want my grandchildren to be ashamed of me. I want to do something with my life. College can wait.'

Jessie was never one to hang around once she had made up her mind about something. She planned to leave on the early ferry the next morning, so we went out on the town, to mark her last night. Gorgeous Georgios gave us all the night off. 'I get someone to help here. You have good time.'

We ate in town (pizza for a change), and then went for a drink. It was a lonely kind of a night. The rush and bustle that had been in the town all summer were now gone. Bars that had been buzzing every night now played host to just a few, scattered customers. One of the bars we used to frequent had even closed down altogether, shuttered up for another long winter. We reminisced about previous nights, the wild times, the good times, but this was done without joy. Now that Jessie was leaving, it marked a change – an ending. We all had to admit that the summer was finally at an end, and, in our various ways, we had to go back to the drab and dreary life that was our true existence. Of course, I had added problems which didn't help, but whenever I thought of home, all I could think of was greyness, dampness and – worst of all – responsibility. Jessie was escaping for a time, but in the face of the pessimism of Grace and myself, it was hard for her to feel anything but gloom. There was no sense that she was going to a wonderful place; it was just that she was getting away. It was the escape that mattered, not the destination.

So we sat in what had been our very favourite bar, the one where we had spent many a carefree evening, watching tourists streaming past, eyeing them up, and selecting likely targets for our innocent, girlish romantic dreams. Now, however, there was no stream of tourists. The odd person strolled by, but we couldn't summon any enthusiasm, any interest, and rarely took our eyes from the single drink we each had that evening. The buzz was gone, and even though we were still there, we were only marking time. We knew it was gone past the time to leave.

Next morning, one of the very few we experienced hangover-free, was also one of the very few dull, drizzly days of that Greek summer. This suited our mood perfectly, as Grace and I lay on our beds, watching Jessie packing up her few belongings. She shook sand out of each item before carelessly tossing it unfolded into her rucksack. It was like watching a silent movie, telling the story of our shared summer.

She reached into the wardrobe and pulled out the pale pink t-shirt with 'I love Mykonos' in silver print on the front. She smiled ruefully. 'God, remember this.'

Grace smiled. 'Yeah, what was the name of the guy who gave you that?'

Jessie wasn't sure. 'He was Swedish. Something beginning with "b".'

I remembered. I'd kind of fancied him myself. 'Benny.'

Jessie laughed. 'Yeah, that was it. I met him the first week we were here. Bet he's back at his boring banking job by now. Bet he's forgotten all about me.'

She shoved the t-shirt into a side pocket. 'That'll be a great present for my kid sister.'

She pulled out the green striped shirt she'd worn every time she'd had a special date. 'Ha, look at this. The back of this has been pawed by a representative of every country in Europe.'

Grace gave a supercilious smile. 'Yeah, and the front had its share of action too, I've no doubt.'

Jessie threw the shirt at her in mock anger. 'Here, you prissy wagon. Would you like it as a memento of me?'

Grace threw it back in equal spirit. 'Thanks but no thanks. It's forgetting you I'll be trying to do. Anyway you'll need your lucky shirt in the kibbutz.'

Jessie took the shirt and shoved it into the rucksack. It was quickly followed by the loose blue cheesecloth skirt she had worn over her bikini on almost every one of our daily trips to the beach. Then the blue-and-mauve bracelet woven out of cotton threads, which Grace had given her in gratitude for switching work nights, when Grace had wanted to spend a special evening with a suave Frenchman. Finally, from the very bottom of the wardrobe, Jessie pulled out the dress I had worn on the night out with Kevin. It had a small tear in the front where one of the buttonholes had been pulled apart. It hadn't been worn since then, and had lain there, crumpled up, all this time.

'Anyone want this?' Jessie asked, not looking at me.

'No way,' Grace and I replied in chorus, and Jessie tossed it into the corner.

'I never really liked it. The pattern reminds me of old ladies going to a bridge conference. Georgios can make curtains out of it.'

We laughed for a moment, and then lapsed into our own thoughts again.

Jessie finished her packing, and, placing her rucksack on the floor, used her full body weight to try to keep it closed as she pulled the laces tight around the top. She then carefully rolled up her straw beach mat, and tied it under her rucksack, commenting that it would surely come in handy on the journey home. She donated her share of the suncreams to us, as she did also with her share of the red metal flask. That was it. All of her belongings fitted into the not-so-large rucksack. She double-checked that she had her passport and her money, and she was ready to leave.

Georgios came to say goodbye. He gave Jessie a small bottle of ouzo, 'to remember Greece.' If he had known the rate of which Jessie could drink, he'd have realised that she wouldn't be remembering for long. He then gave her one of his health-endangering hugs, and stood and waved as we set off towards town.

We knew that road so well. I could not have counted how many times we had walked it. We had walked it in the daytime and in the early hours, and more than once we had walked home accompanied by the rising sun. Sometimes, alcohol had caused us to sway a little, and walk in not quite straight lines, making the journey somewhat longer. Sometimes we had sung as we walked.

We knew every stone, every bend, every inch of the grassy verge of that narrow road. Especially the verge. Between us, we had weed on it seven times and vomited on it twice. Once Grace had lain down on it in a drunken sulk, declaring that she'd prefer to sleep there rather than walk the last few hundred yards to her bed. Jessie and I had had to bully and drag her the rest of the way home.

When we arrived in town that last morning with Jessie, we headed straight for the harbour. Petros the pelican waddled past. We were now so used to him that we barely acknowledged him. Jessie alone commented, 'Goodbye, Petros, I'll miss you.'

Petros waddled on, unimpressed, and went towards the boats in hopes of getting some fish.

Jessie's ferry was just arriving. Only a few tourists and locals disembarked, and Jessie was one of only six passengers to board. We embraced briefly, and she kissed my cheek. Suddenly there didn't seem to be much to say.

'Good luck with it,' she said, as she patted my stomach. 'I hope it turns out well for you.'

I tried to sound bright and breezy. 'Good luck with your trip. And with your parents. See you at registration in the Aula Maxima next year.'

'Yeah,' she replied, but once again, she didn't sound convinced. She hugged Grace and stepped on board.

The boat left almost immediately, and Jessie waved until it was out of sight. Grace and I sat on a warm stone wall and waved back. Soon Jessie and the boat were gone. For the second time that summer, I sat and gazed at an empty horizon. I had never felt so lonely.

I looked at Grace who was idly plaiting her hair in long golden strands. All of a sudden, I realised that I didn't like her very much. I had always been so in awe of her perfect beauty that I had failed to notice this. I suspected that the feeling was mutual. I was too plain and dull for her exotic tastes.

Tough. We were stuck with each other for the next two weeks, until we too could pack up and leave. Grace stopped her plaiting. 'Should we go back to the taverna?'

I shrugged. 'I suppose. Nothing else to do, is there?'

She shook her head slowly, and the plaits began to unravel in a cascade of gold. 'Let's go then.'

The drizzle had stopped, but the air remained dark and oppressive. I slouched along, thinking of Jessie embarking on her great adventure, and I felt particularly sad. I liked her a lot, but we had never been terribly close, and now I could not explain the awful desolation I felt now that she was gone. Maybe it was just self-pity. A trip like hers was totally out of the question for me. I felt I had nothing to look forward to, nothing to hope for.

When we arrived at San Stefanos, the beach didn't tempt us, so we headed for home. Georgios appeared, and tried to cheer us up by doing what he did best.

'I make omelette,' he suggested brightly. 'With cheese. And peppers.'

We hadn't the heart to refuse. We normally ate in the kitchen, but this time Georgios insisted that we sit on the terrace that was usually reserved for customers. He made a big ceremony of presenting us with the food. He sat with us, but had to watch us pushing the food around the plates, neither tasting nor enjoying it. He tried to lighten our mood, with little jokes and kind words, but we couldn't manage any enthusiasm. In the end, he gave up, retiring to his room with a small, hurt shrug of his shoulders.

I never saw Jessie again. She spent the greater part of a year on the kibbutz, and went from there to India with a boyfriend. He was a drummer from a faded rock band. Word filtered back to Cork that he had once been almost famous.

The last I heard of her was a postcard from Goa. It arrived a few months before Lizzie was born. I sat in the chaos of my suburban home and read Jessie's final words to me. I could picture her, sitting on a beach, flowers in her hair, wearing her blue cheesecloth skirt, taking deep puffs from a dodgy cigarette, humming sad melodies, and dreaming. Still living the simple, irresponsible life that we had shared in those first weeks in Greece. The message on the card was strangely disjointed, as if she were somehow detached from reality.

Or maybe it was just that by then her reality was so different from mine that I couldn't understand it any more.

About a year after that, I met an old college acquaintance who told me that Jessie was dead. He wasn't sure how, or where, but he thought she had drowned. Apparently her boyfriend died too. The bearer of this news didn't look terribly upset as he told his story.

'I think she was on drugs.'

You would think that, I thought, as I looked at him standing pompously in front of me, in his grey suit which perfectly matched his grey face. This Harp-and-lime-drinking life-insurance salesman had probably never been anywhere more exotic than Magaluf in his entire life. I was cross with him, and wanted to defend the friend I hadn't seen in over ten years.

'Well, I bet she was happy,' I replied rather sharply. 'Happier than you are ever likely to be.'

He gave me a pitying look before stalking away. I suppose he thought I was on drugs too.

I felt a new wave of guilt. I still felt it was my fault that Jessie had never managed to make her way back into what I called 'real life'.

Still though, maybe I did her a favour. She never came home to responsibility and drudgery. She never had to worry about a mortgage or car tax or pension plans. She never reigned in an apple-white kingdom on the outskirts of Cork. She didn't spend her days answering the door to men who wanted to tarmac her driveway or trim her trees or power-clean her fascias and soffits. (I don't actually know what a soffit is, but I regularly tell men with moustaches that I don't need them to clean mine.) Jessie turned her back on attic insulation and tried to find a land of freedom.

I hope she found it.

And if she did, I hope it wasn't peopled by dodgy-looking men in Hiaces, offering to cobble-lock her driveway.

Chapter Twenty-Five

A few weeks after Jessie left for her kibbutz, I went home to visit my parents. If they noticed that I was unusually quiet, they didn't comment – or at least they didn't comment to me. When I got around to telling them that I planned to spend the year in London, I encountered a bewildered silence. I knew they didn't want me to go, but they didn't know how to express this. I didn't make things easy for them. I packed my bags for the winter, and set off once more.

My year in London was dreadful. My cousin was kind, but I rejected her kindness. I wallowed in my misery. My parents telephoned regularly, and I tried to be bright and breezy when I spoke to them. Looking back now, I doubt if they were fooled.

When Christmas came, I didn't go home. I told my parents I was doing shift work in a hospital canteen, and couldn't get away. My mum sent over mincemeat and puddings, and a pretty, hand-knitted jumper with a Fair-Isle yoke. It was too small. I gave the food to my cousin's boyfriend. I couldn't face it.

In the summer, my cousin announced that her boy-friend was moving into the flat. There would be no room for me in their new domestic arrangement. I couldn't face the thought of finding a place of my own. So I went back home. My parents greeted me with open arms. The prodigal returned.

At the beginning of another October, I was back in college, queuing in the dark, dusty Aula Maxima to register for another year's study. I didn't feel much like studying, but I couldn't think of anything else to do. I looked around at my fellow students, jostling and laughing in the long queues. I tried to hold my head high as I wondered bitterly if any other girl had experienced anything like I had, since my last registration day, two long years earlier.

I filled in all the forms, and then sat for the annual photograph for my college identity card. I still have that card. Once, in an idle moment, I laid it next to the photo of me taken on the boat to Mykonos. Of course, my features had not really changed in the year that separated the pictures, but even so, it is like looking at two different people. I suppose that is only right. After that year, I was a different person. And while the old me hadn't been anything special, I'd have welcomed her back.

Grace was there that October day too, registering for her fourth year. She tossed her head and rearranged her already perfectly arranged golden locks. She beamed for her photograph, showing off her even, white teeth. Already she had a small entourage of mousy girls and ardent male admirers who sighed over the perfect image that appeared on the photographic paper two minutes later.

It's tempting to say that Grace and I were no longer close, but that wouldn't really be true. We had never been close, and now we were less so than ever. She was unfortunate really to have become entangled with me. It was a rare poor decision to get herself saddled with me for those long months in Greece. I bet she was sorry she hadn't gone to America that summer. To be fair to her, she was a decent, if rather shallow person. She did make some vague efforts in the next month or two. She gave me the photographs she had taken of me in Greece. (I bet she thought long and hard about that one.) Afterwards, she rang me a few times and we went out together, for a drink, and once to an arty, black and white film. It wasn't a success. She reminded me too much of Greece, and all the things I was trying so hard to forget.

Grace tried not to show it, but I was clearly an embarrassment to her. I was too dour and intro-spective, given to long silences. She wanted life and fun and good times. I was hardly a barrel of laughs. Clearly, after a few attempts, she felt she had fulfilled her duty towards me, and she stopped making the effort. I was glad. We still bumped into each other now and again, and we'd exchange a few words and make a few vague promises to meet for a drink – promises we never kept, never meant to keep.

She did well for herself in the end, doing all the things I had once hoped to do. She graduated with honours, got a great job, went to lots of glitzy parties, travelled the world. I heard that she married a rich, handsome dentist, and moved to a big house in Foxrock in Dublin, which had an ornamental fountain, an avocado-coloured bathroom suite, and a double garage with electric doors. I bet she got invited to the kind of dinner parties where the linen tablecloths were strewn with rose petals, and where candles with four wicks were burned on understated pewter trays. I can picture her flicking her blonde locks as she idly polished her stainless-steel kitchen cupboards which were full of Nicholas Mosse bowls, plain white ramekins from Habitat, and arty little knick-knacks brought back from Tuscany. After a respectable interval, I'm sure she had two perfect children who inherited her good looks, and excelled at the violin.

Grace is all set for the happily-ever-after scenario.

My own path was not quite so easy. But I suppose I shouldn't complain really. After all, I got one of my wishes – no one else ever knew of my pregnancy. Georgios wasn't likely to surface in Cork ready to sell my story to *The Examiner*. He was hardly going to appear on my doorstep, hug my mother and say, 'Put on the kettle quick, and I'll tell you what your daughter got up to in Greece.'

And Grace wasn't telling anyone – that was for sure. She was very quick to dissociate herself from such a nasty, messy business.

Jessie was safe on her kibbutz. Far away. She wrote a few times, that first year, but didn't mention the pregnancy. When I wrote back, I didn't mention it either.

So I never spoke of it to anyone. Probably not a terribly healthy strategy, I suppose, but it seemed easier that way. I never consciously thought of the baby, but it must always have been there somewhere, colouring my moods, influencing my life, condemning me to hours of useless self-pity.

I still lived with my parents, in their comfy suburban home in Douglas, but if they were aware of what was happening to me, they never showed it. We ate meals together every evening, and watched television. We discussed *Dallas* and *MacGyver*. We talked a lot about the weather.

My mum and dad were good, kind people, and I never doubted their love, but during my teens we had sort of fatally diverged. Their precious only little girl grew up with a bang. The summer I was fifteen, I found pop music and left their world behind. I spent three months with a transistor firmly glued to my ear, singing along to 'Tainted Love', and 'Don't You Want Me?' All of a sudden, I didn't want to spend my Sunday afternoons on a 'nice drive in the country', followed by tea in my aunt's house. My idea of life was to lie on my back in the garden, my body covered with Mazola cooking oil, savouring the few pop songs that would be played on the afternoon shows. I spent much of that summer bemoaning the fact that Radio

Luxembourg didn't come on air until evening, wondering how I could possibly last until I would hear the first Aqua Manda ad, or the first Timex jingle.

My parents, like so many before them, scratched their heads and wondered what had become of their baby. They reached out to me, in their humble, tentative way, but I shook myself free of their well-meaning, misguided efforts. Slowly it began to dawn on me – I didn't want their lifestyle, and they didn't understand mine. This caused a distance to grow between us, and often it seemed as if we were nothing more than an embarrassment to each other.

Then, when I came back home from London, when I really needed them, the generation chasm came between us. When they expressed concern, or asked about my welfare, they were easily fobbed off with half-truths and mumbled non-answers. By then I'd had years of practice at keeping them at arm's length. I'm sure they worried about me, but they were passive in their worry. Basically they stood back, stayed in the background, and let me get on with the mess that was now my life.

And the terrible thing is, I know they loved me with a strong, unwavering love. I could see it in their troubled eyes, every time they spoke to me.

And I loved my parents too.

Every night in the weeks after I came home from London, I buried my head under my pillow, trying to muffle the sound of my helpless sobbing, but all the time I half-hoped that my mother would somehow hear me. I half-hoped that she'd shuffle in, in her old pink slippers and her candlewick dressing gown. I half-hoped that she'd sit on my bed, and rub my back, and whisper nice things and make everything all right again, like she used to when I was a small child. But she never came.

And sometimes, at quiet moments, I thought about telling her the whole, terrible story. But I couldn't find the words. I just didn't know how to talk to her about anything more personal than what to have for tea.

Picasso got to have his blue period, and his rose period. Van Gogh mightn't have had an official yellow period, but he sure got through a fair few tubes of yellow ochre and cadmium yellow in his day. Why can't I be dramatic too? I couldn't paint to save my life, but still, I think of the following years as my black period, which ever so slowly merged into my grey period, which lasted for years. Gradually I shrank from the outside world. I kept up the pretence of going to college, but I neglected lectures and study, eventually abandoning them altogether. When the weather allowed, I sat outside on the grass at the edge of the quad, watching people with lives pass me by. Other times, I would sit alone in one of the college restaurants, craving company and friendship, but frightening people away with my obvious despair.

There were some people I used to socialise with before I went to Greece, and they did their best to draw me out at first, but, when I made no effort at all, they tired of this, preferring to get on with their own hectic lives, leaving me to myself. People were kind, but they were only human, and they were bound to give up in the end. Before long, I had efficiently armed myself with a cold, forbidding air which successfully frightened away even the most saintlike of my acquaintances.

When spring rolled around again, and the frenzy of study for exams began, I remained aloof, detached. By the time the grass in the quad was cut for the first time, and I should have been on the third revision of my course, I had completely cut myself off from college life and college work. I hadn't studied or attended a lecture for many months. While the other students planned their revision strategies, contemplated post-graduate courses, and reluctantly cut back on their social lives, I sat back and watched through helpless, half-jealous eyes.

Then May came, exams began, and I had to admit that I was no longer following a course. I was not now going to get a degree. I confessed to my parents, and they were devastated. But by then it was too late to do anything about it. I stayed at home for weeks, not talking, not joining in family life, like an awkward ghost, haunting their days.

The summer passed slowly by. I spent most of it in a green-and-white striped deckchair in the back garden, looking at the sky, listening to Genesis and Fleetwood

Mac. Then I think I just got bored. How long can an almost-sane person mope for? How long can you sit in the garden for in a particularly dull summer? How long can you drag out a pathetic little drama like mine for?

On the first of September, it rained. In a rare moment of activity, I stirred myself, put on my best, formal clothes, left my mock-suede jacket at home, and went job-hunting. I soon got a job, and while it wasn't a great job, I told myself it was a start, and would do for a while, just for a few weeks until I got myself sorted out. In fact, I stayed there for almost nine years, until Lizzie was born. I never particularly liked the work, but I stayed because it was undemanding, and because I lacked the drive or interest to look for something better.

To a casual, disinterested observer it must have looked as if I was almost normal by then. I made a few superficial friendships with workmates, and went out with them occasionally. After all, I had nothing better to do. I even went on holidays a few times with a large group of them. I was the token oddball on the beach in Majorca. The misfit at the disco in Ibiza. No one seemed to mind. They must have laughed sometimes at my strange attire – my flowery pinafores, my baggy dungarees – and at my almost obsessive attachment to my scruffy mock-suede jacket. But they were kind. They never laughed to my face.

Like everyone else, I drank too much at the Christmas party each year, and vowed never to do it again. Every Monday morning, a few of us gathered for a quick cup of coffee before settling down to work, and I joined in the general moaning about life and the rigours of our completely undemanding, unchallenging jobs.

Years passed by, and I half-lived them. I was no longer in the depths of despair, but I wasn't exactly ecstatic either. I just mooched through my life, head down, no trouble to anyone, no joy to myself. I had lengthy conversations with my parents every morning, over breakfast.

'What time will you be home from work?'

'The usual – six o'clock.'

'What would you like for tea?'

'Anything's fine, Mum, really.'

'Would scrambled eggs be OK?'

'Yes, Mum. That would be lovely.'

'Or would you prefer a fry?'

'Really, Mum, I don't mind. Whatever you want is fine with me.'

'Just say which you'd prefer.'

'A fry then, thanks.'

Then Dad would chip in. 'Will we watch *Dallas* or *Cagney and Lacey* tonight?'

'Really, Dad, I don't mind. Whatever you want is fine with me.'

'Just say which you'd prefer'

And so it would go on. That was the level of our relationship – the level to which I quietly and stubbornly forced my loving parents to sink.

They both kissed me goodbye every morning, and expressed the hope that I would have a nice day. They always sort of tiptoed around me. I suppose they were afraid that the relatively normal daughter would vanish again, leaving them with the pale weeping wreck who can't have entirely escaped their notice.

Then, one fine summer evening, I went for an after-work drink with some of the girls from the shop. We went to one of the pubs off Patrick Street, which was very popular at the time. The pub was all polished brass and wood and red velvet and loud music, and loud rugby players, drinking big black pints, ogling blonde girls in too-tight dresses.

It was one of those beautiful evenings when the late sunshine draws the crowds, which then overflow out the door onto the pavement, gradually spreading outwards. Groups of workers began to intermingle, and soon I found myself sitting at a white plastic table, next to James. In the years since Greece, I had rejected the few offers of romance that had come my way. I had repelled the few brave or foolish souls who dared to attempt to barge through my barbed-wire defences. This was partly because men just didn't interest me, and partly because an involvement would have been too much trouble, too much of an interference with my calm, undemanding, boring life. If James had propositioned me that evening, or spoken of romance, he'd have been rejected like those who had gone before him. That didn't happen though. He just chatted easily about this and that, nothing of world importance. I found myself relaxing in his company in a way that was strange and new. I found myself smiling at his quiet humour. I found myself looking for rather too long at his black curls, and his strong, tanned arms.

He didn't ask me for a date, or an evening out, which was just as well, as I would surely have refused. He just mentioned, as if in passing, that on Sunday he was going fishing, and that he wouldn't mind some company.

So, a few days later, I found myself sitting on a damp riverbank, whispering so as not to scare the fish, getting my jumper snagged on low branches, and getting my new jeans covered with black river mud. After a while, James offered to show me how to use the fishing rod, but I declined, shaking my head so vehemently that my hair broke free of its scrunchy and flopped in front of my eyes. James laughed. I sat with my chin in my hands, watching as he gracefully cast his line, and wound it slowly in, occasionally turning back to smile at me. Each time he leaned forwards, I could see a patch of brown skin under his jumper. And the crinkled waistband of his navy-and-white striped boxer shorts.

I hadn't had such a good time in years.

James and I began to go out together frequently. We never went on 'dates'. It was always just casual occasions. We went for long walks, trips to the beach for evening swims, lazy lunches in country pubs. He was good for me. He was kind and gentle, and he made me laugh. On the rare occasion when I lapsed into my old introspection, he made no demands on me. He just backed off and waited for me to shake it off.

Mum and Dad seemed to like him too. Mind you, it was hard to tell. By then, they were so nervous of me that if I'd brought Attila the Hun home for tea, they'd have clucked approvingly at his adventurous spirit and his interest in foreign travel.

Before long, James had become an important part of my life. Sometimes I lay at night in my little single bed in my parents' house, and dreamed of his warm hands around me, keeping me safe.

James had his demons too, of course. Or demon, to be more precise. His brother Bobby had upped and left for Australia just before I met him, and that, coupled with his Dad's impertinence in dying, had thrown Maisie into her first paroxysms of flamboyant self-pity. She put on terrible acts of hysteria whenever James was around, and had him completely fooled. I suppose he shouldn't have been so naïve as to believe in her antics, but she was his mother. And besides, I shouldn't be too harsh on him. After all, he had the moral courage to stay with me in spite of Maisie's loudly voiced worries that I would never be up to the important job of minding her precious son.

Now, looking back all these years later, I can at last feel some pity for Maisie. She must have been frightened when I came along. I was a threat to her.

She knew her son would leave her for me. And I couldn't even cook or sew or clean.

And, when it came to it, it turned out that she was right. He was too good for me.

Or maybe I wasn't good enough for him.

Then again, maybe his decision to throw his lot in with mine was an unconscious act of defiance. Maybe Maisie's disapproval was the spur for both of us in the end.

I had known James for a little more than a year when I discovered that I was pregnant. I know, I know – yet another stupid mistake by a supposedly smart girl.

James was delighted with the news, and wanted to get married immediately. I wasn't so sure. I dithered for a few weeks, unable to commit myself, while James waited patiently for my answer.

There was an elderly lady at work, who reminded me a lot of my granny. Luckily this lady wasn't half-senile, so her advice was likely to be a bit more useful. I confided in her one morning as we queued for the photocopier.

'Please, Betty. I don't know what to do. Should I get married?'

As I spoke, it suddenly dawned on me that as Betty had never married, perhaps she wasn't the best person to ask after all.

'Is he kind to you?'

I nodded enthusiastically. 'Yes, always.'

'Do you love him?'

I nodded again, perhaps a little less enthusiastically than before. She gave me a shrewd look.

'Maybe this is the way we should look at it. Don't ask yourself if you can live with him. Ask if you can live without him.'

'Hmm.' It was taking me a few moments to work out what exactly she meant.

She continued. 'My mother gave me that advice forty years ago, and I took it. I decided I was better off without him. Good job too, as the man in question turned out to be a thief and a womaniser.'

'Oh dear! That's awful.'

'He died in a motor-cycle accident a few years later. They said he'd just robbed the local sweet shop, and was trying to get away before the guards came.'

'Oh, Betty, what an ending.' I was becoming engrossed in Betty's forty-year-old drama, and forgetting my own.

The photocopier was free at last, and as Betty stepped forward with her bundle of invoices, she brought me back to the present. 'Can you live without this man, Claire? That's what you must decide.'

That settled it for me. I couldn't go back to the way I was before I met James. That thought was more awful than I could bear to imagine. And anyway, there was the Maisie factor. I wanted her to know that James loved me even though I couldn't make bread-and-butter pudding, or do invisible mending, and had no idea how to get grass stains out of white cottons.

So when next we met, I shyly gave the answer James was waiting for. In a rare moment of abandon, he threw his arms around me, picked me up, and swung me round and round, singing all the time, 'She said yes! She said yes!'

I joined in his singing. 'I said yes! I said yes!'

I think we were both a bit surprised by my answer.

We laughed together, very pleased with ourselves, and at that moment I was sure I was doing the right thing.

Six weeks later, we were married. We had a church wedding, and a family reception in Norwood Court Hotel. My mum wanted it to be a bit of an occasion, and I didn't like to refuse her as that was one of the few things she had ever asked of her only child. Anyway, all the fuss was a useful distraction. It stopped me fretting about whether I was being fair to anyone by going ahead with the proceedings.

I wore a borrowed, loose-fitting white dress. The unborn Lizzie was invisible under the layers of viscose and lace. We had flowers, and a big black car and a real photographer. We planted a memorial tree in the grounds of the hotel. A three-bedroomed semi stands there now. I have twenty glossy pictures of our small families lined up on the grass with our backs to Cork Harbour. Everyone is trying to look happy, except for Maisie. In each picture, her lined face is draped with a discontented scowl. Even though she got a new dress twice a year for the bridge conventions, she didn't buy anything new for our wedding. She showed up in an unusually frumpy (even for her), slime-green Crimplene dress. I think it was a form of protest. I'll get her back in the end though. I'm going to wear baggy, flowery trousers and a bright red shirt to her funeral!

A few weeks later, James came with me when I belatedly went to register with an obstetrician. The nurse took a blood sample and checked my blood pressure. James admired the ceiling and tried not to look bored or squeamish. The nurse took out a long printed form and began to work her way through the questions. I had a sudden moment of panic. Why had I persuaded James to come? How could I have been so stupid?

'Is this your first pregnancy?'

Do I need to count the one that came about after a one-night stand with a pompous, rich American? The one I'm trying hard to pretend never happened?

I gave a nervous smile.

She repeated her question. James lowered his gaze from the ceiling and looked at me. I coughed to hide my confusion.

He jumped up. 'I'll get you a glass of water.'

I smiled my gratitude, and while he was gone, I told the nurse the awful truth.

Six months after the wedding, Lizzie was born.

I had a sincere, loving husband, a darling child, and a nice suburban home with a garage, a utility room and television sockets in all the bedrooms. James didn't get quite as good a deal. He ended up with a darling child, a nice suburban home with a garage, a utility room and television sockets in all the bedrooms. And a cantankerous, erratic, insecure wife. Who tried her best to love him as he deserved.

But probably never succeeded.

And that, as they say, was that. That was the summer of 1986, and the events that came afterwards.

It shouldn't have been as traumatic as all that. People survive worse and go on to live half-way normal lives. People emerge from vicious wars, and manage to cobble together some kind of tranquillity for themselves. People shake off hideous childhood traumas, and go on to be happy and fulfilled.

Other, stronger souls would have returned from Greece, rapped themselves on the knuckles, and then put it behind them so that they could get on with their lives.

Not me though. I hated myself, and hated what I had done, and I wallowed quietly in the misery of that for years of wasted life. In the end, I think I came to enjoy being an eccentric misfit.

It was the first thing I ever really excelled at.

Chapter Twenty-Six

If this were a film, at this stage everything would go misty, and there would be a series of wavy lines, indicating to the seasoned film watcher that a flashback was over, and the film was ready to progress. There might be some nice, dreamy orchestral music to accompany the time change. Beethoven perhaps. Or Brahms.

Or it could be a Tarantino movie, and the time change could be marked by a few violent murders and some snatches of discordant music.

I'll just jump forward, without ceremony.

I was sitting on the dusty earth beneath an ancient olive tree, on a small island in the middle of the Aegean Sea. Lizzie was cuddled in my lap, curled up the way she did when she was really tired, like a baby again, ready to sleep in peace. She was stroking my face ever so gently, and looking at me with concern.

'Don't cry, Mummy. Did you hurt your knee? Did you bump your head?'

She began a catalogue of all of the things that would bring tears to her eyes, and I had to smile as the list became more and more outlandish. The smile pleased her and she continued joyfully, knowing that none of her suggestions could possibly be right.

'Did you lose your dolly? Did your mummy smack you? Did you wet your knickers?'

I was filled with love for her, and held her tightly to me, kissing her untidy, dusty hair. I felt as if I could never bear to let her go.

I repeated over and over, 'I love you. I love you. I love you. My precious baby. You know I love you, don't you?'

Lizzie snuggled close, too young to worry that her poor dear mummy might finally have lost her few remaining marbles. After a while, she had had enough of the shady olive grove. She used the palms of her hands to push her hair from her face, which was damp and sticky from a combination of her perspiration and my tears. She tugged at my arm.

'Come on, Mummy. Let's go for a swim. You promised. It's my birthday and I haven't had any swim yet.'

So I took Lizzie by the hand, and we left the olive grove.

I phoned James again that evening, but I only got the answering machine. Maybe it was just as well. Phoning him twice in one day would make him think there was something very strange going on. Still, I was seriously disappointed when I heard the recorded message. My own voice once again telling me I wasn't home. I badly wanted to talk to James, but had to settle for leaving a message. It was brief.

'We'll be back as soon as we can get a flight. We're missing you. We miss you very much.'

All I had to do was see Ross one more time, and then I'd be ready to go home.

Chapter Twenty-Seven

Next evening, Lizzie and I presented ourselves at Ross's house at seven, as we had arranged.

I had done my best to dress up for the occasion, but this hadn't been easy. Since I'd been in Greece, my habits had become even more slovenly than usual. None of my clothes could actually be called clean, so I had to settle for a skirt and top that could, at a push, have been called cleanish. I had showered and washed my hair, and splashed on some perfume, and the underclothes I had chosen were a particularly subtle shade of grey.

Ross greeted me with a good-friends kind of hug that I hoped wouldn't be misinterpreted by my perceptive daughter for what it really was. Then he turned to her.

'Hey it's the birthday girl. You must be at least ten by now.'

Lizzie giggled. 'No, silly. I'm five. I was a big four and now I'm five. And it's not my birthday any more. It was yesterday.'

Ross put on a chastened look. 'I am silly, aren't I? Anyway, did you have a nice birthday yesterday?'

Lizzie launched into one of her headlong speeches. 'Yeah. It was cool. I had sweets for breakfast. And Mummy gave me two dolls and a house. And Sninky was allowed to have his breakfast inside. But he doesn't understand about birthdays. And then we went to a beach place. It was very hot. And Mummy was crying an awful lot. And we had pizza for dinner and I didn't have to have any vegetables 'cause it was my birthday.'

She rambled on, wandering onto the patio as she spoke. Ross took me gently by the arm. I couldn't avoid his eyes.

'Well?' One word. A million questions. I knew he wanted me to tell him why I had been crying, but how could I? I wouldn't know where to start. Or where to finish.

His blue eyes were kind. I gently removed his hand and stepped towards the patio.

'It was nothing. Really. It was just the heat. Can we eat? I'm starving.'

He shrugged, and followed me outside. It was a funny kind of an evening. This time, I actually tasted the food. Chicken stir-fry – and very nice it was too.

We finished our meal, and the children skipped off to the television, just as usual. Ross refilled our wine glasses, and we sat back in one of our familiar, comfortable silences. After a while he launched into his own unique rendition of 'Tunnel of Love'. (Complete with air guitar solo that was sad beyond words.)

I smiled and leaned my head on his shoulder. He stopped singing and stroked my hair. He spoke softly. 'Would you like to tell me why you were crying?'

I shook my head. Rather too vehemently perhaps. 'Honestly. It was nothing.'

He turned towards me. 'Come on, Claire. You might be a bit eccentric on occasion, but I'd have thought that even you wouldn't sit crying huge rivers of tears onto hot Greek sand without a pretty good reason.'

I raised my palms as if in defeat. 'OK, OK. I was crying. I was reliving some terrible memories. I had a bad time the last time I was in San Stefanos. That's all.'

He leaned his face towards mine, examining it closely in the fading light.

'Please, Claire. Don't bottle it up. Tell me. Tell me why you're so sad. Let me be your friend.'

As he spoke, he took one of my hands in his. I knew I needed to tell my awful story. And I knew Ross was the person I wanted to tell it to. I wanted him to be my friend.

The words began to tumble out. 'I was only nineteen. I was very young. And foolish. I came to Greece with two other girls, Grace and Jessie. We stayed in San Stefanos. We had such fun at first. We laughed so much. We drank as if drink was going out of fashion. I was really happy. And then . . .'

I stopped. I'd never told anyone this before. My parents never knew. James had no idea. Why was I telling Ross? I looked into his blue eyes. He held my hand tighter. I knew he'd understand. And I had to get the words out. So I continued.

'I met this guy. Kevin. He was American. I thought he was like a film star. He was the best-looking guy I'd ever seen. And when he picked me over Grace and Jessie, it sort of went to my head. I wanted to be the best for once. They were always so cool and sophisticated, and I was just the quiet one in the corner. I couldn't believe he liked me the most. So I went out with him. He took me out to dinner. I got drunk.'

I was on a roll by now. I didn't hold back, as I described every pathetic detail of our fumblings on the beach. Ross's face was serious, almost stern, but he said nothing.

'And then I tried to forget all about it. Put it down to experience, you know? But I couldn't in the end. Not when I discovered that I was pregnant. I only knew him for a few hours, and I managed to get pregnant. How could I have been so bloody stupid? He never knew. I bet he never once thought of me again, and yet I was going to have his baby. And I didn't know what to do. Oh, Ross, I didn't know what to do.'

Ross leaned towards me, and wrapped his arms around me. I cried again. More hot, wet tears. All over his clean white t-shirt. Eventually, my wails turned to little hiccupy sobs, and I began to feel a little calmer. He moved away slightly, and looked me in the eye.

'And the baby?'

As if he had pressed a switch, the torrent of tears started again. I struggled to get the words out. 'It's been sixteen years. You have to understand. I hated it. I never wanted it. I never loved it at all. Not even for a second. Mothers are supposed to love their babies, but I couldn't. I . . . I . . .'

All the old feelings of guilt and self-hatred came rushing back to me, and I couldn't continue. Ross hugged me again. He stroked my hair, and muttered all the soothing words that I never allowed my mother to speak.

'Shhh. It's OK. Don't talk any more. It's all right now. Shhh.'

He rocked me until my sobs had ceased once again. I rested in his arms, and felt strangely peaceful. I wondered if Grace – wherever she was – felt the burden of knowledge lift slightly.

After a while, I felt strong enough to ease myself from Ross's arms. I supposed my face was all red and blotchy. I never could cry prettily. I went into the bathroom, where a glance in the mirror confirmed my fears. I splashed my face with cold water, which didn't help at all, and I returned to Ross. I didn't want to talk about the past any more.

'Actually, Lizzie and I are going home in a few days. We . . .'

Ross interrupted. He spoke hesitantly, without his usual confidence. 'I was wondering. You know. If . . . if I decided to come back here, do you think you might come back with me? Do you think you could live here? You know, with me?'

I didn't know what to say. I had always thought that we both saw our relationship in the same light. I thought it was an interlude, a holiday romance. It was fun while it lasted, and would provide a nice bundle of happy memories that we could take out and leaf through at times in our lives when things were less rosy. I had never really thought of us having a life together – of more than a few sun-filled weeks.

It was almost like when I watched *ER*. I never seriously dreamed of walking off into the sunset with Carter. It was just a dream. An escape. Not real life at all.

And yet, all of a sudden, it seemed very tempting, the idea of spending more time with Ross. Very tempting indeed. He was a good, kind man. He was witty and fun, and his eyes were still that incredible shade of pale blue that I had trouble resisting. Lizzie was already fond of him. And he seemed to be fond of her. We could have a very nice life together, in his perfect stone cottage. I'd never again have to look at my apple-white walls or my limed oak kitchen. We could keep chickens and ducks. We could live the innocent dreams I had dreamed when I was a teenager. We could be free.

But then, into my dreams of sun and simplicity came James's face, and I knew I wanted to see him again. He was Lizzie's dad, my husband, my first love.

James loved me, even though he knew me. The real me. Ross only knew the pretend me – the happy, laid-back me, who was mostly just a sham.

Ross was waiting for my answer. I twirled a lock of my hair around my finger.

He spoke gently. 'I'll take that as a "no" then, shall I?'

'No. I mean, I don't know. I don't know what to say.'

I twirled my hair so furiously that the tip of my finger began to turn an interesting shade of purply blue. He took my hand, and gently unwound the red strands of hair from my finger, exposing a narrow band of white. He ran one finger gently down my cheek.

'I do love you, Claire, you know. I love every single thing about you.'

'Ross, I . . .'

Suddenly I realised that I loved him too. I loved him very much.

But I couldn't say the words.

I looked into his eyes. I saw my own reflection. Twice. It was as if there were two miniatures of me embedded inside his brain.

Poor man. No wonder he looked so worried.

I took his hands in mine. His strong, warm hands that, given the opportunity, could be incredibly inventive.

'I'm sorry, Ross. I have to go back to James. We have to think of Lizzie. I have to see if we can make things work between us. I owe it to all of us.'

Yuck. I was speaking such garbage. It was as if I was reading from a very poor entry into a radio-play competition. But, I suppose, like radio-play competition entries, there was some truth buried beneath the clichés and the trite words.

I tried to smile. 'Whatever happens, I have to go home. Even if . . . even if it's only to say goodbye to James, and to pack up my things. I have to go back to see. Can you understand that?'

He nodded, but he didn't look convinced. 'I'm afraid, Claire. I'm afraid you'll go back home, and settle down with James. You'll slip back into your old life. You'll forget what we had here.'

I shook my head, almost in anger. 'No, Ross, I'll never forget what we had here. Never.'

He gave a small smile that didn't quite reach his eyes. 'You do what you have to do. I have to spend some time in England anyway. If things don't work out with James, I'll be here . . . or there . . . or somewhere. I'll wait for you.'

As he spoke the last words, he leaned across and held me tightly, almost hurting me with his strong grip. I clung equally hard to the firm cotton of his t-shirt. I felt a sudden sick feeling in my stomach. Why, I wondered, did life have to be so complicated?

Why couldn't it have been Ross who had sailed onto that beach in San Stefanos all those years ago? Why couldn't I have met him then, when I was free? Why did it have to be Kevin? Why hadn't Kevin gone to

France on his holidays that summer? Why hadn't he stayed at home with his cookie-baking mom, having barbecues and garage sales and pool parties? Why hadn't he got some cheerleader pregnant at the age of seventeen, and lived with her in teeth-grinding boredom and frustration? Why had he jumped off that stupid boat and into my stupid, stupid arms?

Ross held me for the longest time. I felt like one side of a strip of Velcro. Peeling us apart was going to be painful.

Eventually, it began to get chilly. I shivered slightly. He immediately let me go, and I shivered again. He took me by the hand and led me inside. Alistair had gone to bed, and Lizzie was in her usual sleeping position, curled up in a huge leather armchair. Ross checked that Alistair was sleeping soundly, and returned to me with a look that could not be misread.

So much for the virtuous wife returning to her husband! Then I thought of sheep, and lambs, and being hung. There would be time enough for guilt in the coming weeks and months.

I took Ross's outstretched hand and led the way to his bedroom.

We occupied the next thirty or so minutes, just as we usually spent the time in his bedroom.

I'm happy to report that his hands were wasted on making chicken stir-fry. And that my imagination wasn't confined to writing soppy love poems on the backs of envelopes.

Some time later, Ross, as usual, carried Lizzie home and laid her in her bed. Then he and I stood in the courtyard for our goodbye.

He scrabbled in his pocket for a piece of paper and a pencil. 'This is my e-mail address. Please don't just vanish from my life. Let me know if you think there's a hope for us. Or if there's not.'

I took the piece of paper from him. I hadn't the heart to tell him that I hadn't the first notion of how to send an e-mail. I supposed I'd figure it out somehow.

He kissed me gently on the cheek. A funny, chaste little kiss. Then he stepped away from me and went through the narrow gate. He turned at the last second and we each gave a small wave.

I wanted to run after him, and fling myself into his comforting arms.

But of course I didn't.

I stood outside until the hummed 'Hungry Heart' could no longer be heard.

I thought of Kevin, and how he had walked away from me after ruining my life. Now I was letting Ross walk away. Had I ruined his life?

Had I ruined James's life?

Was life just one big circle of everyone ruining everyone else's lives?

Was every life ruined in some way?

I thought about writing a poem, but I resisted the urge. Instead I went in and ate half a tub of chocolate ice cream. After that, I slid into bed beside my sleeping daughter, and wondered how on earth I would rebuild my ruined life.

Two days later, we were ready to go.

Packing hadn't taken us long, and cleaning up the small room hadn't exactly been an arduous task. I had been worried about Lizzie's pet, Sninky, because of course we couldn't bring him with us.

In the end, she solved the problem herself. She was adamant that she wouldn't leave for the ferry without saying goodbye to her old friend, Grandad, so we waited for him to pass by on his morning stroll. At last, he arrived, and Lizzie ran to him. He fished around in his bag, as he always did, pretending he had nothing for her. He eventually produced a small red lollipop, and she gave him a hug. Then she pointed to our bags, which were packed and ready in the courtyard. She held up her cat and Grandad under-stood at once. He smiled and said something, but of course it was all Greek to me. Then he rearranged his belongings, and slipped the small animal into his bag. Sninky wriggled a bit, then popped his little black nose out. Lizzie kissed him once, and warned him to be good. Then she hugged Grandad one more time. He solemnly shook my hand, and we spoke our goodbyes in our own languages.

In the time we had known each other, we had never communicated in words, but I felt as if this kind old man had somehow been looking out for us. I was sad to think that I'd never see him again. Sometime, perhaps soon, he'd die, and I wouldn't even know.

Lizzie stood in the shady street, holding my hand, calling her goodbyes, as we watched him trudge up the hill. Children seem to lack the sense of nostalgia that besets many adults, especially me, so as soon as Grandad was out of sight, she was ready to move on. No foolish brooding for her.

'Come on, Mummy. We've got to get home. Daddy will be waiting.'

Chapter Twenty-Eight

I was incredibly nervous as our plane approached Cork airport. I had been jumpy since we boarded, making the passengers around me eye me warily. The closer we got to home, the jumpier I became. In the end, one poor timid-looking lady sat with her hand poised over the button for calling the flight attendant, ready to summon help if I finally flipped and started to throw soggy bread rolls and plastic knives and forks around the place. I wondered what she'd do if I pulled the life jacket from under my seat and put it on. If I inflated it, and blew into the attached whistle, would the poor lady ever recover? If she did, she'd have a great story to tell at parties, and maybe the trauma would turn out to have been worth it.

(Still, nervousness was an improvement on my previous form. When Grace and I returned from Greece in 1986, I cried all the way. And we travelled by train and boat. It took five days. That was a lot of tears. Even for me.)

I stroked Lizzie's hair and told myself that this nervousness was utter foolishness. After all, I'd gone back and faced down my demons. I was supposed to be a new, confident person. And anyway, it was my husband of five years I was going to meet, not a total stranger.

I wasn't really convincing myself though. I had no idea how James was feeling. Would he welcome me back with open arms? Did I want him to welcome me back with open arms? Or should I just stay on the plane and hope it would eventually fly me back to Greece?

I could somehow send a message to Ross. I could sneak into the little stone cottage, and wait for him in the fragrant dusk. In many ways, this would be simpler.

I had left a message on the answering machine asking James to meet us, but didn't know if he had got it. Even if he had picked up the message, I had no idea whether he was going to be there. Maybe he'd got a crazy notion himself and gone off to climb the Himalayas and find himself. Maybe he'd gone on a round-the-world rafting trip, just to get away from me.

I shouldn't have worried. He was there all right. Good reliable James, waiting in the meeting area, hands jammed into the pockets of his denims, comfortingly the same. Scarily handsome. How had I managed to forget that?

How I wish this could have been the happy ending, with the three of us skipping off into the sunset, arm in arm. Perhaps that was a bit optimistic, considering the events of the past months, but I felt so good about myself, I was sure we could be happy. I was sure that I could forget all about Ross and be truly, uncomplicatedly happy for the first time in many, many years.

Lizzie threw herself into James's arms, and, as he swung her around, I thought I could see the beginnings of tears in his eyes, giving me more pangs of guilt at our long absence. Reluctantly he set her down (though she still clung to his leg), and he turned towards me. I went to hug him, and he briefly returned the hug, but I found myself kissing his half-turned-away cheek. He smelled just the same as before. He asked how I was, but I noticed, with sadness and fear, that he didn't meet my eyes. He busied himself with our bags, and led us to the car.

Lizzie distracted us on the short journey from the airport, as she prattled on about Greece, and asked question after question, never waiting for answers.

'Did you miss us, Daddy?'

'Did you get my letter with the picture I did of Sninky?'

'I gave Sninky to Grandad.'

'Can we go to Greece again?'

'Will you come with us next time?'

'Why didn't Granny come to meet us?'

I watched the city unfolding beneath us as we travelled down the airport hill. This scene always reminds me of my childhood, when on the way back from Sunday trips to Kinsale or Oysterhaven, I had to beat Mum and Dad by shouting, 'I see the city, the first,' before they did. (I suppose this game would have been more fun if I'd had a car full of siblings to compete with, instead of just my indulgent parents who always let me win.)

As we drove into the city, I sat back and surveyed the familiar streets, so grey and drab after the glowing brightness of Mykonos. I had the strange sensation I always feel when returning home after a long absence. I felt I had been gone so long that everything should be different, but it seemed that life had gone on without me, and nothing had changed just because I wasn't there.

We pulled into our driveway, back to suburbia again. James had tended the garden while I was away. The grass was freshly cut, the edges trimmed, and the flowerbeds almost weed-free. The pots on the doorstep had always been my domain, and these sported the sad remains of the tulips that had been blooming when I left. A few ants crawled over the dried brown stems.

James carried my rucksack out of the car and to the doorstep. I had no keys with me, so he had to open the front door, chivalrously standing back to allow me to enter first. I hesitated. I had the bizarre notion that James should carry me over the threshold. Probably not appropriate.

I stepped into the old, familiar hall. How many times had I mopped the wooden floor and wiped dirty fingermarks from the glass door? (About half as many times as I should have.) How many times had I sulkily polished the brass light switches, wishing I was elsewhere?

I went into the kitchen, and was pleased to find that it was clean and tidy. But why wouldn't it be? In the mediocre battle for housekeeper of the year, James would always win with his dogged, neat ways, over my slapdash make-do efforts.

I sat on a high stool and leaned on the clean, strangely uncluttered worktop. I suddenly felt very tired. I was glad to be back, but I was wary of James. He was an honest man, far too honest to be able to hide his true feelings. I realised that I was very much afraid of his true feelings. I didn't have the energy for a row but I wouldn't have minded some undemanding small talk. Then later, maybe after a bottle of warm, red wine, we could get to the serious stuff. And later again, when Lizzie was asleep, we could have the proper reunion in bed.

Lizzie ran off to see her bedroom and her toys and her hamster, and James and I were alone for the first time in months. I was afraid to speak, afraid to ruin everything, afraid that everything was ruined no matter what I said or did.

James spoke first. 'I'm sorry, Claire. I've moved some of my things.'

I was relieved at this seemingly mundane comment, and rushed to answer him. 'Don't be crazy. I wasn't here.

How could I expect you to keep the place just as it was? We can rearrange them later. A change would be . . .'

I trailed off as I looked up and saw his stricken face.

'I mean, I've moved them out.'

I still wasn't quite sure what he was saying. 'What do you mean, you've moved them out?'

'I mean, I've moved my belongings from this house. I'm not staying. We can't just go on as if nothing has changed. You left me. You took Lizzie. You've been half-crazy since you won that stupid lottery prize. How can you expect me to pick up the pieces and go back to where we were? How can you expect me to act as if nothing has happened, just because you've decided to come swanning back into my life? How long have I got? When will you get another crazy notion, and skip off again? What kind of a fool do you take me for?'

He spoke quietly, but I could see that he was angry. He had been angry when I left, and he was still angry now, months later. The difference was that now I could see why. I was no longer so wrapped up in myself, and I could see for the first time how unreasonable, how difficult, I had been. James was a patient man, but I had driven him to his limit and beyond. I didn't deserve him.

(And, of course, he didn't know about Ross. I tried not to imagine how cross he'd be if he knew that as well as foolish and unreasonable, I'd been unfaithful too. Repeatedly and unashamedly and gloriously unfaithful, for weeks on end.)

I cried and tried to explain why I had left. I had been sick. I couldn't help myself. I was different now. Things would be better now. But all my explanations sounded contrived. They were true but they had no ring of truth. It was as if I had lifted them from the pages of some cheap novel. I hate cheap novels.

James had never been good at arguing. He didn't like tears and passion, and he usually sat back until I had finished, but this time he didn't want to hear me. He quietly picked up his keys and went towards the door. He delivered the final blow.

'I've moved in with Mum. She hasn't been well. She needs me. You don't appear to need me at all. I'll drop by tomorrow to see Lizzie, and to make some arrangements.'

So she'd won at last. I knew it would be foolish to start on about Maisie, and I was too weary to begin to try. And it wasn't her fault anyway.

I heard James talking to Lizzie in the hall, and then the front door slammed.

Lizzie ran in with her hamster in his cage in one hand and a furry dinosaur in the other.

'I'm hungry, Mummy. What's for tea?'

How was I supposed to know? I felt like an alien in this small, neat kitchen. I hardly knew where to look for food. Lizzie took the initiative. She put her hamster in the corner of the room, and went to the fridge. James, considerate man that he was, had filled it up with essential foodstuffs, more than enough to do us for the evening. Lizzie pulled a packet from the fridge with a little cry of delight.

'Look, Mummy. Tankly telly. It's soooo long since I had tankly telly. Can we have it now?'

I smiled as I took the packet of tagliatelle from her, and filled the kettle. Then I warmed a jar of tomato sauce in the microwave. Seven minutes later, tea was ready.

Lizzie set the table, smiling over the plastic Barney plate she hadn't seen for such a long time.

'You have Teletubbies, Mum. And you can have the Barbie cup.'

I smiled at her. She had slipped so easily back into her old world of trademarks and merchandising. She sat naturally back in her old place beside the window, and I took my old position opposite her.

Just the two of us.

While she ate, I rooted in my handbag for Ross's e-mail address. I unfolded the scrap of paper carefully. It was very neatly written, considering he'd been leaning on a bumpy wall when he written it.

Ross and Greece and that bumpy wall suddenly seemed very far away.

On the paper was the address, and under it Ross had written one small 'x' and a single word. 'Please'.

Chapter Twenty-Nine

The next few weeks were very strange. I woke up each morning, rather surprised that I had somehow got through another night and day. I was surviving. I wasn't falling apart after all. I was relieved that the new confident me wasn't a total sham.

James was relieved too. He was glad that I wasn't making a fuss, and he began to relax a little. No doubt, Maisie was giving him terrible grief with her attention-seeking shenanigans, but he was wise enough not to share this with me. His life would be doubly ruined if he stayed with her, but for the moment I couldn't deal with that. I needed to get myself sorted out before I tackled her – the great misguided Irish mammy.

He called to see Lizzie most days. Sometimes he took her out, but quite often he stayed in the house and played with her there. I suppose there's only so many times you can go to the pictures, or to McDonald's. And people start to talk about you if you show up too often at the bowling alley. And let's face it, it's embarrassing when the cashier at Fota Island is on first-name terms with you.

James's coldness towards me was lessening, but it wasn't exactly turning to warmth. He treated me with respect, like a casual acquaintance. He was willing to pass the time of day with me, but I felt as if he didn't really care whether or not he ever saw me again. This hurt me deeply, but I was so glad to be somewhat on an even keel that I made no fuss. I tried to enjoy his visits, and began to think that perhaps, in time, if he could believe that the crazy me was gone forever, he would mellow and would be able to see a way forward.

Every now and then, I took out Ross's e-mail address and looked at it. Could I go to Greece and live happily ever after with Ross? What if he wanted me to be lady of his manor in England? Did the answer to all my problems lie on that crumpled page?

Then I would put it away again. I knew I had to be sure about James before I had any more contact with Ross. I wasn't the sophisticated kind of person who could successfully juggle two relationships – one at a time was more than enough for me.

Lizzie and I had led a frugal existence in Greece, so there was still plenty of lottery money left. Sometimes I half-entertained notions of going away again, perhaps to America, with Lizzie. But then I decided that that would only prove to James that I really was a hopeless case. So I put the remaining money in the bank, vaguely figuring that James and I would spend it together, when he came back home.

Or, if I ended up going back to Greece, at least I wouldn't be arriving with my hands hanging.

I kept myself busy, afraid to allow too much space for brooding. In the mornings, Lizzie and I went for walks, or cleaned the house, which seemed so unnecessarily large after our little home in Greece.

I even sorted out all of our photographs, and displayed them in albums. I was proud that I managed to do so without shedding too many tears, just becoming a little misty-eyed when reminded of particularly happy occasions. I figured that was allowed.

Lizzie and I spent one happy afternoon sitting in the driveway, using blunt knives to prise weeds from between the paving stones. It's a bit sad that such a mundane task gave me a small measure of satisfaction. And even sadder that we made no visible impression at all on the weedy driveway.

One afternoon, I decided to clean out the hall cupboard – slightly overdue, as I couldn't recall ever having done so before. I hauled everything out and piled it in huge heaps in the hall. Very impressive. Then I decided to have a cup of coffee. Then I read the paper, did the crossword and wrote two poems. 'Ode to an odd glove', and 'How dust gets into corners that light can't reach'. Then it was time for tea. After tea, I tried again. Really. I lined up all the gloves and matched them. Five were like me – partnerless. These I threw into the bin, very pleased with myself. Unfortunately, they were no sooner in the bin than Lizzie appeared and announced that there were lots of gloves under her bed. She happily produced the matches for the gloves that were in the bin. Frugal person that I am, I decided to rescue the binned ones. Did you ever try to get something out of the bottom of a wheelie bin? Not easy, I promise. Eventually, I managed to upend the bin, but then the path outside the backdoor had to be hosed, as it was covered with a stream of black, bin-sludge. Then the odd gloves had to be washed, as they too were a bit sludgy, but I used too hot water, and they shrank, so they had to go back into the sludgy bin, along with their still-perfect partners.

By then, it was my bedtime, so the piles of rubbish that I'd dumped in the hall many hours earlier were shoved unceremoniously back where they came from. Only difference was that nothing seemed to fit as well as before, and I had to lean my full weight on the cupboard door to get it to close.

I threw myself in front of the telly with a beer and a huge box of Pringles, not quite sure why I suddenly felt so inadequate.

Lizzie slipped easily back into her old life, dragging me along in her wake. During this settling-back period, Jason's mum, Maureen, was particularly kind. She had every right to turn her back on me, but she didn't. I felt dreadfully guilty when I thought how I had rebuffed her friendly advances in the past. I had been positively rude to her on more than one occasion, and yet here she was introducing me to her friends and making sure I was included in anything that was going on.

A week after my return, she came to my house for coffee, and we chatted while Lizzie and Jason splashed in the paddling pool on the grass outside. Maureen told me about a book she'd just read, surprising me with her insight. I began to feel very bad indeed. Just because she usually spoke about humdrum, everyday stuff, I'd presumed that she was a dull, not-very-smart person. I had always thought that she had no interests beyond her son and her soap operas. Perhaps there was more to her than I realised. The barbs that I thought would have sailed unnoticed over her head might well have struck home. I tried, in my flustering way, to apologise.

'You know, Maureen, before I went to Greece, I was very mixed up'.

She sipped her coffee and looked at me with clear, honest eyes.

'I had a lot on my mind,' I continued. 'I might not have been a very nice person.' Maureen didn't speak, but her look was not unkind.

'I think I was quite mean to you. I don't know why. You were always so kind to me, and I didn't know how to respond to that.'

Maureen nodded slowly. 'OK, Claire. I'll be honest too. There were times when you overstepped the mark a bit. But you always looked so sad. I knew you didn't mean it.'

This kind of cleansing chat didn't come easy to me, but I didn't want to leave it only half-sorted.

'That's not the point, Maureen. I shouldn't have been rude to you. It wasn't right.'

She surprised me again with her perception. 'It's fine, Claire, really. I always knew you weren't cross with me. You were cross with yourself. And I don't know what happened you in Greece, but that anger is gone. The hot sun must have made it evaporate or something. Or maybe it got drowned in ouzo.'

She smiled. 'You're actually quite nice now.'

I felt like crying. I wondered if I should hug her. I wondered if I should offer her a glass of wine so that we could toast our new friendship. I wondered if that would convince her I'd finally slipped off the rails, and make her leave me alone forever.

We sat in silence for a while, sipping our coffee and chewing on the crumbly home-made flapjacks that she had brought. I was still wondering whether a hug would be completely inappropriate, when Lizzie and Jason came tumbling in the back door with a contorted tale about a spider, a worm and a bucket of grassy water.

I chased them outside, and as I went out the door, Maureen said quietly, 'I'm glad you're back, Claire. I missed you.'

Of course, many of the other mothers on the circuit might not have been so understanding, and I'd offended them all at some stage. Maureen's friendship protected me like a magic cloak though, and I found that everyone seemed prepared to overlook the fact that a few short months earlier, I'd been the cranky wild-haired oddball they had crossed the street to avoid.

Soon I found myself fitting into a group of women who met one or two afternoons a week. Different houses were visited, and mothers indulged in coffee and biscuits while the children played in back gardens or playrooms. I found this routine restful and reassuring in some way, though I had always eschewed it before. I enjoyed the feeling of being part of a group, and these sociable gatherings, which I would once have avoided like the plague, became the highlight of my life.

I discovered that it was possible to talk about nappies and weaning and tying laces, without abandoning your brain forever. These women spoke happily of everyday domestic trials, and then switched with ease to discussions of politics and world peace. Some of the children were so challenging I felt that the mothers would make admirable representatives to the United Nations – so adept were they at mediating between screaming, flailing bundles of fiercely determined humanity.

I returned to my old card game too. Lily and the others welcomed me back with open arms. (My replacement must have been really pathetic. Or maybe she was too good, spoiling the game by winning all the time.) On my first Wednesday, I found myself hanging back with Lily after the others had donned their matching brown raincoats, and set off on their way home. As soon as she had closed the door behind them, Lily gave a mischievous laugh, and dived into her fridge, returning with bottles of strong fruit-flavoured alcohol – the kind that is usually marketed at spiky-haired, baggy-trousered ravers some thirty years younger than Lily. Having handed me a bottle, she sat on a beanbag opposite me, then raised her bottle and declared loudly, 'Let's drink to holidays in Greece – the new face lift.'

I politely raised my bottle in the air, and drank deeply, but couldn't hide my puzzlement. What kind of a toast was that?

She laughed. 'Do you not know what I mean?'

I shook my head.

She laughed again. 'Do you never look in the mirror, child? You look ten years younger than when you left.'

I smiled, but I knew I was blushing.

Lily looked at me with her clear, calm gaze. 'Don't worry. I don't want to know who or what caused the change – I'm only commenting on it.'

All of a sudden, I felt I could confide in her. 'Lily, can I tell you something, just between ourselves?'

'Of course.'

I could see that she was delighted. She leaned forward, threatening to slide right off the beanbag into a pile of 'interpret your dreams' part works.

'Well, you see, something bad happened me before, the last time I was in Greece. You don't mind if I don't tell you about that, do you?'

She shook her head defiantly, spectacularly failing to hide her disappointment.

'Thanks. It's a bit sensitive, and anyway, it doesn't matter. I realise now that I can put it behind me. That's part of why I feel better.'

Lily nodded. She was edging ever closer, and I had a funny feeling that if my tale went on for too long, she'd end up sitting on my lap.

I continued. 'And also, I met someone in Greece. A man. We had a bit of a fling.'

Lily grinned. 'I thought so. I knew it had to be something like that. What was he like?'

I closed my eyes for a second. I could picture Ross clearly. Leaning back on his patio chair. Looking at me with that half-smile I so loved. Making sandcastles with Al and Lizzie. Reclining on his bed, watching me undress. I could see his hands, his hair, his teeth, his pale blue eyes.

I spoke softly. 'He was handsome. Very handsome. And kind. And gentle. And funny. And he could cook and he couldn't sing, and he made me feel so special, you know? And at first it was like a dream. I thought it was just a holiday fling. And then he asked me to come back to him, to come and live with him. And part of me really, really wants to go back. And I haven't said yes or no. And I don't know what to do. Lily, what will I do?'

306

By now, Lily was sitting on the floor at my feet, with her hands wrapped around her knees. She leaned across to the fireplace, and lit a long line of scented candles.

'I don't know about you,' she said sighing, 'but I need something to calm me down. This is all far too exciting. Run out to the fridge, there's a dear, and get us more drink.'

I obliged. As I passed back through the hall, I saw my reflection in the hall-stand mirror. She was right, I did look younger. My skin had an unusual glow, and my hair, though wild as usual, seemed to suit me for a change. (If Nicole Kidman looked in a mirror and saw me, she'd probably kill her hair stylist and book herself in for a face transplant, but my standards were lower and I was pleased with what I saw.) I handed Lily her drink, and sat down again. I began to peel the silvery label from my bottle, half-hoping that Lily would suddenly want to talk about the weather. No chance. She dived right back in at the deep end.

'And what about James? Where does he fit into all of this?'

I picked at the sticky residue from the label, and wondered how to answer.

Lily continued. 'Sometimes I get up to do my yoga at sunrise. I happened to notice some mornings that James's car isn't in its usual place in your driveway.'

I looked at her with doubt and amazement. She was gracious enough to look embarrassed.

'OK, I'm sorry. I don't actually do that much yoga. But I worry about you, so sometimes when I get up to go to the loo in the night, I peep out to see if he's home. He never is, is he?'

I didn't like the idea of being spied upon, but how could I be cross when she was being so honest?

'He's left me. He's angry, and he can't forgive me for leaving. He thinks I'm a bit unstable. I don't blame him really, but he's wrong. I'm fine now. Well, I'm all mixed up, I admit, but basically I'm fine. And I know now that I love him too. Lily, can you understand? For years, I didn't think I could love anyone. And now I think I love them both – James and Ross. But maybe it doesn't matter anyway. I'm afraid James is going to stay with his mother forever, and never come back to me.'

Lily nodded, and put on a wicked face. 'Ah, the dreaded mother-in-law.'

I smiled at her. 'She's not so bad really. She's just lonely. James and I always row about her, but we shouldn't. She's just a sad, lonely old woman. None of this is her fault.'

Lily was beginning to look impatient. Clearly she didn't want a lengthy discussion about Maisie. 'Let's get back to the guy in Greece. What's his name?'

I sighed. 'Ross. I don't know, Lily. He was lovely, but I think he might just have been a dream, you know. If things worked out with James, I think I could forget Ross . . .'

Lily fixed me with a strangely intense look, forcing me to finish my thought.

'. . . eventually.'

There was silence for a few moments, and then I continued. 'But I have a feeling that Ross and I could be happy too. Oh, Lily. It's an awful mess. What will I do?'

Lily stood up.

'It's very late. You go home, and sleep well. I'll see you next week. I'll get more alcopops in, and we'll have a nice chat.'

I wasn't quite sure if that was a threat or a promise. I stood up and she walked me to the front door. She gave me a big hug. Her body was large and flabby against mine. She smelt just like that Indian shop that used to be in Market Arcade. I gently removed myself from the comforting folds of her arms, and walked the short distance home.

Chapter Thirty

The weeks slipped by, and soon it was September, time for Lizzie to start at the local primary school. The first morning, she was up bright and early, eager to get started. She looked so sweet and vulnerable in her school uniform of bottle-green gymslip and cream-coloured shirt. Her bright new schoolbag was ready, together with a whole set of books. She helped me pack her lunchbox with a small red apple and a mini-Crunchie as a treat for her first day. Then she paraded proudly around the kitchen, very pleased with her new, grown-up status.

I was pleased that she was so happy, but was struck by the contrast between this Lizzie and the one who had danced barefoot around Mykonos, dressed in faded cotton, tanned and carefree, with no worries, no obligations. Now that she was starting school, she was taking her first step on the treadmill of life. Of course, she would have holidays again, but from now on, she would always have the next year of school, or work, looming ahead of her whenever she took a break.

From now on, she would be bound by someone else's rules, not just mine and James's. Now her real freedom was coming to an end.

James called to pick us up, as, of course, he wanted to be part of this special day. Lizzie skipped out to the car, and was her usual lively self throughout the short journey. James parked the car a few streets away from the school, as we were a little too early, and we walked the rest of the way, each of us holding one of Lizzie's hands. I had the bizarre notion that I could somehow transmit a message of love through my daughter's thin arms, so that James could feel some charge or tremor that would make him realise how much I loved him. Luckily Lizzie was oblivious to this craziness as she skipped along between us.

We walked through the school gates, and Lizzie watched the bigger children in the yard, running and pushing, playing and shouting. Her step slowed a little, and I could feel her grip on my hand tightening as we approached her classroom.

The classroom was a scene of total chaos. Anxious children and even more anxious parents milled around. The teacher had set out boxes of Lego, and beads and straws on each table, but the children were reluctant to sit down. The wild ones wanted to run around demolishing the place, while the timid ones clung to their parents, sobbing with abandon. One serious, pale-faced little girl was systematically removing all of the books from the library shelves and stacking them in the corner of the room. Though it seemed that order could never be imposed on such a scene, eventually things began to calm down. Lizzie sat next to a little girl called Jennifer, and they began to play with a big box of modelling clay, rolling it and cutting it into shapes. James and I smiled at Jennifer's parents, all four of us a little smug that our children were so well-behaved. Most of the other children also settled down to work, though one child could not be consoled as he stood in a corner sobbing.

'This is only baby work,' he wailed. 'I want to do sums and reading.'

The teacher, Mrs Browne, who after only twenty minutes of term already deserved a medal for patience, took him aside, and spoke quietly to him. I don't know what she said, but it was very effective, as the little boy beamed and began to play with a box of Lego.

James and I stood apart, both of us watching Lizzie, ignoring each other.

Many stay-at-home-mothers rejoice when their child starts school, glad of the freedom it gives them. They revel in all the free time they have for visits to the hairdresser and the gym, and for trips to the shops. I could never be like that. I was pleased that Lizzie was happy, and developing normally, but I was terrified because her childhood was slipping by me so fast. I stood in the classroom, looking at her, and fervently wishing that she was a baby again, so I could relive all of the wonderful moments we had had together. I longed to grab her, take her home, and spend the morning making grey pastry, and watching *Barney* videos, cuddled together on the sofa.

Soon, parents began to leave, led by those who had to go to work, and who had something more fulfilling than the week's ironing to entice them away from the scene of their child's first step towards independence. James kissed Lizzie goodbye, and I quickly followed suit.

'Be a good girl. I love you,' I whispered, and then I left.

I peeped in the window as I passed and was guiltily rather disappointed to see that she was laughing heartily at something Jennifer had whispered to her. She whispered back, prompting more giggles, and then they settled back to their modelling, frowning in concentration as their pudgy fingers moulded the soft clay.

I walked back to the car with James. He had offered me a lift home, and though it was only a short walk, I had accepted, as I wanted the company. We chatted about Lizzie, both glad that she had separated from us so easily. We were pleased that despite the differences between her parents, she seemed to be perfectly happy and well-adjusted.

James pulled up outside our house, not even driving into the driveway. I unbuckled my seatbelt but was reluctant to leave him. I longed to throw myself into his arms, and beg him to come back to me. I longed to stroke his hair, the way he used to like. I longed to push aside his shirt collar, and kiss the hollow of his neck. I didn't dare though. I was too afraid that I'd frighten him away forever.

We sat in silence for a few moments. I could see that he wanted to leave.

'Have you time for a cup of coffee?' I asked.

He replied too quickly. 'Sorry. I'm late already. I have to go.'

I wasn't surprised. 'Even a very quick one? The kettle is still warm.'

He shook his head. I felt like grovelling. James is a kind man, he'd have come in if I'd begged. I decided against it though. I got out of the car and closed the door behind me. James put down the electric window on my side. He reached out and touched my arm lightly. He gave me a warm smile.

'Don't worry, Claire, She'll be fine. You'll see.'

Typical, misguided, stupid, stupid man. Of course she'd be fine. I knew she'd be fine. That was never in doubt. It was me I was worried about. Would I be fine without her? I felt like crying.

James looked at his watch. 'I really have to go, Claire. See you tomorrow. I'll call at ten to nine.'

'OK, see you then.'

He smiled again. 'Trust me, Claire. She'll be fine.'

He flicked up the window, and drove off quickly.

A sudden fit of temper made me stamp my foot on the hard pavement. It didn't help at all.

Foolishly, I had made no plans for the morning. I knew that Lily would be gone to work in the healthfood shop, and wouldn't be home until afternoon.

I'd have liked to have spent some time with Maureen, but she wasn't available. Jason had started school too, but he was going to the all-Irish school, and Maureen had been invited to a coffee morning for the parents of junior infants. The few other women I knew well enough to invite over were all otherwise occupied, so I was condemned to an entire morning stretching ahead of me, with nothing to do.

I went into the garage and pulled my bike out from underneath the lawnmower. My poor bike. My trusty, faithful steed. Lizzie no longer liked to be carried on the back carrier, so it was months since I'd been for a cycle. I wheeled it outside, into the unforgiving sunshine. It was a sorry sight. Dusty and cobwebbed, and more chipped than I remembered. I had always thought of my bike as being pink, but the sad truth was that it was now black again, with occasional speckles of pink, as if a small child had half-heartedly flicked a pink-soaked paintbrush in its direction. I thought of the lottery money, sitting in the local bank. I could easily liberate some of it and buy myself a shiny new mountain bike with twenty gears and thick, ridged tyres. But that would have been a betrayal.

I grabbed a damp cloth, and wiped off the worst of the dust and cobwebs from my old steel friend, then I jumped aboard, and headed for the hills.

The old rush of the wind in my hair and the warm air in my face was better than any drug. I cycled for miles, almost laughing with the exhilaration and the freedom. I stood on the pedals, straining as I struggled up hills, and then whizzed down again, my skirt billowing behind me, like a crazy, flower-patterned sail. Eventually I stopped on the side of a gentle hill. I sat on a grassy verge, and breathed deeply. Shiny, fat blackberries shone healthily from the hedgerow. Birds chirped all around me.

I turned my face to the sun, closed my eyes, and daydreamed of a dark-haired lover. It was a nice dream. Suddenly I snapped my eyes open again. Oh dear. I wasn't sure if my dream-man was James or Ross.

Ross. I felt a sudden urge to phone him. To hear his voice.

No chance though. What good was an e-mail address? Was I supposed to head into the nearest Internet café and say to the pale, geeky assistant, 'Please send this message of love to the rich bloke I met on my holidays'? Was I supposed to wait for hours amongst the hunched, sweaty clientèle in hope of a response?

Anyway, I was being unusually foolish. Ross was probably already courting some horse-faced heiress, with big thighs and a booming laugh and a wardrobe full of tweed and cashmere. He'd probably forgotten me already.

I felt suddenly deflated. I climbed aboard my trusty steed and set off for home. I propped my bike against the side-wall of the house. Maybe later, if I could work up sufficient enthusiasm, I'd get some pink paint and try to restore it to its former, rose-coloured glory.

I let myself into my lonely house, closed the door behind me, and leaned against it. How would I pass the next two hours? I had absolutely nothing to do.

Well, actually I had lots to do. The refrigerator needed to be emptied and cleaned out, the oven needed a good scrub, and I had enough ironing stacked up to keep me going for hours. There was always the hall cupboard to sort out. I could have read one of the many unread books that were on the locker next to my bed. I could have taken a brisk walk. I could have watched any one of three chat shows on television. I could have walked to the shopping centre and bought the few groceries I needed for the coming week. All the mundane jobs that awaited me would have filled my morning several times over, but that wasn't the point. The truth was there was nothing I really wanted to do. I sat on the couch in the living-room, staring into space, threatening to fall into a serious bout of self-pity.

Luckily I was able to pull myself back from the brink, and I jumped up, determined to be positive. I whizzed around the house, half-did all my jobs, and then indulged in a cup of coffee, a whole Mars bar, and fifteen minutes of daytime television. I wrote a poem. It took me twenty-five minutes, and it was only four lines long. I called it 'The Passage of Time'. I got myself another cup of strong black coffee, and started the crossword. I thought for the first time that mornings to myself might not be so bad after all. Then it was time to walk to the school to collect Lizzie.

I arrived ten minutes too early, but the schoolyard was already full of parents, keen to reclaim their babies, to hear the story of their first day. Soon, the double doors opened, and an orderly line of children edged its way into the schoolyard. The anxious little faces scanned the waiting crowd, searching for familiar people, then as each spotted their parent, recognition dawned and wide smiles appeared. For one or two, the joy of recognition prompted great tears of relief. Lizzie ran to me, and hugged me, bursting with news.

'One boy wet his knickers. He had to change into a horrible brown trousers. I ate all of my break. I played outside. We learned a poem about a chicken. Jennifer has a baby brother. He got sick on her mummy's new dress last night. And her mummy said a rude word, and then her daddy got cross and they had a big fight. And then her mummy said sorry, and they were kissing, and Jennifer had to go to bed, but it wasn't even bedtime, and she hadn't been bold or anything, so that wasn't fair, was it? And Billy's dad smokes cigarettes in the garden when his mum isn't there, and his mum thinks that he doesn't smoke at all and . . .'

Lizzie's story rushed on, as she blithely revealed the private lives of every family in the parish. I squeezed her hand tightly and tried not to imagine what secrets of mine she had revealed in exchange for these interesting stories.

We arrived home, and I gave her some lunch. She yawned as I put the plate in front of her, then smiled as she saw her favourite food – fish fingers and baked beans. I sat at the other side of the table and watched her as she ate. She had a set ritual for eating this meal – first she ate the beans, displaying perfect manners as she carefully used her knife and fork to scoop up every last one. Then she laboriously cut up her first fish finger, and ate it with her fork. Finally, as if tired of such good behaviour, she picked up her last fish finger, carefully bit off the breadcrumb coating, and stuffed the naked greyish-white fish into her mouth, pushing it in with her fingers.

She was silent, engrossed in her task, and she was seemingly unaware of the way I was watching her. I watched her small fingers clutching the fork, and her tiny baby teeth biting into the food. I watched as some of her hair strayed into her mouth and she patiently removed it before shoving another forkful of food in in its place.

I could think of nothing to say to her. I just gazed, overcome with love. I was filled with a sudden fear of a future in which my daughter would no longer need me.

Lizzie stopped eating and looked up. 'Mummy, will you help me with my homework? I have to find pictures of red things.'

Ah, homework. I sighed happily. It looked as if I'd be needed for a few more years yet.

Chapter Thirty-One

Lizzie's first term at school dragged by. She had gone to playschool only three mornings a week, and that had been just enough for me to do boring jobs like going to the supermarket, or to the dentist. Now that she was gone five mornings a week, I missed her terribly.

One night, when I was putting her to bed, she complained of a sore throat. I didn't sleep well that night, and I found myself hoping that she would be too sick to go to school the following morning. I didn't want her to be seriously ill, of course. I just wanted her to be slightly off-colour, so she could spend the day on the couch, wrapped in a soft blanket. I could make her hot drinks and read to her. We could colour in pictures in her colouring books, and I could pretend that her colouring was better than mine. I could make her eggy bread and chocolate crispie cakes. She could snooze in my arms, and I could stroke her hair and kiss her nose.

Of course, when morning came, she bounded into my room with her usual energy.

'Get up, Mummy! Get up! It's time to get up for school. We're doing painting today. Jennifer and I are going to paint a farm with pigs and chickens and a big black horse.'

I sighed, and hauled myself from the bed, my happy dreams evaporated.

I missed James terribly too. He still visited almost every day, and I fantasised about him coming one day with all of his bags, back to stay, rushing into my welcoming arms. This, of course, never happened. He stuck firmly to his air of kind coolness towards me.

He was generous in his financial support. He never asked about the remains of the lottery money, which languished in my deposit account. Of course, there was no reason why I couldn't get work, but James never pressurised me in this direction. Our joint bank account operated as before, and I was free to spend whatever money I needed. Our only transport was the car, and James needed this for work, but each weekend he offered it to me. I never accepted. I had become used to a simpler life while I was away, and no longer felt the need to go dashing around the countryside, trying to make leisure time more meaningful. Our house was well located. I could walk to Lizzie's school, and to the shops. If I was on my own, I could cycle pretty much anywhere I needed to go. On the rare occasion when I needed to go further afield, there was a good bus service, or, as a real luxury, sometimes I called a taxi.

At that time, I was probably having a far better life than James. While he didn't complain, I knew that he was finding it hard to cope with Maisie's fussing. I was sure she must be glad to have her willing slave back, and she would be determined not to let him escape a second time. In my dreams of James returning to me, Maisie never featured, but in the cold light of day I had to accept that he wouldn't leave her. He was stuck with her, and since we both knew that I couldn't live with her, there was little point in our pursuing any kind of a reunion.

I thought a lot about it, but I could never see how the Maisie issue could resolve itself. In my darkest moments, I used to finish her off with a quiet death in her sleep, but I figured that she wouldn't even oblige me by dying. She'd live forever, just to spite me.

I felt bad for harbouring such evil thoughts, of course, but managed to live with it. After all, I'd had years of practice.

I suppose it was a sign of the times that Lizzie didn't feel strange about not living in the same house as her dad. Her schoolbooks allowed for all types of family set-ups, so very different from my old texts. In mine, all families had a mum at home, working in the kitchen, wearing a frilly apron and a slightly flustered expression. The dad, who invariably wore dark-rimmed glasses, always seemed to be going off to work in his suit and tie, carrying a shiny new brown leather briefcase. There were always two perfect children, a boy and a girl, carefully filling stereotyped sex roles. Though Lizzie was a child who so loved to ask questions, for some reason she never once asked why James no longer lived with us. She looked forward to his visits, loved his company, but when he left, she seemed quite unfazed by his departure – confident, I suppose, that he'd show up again the next day.

I wondered over and over how such a dysfunctional mother had produced such a well-adjusted child. Maybe it was just luck.

And so, life trundled along. It wasn't such a bad life really. Though I missed James so much, and found it hard to see him each day without the old closeness we had once shared, I still looked forward to his visits. I realised he wasn't being deliberately unkind when he kept his distance. I think he was trying both to protect himself from further hurt, and at the same time, to avoid giving me false hope. Maybe I felt so calm, because, deep down, I never gave up hope. I was sure that if I stayed calm, and didn't put pressure on him, he would see how I had changed, and be prepared to try again.

And all the time, Ross's e-mail address lay gathering dust and rubbish at the bottom of my hessian bag. While I still had hope that things would work out with James, what could I say to Ross?

'I'm not sure if I love you or not. I just have to wait and see if my husband loves me at all. I'll let you know as soon as I can. In the meantime, please keep away from horse-faced heiresses in Range Rovers.'

Hardly.

323

I did my best to keep myself busy. I did lots of house-work. It never made any difference though. The house always looked as if it had been turned over by a gang of very messy burglars. I fear that in my case the housework gene was recessive. In October, the fridge broke down, and the prospect of a visit by the repair-man prompted my usual panic. I knew he'd move the fridge only to be faced with a greasy accumulation of crumbs and tissues and chop bones and dried-up peas. When the time came, it was worse than I had feared. The floor where the fridge had stood was mostly covered with a sticky grey mess, which might have been years-old orange juice, dotted with decaying flies.

I smiled bravely and pretended to be the babysitter.

When Lizzie came home from school each day, I wore her out with further activity as I tried to use up all of my pent-up energy. We painted, modelled, baked and sewed. I was spectacularly bad at all of these things but my sweet Lizzie either didn't notice or didn't care. Or maybe she was just humouring her mad mummy.

Christmas approached, but as it came closer, James carefully avoided any mention of it. Maisie the mad meddler had always spent Christmas in a hotel with two of her widowed cronies – reluctant, I suppose, to subject herself to my dodgy cooking. James and I had always spent Christmas together, in our own house. We had developed our own little traditions and practices, an amalgamation of things we each remembered from our childhood, with a few of our own ideas thrown in.

I always felt slightly sad when I thought of my own childhood Christmases. Mum and Dad always tried so hard to make things special for me, centring their activities around the little things they misguidedly thought would interest me. Unfortunately, despite their selfless efforts, once I'd passed the age of twelve, I found Christmas day to be tedious beyond belief, and I usually spent it glued to the television, watching *Chitty Chitty Bang Bang*, eating too many Cadbury's Roses, and wondering when I'd be considered old enough to have wine with my dinner.

The big day came closer and closer, but still James never once mentioned it. It was clear that we both would want to spend it with Lizzie. I began to picture a dreadful scenario – me and Lizzie together for the first part of the day, and then James taking her away, leaving me with my festive house, festive food, festive television programmes, and a broken heart. I could picture a weeping me sitting amid the discarded wrapping paper, wringing my hands and dreaming of happy past Christmases.

I suppose that scenario wouldn't have been much fun for James either. I knew he would want to witness Lizzie's joy in the morning, laughing as she dived onto her presents. He would hate to take her from her warm, cosy home to Maisie's dreary one. He wouldn't want to spend his Christmas night sitting on a straight-backed chair in Maisie's chilly parlour, warning Lizzie not to spill food on the ugly Axminster carpet, or to chip the china that Maisie's aunt had sent from America in 1922.

One cold Saturday, a few weeks before Christmas, James dropped Lizzie home after a trip to the cinema. He was in a good mood, and had agreed to stay for a sandwich and a cup of tea. I had a sort of speech prepared, about how difficult the separation would be for Lizzie on that special day, how we had to be civilised and amicable for her sake, how we had to put her first, and so on, and on.

The speech didn't come out though. Partly because I hadn't rehearsed it that well, and partly because it was a pack of lies. I knew well that Lizzie, in her charming easy way, would adjust quite happily to whatever James and I suggested. It was once more a case of me hiding behind her non-existent needs, pretending to think of her when I was really thinking of myself.

Instead of the half-prepared speech, I blurted out my request. 'Why don't you spend Christmas day here, with Lizzie and me?'

I was half-expecting him to have a hundred reasons not to accept. Instead, he gave me his old guileless grin. 'I'd love that. I'll come over first thing in the morning.'

I felt like kissing his handsome face. I was relieved it had been so easy.

'That's great, James, really great. It's fantastic. Super. Wonderful.'

I was so happy, I struggled to find another word. At last it came. Lizzie's new favourite expression for everything nice. 'It's brill.'

James made a face. 'No thanks. I don't think I'd fancy fish for Christmas dinner. Can't we have turkey?'

'No, I mean, brill – you know, brilliant.'

He laughed, and touched me lightly on the shoulder. 'Gotcha.'

I laughed too. He was always good at winding me up. Funny how I could miss even that.

For a moment, I thought of Kevin. The first time I'd thought of him in a very long time. I remembered that he had no sense of humour. Absolutely none. How sad for him.

I babbled happily at James. 'I mean it though, James. It is fantastic. I'm very glad you're going to join us.'

He smiled at my enthusiasm. 'Will I get a tree from Liam at work? He always gets great ones.'

I nodded happily. It was all settled.

When I told Lizzie of our decision, she was un-impressed. I think she had presumed all along that that would happen, and had never thought about an alternative.

I began to make plans immediately. I toyed briefly with the idea of doing the traditional Christmas, home-baking and all. Then I realised how foolish that was. My baking skills were about as good as my housework skills, and food-poisoning can be fatal.

And if people were going to be throwing up in the toilet, I'd only have to clean up after them, and I didn't fancy that.

So I did the decent thing and took a taxi to Marks and Spencer's, and returned home with eight carrier bags full of cardboard-clad festive fare.

I consulted James about buying presents for Lizzie, but we decided that since I had always done this, there was no reason to change now. In our worldly-wise, newly separated state, we agreed that any presents we gave her should be from both of us together. We weren't going to fall into the trap of competing for her abundant love. I occupied many happy hours in toyshops and bookshops trying to find things she would like, though I knew she was easily pleased, and not yet too caught up in the need to possess every toy she saw advertised on television.

In a feeble effort to be a good home-maker, I got craft books from the library, and I made a wreath for the front door, and glittery ornaments for the tree and for the mantelpiece.

Yes, the arty gene was recessive too. I struggled on and tried not to wonder whether I was actually any good at anything at all. No matter how I tried, the wire hanger remained defiantly visible in the centre of the wreath, and some of the supposedly smiling angels were definitely leering as they stood lopsidedly against the minimalist wire candle holders. Still, Lizzie was impressed, which was the main thing. Well, maybe impressed is too strong a word. But she didn't laugh, which was kind of her.

I saw a poster in the local shop, advertising a half-day course in wrapping Christmas presents. It promised such delights as printing your own paper, and incredibly clever things involving newspapers and leaves and gold paint. The course cost seventy Euro, which was more than I usually spent on all my presents put together. I wondered if there was a method of gift-wrapping that was so creative that the dazzled recipient would fail to notice that the elaborate frothy concoction didn't actually contain a present at all. Or was there a way I could give Maisie a present that looked like a new car, and when unwrapped would turn out to be a box of out-of-date chocolates.

Frivolous as it sounds, I found I was tempted for a few minutes before I regained my senses. But, in the end, no gift-wrapping course for me. It was back to the cheap wrapping paper – five sheets for a Euro.

On Christmas Eve, Lizzie hung up her stocking. She did this with difficulty as it was hard to find room on the over-decorated mantelpiece. Two particularly drunken-looking angels had to be retired to the kitchen. Then Lizzie went to bed, full of an anticipation and excitement that adults find it so hard to recreate once childhood is past.

An hour later, James arrived, as arranged, as he had not wanted to miss the fun of filling her stocking. I had collected all of the things we needed, the things she got every year – the mandarin orange, the chocolate Santa Claus, the new toothbrush, the bubble bath, the novelty soap, and a few small toys. Then we set about assembling her main present. This was a doll's pram, an expensive one, but one I had fallen for because it so resembled one that I had wanted very badly as a child, but had never received. James was good at this type of work, so after a few minutes I left him to it. I sat back in the firelight, enjoying the domesticity of it all.

The job seemed to be a lengthy, complicated one, so I fetched us each a glass of red wine. James was engrossed in his task, and he relaxed a little and began to reminisce about past Christmases. We laughed together as he reminded me of the year (our first year together) that I had bought a huge frozen turkey, and expected it to defrost on Christmas morning. Then there was the year that James the electrician managed to trip the electricity when he plugged in a very dodgy set of fairy lights. There was Lizzie's first Christmas, when, at only a few months old, she completely ignored all of the toys we had bought for her, and spent the day eating her sock.

For the first time in many months, James seemed to be at ease in my company, but I couldn't relax. I was too conscious of the delicate balance of our relationship, too afraid that I would say something that would break the spell. I decided to sit back, say little and try to enjoy the moment.

The poorly translated assembly instructions for the pram were soon discarded. ('On the left proong fix the over nut with the small screwing.') James worked steadily, matching nuts to bolts, and hooking springs onto the frame. Finally it looked ready, and James didn't seem too worried about the three remaining metal pieces which didn't appear to have a place on the finished article. I put Lizzie's current favourite doll into the pram and tucked her in with the small, patchwork-effect blanket, decorated with ducks and teddies, that I had knitted in the evenings after she had gone to bed. Well, they were meant to be ducks and teddies anyway. In reality, they were more like octopi and spiders, but I knew my loyal Lizzie wouldn't complain.

James finished his wine. He stood up and stretched. I eyed him, afraid to speak, afraid to rush things, afraid to let him leave, afraid to ask him to stay. After all the foolish mistakes I'd made in the past, I wasn't taking any chances. Forget my poor granny's ancient wisdom. When in doubt, keep your mouth shut, was my new philosophy.

James didn't give me much time to dither. He came over to where I was sitting in an armchair near the fire, and he kissed me lightly on the cheek. 'That wasn't so difficult after all. I'm going to meet some of the lads in the pub. See you in the morning. Around eight.'

Then he left before I could think of a better reply than, ''Bye. See you in the morning.'

I poured the remaining wine into my glass, and swirled it around in the firelight. The fire crackled and hissed. It was warm and comforting. In the poor light, the drunken angels almost looked good, in an inventive, arty kind of way. The fridge was full almost to bursting point with the finest pre-packed food Cork could offer. My beautiful daughter slumbered upstairs, dreaming happy, Christmas dreams. I sipped my wine, and tried not to acknowledge the sadness that washed over me.

Chapter Thirty-Two

Almost everything went according to plan on Christmas day.

Lizzie ran into my room, at some dark, early hour, but was easily persuaded to snuggle into my bed for another snooze, agreeing with me when I suggested that Santa might not be finished his work yet. Amazingly, she fell asleep again, and I did too, enjoying her closeness, as she lay with her warm little body cuddled up to mine. Neither of us awoke again until I heard James's car pull up outside. I nudged Lizzie, and she awoke at once, ready for the best day of the year. Impatiently, she donned the dressing gown and slippers I insisted on, and she galloped down the stairs, to be met by James who had just let himself in.

He looked at me apologetically as I appeared at the top of the stairs, struggling into my fleecy yellow dressing gown.

'I didn't like to ring the bell. I thought you might be still asleep.'

I buttoned my gown and tried in vain to flatten my hair. Even though he'd seen me like this a thousand times before, I was embarrassed.

'It's your house too, you know,' I replied, hurt, as always, when he acted as if he had no right to be there.

Lizzie interrupted by grabbing both our arms and dragging us into the living-room, to where the tree was, and where her stocking and presents awaited her. She walked slowly over to the pram, and viewed it carefully. She touched the handle and ran her fingers lightly over the patchwork blanket.

'Polly is in here,' she said solemnly.

'Yes, darling,' I laughed. 'It's for you. Santa Claus brought it for you to play with.'

She didn't seem able to take this in, but she soon began to wheel the pram around the room, talking to Polly as she went. Every now and then, she stopped to rearrange the knitted blanket around the doll's chin, whispering to her, 'It's very cold today. You need your blanky. Your nice spider blanky.'

Eventually, we had to draw her away from the pram to show her the bulging stocking, which she promptly upended onto the hearthrug. She was mesmerised by all of the things in front of her, picking each up in turn, and then replacing it with care on the rug.

'Are these all for me?'

My heart went out to her. She was so innocent and so easy to please. James smiled at me and took her onto his knee. I'd have preferred it the other way around.

'You've been a very good little girl. That's why you got all of this.'

Lizzie thought about this for a moment. 'Zoë won't get any presents then, will she? She kicked Jennifer, and she tore my *Honey Bear* book. I bet Santa just left her a huge dirty bag of coal.'

James looked towards me for help. How was he going to get out of this?

Lizzie wanted to know for sure. 'Won't she only get coal, Daddy. Won't she?'

I decided to help him out. 'Well, maybe Zoë was very good for the last few days, and Santa decided to give her one last chance. She'd be very sad if she only got coal, wouldn't she?'

Lizzie grinned at me. 'Yeah, I hope she got real presents, and then she can be good next year, and she won't tear my *Ginger Giraffe* book.'

Lizzie wriggled down from James's knee and began to load all her goodies onto the shopping tray underneath the doll's pram. She then wheeled the pram proudly around the house until I called her for breakfast.

I had set the breakfast table the night before. There was a new red tablecloth, and our best china, a rarely used wedding present. I had made a table decoration out of pine cones sprayed with gold paint, and red ribbons. (I hoped James wouldn't go outside and notice that a large patch of the patio and one of our wooden benches were now adorned with large abstract spatters of gaudy gold paint.)

Maureen had called a few days earlier with some home-made yeast buns for me to put in the freezer. They were now warming in the oven, filling the house with their wonderful smell.

This smell always took me back to my childhood. My mother had baked almost every day of her life, and I loved to come home from school and peep under the tea towel which protected the baking from flies. I used to breathe in the warm, welcoming scent, hoping to be rewarded with a small taste before my tea. I had often wondered how come I had inherited none of this skill, but I consoled myself with the fact that I too had my own special skills. I just hadn't identified them yet.

James came into the kitchen, and breathed deeply.

'Something smells fantastic.'

'Jason's mum made us buns,' said Lizzie, who was passing through with Polly on her circuit of the downstairs of the house. 'She said that you can weigh a man's heart on his tummy.'

I flinched slightly, but luckily Lizzie's garbled version of the old adage was too obscure for James to understand.

Breakfast was perfect. We had fresh orange juice (something even I could prepare without mishap), the yeast buns, jam that Lily had allegedly made from organic raspberries, and strong fresh coffee. It was strange to be sharing a proper meal with James. He was in good form again, like the night before, and I had great hopes for the rest of the day. We lingered over our coffee, smiling at Lizzie whenever she wandered in, indulgently letting her eat her chocolate Santa, and her little bag of chocolate coins, even though she had had no proper breakfast.

We cleared the table together and the day began to unfold like Christmas days usually do – not terribly exciting, sometimes even a little boring, but special despite this. Maybe it's because of the memory of magical childhood Christmases, anticipated for weeks, and then rushing by in a haze of presents, flashing lights, chocolate and fizzy drinks.

Or maybe it's that after all the weeks of frenzied work, everyone has to enjoy Christmas, whether they like it or not.

Despite our recent differences, I couldn't let Christmas go by without buying a present for James. In any case, Lizzie had been hounding me for weeks, pulling at things in shops, crying, 'Buy this for Daddy. He'd love it.'

He had never liked me to buy clothes for him as his taste was rather conservative, and he lived in fear of me buying him a suede waistcoat, or a loud shirt, so I resorted to the unoriginal and terribly unromantic – a compact disc, and a heavy-duty torch. He presented me with a bottle of perfume. Not the most original present in the world, I'll admit, but I was touched that he remembered the kind that he'd always mistakenly thought I liked.

As well as the jam, Lily had given me a tin of joss-sticks. I'd given her a book on feng shui. I had bought

337

Maureen a book, too pleased to have another friend to buy a present for. I'd found it the week before Christmas, and decided it was perfect. It was a wry, witty book about the perils of parenting in the twenty-first century. I'd dropped it over to her the day before Christmas Eve, and was strangely touched when she hugged me and produced a similarly book-shaped package.

I opened Maureen's present after I'd enthused over my perfume, and laughed out loud when I realised that she'd bought me the same book I'd bought her.

'Look, James. Of all the books in all the world, she bought me this. It's the same as the one I got her.'

James shook his head and spoke in a mock cynical fashion. 'Must have been on special offer.'

I gave him a light punch on the arm. 'It wasn't actually. It's hardbacked and full price. She just knew I'd like it. Isn't that incredible? We must be like-minded.'

'Or terribly lacking in imagination.'

He was ready this time, and managed to duck my punch. Just as well. The second one would have been harder. After the way I used to mock Maureen to James, I now felt fiercely loyal.

'She's actually very nice, you know. I just never took the trouble to notice.'

James spoke easily. 'You should have asked me. I'd have told you that years ago.'

I gave a wry smile. I think we both knew how pointless that particular exercise would have been.

In the first years of our marriage, I grudgingly used to buy Maisie something cheap and nasty, which she used to accept greedily, while saying, 'I didn't get you anything, Claire. What more could you want? You've got James, and this lovely house.'

After a few years of this, I had decided not to waste time or money on her, and used to greet her before Christmas with a blithe, 'I didn't get you anything Maisie. I knew you wouldn't want anything from me.'

This would produce a dissatisfied grunt from my beloved mother-in-law, and a sigh from my poor long-suffering failed peacemaking husband.

This year, in a moment of generosity, I had bought her a pretty china plant-holder. I handed it to James. 'This is for Maisie. Could you give it to her tomorrow?'

He took it and placed it carefully beside his chair. He didn't speak, but his quiet smile made me suddenly very glad that I'd given in to my generous impulse.

After unwrapping our presents, we sat back and watched Lizzie play. I thought back to the previous Christmas, and how happy we had been.

Or as happy as I knew how to be back then.

Which, now that I think of it, probably wasn't all that happy at all.

We had begun to talk about having another baby, that Christmas, but before anything could happen, I had got caught up in the Greece thing, and now we had finished up in the separated-but-aren't-we-so-adult-and-amicable scenario.

Before I got sucked into too much introspection, Lizzie demanded more attention, needing help with the arrangement of her treasures around her poor squashed baby. Then the three of us settled down in front of an early movie, and before we knew it, the morning and a box of Milk Tray were gone.

Our house was one of eight in a small cul de sac. Every Christmas, the O'Connells, the couple in the corner house, hosted a small drinks party, and every year we were invited. Every year, we attended out of a sense of duty. When we bought our house, we thought it was perfect, but, naïvely, we didn't look too closely at the population of the road. They were all close to retirement age, or already retired. The men played golf and the women pottered around the gardens with little pruning clippers in their hands, seemingly busy, but somehow never managing to get their hands dirty. They were all very friendly and nice, but we had little in common with any of them. When Lizzie was a baby, the women stopped to admire her when I wheeled her out in her pram. One or two people even knocked on our door with baby gifts for her, but we never went beyond that level of acquaintance. I have to take some responsibility for this, as I was so wrapped up in my own cosy, eccentric little world, and had little time for anything outside it. One woman, Mrs Moriarty, called a few times and offered to baby-sit, so I could have a few hours to myself, but I never took her up on her offer. I was slow to accept help from anyone, and anyway, I didn't really want to have any time away from Lizzie. Soon, Mrs Moriarty stopped offering, and our relationship never developed beyond polite greetings when we met in the street. Then, she sold her house to go and live with her daughter, and Lily moved in, and I made my first sort-of-friend in the neighbourhood.

The Christmas party was always a bit of an ordeal. I always felt shabby and underdressed in my usual best clothes of long black skirts, and flowered tops. I put on a brave, defiant face, but was secretly half in awe of the sophisticated women guests with their designer trouser suits, heavy gold jewellery, and perfectly coiffed, dyed hair. (Only Lily, the recent arrival, ever vied with me for title of the least suitably dressed.)

James and I set off for the annual Christmas penance, clutching a box of chocolates someone else had given us, hastily wrapped in some second-hand shiny gold paper.

We stepped onto the O'Connells' doormat, prompting a weak, electronic version of 'Deck the Halls with Boughs of Holly'. We rang the doorbell which produced deep tones of 'Silent Night'. Mary O'Connell opened the door, kissed the cold air around our cheeks, and ushered us into the living-room. This was a lush, over-decorated room, with every available surface heaving under the weight of delicate china, or more robust, just-polished silver. The room was papered with deep pink, striped wallpaper, but little of this was visible as there were pictures hanging everywhere. Family photographs hobnobbed willy-nilly with dark, hunting scenes, and a large selection of ugly paintings depicting golf courses of the world. Wherever I looked, I could see huge swags of greenery, looping and diving ostentatiously. An enormous Santa swayed and sang on the mantelpiece. The smell of Christmas (as interpreted by pot-pourri makers) pervaded the atmosphere like a forced sentiment.

The guests were engrossed in their golf tales, or stories about how successful their grown-up children were. Everyone greeted us when we walked in, and most had a few words with Lizzie, invariably about Santa Claus. There was a great fuss made about her new dress, which pleased me, as, uncharacteristically, I had spent a lot of money on it. Then everyone lapsed back into their conversations, and James and I were left with Mrs Latimer, a sweet old lady who was quite deaf and a little out of touch with reality.

Just as we were wondering how to leave, Lily arrived. She was resplendent in a floor-length dress made of about fifty yards of deep red velvet. Pinned to her hair was something that resembled a canary that had spectacularly lost a tussle with a steamroller.

Lily hugged everybody, whether they wanted to be hugged or not. She came to me last, having saved her biggest, tightest hug for me. I was overwhelmed by the thick fabric of her dress, and the strong smell of whiskey from her breath. She laughed a deep, loud laugh, and whispered in my ear. 'I'm half-jarred already. Christy and Helen are coming for the day. I couldn't face that if I were sober.'

With that, she circled the room once more, hugging anyone who wasn't quick enough to get out of the way, and then she sailed out of the house again, leaving behind her an embarrassed silence and a strong smell of patchouli oil and alcohol.

After a few tense moments, Mrs O'Connell asked brightly, 'Now, who would like another home-made mince pie?'

After what we hoped was a decent amount of time, James and I muttered our excuses, vaguely mentioning turkey and ovens, and made our escape. Luckily the O'Connells didn't know that our M&S turkey portions (with real herb stuffing) needed only twenty minutes in the microwave.

When we reached the safety of our house, we giggled like teenagers, hoping, as we did every year, that we would never turn out like them. Lizzie watched bemused as her normally serious parents sighed dramatically at their deliverance from the ghost of Christmas Glitz.

I busied myself with the dinner, and James sat down to watch television. Lizzie saw her opportunity, and she ran to curl up on his knee. After a while, I noticed that she was twiddling her hair in a way that indicated that she was tired and comfortable. Soon she had fallen into a light doze, and I watched for a while as James stroked her hair.

There wasn't much to do for the dinner. After a succession of trips to the recycling bag with mounds of cardboard, and an equally long succession of pings from the microwave, everything was ready. I even warmed the plates.

The meal went well, and if a stranger could have observed us, peering in through our rather grubby windows, it would have seemed that we were the perfect, happy family. Lizzie's presence lightened the atmosphere, and when we weren't joining in her childish chattering, James and I chatted easily about everything except our relationship.

Much later, we had dessert and coffee in the living-room, slouched in front of the fire. Lizzie was snoozing once again in a corner of the room. James and I were mellow after a few glasses of wine each, and I felt like a young girl again.

All the old doubts were there. Did he fancy me? Had I a chance with him? Was he just being nice?

I found myself taking sly glances across at James, admiring all over again his handsome profile. I sat with my husband of five years, and I was afraid to make a move. I felt sure that things could be good between us again, and now that we were having a lovely day together with our daughter, the time seemed right to start, but I couldn't initiate it. I wished it could be like in a soppy film. I wished that I could edge closer to him on the sofa, and we would end up kissing fiercely, declaring what fools we had been. James would hold my head in his hands, and look at me with an intensity that would almost frighten me. He would give a low moan of desire. Then we could creep upstairs and make mad passionate love, with our naked bodies illuminated by the shafts of gentle moonlight filtered through the net curtains that I had never got around to washing.

None of this happened though.

I was afraid of rejection, afraid of frightening him away, afraid of losing the precious little I had. So we watched the big Christmas-night movie from opposite ends of the sofa, and when it was over, James carried the sleeping Lizzie upstairs to bed, thanked me for a lovely day, and left.

I went up to my bedroom and surveyed it. I had been so hopeful that at last I would have the chance to share it with someone other than Lizzie. I had tidied everything, and even changed the sheets. Under the pillow was a new silky nightdress, purchased with only one thought in mind – the seduction of my husband.

I had been so bright and cheery over the last few months. I had tried so hard to banish the old pessimistic me. I had never really faced the possibility that James might not come back into my life. Now, since nothing had happened, it seemed clear that he was happier alone. If he could walk out after such a lovely day, what should that tell me?

Maisie was safely out of the way, inflicting her very poor table manners on her unfortunate fellow hotel guests, before retiring to snore loudly, disturbing the sleep of countless others. So James couldn't use her as an excuse. He had just left our warm, welcoming home to go back to a cold, loveless house. Clearly all hope for us was gone.

Then, for the first time, the dreadful thought struck me that he might be seeing someone else. A picture flashed into my mind. A sick picture of James and a shadowy blonde figure, wrapped around each other on a sofa. Clinking crystal glasses and laughing deep, throaty laughs.

Had James left me to go and make mad passionate love to my replacement?

Was Maisie gloating somewhere, rejoicing in how easily she had prised us apart? Had she found him a beautiful, calm replacement for me? One who could make soufflés and fold napkins into dainty swan shapes? One who could make pretty cross-stitch pictures reading, 'Home, Sweet Home'?

Was my beloved husband now going upstairs, hand in hand with a willowy stranger, chuckling hoarsely at the thought of how they would celebrate their own Christmas feast? Was her hair so soft that it wouldn't snag when he ran his fingers through it? When he rubbed her belly with his fingers, would he rejoice in the absence of scars and stretch marks? Would his dry palm trace the smooth outline of her gently rounded hips, her tiny waist, her cellulite-free thighs? Were the silver shafts of cruel moonlight preparing to illuminate her slim youthful body, as she heaved in the ecstasy of my husband's touch?

I tiptoed in to give Lizzie her final Christmas-night kiss. She stirred, and gave a soft, sleepy smile. Then she turned towards the wall, dislodging Polly who fell to the floor with a dull thud. I returned to my own room, leaving the door slightly ajar, half-hoping that Lizzie would waken soon and join me for cuddles.

I looked out the window. The street was quiet. Fairy lights twinkled in every garden. Chinks of light escaped from living-rooms. Was everyone happy, except for me?

Where was Ross? Was he thinking of me? He said he loved me. Did he mean it? Was it time for me to brave the Internet café and find out? What if he had forgotten all about me? Could I bear to be rejected any more?

Where was Kevin? When did a vision of my face last flit across his selfish mind?

Then, with tears of self-pity trickling down my cheeks, I put on my winceyette pyjamas, and climbed into my lonely bed.

Chapter Thirty-Three

January is a month that I've always found depressing – the excitement of Christmas over, and spring still so far away. This year was even worse as I began, for the first time, to face the prospect of being a single parent.

It wasn't a great prospect. I had always arrogantly thought that single mothers were seventeen-year-old girls with belly tops and pierced navels and babies called after places – Chelsea, Paris and Brooklyn. Why not Ballybofey or Brighton? If babies are called after their place of conception, why are none called Honda Civic or The Lane behind the Chip Shop?

Single parenthood really wasn't my scene. Or so I thought.

You see, I always thought that when I got married and started a family, we'd be like *The Little House on the Prairie*. (Just without the prairie, and the mean girl with blonde ringlets.) I thought I'd be part of a happy family, settling our minor differences with under-standing smiles and huge hugs and tasty dinners served from big copper pots.

Now it seemed as if I'd strayed onto the real-life set of *The War of the Roses*.

I didn't dare to think what was next. Would I soon be playing a part in *Fatal Attraction*? Would James find out about Ross? Would I come home one day to find Lizzie's hamster simmering on the hob?

I still saw James almost daily, but our relationship remained static. We never fell out, but we never grew closer. I began to feel terribly lonely. I still had my Wednesday nights with Lily, of course, but I was struggling to avoid her persistent efforts to read my tarot cards and my tea leaves. Her big, warm personality was threatening to overwhelm me.

Maureen still called to see me regularly, and I was still grateful, but I needed more than this. I engaged in idle chat with the mothers at the school gate, but once the children came out of school, they all disappeared in a mad rush of coats, schoolbags, and still-wet works of art. If I lingered for more than a few minutes, Lizzie and I would find ourselves alone in the schoolyard, except for a few opportunistic pigeons, and Zoë the poor bedraggled child who was always collected ten minutes later than everyone else.

One day, as Lizzie and I walked slowly home, the grey clouds above us shifted and revealed a tiny patch of blue sky. I stopped, transfixed. For a moment, I was reminded of the blue skies that had shone over us in Mykonos the previous year. Then a cloud swirled suddenly and the blue patch began to vanish before my eyes. I felt bereft for a moment, and dreamed of snatching at the blue, like at a lost memory or a fading dream. Moments later, the sky was a uniform grey, and we continued our journey home.

Months had gone by and Ross had had no word from me. What was he thinking? Was he upset? Or was he relieved? Or had he forgotten me completely, and was it time for me to be checking *Hello* magazine for exclusive photographs of his wedding?

I passed the long days by trying my best to be a good housekeeper. My best wasn't very good.

Once, I glimpsed the bottom of the ironing basket. It took me hours to get over the shock.

I'd half-heartedly mop the middle of the floor. No one would notice. It would get dirty, and then I'd mop it again. Still no one there to admire the fruits of my drudgery. It would get dirty again, magically gathering peas and rice to its sticky surface.

No one ever called to the house anyway, except James and Maureen, and I felt no need to impress them.

Hardly fulfilling stuff for a girl who once got 'This girl will go far' on her end-of-year school report. OK, so I went far. I travelled miles every week. Up and down the stairs every day, half-heartedly vacuuming and dusting and sweeping. Walking to and from school. Trudging to the shops to buy food for lonely suppers for Lizzie and me.

I cleaned out the deep freeze one day. That was fun. I'd never done it before. I love deep freezes. With a fridge, whenever you have leftovers like a half-jug of gravy, or a few teaspoons of whipped cream, you can hide them for a few weeks while you work up the resolve to throw them out. The good thing about freezers is that you can keep such useless leftovers for years on end.

On my excursion into the icy depths, I reached right down into the furthest, darkest corner, and my hand closed over a small, smooth pouch. It was a little bag of breastmilk. I took it out and looked at it fondly. I considered defrosting it and putting it on Lizzie's cornflakes. I wondered if she'd remember the taste. I wondered if she would recall the copious amounts of that fatty liquid that she'd put away in her first months. I wondered if she had any recollection of her tiny, guzzling, baby-self.

Still, I figured she wouldn't have been impressed, so I squished the defrosting pouch in my hands for a few moments, and then found the strength to throw it into the bin.

If I'd ever got around to feeding that milk to the baby Lizzie, it would have ended up in a strangely sweet-smelling light-brown mess in her nappy. Nevertheless, I shed a small tear as I closed the cover of the bin, revealing to myself what a truly sad person I'd become.

A few days after the sad, breastmilk episode, I met Maureen on the way home from school. She probably thought I was madder than usual, but I didn't care.

'I need to tell you something,' I began, and continued as she looked at me worriedly, half-afraid of what I was going to say. 'You've been very kind to me. I would have been lost without you, these last few months. I'd like you to know that I'm very, very grateful. Thank you.'

She began to shrug it off, muttering, 'It's nothing.' But I could see a slow smile beginning, and it was clear that she was pleased, and that pleased me. Suddenly I thought of a way to pass some of the long morning.

'Maureen. How about coffee? Would you like to come back to my place?'

'Sorry, Claire, I can't. The tiler's coming.'

Oh, no. Her expression was inscrutable. Was she mocking me? Had she known all along, that I had been deliberately inventing tradesmen so I wouldn't have to have coffee with her?

'Oh, OK, then. Another time perhaps.' I felt about one inch tall.

Then she burst into a huge peal of happy laughter. 'Come on, Claire. Don't you know when you're being wound up? I'd love to come. Anything to avoid the ironing.'

I couldn't join in her merriment. 'Do you mean that you knew all the time? All those times when you used to ask me over to your place? You knew?'

She laughed again. 'Of course I knew. You weren't one bit convincing. You didn't think I believed all those stupid excuses, did you?'

So why was she here now, laughing with me, as if she were my friend?

'But . . .

She stopped in the middle of the street and gave me a big hug. 'You big eejit. I knew it wasn't personal. It wasn't about me. I liked you, and I decided to sit it out until you realised that you liked yourself.'

Oh dear. Too perceptive for someone I had dismissed so easily.

'Maureen, I am so, so sorry.'

She stopped again, and looked me in the eye. You've been apologising for months now. Please stop. It's forgotten. Now, do you have any nice home-made cakes?'

This time I knew she was teasing.

I laughed with her. 'Not a one. But I have the finest of fig-rolls and chocolate Kimberleys, just waiting for you.'

So we set off, chattering about God knows what as we covered the short distance to my road. As we turned the last corner, Maureen was making me laugh as she wickedly mimicked the principal of Jason's school, reprimanding parents for double-parking in the bus lane.

I wiped a tear of laughter from my eye, then stopped suddenly, and wiped my eyes again. Maureen stopped too.

'What is it, Claire? Have you something in your eye? Let's see.'

I could feel a flush spreading through my body. Maureen was rooting furiously in her pockets.

'I know I have a clean tissue in here somewhere,' she muttered, as she pulled out an assortment of very grubby ones.

'Hah!' She gave a crow of triumph. 'Here, use this.'

I didn't answer her. I was looking towards my house.

There was a strange car outside it. There was a man in a bright blue parka sitting on the garden wall.

It was Ross.

Maureen looked from me to him, and back again. She put her tissue back into her pocket. 'I take it from your somewhat bemused expression that that's not your tiler or your plumber.'

I shook my head.

'Will I stay, or will I go do my ironing?'

I smiled at her in gratitude. 'Maybe the ironing. Do you mind? I'll explain later.'

She gave me an inscrutable gaze, and with one wave of her hand, she set off towards her own house.

I walked towards Ross. It was strange to see him in winter clothes. His tan had faded to a lighter shade of gold. Even from a distance, I could see the pale blue of his eyes.

He stood up as I approached.

I spoke first. 'What are you doing here? How did you find me?'

'Interpol.'

'Interpol?' I repeated the word after him, rather foolishly.

'Do they . . . ? I mean, can they . . . ?'

Ross was laughing. 'Actually, I looked you up in the phone book. You have an unusual surname.'

'Oh.' I looked at him, wondering what should happen next.

He took the initiative. But then I suppose since he'd taken the initiative and come and parked himself on my doorstep, the next move was a small one.

'Any chance of a cup of coffee?'

'Yes, yes of course. Come on in.'

I led the way up the driveway and fumbled terribly for my keys. When I finally got the door open, I went in first and led the way into the kitchen. I indicated a chair and Ross sat down. I gathered the worst of the clutter in my arms and threw it into the hall cupboard. I heaped the breakfast dishes in the sink, and filled up the kettle. I put the pathetic paper sculpture Lizzie and I had been making onto the floor in the corner of the room, where it collapsed slowly, into a messy heap of too-wet papier-mâché, and crumpled egg boxes. I rooted in the back of the cupboard for two clean, unchipped mugs, and a jug that wasn't too badly stained with residues of instant gravy mix. I opened the fridge. The first thing that met my eyes was a bowl of something green. I picked it up without thinking. Clearly it had once been food. Clearly it was somewhat past its eat-without-dying-by date. Ross was looking at it too.

I shoved it back to the furthest corner of the fridge.

'Just Lizzie's science project,' I muttered, as I reached for the milk.

I made some instant coffee, and then, unable to fluster any more, I sat at the kitchen table, facing Ross.

We didn't speak for a few moments. He busied himself with stirring his coffee, and finding a porridge-free piece of table for his elbows. I busied myself looking at him, remembering all of a sudden how very handsome he was.

I cracked first. 'I'm sorry, Ross. I should have sent you a message. It's just . . . I just didn't know what to write.'

He smiled, showing his even white teeth. I resisted a sudden urge to touch his face.

'That's OK. And I should apologise for showing up like this, with no warning. I just came on a whim. I didn't think too much about it. Maybe I should have given it some more thought.'

I considered asking him about Alistair, but resisted. Clearly he hadn't come all this way to make small talk about his family. 'Have you decided what to do about the factory? Are you going to go back to Greece?'

He relaxed a little, alerting me for the first time to how tense he was. 'Yes. It's going to be fine. Dad and I have set up a management company. I can live in Greece, and, as long as I travel back to the factory for a few days every four weeks or so, there shouldn't be any problems. Dad's happy with the arrangement. I think he knows I'd never be happy to spend all my time in the factory. It seems like a perfect solution.'

'I'm very happy for you.'

'And you? How are you? Did things work out?'

'You mean with James?'

He gave a wry smile. 'Yes, I mean with James.'

How could I answer that? Could I tell him that I thought I loved James, but that the feeling didn't appear to be mutual? Could I say that my marriage was going nowhere, and might I please jump into the back of his hired car and skip off to Greece, to live happily ever after in his stone cottage by the sea?

And was my marriage going nowhere?

I decided on a half-answer. 'James is living with his mum at the moment. We haven't really worked things out just yet. I'm not really sure what happens next. But we're getting on fine.'

Ross leaned across the table and took my hand. I removed it briefly and handed him a piece of kitchen paper to clean the porridge from the underside of his sleeve. Then he took my hand again.

'Is there any hope for us, Claire? For you and me? I love you, you know. Could you bring Lizzie to live in Greece with me? Could you leave all of this?'

As he spoke the last words, he waved his free hand in the air, indicating the filthy kitchen. I could even see into the utility room to where there were two huge multi-coloured mountains – one waiting to be washed, the other waiting to be ironed. A stray cat had chewed the bottom of the recycling bag, and every piece of cardboard we had used in the past three weeks was strewn around the back garden.

Yes, I thought. I could quite happily leave all that behind. I didn't mind if I never saw that again.

But James? Could I leave him behind? I wasn't so sure.

I looked at Ross. His handsome face was serious. His intense look almost frightened me. He was gripping my hand rather too tightly in his. He leaned closer, as if he were going to kiss me. Then he pulled back. 'I'm sorry, Claire. I shouldn't have come.'

God, this was difficult. It was like a soap opera. Only in soap operas, people don't have to make up their own lines. And they get to do the scene all over again if it doesn't work out right the first time. And if you get things really wrong, you just get clocked with a shovel and buried under the patio. Or driven into a canal. It's all over quickly. You don't get to stew in your mistakes.

'I'm sorry, Ross. I just don't know what to do. You know I feel strongly for you. I just . . . I just . . . want to make it work with James. And yet . . .'

Ross looked slightly happier. 'And yet what?'

'And yet, I think I could be happy with you too.'

I put my head down on my arms and whispered the next words. 'I think I love you too.'

Ross got up and came around to my side of the table. He went to put his arms around me, but I pulled away. 'I'm sorry, Ross. Please don't.'

If he put his arms around me, I wasn't sure I could resist him, and that wouldn't have been fair on anyone.

He sat down again at his own side of the table. He was giving me that intense look again. He'd only been in the house for ten minutes, and already it seemed as if we had said all there was to say. I felt dreadfully insecure under his clear gaze. I didn't know whether to cry, or to beg him to leave, or to tear my clothes off and race him to the bedroom.

I got up. 'I'm sorry. Do you mind if I wash the dishes?'

He shrugged. Of course, he had no idea how out of character that suggestion was. And he kindly didn't point out that I had a dishwasher. I piled the dishes on the draining board, and filled the sink with hot water. Ross rooted in a drawer and found a clean(ish) tea-towel, and we began to work. We chatted as we worked. It was slightly easier with the washing-up to occupy our hands and eyes. He told me about Alistair and his new school. He told me of his plans for the factory. He told me how he planned to improve the stone cottage in Mykonos. He told me of an idea he had to use his graphic-design skills to help small charities.

Of course, I had no plans for the future. I didn't even know what I was having for tea that night. So I talked about Lizzie, and her new school.

I dragged out the washing-up for as long as I could. I wiped out the oven, and cleaned the hob, and removed the mountain of crumbs from under the toaster. I emptied all the cutlery onto the kitchen work surface and cleaned the drawer. Ross swept the floor, and rearranged the ware on the dresser. He wiped the grubby seats of the kitchen chairs, and when he was finished, they were a different colour.

Finally, unless we were to take down the net curtains to wash them, or start emptying out the cupboards, there was no work left. I threw my cloth onto the drainer, and leaned against the sink. Ross stood against the unusually clean oven door. He put his arms out to me. I had a sudden glimpse of my own happy childhood, with my mum laughing and holding her arms out – 'Who'll come to me the first?'

I hesitated for a second before I went to him. He held me tight, while I buried my nose against his shoulder. He felt just the same. He smelt just the same. I could see time passing in slow green digital minutes on the oven clock. I closed my eyes and tried to make time stand still. He lifted my head and pressed his cheek against mine. I could feel his breath on my ear. I felt weak.

I pulled away from him. Desire for him was making me dizzy. I felt like I used to when I was a child after spinning around in circles. Back then, I used to finish by throwing myself on the ground in fits of crazy laughter. That was hardly appropriate here.

I backed away and used the kitchen table for support. Ross stepped towards me again. He put one hand on the back of my head. He brushed my lips with his. I gave a choked sob. Or a sigh.

And then the doorbell rang. I wanted to ignore it. I looked over my shoulder through the open kitchen door. Whoever it was would have seen us through the hall window. Better to answer the ring.

It was a dirty, rough-looking youth of about sixteen.

'Clean your gutters, Missus?'

'No, thanks.' I went to close the door.

'They're well full of weeds. You'll have problems. Dreadful problems altogether.'

I didn't need that scruffy-looking article to tell me that I had problems. 'No, thanks.'

'I have me own ladder, and me own insurance. I did your neighbour's. A hundred Euro.'

Ross appeared behind me. He looked at the youth with disdain. 'If I give you ten Euro, will you go away?'

A sudden smile lit up the young lad's face. It made him look even younger – about twelve. Before I could stop him, Ross handed over a neatly folded note, and the boy almost skipped out the garden gate.

Ross closed the door. He looked sad. 'Maybe the interruption was for the best.'

I wasn't so sure. My dizziness had evaporated, but I was sure it wouldn't take much to rekindle it. I put one hand on his shoulder. He covered my hand with his.

'Claire, I want you so much. But you need to sort yourself out. Sex won't help.'

Maybe not. But it would have been fun.

He was right though. How could I sort out my feelings if all I could think about was Ross's passionate touch? It might further distort my muddle-headed vision.

He sighed deeply. 'I think I'd better go. You know how I feel about you. I want to spend the rest of my life with you. I want us to grow old and cranky together. Make up your mind, and let me know.'

He reached for the doorknob.

I felt as if I was being torn in two. If he stayed, I'd be saying goodbye to my marriage, and I wasn't quite ready for that. If he left, would I ever see him again?

I remembered to confess. 'I'm sorry, Ross. I couldn't send an e-mail to save my life. Could you give me an address, or a phone number? Something I could actually understand?'

He rooted in his pocket, and produced a leather-bound notebook. He scribbled something on a page, tore it out and handed it to me. 'I'll be in England for a few days. After that, I'll be in Greece. Both numbers are here. And the addresses. Just let me know. Please?'

I nodded. I had a horrible feeling that I was making a big mistake.

He leaned forward and kissed me on the lips. Then he opened the door and almost ran down the path. He jumped into his car, and reversed into the driveway to turn around. As he drove out, he nicked the side mirror on the gatepost. (I suppose the gates were a bit smaller than he was used to.) He stopped the car for a moment, and gave one small wave. Then he accelerated, and drove out of my sight.

I closed the door, and went inside.

I switched on the television and watched two consecutive chat shows in an effort to punish myself.

When I went into the kitchen later, I spotted an envelope on the table. Ross must have left it there when I went to answer the door.

My fingers shook as I opened it.

Inside were two plane tickets to Mykonos via London. One for Lizzie, one for me. The outward date was just over two weeks away. The return section was undated.

I sat and looked at the tickets for a long time. Then I put them carefully into a cupboard behind a mountain of old ESB bills.

What on earth was I going to do?

Chapter Thirty-Four

I just about remembered to collect Lizzie from school that day. She skipped home beside me, distracting me with idle chatter. When we got home, I planted her in front of the telly, where she slipped into a trance while watching Disney videos.

I too fell into a trance. I sat in the kitchen and fiddled with my hair, and watched the rain stream down the windows.

What was I supposed to do?

I couldn't cope with all my conflicting emotions. All I wanted was a simple life. I thought of phoning Maureen and asking her to come over. Trouble was, I hadn't told her about Ross, and I wasn't quite sure where to start. So I sat and watched the drizzle until it was time to microwave the dinner.

Lizzie slept in my bed that night. I hoped that her peaceful warmth beside me would distract me from thinking about James and Ross.

I was wrong.

After I dropped Lizzie at school next morning, I mooched home alone. Life was too complicated. Why couldn't I skip back a year, back to when it was just James, Lizzie and me? I wouldn't go away, and everything would be all right.

I went upstairs and half-heartedly began shaking out my duvet. Three socks, a knickers and an Argos catalogue fell to the floor.

My scrambled thoughts were interrupted by the doorbell.

Who could it be? Who did I hope it would be?

I peeped out the bedroom window. The figure on the doorstep didn't have black hair – not James or Ross then. I was almost relieved. It was a young backpacker type with floppy blond hair and torn jeans. I ran downstairs and opened the door, all ready to say that he was at the wrong house. I was met with a boyish, open smile.

'Carla. Good to see you, mate. How've you been.'

He dropped his rucksack heavily onto the step and gave me a huge, painful hug. He smelt like he needed a good bath.

Luckily his acquired Aussie accent, and the fact that he managed only a vague approximation of my name, gave me enough clues to his identity. It was the prodigal son returned. The long-lost Bobby, James's brother, was found again.

He released me, and I smiled weakly at him.

'Bobby, good to see you. Won't you come in?'

'Don't mind if I do. Thanks, mate.'

He picked up his rucksack and stepped into the hall. He'd forgotten my name, but he still remembered the way to the kitchen. I followed him, and invited him to sit. But he was seated already, with his dirty climbing boots propped up on the chair opposite. He still looked like an innocent little puppy dog. James might have had reason to be cross with his brother, but I decided to leave that to him. I had always kind of liked Bobby. He was like a fresh version of James. A less serious model.

'Am I too late for breakfast?'

Bobby was treating me to one of his charming smiles, all shining eyes and crooked teeth.

I smiled back. 'It looks as if the second sitting is just about to begin.'

I grilled rashers and sausages, and made a stack of wholemeal toast. Bobby ate quickly and hungrily. It looked as if his last meal had been around the time of his last bath. As he ate, he told me a rambling tale about a crocodile, Ayers Rock, and the girl he'd fallen in love with.

He finished, and pushed the plate away from him. He had all but licked it clean. He gave a deep sigh, then leaned down and loosened his hiking boots, releasing an aroma of the kind of strong pungent cheese that some people appear to like eating.

'What time does our Jimmy get in? Does he come home for lunch? Can't wait to see him.'

Aha! Bobby phoned Maisie regularly (at least twice a year), and yet he didn't appear to know that James and I had been separated for so long. Either Maisie didn't think it worthy of mention, or Bobby didn't think it worthy of remembering.

I tried to speak casually. 'Actually, Bobby, James won't be home for lunch.'

That didn't bother our Bobby. He slouched even further into his chair, and kicked one boot off. Parmesan definitely. That dry, ready-grated stuff that should surely be illegal.

'OK. I'll see him at tea-time then, won't I?'

'Well, you won't actually. He doesn't live here any more. We've separated. He's gone back to live with Maisie.'

Bobby and James hadn't a whole lot in common, but they shared a dislike of conflict. Of drama. Of anything that might require them to take sides or express a contentious opinion.

Bobby began to look decidedly uncomfortable. He certainly didn't want to be caught in a possibly vicious love tangle. He sat up straight and pulled his boot back on. As he jumped to his feet, the chair clattered loudly on the tiled floor.

'You know, Carla, that was great. Just great. I must get over to Mum's now. She doesn't know I'm coming. She doesn't know about my girlfriend yet.'

He gave me a quick kiss on the cheek, grabbed his rucksack, and all but ran out the front door. The cheesy aroma lingered in the air for some time afterwards.

James rang that evening, as I knew he would.

He got straight to the point. 'I hear you've met the prodigal son.'

I laughed. 'Sounds like you've met him too. Has Maisie killed the fatted calf yet?'

James groaned. 'That's the trouble. Apparently Bobby has a girlfriend, and she's arriving in Cork tomorrow. Mum wants us all to go for a family celebration meal tomorrow night. We'd love you to come.'

That didn't sound quite right. I knew Maisie would be much happier if I wasn't there for the big 'family' get together. Her idea of a happy family was one that didn't include me. And Bobby wouldn't care either way. He'd be happy to share his table with a swarm of flea-bitten rodents as long as there was enough food, and a few beers to wash it down with.

James spoke into the clear silence that hung between us. 'I mean, I'd love you to come. Please come. If you and Lizzie are there, it might just about be bearable. Without you, I know it will be a nightmare.'

He was right of course. 'I don't know, James. You know Maisie wouldn't want me.'

James gave a small laugh. 'Isn't that reason enough for you to go?'

I laughed too. 'Let's not go there, shall we? I don't really know if it's a good idea for me to be there.'

'Please, Cee. Please come.'

That clinched it. James was the only one who ever called me Cee, and he hadn't called me it for many, many months. I softened at once.

'OK. OK. I'll come. Anyway, Lizzie would love a night out with the grown-ups.'

James sounded truly grateful. 'Fantastic, Claire. I'll pick you up at half-seven.'

I hung up and wondered if I'd been foolish to agree to go. I'd had very little contact with Maisie since coming back from Greece. Just the odd accidental meeting when James was driving her around. Our contact was limited to her frostily waving from the front seat of the car, and me responding with a pointedly small nod in her direction.

Still, I consoled myself, a full night in her company would be interesting, if nothing else. And it would be nice to have something to distract me from the big decision I had to make. And with Bobby and a new girlfriend added to the mix, sure anything could happen.

I thought back to the first time I had met Bobby. He had flitted through our lives when Lizzie was a very small baby. He arrived unannounced, clutching a present. It was a pair of dungarees with 'Best Boy' embroidered on the bib.

He tickled Lizzie under the chin and cooed, 'What's his name then?'

'Lizzie.'

He looked puzzled. 'Bit unusual for a boy, isn't it? Lizzie?'

I thought he was joking, and watched with amusement as the truth dawned.

'Sorry, Carla. I thought Mum said you'd had a boy.'

'It's a sweet present anyway,' I replied.

He tossed his boyish fringe from his eyes and laughed. 'Maybe you'll have a boy next.'

James shook his head impatiently. Clearly this wasn't going to be the reunion that would bring the faintly warring brothers to a happy relationship.

Bobby stayed for two nights that time, and then left promising to visit the following year. Of course the promised visit never happened. He sent occasional postcards, from far-flung corners of the world, but never sent an address. This prompted gruff complaints from James. 'He's only afraid we'll want to visit him. That's why we never know for sure where he is.'

I couldn't defend Bobby. After all, I hardly knew him.

The night in the restaurant was interesting. James dropped Lizzie and me off and went to collect his mother. He was gone for ages. I knew what was happening. He'd have to endure a half-hour of her complaints. She'd detail a hundred reasons why she wasn't well enough to go before leaping with alarming alacrity onto her throne in his car.

Bobby and Charlene were already in the restaurant when Lizzie and I went in. Bobby had brought a present for Lizzie, and was very pleased as he handed it over.

'No mistakes this time. I knew you were a girl.'

Lizzie took the present eagerly, and ripped the wrapping paper off. True, it was a present for a girl. A girl of about two years old. It was a cute little shorts and top set, which would have suited Lizzie very well, if only she'd had it three or four years earlier.

Lizzie looked bemused. Even she could see that this wasn't right, but she remembered her manners. 'Thank you, Uncle Bobby,' she whispered.

I spoke brightly. 'Isn't that just lovely? It will be perfect for your dolly. Polly will look sweet in it.'

Lizzie looked a bit doubtful. 'Is it for my dolly?'

Bobby looked as if her were about to contradict me, then I could see him comparing the scraps of bright pink cotton with the lanky limbs of my tall five-year-old. He nodded enthusiastically. 'Yeah, Lindy. It's for your dolly. I'm sure Molly will love it.'

Lizzie was too young to ignore his slips. 'No,' she corrected him. 'I'm Lizzie and my dolly is called Polly.'

Bobby smiled weakly. This was too much trouble for him.

'Carla, I haven't introduced you to Charlene yet.'

At least he could remember his girlfriend's name. I figured he must be very much in love. Charlene looked about fifteen years old too, though apparently she was twenty-three. She was American. She had her nose and her eyebrow and her tongue pierced. Probably her nipples too, but I didn't get to see them. Her short hair was dyed a deep wine colour, with bright pink tips. She wore a tight Lycra t-shirt, about the size of the one that

Lizzie was carefully folding, and trousers which betrayed the fact that she'd never been pregnant. Or eaten a square meal within recent memory either.

Next to this girl, I was the picture of conventional dressing and normality.

I had to know. 'Tell me, Charlene. Have you met Maisie yet?'

She beamed at me. 'Yeah, I have. Isn't she just great?'

I thought I'd misheard. 'Pardon?'

'She's great. You must just love her.'

Seems like my hearing was OK. I looked closely at her. Perhaps she was joking. I looked at Bobby, but he had switched out of our conversation and was paying close attention to the menu. Bet he wasn't looking at the prices. I knew for sure that he wouldn't be coughing up when the bill came.

Charlene repeated her question. 'Don't you just love Maisie?'

I could hardly tell the truth, so I muttered non-committally, 'Mmm.'

Charlene couldn't stop. 'She's such good fun. A real laugh.'

Suddenly the truth dawned. The ever-irresponsible Bobby had introduced her to some stray old lady he'd met in a car park somewhere and pretended she was his mother. Some baffled granny had probably found herself hugging this burgundy-headed, multi-pierced apparition. Now James, the sensible one, would have to produce the real thing, and the fun would start.

Just then, James and Maisie arrived. She was leaning on him, threatening to topple him over with her hefty bulk. I waited for the surprise on Charlene's face. I was wrong though. She jumped from her seat and helped to guide Maisie to the table.

'Here, Maisie, let me help you. Why don't you sit by me, and we can have a nice talk?'

Maisie spoke as if she'd been through a terrible ordeal. 'Thank you, Charlene, dear. You're so kind.'

She shot me a strange look of triumph, as she eased herself into her seat. I sat and watched as she and Charlene engaged in a spot of mutual worship. I couldn't figure out what was going on. I lit up a cigarette to help me to concentrate.

I only smoked to annoy Maisie. In fact, I only ever smoked in her presence, just because I knew she hated them. I blew a cloud of swirling smoke in her direction, and this didn't even produce a reaction. She just went on prattling at Charlene, rubbing her arm occasionally. I stubbed my cigarette out. It was time I gave them up. How petty was it to kill yourself out of spite?

We ordered, and the meal arrived. We were occupied for a few minutes with the passing of plates, and the serving of overcooked carrots.

At last, the truth dawned on me. The wily old bag. She was always one step ahead of me. She knew she'd burned her bridges with me. She and I were never going to aspire to anything more than a strained, barely-polite relationship. Then poor innocent Charlene appeared. A lamb to the slaughter. She was easily fooled by Maisie's charm offensive. A perfect victim.

James caught my eye a few times during the meal. He could see perfectly well what was going on. I looked at Bobby a few times. He was shovelling food into his mouth at a frightening speed. I wondered if he could see what was happening. He smiled at me with his little boy's smile. He was hard to read. I figured he'd go along with anything as long as no one hassled him.

The time passed quickly. The boys and I didn't have to make much of an effort. We just sat back and watched the Charlene-and-Maisie-mutual-admiration-society at work. We finished our coffees, and Lizzie gave a huge yawn. Clever girl. I was becoming weary of the gushing compliments that were flitting through the air opposite me. James offered to drive us home, but I insisted that Lizzie and I would take a taxi. After all, they were his family, why should he escape so easily?

I slept a bit better that night. Maybe it was the wine. It had been nice to see James so relaxed and happy. If Bobby stayed around for a while, Maisie would be happy, and she might release her strangle-hold on James.

That night I had lots of dreams. But they were very democratic. In some, James was the hero. In others, Ross starred. They never overlapped.

Next day, however, it was back to decision time. I took out a piece of paper and a pencil. That's what they do on the telly, when it's decision time. I started to write a poem. I scribbled it out in anger. This wasn't a time for poetry.

I got out a new piece of paper and divided it in two with a crooked, freehand line. At the top of one column, I wrote 'James'. At the top of the other, I wrote 'Ross'.

Fifteen minutes later, nothing had been added to either column.

I went to the garage and hauled out my bike. I went for a long cycle in the cold air. When I got back, I was flushed and breathless. But no wiser.

I drew a smiley face under each name. Then a sad one. Then a few question marks. I got out Lizzie's markers and coloured in the smiley faces. The page looked very pretty, in a modern-arty sort of way. But I still didn't know what to do.

How could I choose between two such lovely men? Did Ross get extra points because he loved me back? Or did James love me too, and was he just too afraid to show it? Would Ross love me if he really knew me? What about Lizzie? What would James do if I decided I wanted to take her to Greece?

I wrote a poem after all. 'Torn between two lovers'. I don't know why the title seemed so familiar.

Luckily it was Wednesday. Card night.

I gave the baby-sitter her instructions, and closed the door behind me. I was glad to be out of the house, and I enjoyed the fifteen-second walk to Lily's. Lily greeted me with her usual hug. I thought perhaps it was my imagination, but her smile seemed even more mischievous than usual.

We played only one game of cards. Helen had a headache and wanted to leave early. Lily was almost indecently hasty, as she held her guests' coats, and ushered them through the front door. When they were safely gone, she rushed to the fridge for the alcopops. Lurid green this time, made with some fruit I'd never heard of.

We settled into our usual positions, and Lily took about three-and-a-half seconds to get to the point.

'Did I see a strange car outside your house the other day as I left for work?'

Ha! So that was it. She'd seen Ross. Luckily it looked as if Bobby had managed to sneak past her unnoticed.

I decided not to make it easy for her. 'I don't know, Lily. Did you?'

'And there was a guy sitting on your garden wall. A handsome kind of a fella. I never saw him before. Was he waiting for you at all?'

Dear Lily. Never one to beat around the bush. Or around the garden gate.

'Yes. You're right. There was a strange car. And a handsome fella. And he was waiting for me.'

Lily took a long drink from her bottle.

'Was that him? The guy from Greece? What was his name again?'

I couldn't help laughing at her. We'd been sharing sweet strong drinks, and confidences, for months now. Of course she knew his name.

She had the decency to blush, knowing why I was laughing. 'Oh, yeah. Ross, wasn't it? Was that him?'

'Yes, Lily. That was him.'

She looked as if she was going to explode with delight. She rubbed her hands together.

'Oh, I knew it. I knew it. What did he want?'

'He was selling encyclopaedias actually.'

Lily got up, and punched me lightly as she went past. 'I'm getting more drink. Then I want the whole story. Every gory detail.'

I told her part of the story. I skipped the small detail about nearly taking Ross to my bed. After the third alcopop we were still talking, but I was no wiser.

'What will I do, Lily?' I wailed. 'I love them both. I think. Ross says he loves me. James used to love me. I think maybe he still does. But I'm not sure. And I want to do what's best for Lizzie. It's all just so . . . you know, so hard.'

We were sitting at the card table. The cards were pushed to one side. Lily looked rather creepy in the light of the candles she had arranged around us. Her wild hair cast strange, flickery shadows on the walls. She picked up the cards and began to shuffle them meditatively. I suddenly got a nasty feeling. It must have shown.

Lily gave a big loud laugh, which extinguished the two candles closest to her.

'You thought I was going to suggest that you cut cards to decide.'

I nodded sheepishly.

She gave a mock-offended shake of her shoulders. 'As if.'

She pushed the cards aside. 'I was only tidying up. Anyway, forget for a moment who loves you. What you have to decide is who you want to spend your life with. Then you have to find a way to make it work with him.'

She was right of course. But how could I decide?

She leaned across the table and took my hands, pulling me towards her. My hair fell forwards, coming dangerously close to a candle flame. Lily released my hands and pushed all the candles clear. Then she rooted in her pocket and pulled out a small brown bottle. She uncorked it and poured a few drops onto a small oil burner. She placed one candle into the burner. Immediately a strong, sweet scent wafted into the air. It smelt like holidays and medicine and chanting. She took my hands again.

'Close your eyes.'

I obeyed. I felt like a right loo-laa, but so what? It couldn't hurt.

Lily continued in a soft voice. 'You're in your bedroom. You've just bathed in scented oils. You're putting on your best clothes. You're brushing your hair. You're getting ready for a night out. You're going to dinner with the man you love.'

Her voice was strangely hypnotic. I could almost feel the hairbrush tugging at my curls. I could almost smell the perfume I wore on very special occasions.

'You take one last look in the mirror. You look beautiful. You're happy. The doorbell rings. You turn off the bedroom light, and almost float downstairs. You can see a shadow on the porch. You wrap a silk scarf around your neck. You reach for the door knob.'

I sighed deeply. I could feel the cold steel in my hand. I could see the hammered glass of the hall door. I could see the shadow outside, waiting.

'You turn the door knob, and it clicks. The door swings open.'

I could hear the click, and then the squeak of the un-oiled hinges.

Lily was gripping my hands very tightly now. 'Who's there, Claire? Who is there?'

And all of a sudden, I knew. I knew for sure.

I opened my eyes and jumped up. Lily was grinning at me.

'Did it work? Do you know?'

'Yes. Yes.'

I laughed and hugged her tightly. 'Thank you, Lily. Thank you so much.'

I knew she wanted to know who I had chosen. I didn't want to say though. I didn't want to break the spell.

Lily stood up and flicked the switch by the door. The room was filled with harsh light. She blew out the candles, and began to gather the empty bottles. I pulled on my coat, and headed for the door. I was in a hurry to get started with my plans.

Maybe there was something in all that mystical stuff she practised. Maybe it wasn't all airy-fairy loopiness.

'Tell me, Lily. Did you get that idea on the meditation course you went on last month?'

She shook her head ruefully.

'Actually, Claire, I decided against the meditation course. I got cheap flights on the Internet and I went to Las Vegas instead. I won a fortune on the slot machines.'

The old devil. Still, one lapse was OK.

'Was it from one of your part works then? Is that where you got the idea?'

She shook her head again. 'Actually, I saw it on the telly. They did it on *Cold Feet*.'

I stepped into the night and Lily closed the door behind me. As I went down the garden path, I could hear her huge laugh, and the clinking of alcopop bottles. There was a stumbling noise, and then a loud crashing sound. I hesitated until the rush of expletives convinced me that she wasn't seriously hurt, then I skipped all the way home.

Chapter Thirty-Five

Two days later, I stood in my bedroom, dragging a hairbrush through my tangled curls. (This part had been much easier in my dream-vision.) I had a new dress on. (Well, new to me anyway. I'd bought it in the charity shop.) I had liberally splashed myself with my favourite perfume, and I'd rubbed on some pink lip-gloss that Lizzie had got free with a comic.

The takeaway dinner from the local Italian restaurant was warming nicely in the oven.

Lizzie didn't know he was coming. I didn't want any distractions. So, at six-thirty, I'd told her it was bed-time. Luckily she couldn't read the clock, so she went off with no complaint, and as she was tired anyway, she was soon fast asleep.

The doorbell rang. I switched off the bedroom light. I didn't float downstairs. I was too nervous. I sort of half-skipped, and half-stumbled. I grabbed the hall-cupboard door handle to support myself. The cup-board door flew open, and a heap of coats, scarves, umbrellas and a tennis racquet tumbled to my feet. (No one in the family plays tennis, and I have no idea where the racquet came from.) I kicked everything back into the cupboard, and used brute force to jam the door shut again.

There was a shadow on the porch. I opened the door. He was smiling. A rather nervous smile. His black hair was combed neatly. He was holding a bottle of wine.

I smiled nervously back at him. A sudden cold blast of air pushed past him into the house.

I shivered. 'Come in quick. It's freezing out there.'

He stepped in and I closed the door behind him. We were both a bit unsure of ourselves.

I smiled again. 'Come on into the kitchen. It's warmer there.'

He followed me through.

'You look lovely, Claire.'

'Thanks,' I replied. 'You don't look too bad yourself, James.'

I'd phoned the day before to invite him for dinner. He must have thought it was unusual, but he didn't say so. Before he hung up, he said quickly, 'Oh, Claire. I just want to say something.'

I suddenly felt my heart sink into the toes of my Doc Martens. For a minute, I worried that he was going to drop some terrible bombshell, like telling me he was moving to Australia, or that he wanted full custody of Lizzie, or that he was in love with the brazen hussy with the thick black eyeliner who worked in the post office. (The hussy who wore slinky black tops and a bra three sizes too small. She looked like she had four breasts. But hey, maybe that's the kind of thing men go for.)

Luckily I was wrong. 'I just wanted to thank you again for coming out with us the other night. I'm glad you came.'

I smiled to myself. 'That's OK. See you tomorrow. Seven-thirty.'

We ate at the kitchen table. The food was fine. Predictable. It tasted mostly of garlic and tomato. We chatted easily, like an old married couple. James told me about Maisie's latest exploits, and of Charlene's innocent charm. I told him about Lizzie's class trip to the fire station, and my failed effort to clean out the garden shed.

When the meal was over, James stacked the dirty ware in the dishwasher, and I carried a fresh bottle of wine and two glasses into the living-room. I poured us each a glass of wine and sat back on the sofa. James sat next to me, and we remained for a while, sipping our wine in companionable silence.

After a while, I took a deep breath and I began to talk. I told James about my first trip to Greece with Grace and Jessie. I described how I felt as we set off for the islands – how the world seemed mine for the taking. I told him about San Stefanos, about the little taverna, about Georgios.

James must have realised that this was important, that it was leading somewhere, because he didn't comment; he didn't interrupt – he just sat and listened intently.

Determined to continue, I told him about Kevin. I briefly recounted the scene on the beach, skipping the details, and I described the way he had left me afterwards. I told him how I had discovered that I was pregnant, and the feelings of despair that had come with that knowledge. I told him about Jessie leaving, and how I had spent the next few days wishing that the baby was dead, just so I could go back to college as if nothing had ever happened.

I stopped then. I wasn't sure if I was strong enough to continue. The next part was the worst part. This was the part that I hadn't told Ross. The final truth.

I put my face in my hands. James gently pulled my hands away, and leaned towards me.

'I think you need to finish, don't you? Please tell me everything, Cee. Please.'

So, I took another very deep breath, and continued. And as I spoke, every detail came back to me once more. I closed my eyes, and it was as if I was there again, living through every horrible moment, one more time.

'I was desperate, James. You can't imagine how desperate I was. It happened one afternoon, about a week before I was due to leave the island. Grace had gone off somewhere, probably to get away from me –

she was really fed up of me by then – and there was no sign of Georgios. I lay in the bedroom moping. I felt unbelievably tired. I wanted the rest of the world to vanish, so I could just stay there forever, and never have to have the baby, and never have to go home.

'I remember I watched a fly struggling to escape through the glass of the bedroom window. I knew how he felt. I dragged myself up and opened the window, and shooed the fly. He flew off, and vanished into the warm air. I wished that I could escape so easily.

'I lay back on my bed then and closed my eyes. The air was warm, and my skin felt clammy – you know, like Lizzie's felt when she had that ear infection last year. I lifted up my t-shirt and put my hand on my stomach. It felt huge, but that was probably from too many pizzas. I breathed deeply and tried to relax. Another fly flew into the room, but I ignored it.'

I stopped speaking for a moment. I was getting to the point of no return. This wasn't a story that I could easily abandon in the middle. So I struggled on.

'I'm not sure how to describe the next few hours. I felt very strange. You know, as if I was half-asleep. It was as if some force had taken over and was directing everything I did. Or maybe I'm just saying that because I feel so guilty about what happened next.'

James muttered something then. I opened my eyes. He looked half-afraid. I suppose he was right. He must have dreaded my next words. I put my head down, so I wouldn't have to see his worried face, and I went on.

I spoke in a whisper, prompting James to lean closer in an effort to catch each dreadful word.

'I took my rucksack from where it had been thrown on top of the wardrobe since we'd arrived. I filled it with all of my clothes, and pulled it onto my back. It wasn't all that heavy – my clothes were only rags, I suppose – so I dumped everything onto my bed, and went outside to the little yard behind the house. I half-hoped that Georgios would appear and stop me, but he didn't. The yard was hot and dusty, and there were stones everywhere. I filled my rucksack to the top with the biggest ones I could find. I got covered in dust. Then I hauled the rucksack onto my back again. It was awfully heavy. I could feel the straps biting into my skin. I went back indoors. I climbed slowly upstairs, to an empty storeroom, then back down, then up again. I did it again and again and again. I don't know how many times. After a while, I kind of collapsed at the bottom of the stairs.'

I sneaked a look at James. He had a hand to his mouth, and his face seemed to have gone paler. I briefly wondered if it was right to burden him with my story, but I pushed the thought away. I needed to say the words.

'I wriggled free of the rucksack straps, and half-staggered to the larder where Georgios kept the alcohol. I rooted around and then helped myself to an almost-full bottle of ouzo. It was really awful, like liquorice. I drank until I started coughing, and I couldn't drink any more. I took a deep breath and drank again. I felt sick. I dropped the bottle, and it broke on the floor tiles. A piece of glass flew up and cut my ankle. I didn't care.

'I looked up at the hooks over the cooker, where Georgios kept his cooking things. I reached up and got a large, sharp skewer-like thing. My hand was shaking.'

James gave a sudden gasp. 'No, Cee, no.'

I gave a wry smile. 'Don't worry, James. I was too chicken for that. I dropped it on the floor and it rolled under the cooker, out of my reach.

'I went through our bedroom and into the bathroom. The bath was full of Grace's white knickers and socks, soaking in bleach. I fished out the clothes and threw them on the floor. There was an inch of bleachy water in the bottom of the bath. I left it there. Then I turned on the tap and filled the bath with water, hotter than I could comfortably bear. I knew that I was being really stupid, but I couldn't stop myself. I climbed into the bath and lay there. My hands were shaking and I couldn't breathe properly.'

I stopped speaking again. This was nearly too real. As I described the scene in the bathroom, it was almost as if I was there, lying in that stained bath once again with the hot water burning my skin.

I looked at James. He said nothing. I closed my eyes, and continued to speak. 'I watched as my skin turned blotchy and red. I felt like I was watching someone else, like in a film. The small room was filled with steam, which hit the tiles and became tiny rivulets. For a long, long time I watched those rivulets as they raced each other to the ground. I wasn't shaking any more. I felt sort of peaceful. I thought it would be nice to slip under the water, and stay there, but I couldn't do it. Then I closed my eyes and waited for the alcohol to reach my brain.

'Soon I began to feel dizzy, I remember I tried to concentrate on one tile under the window. It was blue – blue like the sky. It had a big crack in it. But I couldn't focus on it. It kept spinning out of control, whipping round in circles. Still I lay there in the cooling water, trying not to think about why I was there. Eventually, I climbed out of the bath. I felt really dizzy. I pulled my skirt and t-shirt on over my wet skin and went back into the bedroom. My bed seemed very far away, so I lay on Jessie's. The pillow smelt of her musk perfume. I wished she was there. I started crying. Then I must have fallen asleep.

'I woke up in pain. It was as if someone had taken one of Georgios's long thick-bladed knives, plunged it deep into my tummy and was now twisting it round and round.'

I looked up just in time to see James flinching. Still though, I couldn't stop.

'Sorry, but it really felt like that. I curled up in the bed, and tried to breathe deeply, but the pain was too intense. I lay there, helpless and afraid, and the pain kept coming in waves.

'Some time later, I heard happy, laughing voices. It was as if they came from another world. It was Grace and Georgios, chatting just outside my bedroom. I called out to them. I was suddenly afraid that they would leave, and abandon me to my fate. I called again, louder this time.

'Grace came in, and stopped in horror when she saw me. I can't have been a pretty sight. I begged her to get help. I told her I thought I was dying. I half-hoped I was.

'She ran out of the room. I heard her whispering to Georgios, and then she came back in and held my hand. You know, I never liked her all that much, but I will always remember that small kindness. I remember her hand was lovely and soft.

'She told me that Georgios was gone for help. And then we waited.

'After what seemed like ages, the door was pushed open by an old woman. She shook her head when she saw me, muttering something in Greek. She looked crossly at Grace, who edged towards the door. I didn't fancy being left alone with the witch-like woman, but I was too weak to protest.

'All I remember after that is lots of pain and lots of blood. I could sense the old lady's disapproval as she sat by the bed and waited for it to end. Every now and then, she pressed hard on my stomach. Her old hands felt rough. I felt that she was deliberately hurting me. Her fingernails were all black.

'Eventually it appeared to be finished. She stood up and began to clear up the mess. She went outside and came back with a big black plastic sack. She filled it up with all of the bloody sheets and towels. I could see no sign of a baby, but didn't know if it would have been recognisable at that stage.

'I begged her to tell me if it was a boy or a girl. She turned back from the door, and almost spat out the word. "Girl." I know now there can't have been much to see. I think she said "girl" because she thought it would upset me more. Then she left.'

I stopped talking. The worst was over. James still looked shocked. He took my hand, and squeezed it. I felt like throwing myself into his arms, but I resisted the urge. It was better to finish the story properly.

'Grace came back. She sat down on her bed. I could feel blood seeping from me. I thought perhaps I was bleeding to death, but I didn't really care. I just felt empty, as if my emotions had seeped out of me, along with all the blood and gunge. I could see that Grace was afraid. She looked at the black plastic bag which still lay in the corner. She asked what we should do with it. I was so sick and weak, I could do nothing, so it was going to be her problem, whether she liked it or not.

'And then she left, escaping back out to the clean air. I could hear scraping sounds. Then she returned, flushed and out of breath. She picked up the bag and went to the door.

'She asked me if I wanted to say goodbye. I shook my head, and she hurried off.

'The bedroom window was still open, and I could hear her footsteps outside, at the back of the house. I raised myself up to my knees and looked out. She had gone to the olive grove behind the house, and had managed to dig a shallow hole under one of the trees. She put the bag in the hole, flattening it so it was hidden from my view. She took a shovel, and filled in the hole. She stood back and wiped her forehead. Then she bent again and used her hands to smooth out the soil.

'Then, Grace, the vociferous atheist, the one who argued long and loud about the impossibility of the existence of a god, knelt in front of her work and made the sign of the cross. She bent her head and I can still see a lock of her beautiful golden hair falling forward and skimming the dust. She stayed there, as if she was praying for a few moments. Then she blessed herself again.'

James interrupted for the first time, with a typical, James-like comment. He always tried to see the best in people. 'Well, that was nice of her anyway, wasn't it?'

I gave a wry laugh. 'You didn't know her. She was probably praying that such a thing would never happen to her.'

James gave a small laugh too, and then I rushed out the last few words.

'I remember Grace went off towards the beach then. She didn't come back for hours. I dropped back down on my bed and fell asleep. When I woke up and remembered, I thought that all my problems were over. I thought I could just forget about it. Act as if it had never happened. Like you forget a bad dream.'

I stopped again. James gave me a brief tight hug.

'Cee, my poor, Cee. I'm so sorry. I wish you'd told me before. Why didn't you tell me?'

'I'm sorry, James. I just couldn't. For years I tried not to think about it. I've always felt so guilty. Whenever I saw a mother with her baby, I felt like an evil murderer. Then you came along, and I loved you so much. I loved you all the time. But I was afraid. I didn't deserve you. I felt . . . I felt kind of detached and locked in. I couldn't get close to you.'

James ran his hand through his hair, in a gesture of bewilderment.

'Cee, I'm so sorry. I never knew. How could I have known?'

I tried to smile. 'You couldn't have known. It was all my fault. I always knew that. And then, last year, I just felt as if I was going crazy. I thought I was going to lose my mind, if I didn't go back. I had to go back. And I didn't know how to tell you why. And I did go back. I went to the beach. I saw the olive grove. I even found the tree.'

I sat there, with tears in my eyes. I was crying for the young me who had been so badly hurt. I was always able to find a few stray tears for the foolish, young, wronged me.

And I was crying because I had a horrible fear that I had frightened James away again. I had called it wrong. I shouldn't have told him. I felt sure that he couldn't cope with all this raw emotion. The crazy Claire had come home to roost again, and it was time for him to make his excuses and go.

Still, I could hardly unsay all of that sorry tale, could I? I couldn't laugh and say, 'Just kidding.' I couldn't calmly pour us some more red wine as if we'd been discussing new tiles for the bathroom, or our income-tax returns.

So I waited, with my eyes down, for James to mutter polite sympathies and leave. For what seemed like ages, we sat there. I examined every detail of the carpet I had always hated. My eyes traversed the grey and pink pattern, over and over, following the motifs, as they blended into each other. I could see scatterings of white rice, like small dead maggots, gathered under the coffee table. (How long had they been there? I hadn't eaten rice in weeks.)

I read and re-read the headlines of the sports section of a Sunday newspaper that nudged out from under a cushion. Apparently Liverpool won two–nil.

I picked some potting compost from under my left thumbnail.

Finally I looked up. James was crying. Tears were dripping onto his grey shirt, and he was making no effort to stop, or hide them. He gave a little sob, which may have been an effort to say my name, and then he leaned towards me, and held me tight. I clung to him, gripping his shirt with my fingers, afraid he would slip out of my grasp. We cried together, in big, choking sobs. I cried until I feared that Lizzie would come down in the morning to find her parents dissolved into a salty, garlicky puddle. Only our wine glasses would remain to tell our story. And since we weren't Princess Diana and Dodi, some kind neighbour would throw them into the dishwasher, and there would be no evidence of our last night on earth. There would be no monument in Harrod's to the memory of James and me.

Eventually my tears were exhausted, but I wasn't letting go of James. No way. Not after all that time. I could feel the warmth of his skin through the fine cotton of his shirt. I could smell washing powder, the cheap kind Maisie favoured, and the faint traces of his shampoo. While he held me, I knew everything would be all right – he would take care of me, and life would be good. It was like coming home after a hard day. This was where I belonged. Warts and all.

James was the first to interrupt the moment.

'I'm really sorry, Claire,' he said. 'I have a cramp in my leg. I need to stretch it for a moment.'

I couldn't argue with that, so we disentangled ourselves, and he limped towards the hall. He looked over his shoulder as he reached the door.

'Don't go away. I'll be right back.'

He was back in moments. I could see a large damp patch on his shoulder where my tears had soaked into his shirt. His eyes were red, and his skin was blotchy and damp. He looked too young to be so sad.

This time we sat so we could see each other's faces. James held my hands in his. He had lots of questions to ask, and I answered gladly. I had the feeling that we wouldn't be discussing this again, and I was keen to be finished with it. I didn't want him to be left with un-answered questions that would always hang between us.

Around midnight, he got to a question that had always sort of bothered me too.

'How come you went to London, Cee? You know, after . . . well, after it was all over. You could have gone home, back to college, like you had hoped.'

I thought for a moment before replying. 'I think it was the guilt. You see, all the way home, all that long train and boat journey with Grace, I tried to picture myself back at college. But I couldn't do it. I couldn't see myself hanging around the bar or the Rest, as if nothing had happened. I knew I couldn't go back to the way things used to be.'

James protested. 'But that wasn't fair. It wasn't your fault. You didn't know what you were doing.'

I shrugged. 'Maybe so. But anyway, I think I went to London to punish myself for not wanting the baby. I thought I didn't deserve to be happy any more.'

James held me tight, and whispered, 'You poor thing. My poor, poor girl.'

I was tempted to stay within his embrace, but I knew we weren't finished yet. I gently freed myself from his arms, and waited for his next question.

The conversation went on for hours. Then James began to talk about himself.

'I never stopped loving you, you know. Not even for a second. But I couldn't bear the fighting. I was afraid all the time. I thought I was losing you. It was as if you were locked inside a single idea. I couldn't reach you. You were going crazy, and I didn't know how to help. I wish you'd told me about . . . about that first time in Greece.'

I spoke softly. 'I'm sorry, James. I wasn't ready.'

He nodded. I think he understood.

Something else occurred to me. 'And you let me take Lizzie.'

'What else could I do? I was afraid that if I objected, I'd lose you both.'

He put his head in his hands. His fingers looked white against his dark hair.

'I'm so sorry, Claire. I didn't know what else to do.'

I rubbed his shoulder. He needed consolation too.

'Anyway,' he added. 'I wasn't much help to you. I could have been more sympathetic. I wasn't listening. If I had been listening to you, you might not have gone.'

'But I had to go, don't you see?'

I knew I was right. I had to deal with my pain sometime. It had been like a great dark cloud over my life. I wasn't always aware of it, but it was always there, and like all dark clouds, until the heavens opened, and the downpour came, it wasn't going anywhere. It was just going to hang there, blighting my days.

Now that the storm had been, and passed over, everything seemed so much better and brighter. All the sadness was washed away, like vomit from a rainy Sunday-morning footpath.

It got past three o'clock in the morning, and we were still sitting together on the sofa. Still close, with my head resting in the hollow between his head and neck, which I had always felt to be my special place. My brain was fuzzy from emotion and tears. All I knew for sure was that I didn't want James to leave. Ever. Once or twice, I dozed off, and awoke to the great pleasure of finding that it wasn't a dream.

Then, without discussion or anguished soul-searching, we were going upstairs together, just like we used to.

There had been no forward planning on my part. I had never dared to hope that it would come to this. The bed was unmade, the sheets crumpled. The damp towel I'd used earlier was thrown on the floor. My unsexy nightdress was tossed on the pillow, and a pile of unread newspapers adorned the bedside lockers. On the spare pillow there was an unfinished crossword, with the scribbled lines of a poem in the margins.

For the first time in a long, long time, James and I slipped between the sheets together.

It was, as they say in the movies, like the first time. Or like the first time should have been.

It was like a wedding night without the sore tummy from too many egg sandwiches and cocktail sausages. Without the worries about whether the florist had been paid, or whether the grumpy mother-in-law had managed to ruin every single photograph with her ostentatious scowl.

I had forgotten James's warm strength. I had forgotten his worryingly good techniques, his inventiveness.

It all came back to me in a rush.

So to speak.

When it was over, and we lay together hot and sweaty after our exertions, I knew for sure what I wanted in my life.

My Juliet had found her Romeo. My Barbie had found her Ken. I turned my head to where my Ken lay panting on the pillow beside me. He beamed at me.

He looked happy to have been found.

Chapter Thirty-Six

I slept for the rest of the night – a restful, sweet and dreamless sleep. Then I awoke to what felt like a dream. I could hear Lizzie, playing in her bedroom, talking to her toys. I could see the morning light glimmering through the thin floral fabric of my bedroom curtains. I could taste the garlic from last night's meal, strong in my mouth. I could feel a very strange bruise just above my left hip. I could hear my husband snoring in the bed, next to me.

I snuggled close to him, almost overcome with the joy of it all.

Lizzie pushed the door open, and put her little tousled head around it. She looked at me, and she looked at James. Then in the wonderful way that children have, she made nothing at all of the scene.

'Hi, Mum! Hi, Dad! Who's going to make my porridge?'

James awoke, and rubbed his eyes. It seemed to take a few moments before he remembered the night before, and then he gave a slow smile. 'That was some night.'

He gave a long, low whistle, and then groaned as Lizzie jumped on top of him, on her way to her old position, wedged between the two of us. We lay close together, enjoying the old familiar warmth, enjoying the feeling that everything important to us was there, in that five feet of bed, huddled under our old, faded duvet.

Just like in the old days, Lizzie tired of the cosiness before we did. She was soon begging for her breakfast as if she hadn't eaten for days. 'I'm so hungry. Pleeeeeeease make me my porridge.'

James summoned the energy to spring out of bed, saying wryly as he did, 'I suppose it's my turn. Anyway, it's Saturday, so no porridge.'

At these words, Lizzie gave a squeal of joy, and skipped off, giggling as James chased her across the hall.

I rolled over into the warm spot where he had lain, and savoured the moment. Then, not wishing to waste any of this precious new day, I slid out of bed, and headed for the shower.

We slipped into the old Saturday-morning routine. James nipped to the shop for the papers, and we read them over breakfast. I got the crossword and the books page. He got the sport and the gardening. Lizzie got to mess with her cereal without censure from either of us.

When the lingering breakfast was over, and the table tidied, I looked at James.

'Now what?'

James looked at his watch. 'I'm sorry, Cee. You know I'm going to England this afternoon, don't you?'

I had forgotten. He and his partner Liam had agreed to go over to do a big electrical job for an old friend of Liam's. He'd be gone for two or three weeks.

He saw my disappointed face. 'I'm sorry, Claire. I can't get out of it. I promised Liam. We'll work as fast as we can, and get home quickly.'

He hesitated. 'Can I come home to you? Here?'

I stood up and went to him. I gave him a long, deep kiss before I spoke. 'Of course you can. You big eejit.'

He finished his tea and we had a lingering hug in the hallway. Then he set off for Maisie's to pack for his trip.

He was gone for three weeks. I missed him terribly. He phoned me every night, and we whispered sweet nothings across the Irish Sea. Lizzie and I planned for his return, making cards that opened back-to-front, and banners that always broke in the middle, and cakes that sank terribly the moment they escaped the heat of the oven.

It's time now for the wavy lines, and the sudden change of time again. We need some more music. Something romantic this time. Sinatra perhaps. Or Robbie Williams.

I'm back to the beginning of my story again. Back to the day of the pregnancy test, and yes, I'm still pregnant.

This didn't come as a great surprise to me, as James and I had had serious sexual activity, right at my most fertile time. If we'd thought about it, we might have found reasons to delay having a baby, but now, with no thought at all, no forward planning, it had happened.

There still lurked, at the back of my mind, a few cold shards of fear. I was afraid that James would back off again, intimidated by the new commitment. He might think that I was rushing him into something he wasn't ready for. He might feel trapped. Would he feel that I had deliberately trapped him? Had I ruined everything by my lack of caution?

The positive me – the new, confident me – took over and firmly pushed these negative thoughts away. Everything would be fine, I told myself. This would be a new beginning.

James got my message as soon as the boat docked in Ringaskiddy that afternoon. He came straight over. I met him at the door, and spoke with no preamble, no little introduction to soften the news.

Just two words. 'I'm pregnant.'

Three syllables that change peoples lives forever.

James's first reaction was one of surprise. Funny how men can react when they hear news like this. They deposit several million sperm inside you, and then they seem surprised when you tell them that just one of these millions has gone ahead and done what it was meant to do.

Then, to my great joy, he beamed and hugged me. After a while, I reluctantly pushed him away. I had to breathe.

He seemed full of nervous energy. ' I'm going to get my stuff. I won't be long,' he called over his shoulder as he ran down the path.

He wasn't long either. I was so glad to see him return with his belongings. There was a pang of guilt too. He had only two largish sports bags, and neither of these seemed to be full. For the first time, I realised how little he had taken from the house when he had left. Apart from his clothes, everything else had been here all the time.

I went upstairs with him, and sat on the bed while he unpacked. I hadn't had the heart to fill the spaces he had left in our wardrobes, and in the drawers he had used, so it didn't take him long to put everything back where it had been. When he was finished, he crumpled up the two nylon bags, and stuffed them at the bottom of the wardrobe, where they always used to go.

We went down to the kitchen, where James sniffed the air.

'Hmmm. I don't smell burning. Is it salad for tea?'

He laughed as he ducked my punch, and our hands touched as we reached together for the Chinese takeaway menu.

Chapter Thirty-seven

Seven months later
An update.

Lizzie has now settled into her second year of school. For a change, her every utterance isn't prefaced by, 'Mrs Browne says . . . ' This year her teacher is called Miss Flynn, and she appears to be equally infallible.

Lizzie has almost forgotten her sojourn in Greece. I don't know why, but since we came back, she has never once mentioned Ross or Alistair. Similarly, there is no mention of the time when James didn't live with us. She just gets on with her life, living for the present. She is growing tall and strong, and though I may be a little biased, I think she is the perfect child.

Our baby is due soon. It kicks a lot. I like to lie on my bed in the afternoon, with my hand on my swelling abdomen, luxuriating in the wonderful, age-old sensation, the joy of a new life. I don't mind that millions of women have felt like this before me. To me it is wonderful and special. I pamper myself, lying there, rubbing cocoa butter into the skin over my bump, feeling little parts of my baby's body, unidentifiable, but beloved. Sometimes Lizzie lies beside me, hand on my abdomen, waiting patiently for the next movement. We giggle at each kick and argue whether it was an elbow or a heel that made that fleeting imprint on my tightly-stretched skin.

In May, James and I sold our apple-white house in Douglas. The suburban dream wasn't really for us. We found a wonderful new place. It's in Myrtleville. It has a beautiful view of the sea. It's a bit on the small side, but we can extend it – if we ever get around to it. I haven't stencilled pretty swathes of ivy on the walls, but who knows? Maybe one day I will.

(And maybe one day the air will be filled with fat pink animals, snorting and wiggling their curly tails as they fly by.)

The last owner of the house left to go and live in Canada with a guy she met on holidays. I found a photo under a broken floorboard. I suppose it's her. She looks nice. Something tells me we'd like each other. I hope she's happy.

When we were packing up to leave the apple-white palace, I found the bundle of photographs that Grace gave me, all those years ago. The young me smiled out at the older, wiser me. I sighed at my smooth skin and cellulite-free thighs.

Lizzie came and peered over my shoulder as I flicked through the glossy sheaf of the past.

I stopped at a picture of me that was taken in Zagreb. I'm standing against a very ugly monument, and grinning foolishly.

Lizzie giggled. 'Mummy, your hair is awful. And I don't like your clothes very much.'

I pretended to look hurt. Lizzie was instantly apologetic. 'I'm sorry, Mummy. I know that was back in the olden days.'

She picked up the photo and studied it carefully. 'You look happy.'

I smiled at her. 'Yes, Lizzie. I was happy.'

She cuddled up against me, and I continued, 'But I'm much happier now.'

I still see Maureen regularly. I like to think that we are friends. She has a quiet wit and gentleness about her that I value. We have some good laughs together, and I wonder about my shallowness, when I thought she was just a boring do-gooder, with dress sense that didn't happen to coincide with mine.

Maureen is pregnant too. Her baby is due a few months after mine. It's nice to have someone to share the happy times and the aches and pains with. When our babies are born, we are going to go back to parent and toddler group. This time it's going to be different. This time I'm going to make an effort.

On Wednesdays, I still play cards with Lily. Green tea has its own special merits, but it doesn't make me laugh like the alcopops did. Lily has a big stash of lime and purple bottles ready for when I'm no longer pregnant.

In a few years' time, when my baby isn't a baby any more, I might go back to college. I'd like to finish the degree I started all those years ago.

Then again, I might decide to stay at home, baking rubbery cookies, and making lopsidedly creative things out of toilet-roll tubes and egg boxes.

It's nice to have a choice.

In the meantime, I'm writing lots of poetry. I sent one poem to an arts magazine, and they printed it. James was very proud. He framed the page, and hung it in our living-room, next to Lizzie's painting of a green tiger.

A few weeks ago, I gave my old mock-suede jacket to the charity shop. It was worn and frayed beyond redemption. It was time to grow up and part with it. I'm quite sure no one would want to wear the tattered old thing, but I hadn't the heart to put it in the bin. Maybe someone will buy it to keep a pampered puppy warm. What dreams that poor puppy would have.

My bike is in the shed gathering cobwebs and waiting until my bump is gone and I can balance once more. James offered to paint it pink again, but I said no. I've got used to the mottled look. When the baby is born, James will put a special seat onto my bike, so baby and I can go for long cycles when Lizzie is at school.

Poor baby.

Still, maybe having the maddest mummy won't be too hard to bear when you have a big sister to share the embarrassment with.

James too has spread his wings a little. He plays indoor soccer twice a week, and often goes for a drink with the lads afterwards. In the old days, when I was so insecure, I would have seen this as a serious threat, half-afraid to let him have a place in his life that didn't include me. Now, though, I quite enjoy these nights. I put Lizzie to bed, with an extra few minutes of stories and cuddles, and then I relax with a book, or my smug thoughts of happiness.

Our timing was good. Bobby's return was as unexpected and as unlikely as the arrival of a new character in an Australian soap opera. It turned out to be just as convenient too. He and Charlene moved in with Maisie. They still live together. The love affair between Charlene and Maisie continues. Maisie has hidden her nasty selfish side, and continues to charm poor Charlene. Now that I'm so calm and nice, I've begun to mellow a little towards my dreaded mother-in-law. I wouldn't fancy living with her – Charlene is welcome to that – but I find myself being generous in my dealings with her, and her hatred of me has mellowed a little into grumpy impatience which doesn't bother me in the least. Perhaps one day we will work through indifference and end up with a grudging liking for each other.

I never told James about my fling with Ross, and I don't intend to. I nearly said that I don't want to burden him with my guilt, but this wouldn't be true. I feel no guilt about Ross. Guilt is a useless emotion, like regret, and one I'm trying hard to live without. Life's too short, as I might have said long ago when I was young.

I wrote to Ross to tell him what had happened. It wasn't an easy letter to write. But then I suppose receiving it can't have been much fun either. I hope I didn't hurt him too much. A few weeks ago, when I was waiting for my ante-natal appointment, I flicked idly through *Hello* magazine. Ross was in it, pictured at a race meeting. His arm was resting on the shoulder of a pretty girl. She wasn't dressed in tweed and she didn't have a horse face. They were both laughing.

I hope she likes Bruce Springsteen.

I don't know if I really killed my first baby, way back then, in Greece. Maybe it was a mass of disfigured cells that never could have lived without me. Maybe it would have died anyway, and I just speeded matters up a little bit. Maybe all those old tales of gin and hot baths are myths. I don't really want to know. Maybe that old Greek woman lied when she said it was a girl. It might have been too early to tell, or maybe there was nothing left to see. I will never know the answers to these questions, and a part of me never wants to know. I think it's time to put all that behind me.

James is due home from work soon. He will take off his work clothes of checked cotton shirt, and old denim jeans. He will shower, and change into a plain shirt, and clean denim jeans. As it is Friday night, Lizzie can stay up a little later than usual, but not as late as she would like. She will change into her pink Barbie nightdress, and wash her own face and hands. James will brush her teeth, and then he will sit at the edge of her bed and read her the next chapter of *Pippi Longstocking*.

When Lizzie is asleep, I will prepare our Friday-night dinner. I will take my little basket with the red-and-white cotton lining, and wander out in the late evening sun. I will breathe in the indescribable perfume of the night-scented stock which Lizzie and I planted outside the back door. I will collect the makings of a salad from the vegetable patch, which James has tended all summer. I'll pick red and green lettuce, salad onions, and a few cherry tomatoes. I'll spend twenty minutes removing slugs and greenfly from the scabby articles. In the end, I'll throw James's lettuce into the bin, and sneak out the packaged and washed stuff I bought in the supermarket. I will fry sirloin steak and onions, and we'll have some sautéed potatoes. James will wave a tea-towel at the smoke detector to silence its shrieks. If things are really bad, he'll even go down to pick up a takeaway.

After our meal, we'll clear a space for ourselves on the couch. We'll throw ourselves down and watch a soppy video.

Next summer, James is going to take six weeks off work. We're going to go on a big holiday and blow what's left of the lottery money. James kindly suggested going back to Greece but I said no. Been there. Done that. Bought the Valium. I want to go somewhere new.

I always fancied a holiday in one of those places beginning with 'The'. The Maldives. The Bahamas. The Seychelles perhaps.

James suggested The Aran Islands.

Luckily he was joking.

I will sit in the shade of a palm tree and breastfeed my baby, while James builds elaborate palaces in the sand for Lizzie. Then James and the baby will lie on cashmere rugs and snooze, while Lizzie and I frolic in the impossibly blue sea.

Every night, we'll dine on fish and coconut and salads, served by smiling, barefoot waiters. We'll sip sweet wine and watch the sun set in a blaze of red and gold.

We will talk and laugh and dream of never going home.

And the weeks will pass too soon, and we will pack up our sandals and our shorts and our memories.

And we will go home and we will live as happily as we can, for ever after.